BIG SKY COUNTRY

"Why don't you tell me what you think?" Jill's voice was challenging. This man was too perceptive.

"A beautiful girl like you must be accustomed to lots of masculine admiration," Riordan said mockingly. "So this casual flirtation of yours is just to keep in practice."

"And I'm supposed to have tricked you into coming with me for that reason?" Jill demanded.

"You've picked a romantic setting," he taunted. "A walk in the moonlight, just the two of us . . . alone."

Jill swallowed involuntarily. "If that's my intention, I'd pick a man who was at least attracted to me. You've made your dislike very clear," she answered boldly.

"But I am attracted to you," Riordan said. "I may think you're a scheming little witch—but that doesn't take away my desire to make love to you."

CAN'T *Say* GOODBYE

JANET DAILEY

ZEBRA BOOKS
KENSINGTON PUBLISHING CORP.

http://www.kensingtonbooks.com

ZEBRA BOOKS are published by

Kensington Publishing Corp.
119 West 40th Street
New York, NY 10018

All Kensington titles, imprints, and distributed lines are available at special quantity discounts for bulk purchases for sales promotion, premiums, fund-raising, educational, or institutional use.

Special book excerpts or customized printings can also be created to fit specific needs. For details, write or phone the office of the Kensington Special Sales Manager: Attn.: Special Sales Department. Kensington Publishing Corp., 119 West 40th Street, New York, NY 10018. Phone: 1-800-221-2647.

Zebra and the Z logo Reg. U.S. Pat. & TM Off.

ISBN-13: 978-1-4201-2571-9
ISBN-10: 1-4201-2571-0

First Printing: September 2002

10 9 8

Printed in the United States of America

CONTENTS

BIG SKY
COUNTRY

Chapter One

"Kerry?" Jill Randall tipped her head around the bathroom door, golden curls falling over one shoulder.

A faint smile touched the corners of her glossed lips at the sight of her roommate. Kerry Adams was sitting in the middle of one single bed, a pillow clutched tightly in her arms as she stared dreamily into space. Jill's smile became impish. Slipping a towel from the bathroom rack, she wadded it up and hurled it at her roommate. It landed harmlessly on top of her head.

"Kerry, you're supposed to be getting ready!" Jill stood poised in the doorway, a hand resting on a slim but nicely curved hip, her blue eyes laughing at the girl's dazed expression.

The towel was dragged away from its haphazard position on her head, drawing with it strands of straight brown hair, silky and shimmering like satin.

"Must I?" Kerry sighed. Then she pushed her petite frame from the bed and walked restlessly to the window, pushing aside the curtain to gaze outside. "I wish Todd was coming over tonight."

Jill shook her head and stepped back in front of the bathroom mirror. "Unless you want to fail English Lit, you'd better hope Todd doesn't come over."

"I know, but—" a fervent note crept into her roommate's voice, "—but I keep thinking I'm going to wake up and find it's all been a dream. That it never really happened."

The teasing glint remained in Jill's eyes as she carefully used the sandy-brown pencil to define her light brows more clearly. "Kerry, it's only your *first* proposal."

"And my last! Oh, Jill—" Kerry was in the doorway, a frightened happiness lighting a radiant glow in her somewhat plain face "—Todd asked me to marry him. To be his wife."

"I know, I know. You told me that before." Jill's sensual mouth curved into a wide smile that laughed gently at Kerry. They had been roommates for too long for Kerry to take offense.

"I have to keep repeating it or I'll stop believing that it actually happened. I'm not beautiful like you. I couldn't believe it when he asked me out that first time—or the second or the third or the fourth. But I never dreamt ... Oh, I did dream about it, but l never believed he could actually be serious about me! He never said so much as one word about the way he felt until the other night."

"Didn't I tell you it would work?" Jill winked broadly.

Kerry draped the towel over the rack, a regretful look stealing over her features. A heavy dose of guilty conscience dimmed the light in her brown eyes.

"I still don't know if I should have told him such an outright lie. I have no intentions of leaving Montana to get a job, not even for the summer."

"But Todd didn't know that," Jill reminded her, switching the pencil to the other eyebrow. "Besides, you didn't actually tell him you'd accepted a job out of state, did you?"

"No, I just said that your uncle in California said we could come and work at his resort this summer."

"Then it wasn't a lie, was it? Uncle Peter did write to say we had jobs there if we wanted them." Jill managed an expressive shrug of her shoulders as she maintained her concentration on the image in the mirror. "All you did was fib a little about whether you were accepting the offer or not."

"I suppose so." Kerry sighed and leaned heavily against the door frame. Absently her hand reached up, separating a strand of dark hair from the others to twist it around her finger. "It's just that when you love someone it doesn't seem fair to trick him into doing what you want."

"Todd loves you. And eventually, he would've gotten around to popping the question. You simply adjusted the timetable in your favor. You'd made it so obvious that you were in love with him, and then you found a way to make him declare his feelings."

The first sentence was the only one Kerry heard. "I'll never be able to understand why Todd Riordan would love me. He should marry someone like you who's beautiful and witty, not someone shy and average like me.''

Jill tipped her head to the side, her honey-gold hair curling about her shoulders. Her long hair was expensively clipped to achieve a look of tousled disarray that was very sexy.

''On the outside, Kerry, you're an all-American girl. Nothing wrong with that. Granted, you think your face and figure aren't exactly spectacular, but inside you're a very beautiful person. Opposites always attract, anyway. Todd Riordan has a very strong protective instinct and your shyness brings it out. Plus I think he likes the way you worship him with those big brown eyes of yours.''

There was more that Jill didn't say, but she thought it to herself. Todd liked the idea that he was intellectually superior to Kerry. He needed someone he could dominate—a little, in a nice way. Jill had always guessed that the woman he married would be a pretty moth, not a beautiful butterfly.

He was a very ambitious guy. It wasn't that he would have objected to sharing the spotlight with a beautiful wife. He wasn't that self-centered. But Todd Riordan wanted to be absolutely sure that his wife was sitting at home waiting for him without a gaggle of admirers ready and willing to amuse her in case he was late coming home.

Kerry's ego was very fragile and Jill had spoken the truth when she had said that Kerry was a beautiful person inside. Not for anything would she intentionally hurt her friend by pointing out some of the more callous reasons why Todd Riordan wanted her for his wife.

"I wish you wouldn't talk like that, Jill," Kerry frowned, twisting the lock of hair tighter around her fingers. "You sound so cynical when you do."

"I prefer to think of it as being logical and realistic." Her lashes were already long and curling, but they needed a little improving. Jill artfully stroked the mascara brush. "Men are tall little boys. Oh, they each have their own personality, but inside they're still little boys. Once a female recognizes that fact and treats men accordingly, she's already the winner. All you have to do, Kerry, is praise them when they're good, withhold their treats when they're bad, and play their games when there's something you want them to do for you."

"Easy for you to say. There isn't any man you can't have if you want him." A faintly envious note crept into Kerry's voice as she studied the exquisitely feminine features of her roommate—features that could change from sensually alluring to innocently young with hardly a blink of an eye in between.

"That's true," Jill agreed matter-of-factly. The mascara brush halted in midstroke, the rich azure color of her eyes deepening when she glanced self-consciously at Kerry's reflection in the mirror. "Ooh, that sounded conceited, didn't it? I didn't mean it that way."

"You're not conceited, just confident. If I looked like you, I probably would be, too. As it is, I'm just glad you don't want Todd."

The strand of dark hair was released, Kerry's voice trailing away as she moved into the bedroom they shared. Automatically Jill resumed the application of mascara to her lashes.

"You're going to change into everyday clothes

before going to the library, aren't you?'' she inquired absently.

"Just a sweatshirt and jeans," was the shrugging response.

With the mascara brush returned to the orderly row of cosmetics, Jill stared at her reflection for a long moment. She was never startled by the beautiful girl that stared back at her. It was the same face she had always seen. She had been born a butterfly. From almost the beginning she had been the object of many little boys' attentions.

It was true—she could have any man she wanted. Some were more a challenge than others, but they all could be hers. It was merely a matter of playing a game. Sometimes Jill thought of herself as more of a chameleon than a butterfly, changing into whatever personality the man she was snaring wanted her to be. Sexy, sporty, fragile, intellectual—it made no difference.

Jill never once doubted that she could take Todd away from Kerry if she wanted him. She could appear as helpless and naive as Kerry actually was. With Todd, her beauty would be a handicap, but she could turn that around and show him what an advantage her looks would be to his career. She would never do it. Kerry was the best friend Jill had ever had, and Kerry loved Todd desperately.

Had she ever looked at a man with Kerry's love-starred eyes? The mist of pink hearts had never lasted beyond the initial infatuation that attracted her to a particular man. Once she had him in her power, so to speak, the infatuation disintegrated. The thrill of the chase always excited her, but the actual capture Jill found boring.

A long-sleeved white blouse was on the hanger

on the back of the bathroom door. Jill slipped it on, buttoning it from the bottom up, watching the cotton material discreetly accent the thrust of her breasts.

A butterfly . . . what an apt description of herself. Flitting from man to man, never dallying anywhere too long. Was this destined to be her life, or would some man come along to pin her down?

That was a fanciful thought. From birth she had known instinctively how to get around any man. There wasn't one she couldn't eventually get to do what she wanted. Once she had him dancing attendance on her, she simply spread her wings and flew away.

With a shrug, Jill tucked her blouse into her powder blue denims. She absently fluffed the burnished ends of her hair and stepped from the bathroom to the bedroom.

"Ready?" Kerry tugged a yellow windbreaker over her faded gray sweatshirt. The overall effect was tomboyish, which suited her short hair and average face, but didn't do much for her otherwise.

Jill noted all this with an appraising eye, but she had long ago given up trying to persuade her roommate to dress differently. Kerry had garnered a marriage proposal from the man she loved, so Jill guessed that it didn't really make much difference.

"I'm outta here. Got to research a term paper." Her fawn-colored leather jacket was taken from the small closet, a twin to the one that held Kerry's clothes.

"Look at it this way," Kerry laughed. "A term paper deadline means that summer vacation is around the corner."

Jill swept up her notebooks and bag, walking to

the door her roommate held open for her. "That's a cheerful thought," she agreed with a wide smile.

"Are you taking the laptop?"

"No, but—"

Kerry's question started a comparison of schedules between the two as they descended the stairs leading to the entrance hall. The used laptop had been a joint investment, but they invariably needed to use it at the same time.

Another student appeared at the base of the stairs, took two quick steps, glanced up, then paused at the sight of the two girls coming down. "Hey, Jill. I was just coming upstairs to get you. You have a phone call . . . sounds like Bob Jackson."

The breathless announcement ended with a conspiratorial grin before the girl turned around to retrace her steps. Jill concealed a grimace. Bob Jackson was a recent conquest, one she was now trying to fly away from. He couldn't seem to take the hint.

"Tell him I'll be right there," Jill called after the retreating messenger and hurried her steps.

"He's persistent," Kerry murmured.

"Tell me about it!" She made a face. "This shouldn't take long, though."

The girl who had come to get her pointed to the telephone booth in the dorm's entrance hall. Jill walked quickly toward it while Kerry settled into the lumpy sofa nearby. A hurried, busy tone was easy to adopt.

"Hi, Jill. What are you doing?" The male voice belonging to Bob Jackson responded to her rushed greeting.

"Oh, Bob, it's you. I was just on my way to the library with Kerry trying to finish up the notes for my term paper. It's due on Monday . . . I'm going nuts."

"Oh." There was a hesitating pause and Jill knew her statement did not coincide with his plans for the weekend. "All work and no play, huh?" he offered in tentative jest. "Big dance this Saturday, remember?"

"If I don't get this term paper done, I'll flunk." It was a plausible excuse, although Jill was fully aware that it was not going to take her the entire weekend to complete the paper.

A night out wouldn't hurt anything. She simply didn't want to spend it with Bob. Besides, Kerry had mentioned that the three of them—Kerry, Todd and Jill—might go out to dinner this weekend, a miniature engagement party.

Her roommate was sensitive about the fact that she had no family except for an aunt and uncle in Billings who had raised her when her parents died. Kerry never said anything specific, but Jill had sensed it had not been a mutually happy arrangement.

"You love to dance, Jill," Bob wheedled. "Come on, honey. We'll have a great time. Let's get sweaty."

The front door was slammed shut. Jill glanced automatically toward the noise. Absently she made some objection to Bob's statement as she stared curiously at the stranger who had made such a loud entrance.

Her gaze swept over his appearance, taking in the well-worn sheepskin jacket unbuttoned to the coolness of the late spring night. He looked like he'd just come in off the range and had been working hard. Dark blue Levis hugged slim hips and long legs, stopping on the arches of a pair of cowboy boots, dirty and worn with much use. Yet there was something about his erect bearing that said he wasn't an ordinary cowboy.

Bob was saying something again and Jill let her gaze fall away from the stranger to concentrate on what was being said in her ear. Then the stranger's voice penetrated the glass walls of the old-fashioned booth.

"I was told I could find Kerry Adams here."

The announcement was made to Connie Dickson, the same girl who had come to let Jill know about her telephone call. Jill's blue eyes darted swiftly back to the man, watching as Connie pointed to Kerry sitting on the sofa. Jill would have sworn she knew everyone that Kerry was even briefly acquainted with, but this man who had asked for her roommate was a total stranger.

The harsh planes of his face were impassive as he passed the telephone booth where Jill stood. His long strides reminded Jill of the restless pacing of a caged cougar, impatient and angry. This man wasn't as calm as his expression indicated. The hard line of his mouth was too grim. The way his gaze narrowed on her unsuspecting roommate gave Jill the uncomfortable feeling that he had just sighted his prey. There wasn't any way she could warn Kerry.

Jill didn't even pretend to pay attention to the male voice on the telephone, straining to catch what that man was saying to her friend.

"Kerry Adams?" He towered above her, his low voice clipped and abrupt as his earlier demand had been. Cold arrogance crackled through the tension that held him motionless. There was no flicker of recognition in Kerry's startled upward glance. "I'm Todd's brother."

Jill's eyes widened in surprise. There was a resemblance but not a strong one. Vaguely she remembered that Todd had an older brother. Kerry had mentioned it at some time, or perhaps Todd had himself.

"Of course, how . . . how do you d-do," Kerry stammered uncertainly.

She quickly straightened from the couch to stand in front of the man, momentarily forgetting the notebooks on her lap until they clattered to the floor, loose pages sliding across the linoleum.

Jill's mouth tightened as she watched Kerry's fumbling attempts to recover them, cheeks flaming in embarrassment and the man making no attempt to help in the recovery. He uttered not one diplomatic word to ease Kerry's discomfort nor did he smile to take away the humiliation of such awkwardness. He simply waited with thinning patience until Kerry had retrieved the papers and had them clutched defensively against her chest.

"T-Todd has talked about you often, Mr. Riordan." Kerry seemed unable to meet the man's gaze, her look helplessly falling away.

Standing, the man dwarfed her petite frame, even more completely than when Kerry had been sitting on the sofa.

The tentative, friendly comment was ignored. "Todd called me this morning. He said he'd asked you to marry him."

The disbelief . . . no, Jill recognized it was more

than disbelief. It was cutting contempt that sliced through his words. Kerry swallowed convulsively.

"He did." The admission was made in a tiny voice that was humbly apologetic. If possible, Riordan's expression became grimmer and more forbidding.

"When do you graduate, Miss Adams?" he challenged coldly.

"I . . . I have one more y-year."

His voice became harshly soft. Jill held her breath in an effort to hear him. "Todd has three, possibly four more years before he completes his law degree. Am I supposed to support you and my brother for that long?"

Kerry seemed to shrink visibly away from him. "Dominating bully!" Jill swore angrily beneath her breath. He was domineering, she corrected her choice of words quickly. The kind of man who would use physical strength to impress his will on someone else if need be. Women were an easy target. Shy, timid Kerry didn't have a chance against his slashing sarcasm.

"Bob, I have to go," Jill spoke hurriedly into the phone, her temper seething as she interrupted him. "Call me tomorrow."

She hung up the receiver and racked her mind for the best way to rescue her dear friend. Any attempt to argue on Kerry's behalf would be wasted. That man would never listen to a woman's logic, however right it might be. No doubt he believed that females belonged either in the kitchen or the bedroom—and should be seen and not heard.

Her eyes narrowed for a fleeting moment, a tiny smile of satisfaction edging the corners of her mouth. He had it coming, Jill thought, and she was about to give him a double dose!

Pushing open the folding door of the telephone booth, Jill stepped out, wrapping her arms around her notebooks and holding them to her chest. She paused, adopted her best "dumb blonde" look and walked forward to engage her opponent.

"Hi, Kerry. I'm ready now," she called brightly to her roommate.

She was completely blind to the stricken look from Kerry. She couldn't allow one flicker of concern to cloud her blue eyes at the total lack of color in her friend's face. Her deliberately innocent eyes swept to the man.

Although braced for his look of displeasure, she was jolted by his piercing silver-gray eyes, though he glanced away, obviously dismissing her as being of little importance. Jill blinked for an instant to retain her poise. The jet blackness of his hair and brows had not prepared her for the metallic coldness of his eyes.

A frightened, helpless confusion gripped Kerry. Her beseeching brown eyes riveted themselves to Jill's face. Jill tried to instill a warmth of reassurance in her smile that gently prodded for an introduction. It took an instant for the bewildered Kerry to understand.

"I . . . I'd like you to meet m-my roommate, m-my friend, Jillian Randall." Her shaking voice wavered traitorously. "This is Todd's brother." A wave of red engulfed Kerry's face. "I'm so . . . sorry, but I don't know your first name, Mr. Riordan."

"Just call me Riordan."

His clipped, indifferent tone was reinforced by the lack of a glance in Jill's direction.

"Mr. Riordan, it's totally awesome to meet you." Jill wasn't about to offer a hand in greeting. As rude as he was, he would ignore it, and she didn't intend to let herself to be cut like that. "And please call me Jill. All my friends do."

The quicksilver sheen of his eyes passed over her face briefly and impatiently, openly wishing her gone. It only increased Jill's resolve to remain. "I bet I know why you're here, Mr. Riordan." She smiled widely, darting a warm glance at Kerry, whose face was still pale. "You must have heard the news about Kerry and Todd. Isn't it wonderful?"

There was a speaking glance from Riordan that told her to shut up and get lost. Jill's assumed air of denseness made it clear that she didn't understand. "Everyone here is so envious of Kerry," she rushed on with false excitement. "When you see Todd and Kerry together, it makes you feel all warm and wonderful inside. They're so very much in love . . . it just shines like a golden light. And Todd is so protective of her. No one can say a word against Kerry in front of him. You'll really be proud of him, Mr. Riordan, when you see the way he stands up for her." *Your move,* Jill thought silently. It might be his plan to break up the engagement, but she was confident that Todd would not be as easy to browbeat as Kerry was. His brother's gaze narrowed on Jill's guileless expression.

"Miss Randall!" Impatiently he snapped the words out, his eyes darkening to thunderclouds.

Jill made a silent wish that he could be more

impressed by her blond looks, but he seemed impervious to any attraction to her beauty.

"Jill," she interrupted quickly before he could finish the statement that was undoubtedly intended to dismiss her. "I think it's really terrific that you came all the way into town to meet your brother's fiancée. The two of you must be very close. How long are you going to stay?" He held his temper in check with difficulty as he gazed at Kerry and made Jill wait a long moment for his answer.

"Until I've completed what I came to do," he answered cryptically.

Namely, break things up between Kerry and Todd? Jill wondered to herself. Indignation flashed through her that he should decide that he didn't want Kerry as a sister-in-law without meeting her.

She covered her anger with a soft laugh, letting the battling sparkle in her blue eyes be misinterpreted as happiness.

"That means you can go out to dinner with us tomorrow night," she declared cheerfully. His glowering frown made her rush the explanation that was honey sweet with satisfaction. "Kerry, Todd and I want to celebrate their engagement on Saturday. Kerry doesn't have any family except an aunt and uncle. I feel as if she's my sister— we've more or less adopted each other. It's a pretend family celebration. You lost your parents, too, didn't you, Mr. Riordan? So it's just you and Todd. Now all four of us can have dinner tomorrow and toast the newly engaged couple. Or did you bring your wife along, Mr. Riordan?" Deliberately she blinked her long, curling lashes at his impassively hard expression.

"I don't have a wife, Miss Randall," in a voice

that plainly implied that it was truly none of her business.

Jill tipped her head back, swirling tawny-gold hair about her shoulders, purring laughter rising in her throat. "I just bet you'll be an uncle, then, before you're even a father. And the name is Jill."

His gaze trailed over her blankly happy expression to her throat. Jill was consumed by the sensation that he would like to shake her until her teeth fell out. Kerry moved uneasily beside her.

Jill let her gaze swing to her roommate. Her knuckles were turning white with the death grip she had on the notebooks, loose pages sticking out in crumpled disarray. Jill's airhead routine hadn't helped Kerry regain poise. She was on the verge of breaking, tears welling in her spaniel eyes.

Jill reached out, taking her roommate's left wrist and twisting it to see the watch face. "Wow, look how late it is, Kerry!" she exclaimed, turning an innocently apologetic glance to Todd's brother. "We have term papers to finish by Monday and a zillion research notes to take. Not much time before the library closes." After releasing Kerry's wrist, she dug her fingers into her roommate's shoulder, already turning her away toward the front door. "You'll probably be getting together with Todd. He'll fill you in on the time we're all meeting and stuff. I'm really glad I had the chance to meet you. I know you're just as happy about these two as I am. Good night, Mr. Riordan."

Her cheery departing wave was returned by a look that was broodingly thoughtful. Jill could feel his wintry-gray eyes following their path to the door. She kept up a steady, one-sided chatter until the door was safely closed behind them. Only then did she slacken their pace, drinking in deep gulps of the serene evening air.

The palms of her hands were wet. How strange, Jill thought, wiping the nervous perspiration on the hips of her light blue denims. She couldn't remember any time when she had been consciously or unconsciously intimidated by a man. This arrogant Riordan guy had affected her more than she realized. Her gaze slid to Kerry, still visibly trembling from the encounter.

"So. That's Todd's older brother," Jill breathed aloud.

Her statement released Kerry from the nameless fear that had held her speechless

"Jill, he doesn't want me to marry Todd!" Hysteria strained her voice. Her dream of perfect love had turned into a nightmare. "Before you got there he told me that if I truly loved Todd, I wouldn't hold him to the proposal. He said Todd still had to finish his education and begin his career and that he didn't need the burden of a wife."

"That's a lot of garbage," Jill responded calmly. Her shoulders lifted beneath the fawn leather jacket to indicate that he didn't know what he was talking about. "Plenty of couples get through college together, it happens all the time. Todd knows what he wants and he wants you."

"Todd is a Riordan," Kerry whispered, "and I could tell by the look in Riordan's eyes that he didn't think I was the right wife for Todd." She paused for a fleeting second. "Do you know, I've never heard Todd call him by his name. He either refers to him as his brother or simply as Riordan."

Jill glanced over her shoulder and saw Riordan emerge from the building. "Let's cut across the grass." She tucked a hand quickly under Kerry's elbow and guided her off the sidewalk. "And I wouldn't worry about what Todd's brother thinks. It's only Todd's opinion that counts and he's already proposed to you."

"But I tricked him into that. I made him think I was leaving Montana for the entire summer and we wouldn't see each other until the term started. I shouldn't have done that." Kerry's voice trailed off lamely, heavy with guilt and recrimination.

"What does it matter when Todd proposed to you—now or next fall? Unless you think he should have waited three or four years until he had his degree safely in his hand and a job lined up. Anyway, if Riordan really does think you aren't right, I doubt if time would change his opinion."

The wind tossed a burnished-gold lock of hair across Jill's face and she quickly smoothed it back. Her suggestion that Kerry fib about her summer plans might not have been exactly fair, but Jill wasn't going to waste time feeling guilty about it nor allow Kerry to either.

"Do you think Todd knows his brother is in town?" asked Jill in an afterthought.

As much as she disliked it, Jill thought she had to consider the possibility that Todd was having second thoughts about the marriage proposal and was using his brother as an excuse to break it off.

"I had the feeling that Riordan came straight to see me without talking to Todd except for this morning," Kerry answered.

Jill whispered a silent prayer of relief. There might have been some things about Todd that didn't appeal to her personally, but she had always believed his affection for Kerry was honest and straightforward.

"When we get to the library," Jill breathed in deeply, speaking aloud the battle plan that was forming in her mind, "I think you should call Todd and let him know in a diplomatic way what happened tonight."

"No." Kerry shook her head, the dark brown, straight hair swinging across her cheeks.

"No?" Jill's blue eyes widened in stunned surprise as she stopped to stare at her roommate. "Why not? He's your fiancé."

"But I'm not going to make trouble between Todd and his brother. We haven't been engaged for one whole day yet. I don't want to go running to him just because I might have misunderstood Riordan," her roommate argued. Jill wondered if it was logic that made Kerry reluctant to go to Todd, or an inner fear that Todd might be swayed by his brother's arguments.

"What about dinner tomorrow night?" Jill challenged softly.

"Todd . . . Todd is going to call me in the morning. I'll find out what time he thinks the f-four of us should meet." Her wavering voice indicated that her previous argument hadn't changed her apprehensions. She was unsure of Todd's reaction and wanted to postpone the moment when she would find out.

She felt a strong desire to insist that Kerry call Todd immediately, but Jill subdued it. Her roommate was already subconsciously regretting her interference that had prompted the proposal. She'd better sit back and be ready to pick up the pieces or, with luck, catch Kerry before she fell.

"Well, between now and tomorrow night—" Jill made her voice nonchalant, "—why don't you tell me everything you know about Todd's brother?"

Chapter Two

Kerry knew very little about Todd's brother, Jill discovered. He was Todd's elder by about eight years, which made him thirty-two or three. He had inherited the family ranch when their father passed away some five years ago. Kerry had forgotten where it was located except that it was somewhere near Dillon, Montana. Beyond that, she couldn't fill in the blanks.

The eraser end of the pencil tapped the edge of her notebook with monotonous rhythm. Only half of Jill's mind was concentrating on the paragraph she was reading. The rest was thinking of Riordan.

He resembled his brother in the clean cut of the cheekbones, the sharply defined jawline, the Roman boldness of the nose, the intelligent forehead, but the mouths were different. Todd's was curved and mobile, ready to spring into a smile or a laugh. His brother's was hard and grim, nothing gentle about it at all.

The result, as she visualized it, was night and day. Warm sunshine spilled over Todd to illuminate a smoothly handsome face. The dark shadows of night threw his brother's features in sharp relief to make him strikingly male but never handsome.

Jill leaned against the straight back of the chair, giving up the pretense of interest in the book opened before her. Tonight Riordan had been angry about the engagement of his brother, yet he had seemed curiously detached at the same time. How could a man confront his brother's fiancée with the hope of breaking the engagement and remain aloof at the same time? It was a contradiction that intrigued her.

A sideways glance at Kerry caught her gazing into space, a hollow look of fear in her expression. Jill breathed in deeply and expelled the air in a long sigh. Neither of them had accomplished anything in the two hours they had spent at the library.

She flipped shut the pages of her notebook with an air of finality. "Let's call it a night, Kerry," she murmured so as not to disturb the others studying at the long table. Without a whisper of protest, as if in a trance, Kerry gathered her papers into a stack and followed Jill out of the library.

A round silver-dollar moon hung above the capital city of Montana, its silvery light touching the crowning peaks of the mountains surrounding the city. A cool night breeze ruffled the careless tumble of Jill's tawny hair, the golden color paled by the moonlight. A crisscrossing spider web of streetlights illuminated the sidewalks and the girls walking in tense silence.

The whisper of tires on pavement went unnoticed until a car rolled to a stop beside them, the passenger door opening to block their progress. Kerry was nearest to the street. Steel-gray eyes focused on her.

"Get in. I'll give you a ride," was the curt command. Riordan again! He must have been waiting outside the library for them to leave, Jill decided swiftly as Kerry remained frozen in her tracks. The invitation was meant for her roommate alone and Jill knew it. Riordan intended to have his talk with Kerry, and Jill knew of only one way to circumvent it.

"Why, Mr. Riordan! We didn't expect to see you out here waiting for us." Jill stepped quickly forward, a bright smile curving her mouth. "How thoughtful of you to offer us a ride. Studying can be so mentally exhausting that it just drains all your energy." She slipped into the passenger seat, but avoided his gaze. "I can totally tell you're Todd's brother. He's always doing thoughtful things like this." Only when she was seated and about to make room for the bewildered Kerry did Jill allow her innocent blue eyes to be caught by his gaze. The line of his mouth was forbiddingly harsh. She let her eyes widen and the smile fade from her lips. "Oh," she murmured in a very tiny voice, "you were only going to take Kerry, weren't you? You didn't plan to give me a ride, too. I am sorry, Mr. Riordan. I didn't mean to be so obtuse. You want to talk to Kerry alone, don't you?"

"If you wouldn't mind, yes, I would," he agreed with cynical tautness.

"It's all right." Jill began sliding out of the car, giving him a falsely self-conscious shrug. "It isn't all that far to walk. I've done it lots of times, although never at night and alone."

As Jill stepped from the car, Kerry's gaze moved beseechingly to her face. Jill smiled faintly, not giving her roommate the reassurance she wanted.

"You go ahead and ride with Mr. Riordan," she prompted gently. "I'll see you back at our room."

"Jill, no, not alone!" The frightened protest made it clear that Kerry was afraid to be alone with Todd's brother.

Jill deliberately misunderstood her. "Don't be silly, Kerry. I'm not going to be molested. Except for that one block, it's all very well lit. I'll be okay, really."

As she expected, Kerry still didn't get into the car, hesitating while she silently pleaded for Jill to rescue her. From inside the car, Riordan swore under his breath. "Both of you get in!" he snapped.

Her back was to the open door and Jill winked broadly at Kerry. It was difficult to conceal her smile of triumph, although she knew it was only a temporary one.

She urged Kerry to get in the car first while her mind raced for a way to rescue her friend once they arrived at their destination. There wasn't any chance that she would be able to sit in the car and take part in the discussion as she had done in the hallway.

As they pulled away from the curb, a silence settled in, threatening to become oppressive. An uncontrollable shiver quaked over Kerry's shoulders, signaling to Jill that she couldn't let Riordan's presence dominate them.

"I guess it's the romantic in me that always finds

weddings so exciting." Jill heard the sound of disgust that came from Riordan's throat and smiled securely in the darkness of the car. "Kerry has already promised that I can be her maid of honor. I know Todd will ask you to be his best man. That's why I'm so glad I've had this chance to meet you before the wedding." She rushed on, "We've been talking about what colors Kerry should choose. She wants green and yellow—her favorites—but I was thinking it should be yellow and white or green and white. What's your opinion, Mr. Riordan?" she asked, leaning forward as if she was really interested in his answer, then hurrying on before he could reply. "I guess it really depends on when they decide to get married. Yellow and white would hardly be good winter colors, although I doubt if they would wait that long before tying the knot."

The inanity of her chatter sickened Jill. She knew it reinforced Riordan's opinion that she was a silly dumb blonde. At the moment she was interested only in shielding Kerry for as long as she could. All too soon they had traveled the short distance from the library to their dormitory.

The car stopped in front of the building. Unable to meet Kerry's pleading eyes, Jill glanced around her roommate to the impassive profile of the driver.

"Thanks a lot for the ride, Mr. Riordan," she offered brightly, and received a curt nod of dismissal in reply.

A quick good night to Kerry and Jill was out of the car. She wanted to run to the front door, but she kept her steps unhurried. The instant the door was closed behind her, she raced for the telephone booth.

Excitement had her fingers shaking. Jill had to try twice before she dialed the number correctly. "Todd Riordan, please, and hurry!" Her voice was oddly breathless. She rested her fingers on the steel coil of the telephone receiver as she waited impatiently.

"Todd Riordan here," came his familiar male voice.

"Todd, this is Jill."

"Jill?" His surprise was obvious. "What's wrong? Is something the matter with Kerry?"

"Yes, in a way. I don't have much time to explain. Your brother is here."

"Riordan? Damn him!" was the muttered response.

With a flash of insight Jill realized that Riordan had evidently made his opinion of Todd's engagement quite clear when Todd had made the telephone call to inform him of it. At least she didn't have to make a lengthy explanation.

She took a deep breath. She might as well let Todd know that she was aware of his brother's displeasure.

"He and Kerry are outside the house now. I believe he's giving her a hard time about your engagement. Kerry didn't want you to know about this, so when I go out there to tell her you're on the phone, I want you to pretend you're the one who called and not me."

"I'll take care of it," Todd answered grimly.

Setting the receiver on the small counter of the booth, Jill pivoted sharply out of the glass doors and retraced her path through the front door to the car. Her heart was pounding in her throat as she bent her head toward the window.

"Kerry, Todd's called. He wants to talk to you." In spite of her attempt to relay the message calmly, there was a note of victory in her tone. The sensation was increased by the look of utter relief on her roommate's face.

Kerry nearly bolted out of the car, not offering one word of goodbye to the grim-faced man behind the wheel. Jill couldn't resist a glance at him. There were times when rubbing salt into wounds was very enjoyable.

"Would you like to talk to Todd, Mr. Riordan?" she suggested sweetly.

His mouth tightened harshly. "No, I wouldn't."

The key was turned in the ignition and the powerful engine purred to life. Jill closed the door that Kerry had left open. Satisfaction glittered in her blue eyes as she watched the disappearing taillights that declared her the winner of this round.

At a more leisurely pace, she returned to the building. A glance at the tearfully happy smile on Kerry's face indicated that Todd was doing a very adequate job of reassuring her of his affection.

Riordan's first attempt had been thwarted and Todd was now aware of it. Would Riordan try again? Her brows arched faintly in speculation. Yes, he probably would, she decided. Perhaps he wouldn't be nearly as blunt with Todd, but she doubted if his determination had lessened.

It wasn't part of Jill's nature to inquire later exactly what Todd had said to Kerry. She and Kerry exchanged a lot of confidences, but her roommate was a very private person when it came to her inner emotions. There were personal aspects of her private life she was too shy to discuss and Jill wouldn't probe.

The only sour note in the evening's conclusion was that the dinner the following evening was no longer an uncertainty. Like it or not, Jill had to attend. She couldn't plead the excuse that it was a family affair, not after she had bragged about the dinner to Riordan and invited him herself.

When the hour arrived, Jill discovered that she was strangely looking forward to another encounter with Riordan. She attributed it to curiosity. It would be interesting to find out what his tactics would be now that he was presented with a united front. He had failed to divide Kerry from the rest and conquer her. Would he attempt to take on all three of them?

The hotel's wall mirror told Jill she had chosen her clothes well. The simple design of her dress gave her an air of innocent sophistication while the azure color pointed up the purity of blue in her eyes.

Jill caught Todd's warm smile in the mirror and returned it. They were comrades in arms, united to protect the petite, dark-haired girl walking between them.

"Where is he?" There was a tremor of nervousness in Kerry's whispered question, her brown eyes sweeping the hotel lobby and its open staircase to locate the man they had come to meet.

Todd's arm tightened slightly around her waist. "Riordan said he'd meet us in the lounge."

"Doesn't your brother have a first name?" Jill focused her attention on the closed lounge door. She half expected him to appear with the striding suddenness of the first time.

"Yes, it's John, but I can't remember the last time anyone called him that. He's always been simply Riordan. And I wouldn't suggest that you call him John either. He despises the name."

"John? But that's a great name." Her blue eyes widened in surprise.

"My mother named him after the man she admired most—her father," Todd answered dryly as his hand slipped to Kerry's elbow. He reached around to open the lounge door.

Jill would have liked to pursue that intriguing statement, but there wasn't time for a discussion of the Riordan family history. They were inside the lounge and somewhere in the dim room Todd's brother was waiting for them.

Like Todd and Kerry, her eyes searched the far corners of the room. She didn't recognize Riordan among the men sitting at the bar, nor was he sitting at any of the small round tables.

A light flickered in a corner booth, flaring brightly for an instant as the waitress lit the candle on the table. The flame cast a golden light over onyx-black hair and the darkly tanned, rugged features of the man within the circle of its light.

Jill felt her senses sharpening immediately. Darting a glance at Todd, she saw by the arch of his brow that he, too, had seen his brother. Meeting her glance above Kerry's head, his hazel-brown eyes said, *let's get it over with.* The arm at Kerry's waist turned her towards the booth and the three of them started forward at the same time.

An inner voice told Jill that Riordan had seen them the minute they had entered the lounge, although he didn't visibly acknowledge their presence until they were nearly at the booth. Then he slid with catlike grace to his feet to meet them.

The sheepskin jacket was gone. So were the denims and the cowboy boots. Jill realized, too late, that she had been partly taken in by his western garb in their previous meeting.

She had not anticipated the worldliness and sophistication that she saw now. A stranger viewing this Riordan in a gray Armani suit would see him as a business executive, not a man of the rugged outdoors as Jill had labeled him. She had underestimated him, and it was a mistake she didn't intend to repeat.

The metallic-gray eyes ignored both Jill and Kerry as Riordan met the silent challenge of his brother's gaze. Todd resolutely forced him to acknowledge both of them by making formal introductions. The action brought a twisting smile to the ruthlessly hard mouth, but the look directed briefly at Jill and Kerry in turn was without emotion. "Shall we sit down?" Riordan suggested blandly.

With some misgivings, Jill noted that she was to sit on the booth seat next to Riordan. Naturally Todd wanted to be close to Kerry, although Jill wished he had chosen to sit beside his brother.

The desire to edge as close to the wall as possible was nearly irrepressible. The palms of her hands were beginning to become damp. Jill told herself to relax and stop being intimidated by the man sitting beside her. She had maneuvered him quite easily yesterday. There was no reason to think she couldn't do it again if the need arose.

To break the silence until the waitress came back

to take their drink order, Todd inquired about the ranch and received ambiguous replies from Riordan. In another second, they'll discuss the weather, Jill thought tensely, darting a quick look at the slightly pale face of her roommate.

After the waitress had their order, Jill could see the impatience building in Todd's face. Riordan wasn't angry. There was none of the aloof moodiness that had been evident yesterday in his expression. In fact, he seemed quite content with just making them uneasy.

A pulse throbbed in her throat as unwillingly Jill glanced at the firm line of his mouth, a hint of cruelty in its masculine hardness. It would be no gentle kiss that he'd give a woman.

The drinks arrived, causing a momentary distraction. Jill's fingers closed around the cold glass in front of her. She smiled across the table at Kerry, who was glancing uncertainly at Todd. The electric current flowing from the man beside her needled Jill. She lifted her glass.

"I'd like to propose a toast," Jill declared. From the corner of her eye she could see Riordan leaning back, almost physically detaching himself from the group. "To the future Mr. and Mrs. Todd Riordan."

A shy pink crept into Kerry's cheeks as she peered at Todd's smiling face through her dark lashes. The faint blush of embarrassment made the sparkle of love in her brown eyes all the more radiant.

Three glasses met in the center of the table, but it was the absence of the fourth that was most notable. The gentle smile that had been on Todd's face faded as his gaze clashed and locked with his brother's. Sooty lashes had narrowed to a black screen, throwing shadows to darken the watchful gray eyes.

Todd didn't carry the glass to his mouth. "Riordan?" he prompted firmly.

Riordan appeared unmoved by the reprimand at his rudeness. In fact, he appeared very relaxed and in command.

"I don't approve of your engagement quite. Don't expect me to drink to it, Todd," was the even response.

"It happens to be my life. And guess what. It's my business what I do with it," challenged Todd.

"Being your brother gives me the right to interfere or at the very least, voice my opinion." The broad shoulders shrugged expressively. "I can't stop you marrying Kerry. But I can and I will withhold my support."

"That's not fair, Riordan, and you know it. That money was set aside for my education," Todd snapped.

"It's unfortunate that your father gave me sole control of the trust fund until you're thirty, then, isn't it?" The low voice was lazily calm as Riordan figuratively spread his cards on the table. He held a strong hand.

"It may come as a shock to you, but I think Kerry and I can make it without your support. It will mean sacrifices for both of us, holding down full-time jobs and a full schedule at college, but we can do it." Todd's arm circled Kerry's shoulder, drawing her closer to him.

"And maintain the grade level you have?" Riordan mocked.

"Maybe not, but we would get our degrees."

"Right. Just the two of you, struggling together, completely on your own. The harsh fact is that you'll be so busy struggling to survive that it'll be four or five years before you realize you've made a mistake. The two of you just aren't compatible. By that time there might be a child involved. You and I, Todd, know what it's like to grow up with parents that have separated."

"Kerry and I are very compatible and very much in love," Todd disagreed forcefully.

"That's what our parents claimed, too," was the quiet and silencing reply.

Todd wasn't able to hold the level gaze of his brother, a certain indication to Jill that Riordan's remark had touched a vulnerable spot. He let the silence settle heavily over the table before he continued.

"I'm not trying to make things difficult. I'm trying to appeal to reason, Todd," he said calmly. "Why tie yourself down? The next few years ought to be devoted to your studies and your future career. Todd, just be sure you're not confusing lust with love. Take her to bed. Make her your lover or whatever. But don't be a fool and marry her!"

Kerry's ashen face flamed scarlet. Jill wondered angrily why she had thought Riordan would be any less blunt with the three of them. Todd had started to listen to his brother's arguments, but the disrespect in the last of his statements had fortunately wiped out the inroads Riordan had made. He had overplayed his hand.

"If—" Todd was angry and making no attempt to conceal it, "—you'd taken the trouble to get to know Kerry, you wouldn't be so quick to insult her!"

"I've never pretended to be the tactful one in this family." Riordan's mouth twisted into a cold smile to match the glacial color of his eyes. "Don't waste your time defending her to me. If you feel the necessity for action, go arrange for a table in the dining room."

There was a seething moment of silence before Todd rose to his feet, impatiently signaling Kerry to accompany him. Jill was forgotten as the couple exited the lounge but murderous thoughts were racing impotently through her mind.

"Well?" Riordan's quietly challenging voice hadn't forgotten her.

Her eyes were round and blank when she turned to him. "Yes?"

"You're obviously in favor of this engagement. Aren't you going to defend your girlfriend?" The deceptively soft tone sliced like tempered steel through silk.

"I hate to contradict you, but I've seen Todd and Kerry together," Jill murmured with innocent apology. "I've noticed that their feelings for each other are essentially very strong and tender. And I think their personalities beautifully complement each other and fulfill basic needs."

"Todd takes after our grandfather. He has big ambitions, political ambitions. Can you picture Kerry as a politician's wife? Her shyness is bound to be a problem in a few years." Jill was unable to meet the intense scrutiny for fear her eyes would reveal her partial agreement with Riordan's assessment. "Todd should eventually marry . . . someone like you, who could be an asset to his chosen career," he concluded, surprising her.

"Like me?" A genuine frown of confusion puckered her brows, as she tucked a tawny gold strand of hair behind her ear.

"An attractive . . . a beautiful woman to be his hostess and entertain the important people he will have to cultivate."

"Really?" Jill tipped her head to one side as if considering his statement. "Whenever I see a man in public office who has a beautiful wife, I always have the feeling that he's lost touch with the common people. Besides, I think Todd would rather have a wife waiting at home than working beside him."

Again the sooty lashes narrowed, making his eyes unreadable. "Interesting. So you're convinced that a marriage between those two would work."

"I think it would work very well," she said, trying to be offhand and not forceful with her statement despite her inner convictions.

"Are you in favor of couples marrying while they're still in college? Now Kerry will have to support Todd for a few years while Todd obtains all his degrees. Quite a strain on a marriage, don't you agree?"

"Yes." Jill nodded. A sparkle of battle glittered in her blue eyes and she forced a smile to hide the antagonism he aroused. "Of course, if you were less controlling, it wouldn't be quite as much of a struggle, would it?"

"Is that what you think?" Riordan was leaning back, the ebony color of his hair darkened further by the shadows of the booth, his strikingly powerful features fully illuminated by the dim light.

The unwavering look in his compelling eyes made Jill vividly aware of the sensual charm he possessed. Her heartbeat accelerated briefly under the potent spell of his virility. Averting her head, Jill broke free of the magnetic pull of his gaze.

"I wouldn't presume to tell you what you should do." She laughed softly, giving the impression that the thought was ridiculous that a mere female could influence him one way or the other.

"Wouldn't you?"

The mocking words were said so softly that Jill wasn't sure whether she had heard them or only imagined them. There was no mistake the next time he spoke. His voice was clear and calm.

"But you think I should get to know Kerry better before I make my decision irrevocable."

"Of course. You guys are brothers, after all, and I know Kerry would hate to be the cause of any more harsh words between you and Todd." That was very definitely the truth. Kerry could be too sensitive. "And what if they eloped or something?"

The wide-eyed, "dumb blonde" look was firmly fixed on her face. Arguing with a man as arrogant as Riordan only made him more stubborn. It was better to keep up the airhead act a little longer and not try to pressure him into changing his mind.

His measuring, thoughtful glance trailed over Jill's face. Then Riordan reached for his glass, downed the drink and replaced the empty glass on the table.

"Let's find Todd and your friend," he suggested with a side look. "They may have decided to eat without us."

Jill gave a little nod of agreement and waited until he was standing to slide out of the booth. His gaze swept appraisingly over her when she stood at his side, a silver glitter that was faintly mocking. No guiding hand touched her, but she was very much aware of him walking beside her as they left the lounge.

Chapter Three

The conversation at the dinner table was stilted. It would have taken only a few conciliatory comments from Riordan to ease the tension, but he didn't make them. Jill had thought her offhand remarks had made an impression on him, but looking back, she could see it hadn't made any difference in his stand against Kerry's engagement to Todd.

There hadn't been any further confrontations, if that was a consolation. There again Jill decided it was because Riordan believed he had pushed Todd as far as he dared. But if Riordan's aim had been to make Kerry unhappy, he had succeeded. Jill couldn't remember seeing her roommate's face look so pinched and strained. Todd's look of concern and smiles of reassurance weren't as bolstering as they might have been if they were alone.

While Riordan was occupied paying the check,

Jill made the decision that Todd and Kerry should be alone. The sooner, the better. She could easily catch a taxi.

"Todd," she spoke quietly, not wanting to draw Riordan's attention, "why don't you and Kerry go ahead and leave? I'll find my own way."

"Are you sure you don't mind?" But there was relief in Todd's eyes.

"I suggested it, didn't I?" Jill smiled. Kerry opened her mouth to protest, but Riordan was moving toward them, his deceptively lazy strides covering the distance swiftly. The way Todd protectively nestled Kerry deeper in the crook of his arm made one corner of his brother's mouth lift in a mocking smile. It remained there to accept Kerry's frozen goodbye.

"I'll meet you here at seven in the morning for breakfast, Todd, before I leave for the ranch." It wasn't a suggestion, it was a command. Jill's lips started to tighten at his autocratic tone, but she relaxed them instantly into a smile when the gray eyes swung to her. "Miss Randall." There was an arrogant inclination of his dark head in goodbye.

"Good night, Mr. Riordan." She wasn't about to thank him for a miserable evening.

In the hotel lobby, they parted company, with Riordan disappearing almost immediately, presumably returning to his room. Todd hesitantly suggested that he and Kerry should give Jill a ride, but she airily waved it aside. The pair insisted on waiting until the doorman phoned the taxi company and received assurances that a cab would be dispatched immediately.

Todd's car was pulling out of the hotel parking lot. Jill stared through the glass windows at the dark shape of Kerry's head resting on the driver's shoulder. The course of true love never did run smooth. Wasn't that the saying? It must be true love, because Todd and Kerry had had a really bumpy start.

"Don't tell me they forgot to take you with them?"

Jill turned, her startled eyes focusing on Riordan. One arm held his jacket open, the hand negligently thrust in his trouser pocket. The other hand held a cigarette to his mouth, his eyes narrowed against the smoke curling from the burning tip. "Or did you arrange to be left behind?" Riordan added unpleasantly.

For another full second, speech was denied her but she finally managed a jerky laugh.

"You startled me." Her hair was caught in the collar of her light coat and she pushed it free. "Kerry and Todd weren't going directly back, so I decided to take a taxi. I—I don't like being the spare tire."

Her voice was low and oddly breathless. He surely didn't think she had stayed behind on the off chance of seeing him again.

"I doubt that *you* would," he agreed, with biting emphasis on "you." "But I was just going for a drive myself. I'll give you a ride."

"You don't need to do that. The cab's on the way here." Frantically Jill glanced out of the window, catching the headlight beam as a yellow taxi swung up to the curb beneath the covered drive. "In fact, it's here now. Nice of you to offer, though."

Before she could reach for the door handle, his arm was already in front of her to pull it open. Ducking under his arm, Jill unwillingly looked into his coolly appraising gray eyes, reflecting nothing but her own image. The cab driver was approaching the door as she stepped onto the sidewalk with Riordan directly and disconcertingly behind her.

"Did you call for a cab?"

"Yes," Jill responded quickly.

Riordan's hand closed over her elbow. "But the lady won't be needing one." He pressed a bill into the man's hand. "For your trouble."

The driver glanced at it, his face suddenly split with a smile. "Thank you, sir." And the money was quickly shoved into his pocket as he turned away.

Her lips moved to protest, but it was useless to openly oppose Riordan. At this point, it was better to accept his offer calmly than to make a fuss.

"I hope I won't be taking you out of your way, Mr. Riordan," Jill said as his hand guided her towards the parking lot.

"Not at all, Miss Randall." There was a suggestion of mockery in the deepening grooves around his mouth. "I had no particular destination in mind. I have a tendency toward claustrophobia whenever I spend any time in town." The car door was held open for her. Jill didn't comment until he had slid behind the wheel. "You seem to fit in very well with the city environment." Her gaze wandered over the perfectly tailored gray suit that only enhanced his lithe muscular build.

His gaze flickered to her briefly before he looked over his shoulder to reverse out of the parking space. "Do you believe clothes make the man, Miss Randall?"

"Jill," she corrected absently, then answered his

question. "You don't appear uncomfortable in them."

"That's strange . . . Jill." He hesitated deliberately over her first name, making it come out husky and mocking. "I would have thought you would realize that a wolf in sheep's clothing is still a wolf."

"Are you a wolf, Mr. Riordan?" Unwittingly her voice dropped the facade of innocence and became slightly baiting.

"Call me Riordan. I'm a lone wolf who prefers to travel without the supposed benefit of a pack or a mate."

Jill leaned back in her seat. Was he warning her? Did he think she was making a play for him? Surely not. She hadn't flirted with him once or given him a single indication that she was interested in him as anything more than Todd's brother and Kerry's future brother-in-law.

Maybe he had become accustomed to women pursuing him. A lot of women would be attracted to that dangerous air he possessed. Catching him would be a challenge. Under different circumstances, she might have tried herself, just for the fun of it.

"You can travel faster that way," she agreed. Directing her gaze out of the moving car window, she pretended an interest in the passing scenery. Silence seemed a way to end this uncomfortably personal conversation

"Are you from Montana?" Riordan didn't let the silence last for long.

"Yes. My parents live in West Yellowstone, where I was born and raised."

"You must be accustomed to spectacular scenery."

"Does anyone ever become accustomed to it? I hope not." Jill smiled naturally.

"Do you have any brothers or sisters?"

"Four. Three brothers and one sister."

"Older or younger than you?" Riordan asked, turning the wheel to guide the car around the corner.

"I have a brother who's two years older than me. The rest are younger." She darted a quick glance at his averted profile, curious why he was interested in her family background. A germ of an idea took root. "Andy, my older brother, is the only one of us who's married. He met his wife when he was stationed with the Marine Corps in California. He called my parents up one night and told them he was married. It was quite a shock for all of us, but once we had a chance to get to know his wife, Sally, we all liked her."

He turned his head slightly, running an eye over her face. "Subtlety is not your strong point, is it?" he suggested dryly.

"Well, I don't give up," Jill returned with a malicious sparkle in her azure eyes.

"But your brother is your business and my brother is mine." The line of his mouth was inflexible, the firm set of his features yielding not one fraction to her honey-coated attempt at persuasion.

A thundering discovery vibrated over Jill with the suddenness of a summer storm. An intangible something had been troubling her ever since the first time she had seen Riordan, some little something that set him markedly apart from any man she had ever known. This very second she realized what it was.

Riordan didn't like her. Not because she was

beautiful or because he believed she was dumb. It was because she was a woman. Jill held herself motionless, letting her mind register the discovery. Riordan was attracted to women, but he didn't much like them.

His childhood couldn't have been much different from Todd's, and Todd bore no emotional scars from the evident separation of their parents that Riordan had referred to briefly. Had he fallen in love with a woman at some time and been rejected?

It was possible, Jill conceded. He was a passionate man for all his impassive exterior. Not passionate in the erotic sense of the word, but in the depth of his convictions and feelings. He could carry a grudge for a very long time. Those gray eyes of his sliced through the pretensions of life in the new millenium to leave only the basics. He wore the cloak of civilization when circumstances demanded, as now, but he was a man of the elements—primitive, ruthless, and strong.

Jill brushed a hand in front of her eyes. Was this insight a blessing or a curse? She didn't want to know such things about Riordan. She didn't even want to think them.

Forcing her eyes to focus on the passing scenery, Jill willed her mind to concentrate on it. They had turned onto the main street of Helena, called Last Chance Gulch.

Once it had been a gulch filled with prickly pear and not a main paved street. That was in the beginning when four luckless prospectors had arrived to take their "last chance" at striking it rich. That July of 1864, something flashed in their gold pans and by autumn, a hundred makeshift cabins made up the gold rush settlement and Last Chance Gulch.

A town had been born. Last Chance Gulch was not a dignified name and survived only through the early months of the town's existence. Then the city fathers changed it to Helena; naming the main street, where twenty million dollars in gold was mined, Last Chance Gulch.

The old, weathered buildings had had a colorful history. The south end of Last Chance Gulch had been the site of Chinatown. The Chinese, who had provided much of the labor to build the railroads, also cultivated truck gardens and operated their own stores. They even had a long tunnel beneath their particular section that they had used as a private opium den.

The architecture of the old buildings ran to stone arches and columns, combined with frieze and cornice and heavy timbers. The car was turning around another corner, leaving Last Chance Gulch to pass the Great Northern Depot, which, before the earthquake, had once possessed a tall clock tower. Then Jill's attention was caught by the Moorish style of the former Shrine Temple, now the Helena Civic Center.

"What are you thinking about?" Riordan interrupted the silence again.

Jill kept her gaze centered on the lighted street. "The city, its history." She shrugged.

A shiver danced over her skin as she wished she had never met him, or been momentarily entranced by his harshly handsome looks.

"Really?" was the disbelieving reply.

The car slowed to pull up to the curb in front of the dormitory entrance. The engine was switched off and Riordan partially turned to face her. The metallic glitter of his gaze shimmered over the gold of Jill's hair, burnished by the outside streetlight.

His arm stretched negligently on the back of the seat, his hand only spare inches from her head. Jill tensed slightly, reacting to the latent animal instinct that warned her to be careful.

"I thought you might be thinking of some new tactic to maneuver me into changing my mind." His voice was low and cynical.

"Maneuver?" Jill swallowed. Her lashes fluttered, a gold-brown fringe above deepening blue eyes.

"Isn't that what you've been doing since we met?" The softly dangerous tone dared her to deny it.

"I don't know what you mean," Jill protested weakly. Her naive facade was being penetrated by his intelligent gaze and she was helpless to stop it. "Well, um, have I tried to convince you to give Kerry and Todd a chance? Yes, I have."

"Do you honestly expect me to believe you're as innocent as you appear?" Riordan smiled coldly, his amusement at her expense.

"You're talking in circles." Jill looked at him in uncertain confusion, tossing her hair to the side in bewilderment. "I don't understand what you're saying."

"Your act was very good, but intelligence has a way of letting itself be seen."

"My act?" she repeated blankly.

Inside she knew she couldn't admit that there was any truth to his accusations. If she stopped playing the dumb blonde now, she would end up losing her temper and telling him exactly what she thought of his arrogant ways. That anger would not help Kerry at all, although it would certainly release some of her own frustration.

"Really, Mr. Riordan, you just aren't making any sense." She reached for the door handle of the car. "I'd better be going inside."

It was locked. For a poised instant, her eyes searched frantically for the release before she realized that it was on the driver's side. Unwillingly she had to turn back to his mocking expression.

"Would you please unlock the door?"

Her request was met with silence and a complacent look. Jill nervously ran her tongue over her lower lip. The action focused his attention on her mouth.

"How do butterflies steal the nectar from so many flowers and never get caught?" He smiled cynically, not requiring a reply.

Butterfly! The word shivered over her skin, goose bumps rising along the back of her neck. Only yesterday Jill had used that very word to describe herself. Riordan had chosen the same one. Coincidence? Or had some mysterious something passed between them, giving each the insight about the other?

"Why . . . why did you say butterfly?" She had to ask the question, her voice breathless and at odds with the guileless expression.

"Because," Riordan answered slowly, "you're as beautiful, as fragile, and about as constant as a butterfly." It was a condemnation, not a compliment. The back of a finger followed a strand of tawny gold hair away from her face and down the back of her neck. Jill was pinned, like the butterfly he called her, by his steel-sharp gaze. "I've always wondered if the honey tastes sweeter from the lips of a butterfly."

His hand cupped the back of her neck, fingers twisting into her hair, adding further pressure to draw Jill toward him. Her hands spread across his chest in resistance.

A soft, surprised, "No!" was offered in protest.

A tug of her hair turned her face up to meet his descending mouth, a flash of masculine amusement in its hard line an instant before it captured her lips. A hot fire of humiliation raced through her veins. In another second, Jill felt, she would melt into the seat under the sensual warmth of his kiss.

It was not the way a man would kiss a woman but the way a man would take his pleasure of a prostitute, without a thought or a care to her feelings. But his strength was overpowering. Her struggles were only the useless flutterings of butterfly wings against iron bars.

Beneath her doubled fists straining against his chest, she could feel the steady beating of his heart. Her own was hammering like a mad thing. The bruising kiss was sapping all her strength, taking it from her as if it were nectar from a flower. There was no escape from his erotically charged embrace.

Riordan had attacked with the swiftness of an eagle swooping on its prey. With the same unexpectedness, he freed her mouth and relaxed the talon-hard grip on her neck, his fingers sliding to her fragile collarbone, capable of snapping it at the least provocation—or caressing it. Jill's head sank wearily in defeat, her tousled golden hair cascading forward over his hand to conceal the flaming humiliation in her cheeks.

But she wasn't allowed the precious seconds to regain her whirling equilibrium and take the calming breaths of air. Her chin was captured between his thumb and forefinger and raised so Riordan could study his conquest. Mirrored in his silver eyes was her own flushed and resentful expression, nothing more.

"So which of us is stronger, Miss Randall?" His mouth curled in a tantalizing smile.

"Physically—you are!" she hissed, a fiery glare in her blue eyes. But Riordan was made of steel, not wood, and the fire missed its target.

The grooves around his mouth deepened. "Don't make the mistake of thinking it's only physical," he warned in a low voice.

Releasing her completely, he was once again sitting behind the wheel. A movement of his hand near the control panel was followed by the comforting click of the car door being unlocked.

"Good night, Miss Randall."

Her knees trembled badly as she stepped from the car onto the curb. His assault on her—it could hardly be termed an embrace—had shaken her more than she realized, but it hadn't broken her spirit. With the security of distance between them, she turned, holding the door open as she leaned down to glare at him.

"Don't you make the mistake of thinking it's over, Riordan. I'm going to do everything I can to make sure Kerry and Todd are married as soon as possible!" She hurled the challenge, slammed the door and marched toward the building.

For a few quaking moments, Jill thought he

might come after her. Unconsciously she held her breath, expelling it in a long sigh when she heard the snarl of the car engine. Those were bold words she had spoken, but she was determined to make them fact.

Kerry returned some time past midnight. Jill was in her single bed, feigning sleep. Her mind was too filled with vindictive thoughts. She doubted if she could hold them back in the intimacy of a late-night chat, and it was better if Kerry never found out about what had happened. Fortunately, her dark-haired roommate changed into her night-clothes and made no attempt to waken her, slipping silently into the small bed opposite Jill's.

Morning brought the exhilarating knowledge that Riordan was on his way out of town, if not already gone. Jill's sleep had been plagued by the lurking memory of his supersexy kiss, but the rising sun seemed to burn away the humiliation she had suffered at his hands. Kerry, too, had seemed more relaxed and less troubled when she had dressed to meet Todd for church.

Arching her back, stretching cramped muscles, Jill couldn't help wondering what had taken place during Todd's meeting with Riordan that morning. Whatever had transpired, she could be sure of one thing—Riordan hadn't experienced a change of heart.

She blinked her eyes tiredly. Her mind was wandering from the task at hand again. If she had concentrated on what she was doing, the term paper would have been done an hour ago, she scolded herself, and forced her gaze to focus on the laptop screen. As she printed out the paper, the hallway door opened. Jill glanced around to see Kerry entering the room.

"Excellent timing, Kerry," she greeted her roommate with a smiling sigh. "This is the last page. The laptop is all yours."

"I brought you a sandwich and a Coke, I thought you'd probably be hungry." Kerry motioned toward the paper bag she had set on the bureau top.

"You're a lifesaver!" Jill gathered up her papers and stacked them on the corduroy quilted cover of her bed. With the bag in hand, she returned to the bed, folding her long legs beneath her to sit cross-legged near the head of the bed. "You and Todd must have gone out to dinner after church."

Her comment was met with silence. A curious frown pulled Jill's arched brows together as she glanced up. Kerry was going through the motions of hanging her dusty-rose coat in the closet, but her mind seemed far removed from the task.

"Kerry?" Jill snapped her fingers to prod her friend back to the present.

"What?" Kerry looked around blankly. "I'm sorry. Did you say something?"

"Nothing important." Jill set the Coke on the table between the two beds and took the wrapped sandwich from the bag. "You were in a daze."

"Was I?" The coat was carefully hung in the closet before Kerry walked slowly to her bed. She sat on the edge, staring thoughtfully at the hands she clasped in her lap. "I suppose I was thinking," she murmured.

"That's a safe guess," Jill teased, but her expression was marked with concern. "Of course, the next question is what were you thinking about?"

The hands twisted nervously in her lap. "You remember that Todd met with Riordan this morning."

"Yes." Her blue gaze hardened warily. She unwrapped the sandwich, pretending an interest in it. "What did the great man have to say?" She couldn't keep the sarcasm out of her voice.

"Todd's application for a transfer to Harvard has been accepted. Riordan received the notification at the ranch this last week," Kerry told her.

So Riordan had another ace up his sleeve, Jill thought angrily. All he had to do was keep Todd and Kerry apart for the summer and the distance between Montana and the East Coast would take care of the rest of the year. He was probably counting on out of sight being out of mind.

"You and Todd will have to set the wedding date for sometime in August, then, won't you?" Jill tossed her head back, letting the golden curls trail down her back.

"With your grade point average you could easily transfer to a university out there."

"I couldn't afford the out-of-state tuition, though." Kerry sighed.

As Riordan had no doubt guessed, Jill added savagely to herself. "And Todd wouldn't be able to help because Riordan is still threatening to shut off the money supply." Her fingers tightened on the sandwich, smashing the bread and wishing it was Riordan's neck. "The two of you can't allow him to blackmail you this way!"

"Todd doesn't think we should do anything too hasty yet."

"Does he think Riordan's going to change his mind? This isn't the age of miracles." At the pinched lines that appeared around Kerry's mouth, Jill wished that her reply hadn't been so completely negative. She should have left her friend with a little hope.

"Well," Kerry breathed in deeply, "Riordan did make a proposition to Todd this morning."

"What kind?" Jill was skeptical of any proposition Riordan would offer.

"He . . . he conceded that he might have been too harsh and quick in his judgment."

"That's big of him," Jill grumbled, biting into her sandwich.

"He admits he was prejudiced against me before we ever met and that he should at least get to know me better. He still doesn't approve of the engagement," Kerry hastened to add.

"So what has he suggested?" Jill asked dryly. "A trial period?" Until the autumn term started and Todd was gone to Harvard, Jill completed the thought silently.

"Something like that," her roommate admitted, finally lifting her gaze from the twining fingers in her lap to look at Jill. "Todd works at the ranch in the summer. Riordan has invited me to spend a month there so he and I can get better acquainted."

Total disaster, was Jill's first thought. Kerry was already intimidated by the man. A month in his company would totally subdue her even with Todd's support. Jill did not underestimate Riordan. She knew his capabilities and the lengths he would go to achieve his ends.

She stared at her sandwich. "There's a catch, Kerry. How are you going to stay at his ranch and earn money to pay for your fall term as well?'' Both she and Kerry were going to work for Jill's parents that summer in their motel restaurant near the entrance to Yellowstone Park. ''Mom and Dad will have to hire someone to take your place. You won't even have a summer job after you've spent a month there.''

''Riordan has offered to compensate me for that.''

She should have guessed he would cover every contingency. Jill stuffed the partially eaten sandwich back in the sack. It had begun to taste like cotton.

''You can't be seriously considering the offer,'' Jill protested desperately, pressing two fingers against her forehead, trying to rub away the throbbing ache that had started between her eyes. ''You know it wouldn't work. He'd make your life a total misery. You know what he can be like when Todd isn't around. How long do you think you could take it?''

''I couldn't, not alone. But—'' Kerry's brown eyes became round and pleading, giving her plain features a lost, helpless look, ''—if you were with me—''

''I'll let you in on a little secret,'' Jill interrupted quickly, drawing a deep breath and untangling her legs. ''Riordan doesn't like me and he isn't about to invite me to spend a month at his ranch. Besides I have to work this summer, too.''

''Jill.'' Something in Kerry's voice put her instantly on guard. ''Riordan thought it might not look right for me to stay there at the house for a month with Todd and him. I mean, he does have a housekeeper, but . . . well, he invited you to come, too, as a kind of chaperone—with the same offer of compensation.''

''Oh, no!'' Jill was on her feet, striding away from the bed to the solitary window. She shook her head vigorously as her hands rubbed the chilling goose-flesh on her upper arms. ''No!''

''Please.'' There was a yearning need in the coaxing tone.

Jill spun around. ''It just wouldn't work, Kerry.''

Lord, but that man had a devious mind! He had considered every possible argument she could have made to prevent Kerry from going.

That he had invited Jill confirmed the magnitude of his arrogance. She had challenged him and now he was offering a front row seat for her to watch him tear the engagement apart. Riordan would have his revenge and be aware of any move Jill made to thwart his attempts. Jill had underestimated him again, and she didn't like the sensation of being bested.

Kerry's soulful eyes didn't see any of that. ''You must come.''

''Don't you see,'' Jill protested in agitation, ''if I come I'll end up losing my temper and only make the situation worse for you and Todd. The wisest thing for you to do is refuse the invitation and take the chance that Riordan won't be able to force Todd to break the engagement. That's the most logical thing, because Todd does love you.''

''I can't.''

The dark head was turned away, tears misting diamond bright in her brown eyes. Jill wanted to take her by the shoulders and shake her hard.

''Why can't you? You can't go there alone!''

''Yes, I can.'' Kerry brushed away a tear with her

hand and let her unreproachful gaze meet Jill's impatient look. "I love Todd. I don't want to come between him and his brother. Not having a family I think I know how important it is. If there's only the slimmest chance that Riordan might approve of Todd marrying me after spending a month at the ranch, I'll take it. I'd feel better if you would come with me, but I'm going either way."

"Kerry, this is a stupid time to turn heroic." Jill sighed. Her mouth thinned in annoyance at the way Kerry winced at her impulsive remark. "Besides, my parents are expecting me to work this summer, not have a vacation. I couldn't tell them at the last minute that they're going to have to find someone else to take my place."

"You said yourself that they have more applications than jobs. They could easily hire someone else," Kerry reminded her quietly.

"I suppose they could," Jill conceded grudgingly, "but they would never agree to this plan. Riordan has a housekeeper. You said so yourself, and chaperones went out of fashion with hoop skirts."

"You could call them and see."

Staring into the resigned yet pleading face of her roommate, Jill knew she would have to make the telephone call. What kind of a friend would she be if she let this poor defenseless creature walk into Riordan's lion den without protection? The question was, who was going to protect Jill? She hoped her parents would.

They were infuriatingly understanding.

Chapter Four

This was big sky country. The last of the big-time splendors. That's the way the brochures described Montana. The vast prairielands in the east rolled westward, gathering speed to swell into mountains towering like a tidal wave over the landscape.

Looking over the horizon where majestic mountain peaks tried to pierce the crystal blue bubble of sky, Jill felt the answering surge of her heartbeat. Their early summer coat of vivid green could only be rivaled by the bold splash of autumn or the stark white purity of winter.

Now it was green, a multitude of shades broken only by the dark brown of tree trunks driving upward toward the sky, the rocky faces of the mountains catching the golden sun, and the brilliant pinks, yellows and white of wildflowers dotting the meadows and craggy slopes. Breathtaking and awesome, the scenery remained constant while ever-changing. The tremendous sensation of being released from an earthbound existence to soar to some magnificent plateau was overwhelming.

"I feel it every time," Jill murmured.

"What did you say?" Kerry glanced at her curiously, not quite catching the softly spoken words.

"I was admiring the scenery." Reluctantly she drew her gaze to the interior of the car. "I never tire of looking at the mountains, especially like this, unspoiled and wild."

"They make me feel small and insignificant," Kerry said, "but they are beautiful."

Jill leaned forward to glance around her friend at their driver. "I've lived in Montana all my life, but always in town. What's it like, Todd, to live in the mountains year round?"

He smiled faintly, sliding a brief look to her. "I don't know."

"What?" Her blond head tilted to the side in surprise.

"When I was born my mother moved into town. I only spent the summers with my father on the ranch," he explained. "So I have no idea what it's like to be in the country during the last days of Indian summer or see the first winter storm clouds building on the mountain peaks. I've often wondered, too, what it would be like, but never enough to find out."

"I didn't know. I mean, Kerry did mention that your parents didn't live together, but I guess I assumed they didn't separate until you were older." Jill leaned back, staring thoughtfully ahead. It was difficult to imagine Riordan growing up in a town. The image of him being raised in the mountains under the domination of the elements was much easier to accept. "Of course, Riordan was older than you. The adjustment must have been harder for him."

"He wouldn't try to adjust," Todd replied. "My mother told me that the minute he found out that she wasn't ever going back to the ranch, he ran away. He was nine years old and hitchhiked all the way back to the ranch. That happened three or four times before my grandfather suggested that it might be better to let Riordan stay on the ranch with his father. She finally agreed. When I was older I remembered asking him one time how he'd had the courage to come all the way from Helena, where mom and I lived with her father, to the ranch by himself." The corners of his mouth were turned up in a wry smile. "He said there wasn't any other way he could get home. The ranch has always been home to him. For me, it's just a place to spend the summer vacation."

There was a twinge of envy that Riordan could rightfully call the mountains home. Then Jill considered the single-minded determination of the nine-year-old boy who had traveled the hundred and fifty odd miles southwest of Helena.

That part of him hadn't changed. Now he was determined to prevent a marriage between Todd and Kerry. He wasn't going to let anything stand in his way. He had even invited Jill along to watch.

Drawing in a deep breath, Jill shook her head slightly in angry despair. There were three fools in this car. She wasn't sure which of them was the biggest. Probably herself, since the other two were blinded by their love for each other. The month promised to be a long and trying one—if she and Kerry survived.

"What was Riordan like as a boy?" It was better to find out as much as she could about the enemy.

"I don't know," Todd answered thoughtfully. "When you're a kid yourself, you don't pay much attention to those things. He was always 'big brother,' teaching me to ride, taking me hunting, letting me tag along. He was just Riordan."

Kerry shuddered involuntarily. Todd reached out and covered the small hand on her knee with his own. Out of the corner of her eye, Jill saw the reassuring squeeze.

"Don't start worrying," he murmured softly. "Once he gets to know you, he'll see how great you are."

Jill fell silent. Todd seemed unable to tell her much about Riordan and the mention of his name was only making Kerry more uneasy. A smile tugged at the corners of her mouth. She was concerned about making Kerry uneasy, when she had been sitting on pins and needles for the last half hour herself. The points had grown sharper as they came closer to their destination. It couldn't be far now. They had turned off the main highway several miles back.

As if on cue Todd slowed the car and turned onto a dirt road leading farther into the mountain wilderness. The fence opening had no gate as the tires thumped over a cattle guard.

"This is it," he announced, nodding his head at the window to indicate the land around them. "The house is a few miles back."

Glancing back, Jill couldn't see any sign identifying the ranch as Riordan's property. The only sign she had noticed was one saying: No Trespassing. A prophetic warning, perhaps?

The midafternoon sun shone in her eyes as they topped a meadow rise and Jill caught her first glimpse of the ranch house. Large evergreens stood in a horseshoe guard on three sides of the house, protecting it from sweeping winter winds. The two-story house itself was a tasteful example of turn-of-the century architecture, with its entrance porch a columned portico. Yet its wood and stone exterior was in keeping with its rustic setting.

"It's beautiful!" Kerry breathed, breaking the spell of immobility after the car had stopped in front.

"Just a little cabin in the mountains," Todd joked, opening his door and stepping out. It wasn't a mansion, but its graceful, old-fashioned lines were impressive just the same, Jill decided. She was eager to see the inside.

As she stepped out of the car, her gaze moved to the ranch buildings. There was no sign of any activity either there or in the house. She had expected Riordan to be on hand to greet them, and been bracing herself to meet his cynical, mocking gray eyes.

"I didn't expect it to be so nice," Kerry whispered. Jill glanced at the petite brunette now standing beside her.

"Let's see if the inside lives up to the outside," she replied quietly, turning to walk to the rear of the car where Todd was unloading their luggage.

With Todd carrying the heavier cases and the two girls the lightweight ones, they mounted the steps to the heavy oak door.

The formal entry hall gleamed with hardwood wainscoting below bright upper walls of cream yellow. A carved oak staircase led to the upper floor at the end of the hall. On their left was a fireplace of native granite, the trophy head of a bighorn sheep hanging above the mantel. The hardwood floor beneath their feet was parquetry, inlaid with geometric designs.

Todd set the cases onto the floor. "I wonder where Mary is," he frowned.

Footsteps approached, unhurried and light. Jill's head turned in their direction, wondering what kind of a woman this Mary was. Anyone who kept house for Riordan would have to be a paragon to satisfy him. From the looks of the polished entrance hall, Jill guessed that the housekeeper was.

If she'd had a subconscious image of the housekeeper, Jill wasn't aware of it. Yet astonishment crackled through her at the sight of the young, almond-eyed woman who came into view. Long chestnut hair flowed around her shoulders as the sensuously curved woman glided toward them. Her eyes were a tawny hazel shade like a cat's and there was a purring quality about her smile.

"Welcome home, Todd." She ignored both girls to walk directly to Todd and press a less-than-motherly kiss on his cheek.

Jill doubted if the woman was Riordan's age, although looks were deceiving and it was possible she was in her very early thirties. It wasn't difficult for Jill to believe that her talents went beyond housekeeping.

Todd laughed self-consciously and glanced at Kerry before returning his attention to the woman whose hand was still resting lightly on his arm. "I didn't expect to see you here, Sheena."

Sheena? This wasn't Mary, the housekeeper? Jill's eyebrows lifted fractionally in further surprise. The woman was certainly acting the hostess and not a guest.

The purring smile deepened although it didn't reach the woman's cat-gold eyes. "I've been deputized as your official welcoming committee. Riordan is away from the ranch this afternoon. I'm sorry I didn't hear you drive in, but I was in the kitchen helping Mary with dinner tonight."

"I . . . I hope you're joining us," Todd offered politely but with little enthusiasm.

"I am." Then the woman's gaze swung to Jill, indifferent in its appraisal of her blond hair and blue eyes. "I'm Sheena Benton, Riordan's closest neighbor. You must be Todd's girlfriend. Kerry, isn't it?"

Closest neighbor? Is that all? Jill thought suspiciously as she smoothly shook the artistically long and slender hand offered to her.

"No, I'm Jillian Randall, Kerry's friend," she corrected lightly.

The tawny eyes narrowed fleetingly before they darted to the plain, dark-haired girl at Jill's side. An uncomfortable flush in Kerry's cheeks indicated her painful awareness of Jill's obvious beauty, her golden looks intensified by Kerry's mouse-soft coloring.

Jill wanted to cry out at the haughty condemnation in the woman's eyes. Kerry's beauty was on the inside, but Jill doubted if this feline creature would understand.

Sheena Benton laughed throatily at her own mistake. There wasn't any amusement, however, when the tawny gaze refocused on Jill. There was a glitter of malevolence in the almond-shaped eyes. Instinctively Jill glanced at the woman's hands, half expecting to see them transformed into cat's claws to scratch her face.

"It's a pleasure to meet you, Jillian," Sheena declared in a husky voice. *Liar,* Jill thought to herself. "I must admit you really don't look like a chaperone."

"I'm really here as Kerry's friend."

Her hand was released as the woman turned to Kerry and inclined her head in a falsely apologetic fashion. "I'm sorry about the mistake," Sheena Benton said in a regal tone.

"It's quite all right," Jill murmured self-consciously. Kerry glanced through the corner of her lashes at Todd as though fearful he might suddenly realize how plain and unobtrusive she was. Warm, hazel eyes affectionately returned her surreptitious look.

"You'll probably be very grateful for your friend's company after you've been here awhile," Sheena continued. "At the end of a week, the magnificent scenery around here begins to pale when you have nothing else to do. That's when boredom sets in."

"You don't look bored, Miss Benton," Jill couldn't resist inserting.

"But then I live here. I've had a few town friends stay with me. Invariably they begin climbing the walls after a week." A cold smile was directed at Jill. "And it's Mrs. Benton."

"You're married?" she returned with some surprise.

"Widowed," was the complacent reply. "My husband was killed in a hunting accident four years ago."

"It must have been a shock," Jill suggested dryly.

"In the beginning I was kept much too busy

trying to keep the ranch going, and by the time Riordan helped me find a competent manager, the worst of the shock had passed." Feline shoulders shrugged as if to say the marriage was long ago and forgotten. "As the owner, I still have enough responsibilities to keep me occupied. I don't have time to be bored."

"Neither will Kerry," Todd grinned, indifferent to the invisible sparks flying between Sheena and Jill. "I intend to devote every spare moment to making sure she enjoys this month."

"Spoken like a typical young lover," Sheena laughed throatily, mocking their youth. "You'll find life operates at a simpler level, Kerry. A night out will probably consist of a walk in the moonlight. Todd is a patient teacher, though. Maybe in a month you'll be a country girl like me."

"Not too much of a country girl," Todd qualified Sheena's statement. "We're going to be living most of our life in cities. I want to keep Kerry mainly a town bird."

The light shining in Kerry's eyes said she would be whatever Todd wanted her to be. In that silent second, Jill forgot the chestnut-haired woman with the tawny eyes and remembered the reason she was in this house. Her mission was to do everything in her power to make certain Kerry and Todd lived happily ever after, as the fairy tales put it.

"Let me show you two girls to your rooms," Sheena inserted smoothly, turning towards the staircase at the end of the entrance hall. "I know you'll want to unpack and bathe and rest before dinner. Naturally you have your old room, Todd," she tossed over her shoulder.

Jill and Kerry followed the woman gliding effortlessly over the flowered carpet that covered the stairs. Sheena Benton seemed intent on impressing them with the idea that she was the hostess in the house, and not just for the afternoon.

"I hope you girls don't mind sharing a bathroom." Sheena paused at the top of the stairs for them to catch up. "You have adjoining rooms with a bathroom in between."

"Sounds fine," Jill nodded.

"Good." With a brief smile, the woman walked familiarly down the wainscoted hallway, opened a door and stepped to the side. "This is your room, Kerry."

There was a fleeting impression of delicate shades of green before her petite friend moved hesitantly into the doorway to block Jill's view. Sheena was already pivoting away, indicating that Jill follow her.

"And your room, Jillian, is here," she said.

The door swung open to a room dominated by white with a sprinkling of blue, contrasted by artistically carved woodwork of polished walnut. A Persian rug in an intricate design of blue and white covered the floor. The skillfully styled furniture in the room was, if Jill didn't miss her guess, antique.

Her eyes sparkled with appreciation and admiration as she stepped farther into the room. The large double bed had a white cover hand-crocheted in a popcorn stitch—the perfect touch.

Setting her small suitcases on the floor, Jill turned to the woman standing in the doorway. "It's lovely," she murmured inadequately.

Any further attempt to express her delight with the room was checked by the look in Sheena's face which clearly said not to become too enamored of a room she would only have for a month. Then Sheena's eyes seemed to change from an amber warning shade to an aloof tawny gold.

"The bathroom and your friend's room are through there," she said, flicking a hand toward the door near the fireplace. "Dinner is at seven."

"Thank you."

But Jill's polite words were spoken to a closing door. She pursed her lips thoughtfully. Something told her she had to watch out not only for Riordan but for Sheena as well. The woman didn't like her or want her here.

Shaking her head to rid her mind of its unwelcome thoughts, Jill walked to the connecting door. The bathroom was large and spacious, its fixtures old-fashioned but in perfect condition. The murmur of Todd's and Kerry's voices in the adjoining room made Jill tap discreetly on the door to her friend's bedroom.

"Come in," Todd called.

A flushed Kerry was trying to squirm out of his arms when Jill walked into the room, but he wouldn't let her go, taking delight in her shyness.

"I did knock," Jill pointed out with a teasing smile.

"Todd, please!"

"Oh, all right," he laughed down at Kerry. Partially releasing her with one hand, he captured her chin and dropped a quick kiss on the button nose. Only then did he let Kerry go and turned to pick up the large blue suitcase belonging to Jill.

"I'll carry this into your room. By the way—" Todd paused after taking two steps, "—what did you think of Tiger-eyes, Jill?"

Grimacing wryly, she shrugged. "I didn't realize it was possible to dislike someone on sight."

"Sheena has staked a claim on Riordan. She doesn't like it when anyone gets too near, especially when they look like you."

"Your warning is duly noted, but she hasn't got anything to worry about from me. I'm not interested in her claim," Jill declared. "She's welcome to Riordan. They would make a perfect pair."

"Please, it's bad enough having her as a neighbor," Todd's brow arched expressively. "Don't wish her on me as a sister-in-law!"

"Todd, you shouldn't say things like that," Kerry protested gently. Love filled his face with a tender smile when he glanced at her. "Why? Because I prefer my women feminine instead of feline?" he teased.

"Go and take Jill's suitcase into her room." Despite the ordering tone, Jill could see the glow lighting Kerry's face at Todd's compliment. She very nearly looked beautiful.

"Whatever you say." He winked, and this time made it out of the room.

Kerry stared after him for a moment. Wrapping her arms around herself as if to ward off a sudden chill, she looked away from Jill's inquiring look.

"Well, we're here," she sighed.

"It's a fabulous place, isn't it?" Jill replied to avoid any discussion of the reason they were here.

Her eyes swung admiringly around the room. "Todd told me about it, but I didn't expect anything like this. His grandfather built the house for his wife. Can you imagine how difficult it was back then? All the furniture was shipped by rail to Bannack, then by wagon here."

Jill wandered over to the four-poster bed with its canopy of spring green. Her hand trailed over the quilted cover on the bed. Varying shades of pale green material had been painstakingly stitched together in an intricate geometric pattern joined against a background of almost white green.

"This is beautiful. The one in my room is crocheted. Whoever did these had to have a lot of patience."

"A lot of love," Kerry corrected softly. "It's these little touches that keep the place from seeming like a museum. It's a home because someone cared about the people in it. She took the time to make these because she cared and because she was proud of the home where she lived. Oh, Jill—" her voice trembled with emotion, "—I can hardly wait until I can have a home of my own. I want a husband and children and a place where I can do things like this for them."

"You will," Jill promised lightly. "In the meantime, I suppose we should start getting unpacked, I want to take a bath and change clothes before dinner. Sheena said it was at seven."

Kerry glanced at the slender watch on her wrist. "It's later than I thought. We'll have just about enough time to make it."

"That's probably just as well. I had the feeling Sheena didn't want us sticking our noses outside the door until then." The edges of her mouth turned up in wry amusement as she moved away from the bed toward the connecting door. "I'll leave you to unpack. Whoever gets done first takes the first bath."

"It's a deal," the other girl agreed. Jill was the first to finish unpacking and lazed in the luxuriously deep tub until Kerry was done. In her bedroom, she slid a lace-trimmed slip over her undergarments and walked to the small vanity table. Her tawny gold hair was piled on top of her head, held in place by a tortoiseshell clasp. Releasing the clasp, she shook her hair free with her fingers and reached for the hairbrush on the table.

Refreshed and stimulated by the relaxing bath, she wandered about the room. Her silken blond hair crackled with electricity from the rhythmic and vigorous strokes of the brush. Pausing near the paneled drapes of Prussian blue, she gazed through the lace insets. The window looked out of the rear of the house, giving her a breathtaking view of the mountains rising above the valley meadow of the ranch.

The sun had begun its descent in the vividly blue sky. The jutting mountains caught the golden fire, transforming the rocky peaks into regal crowns. The strokes of the hairbrush slowed to a complete stop as Jill lifted aside the white lace curtains for an unobstructed view.

Deep green forests blanketed the mountain slopes in a thick velvet cape. She felt the witchery of the mountains reach out and capture her in its spell.

A movement in the long shadows of the guardian pines near the house caught the corner of her eye. Reluctantly, she let her gaze leave the majesty of the sun-bathed peaks. The outer ranch buildings were out of her sight beyond the stand of windbreak trees.

It was from that direction the tall figure had come, only now emerging from the shadows into the afternoon sunlight. Long reaching strides carried Riordan swiftly toward the rear of the house.

He was dressed as she had first seen him, in snug-fitting faded denims, a white shirt, dusty now, accenting his muscular chest, and cowboy boots, the sunlight catching the shiny glint of a spur.

One leather glove was off and he was pulling impatiently at the other. It was nearly off when Riordan stopped, halting fluidly almost in midstride. The jet-dark head raised, tipped slightly to the side as his gaze focused unswervingly on the window where Jill stood.

Startled, she started to step back, then realized he couldn't possibly see her at that angle and distance. The glove was slowly removed and folded in the other hand with its mate. Riordan's mouth quirked at the corner as he continued to stare at the window.

A blush of anger at her own stupidity reddened her cheeks. He couldn't see her, but he could see the curtain lifted aside. This was his home. He knew which room the window belonged to and he undoubtedly knew which room had been given to Jill.

Hastily she released the curtain and saw the amused upward curl of his mouth deepen. Then he was striding toward the house again, the leather gloves tapping the side of his leg in satisfaction.

Irritated by her own schoolgirlish reaction, Jill pivoted impatiently away from the window. She should have outstared him. She couldn't afford to let him have the slightest edge in any meeting. She wouldn't back down again.

"What are you wearing, Jill?" Kerry was standing in the open doorway of the bathroom, concentrating on tying the sash of her robe, so she missed the look of anger on her friend's face.

"The, er, rose silk," Jill replied, breathing in deeply to chase away any traces of temper. "It's summerish but not too dressy."

"I thought I'd wear my yellow flowered dress. What do you think?"

"It would be perfect." Her smile was taut and unnatural, but Kerry didn't notice it.

"I'll go and get dressed. Come into my room whenever you're ready," she announced, and turned toward her own room.

Jill walked to the walnut vanity mirror above the table. A few expert flicks of the brush achieved the windswept style of her hair, tousled and sexy. The pale tan of her complexion needed no makeup, a moisturizing cream provided a subdued glow. A very light application of eyeshadow gave a hint of blue to intensify the color of her eyes.

"Applying warpaint?" her reflection teased wickedly. "Yes," Jill smiled, reaching for the mascara.

At half-past six, she was ready and helping Kerry with the stubborn zipper of her dress.

"Do you think we should go down now? It isn't seven yet," Kerry asked, standing quietly while Jill hooked the fastener.

"I don't see why not. It'll give us time to see more of the house before dinner."

Kerry hesitated as Jill walked to the hall door. "Do I look all right?"

"Like a mountain flower," she grinned in a light-hearted response to ease her friend's attack of nerves. "Come on!"

They were three steps into the hallway leading to the stairs when Jill heard the approach of footsteps behind them, and stiffened automatically. It had to be Riordan. She hadn't heard him pass her room, but with his cat-soft way of walking, it was possible she wouldn't. Besides, it was only logical to assume he would shower and change after working all day.

The desire was there to pretend she didn't hear the firm strides of the man walking behind them. She might have ignored them if she hadn't seen Kerry glancing over her shoulder. There was no choice except for Jill to do the same.

No silver-gray eyes met the sparkling challenge of hers. Instead she saw the darker softness of Todd's gazing warmly at Kerry. Relief shuddered through her. It wasn't a welcome reaction. She wanted to be more poised and in command than this when she met Riordan face-to-face.

Todd's hands were reaching out for Kerry's. "You look beautiful, honey."

"Do you think so?" She gazed rapturously into his eyes. The radiant glow of love chased away all her plainness, making her as beautiful as Todd declared she was.

Feeling superfluous, Jill said, "I'll see you two downstairs." Ostensibly her presence in the house was as a chaperone and companion to Kerry, but Jill didn't intend to turn into her friend's shadow. She and Todd were entitled to be alone once in a while, and Jill was going to make sure it was often.

At the base of the stairs, Jill hesitated. Glancing to the rear of the carved banister, she caught a glimpse of a white-covered table through an open door. Guessing it was the dining room, she walked toward it.

The open door ahead of it led into the living

room. She gave it a cursory glance as she walked by, believing she was more likely to find her hostess in the dining room.

The oval table, covered by an intricately crocheted cloth, was set with fragile, flowered china and gleaming crystal. A chandelier hung from the beamed ceiling to illuminate the table. A silken fabric covered the walls above the wainscoting, its white-on-white design alleviating the heavy darkness of the furniture and panelling. But the room was empty and Jill was not inclined to wait in there for the others.

Retracing her steps, she wandered into the living room. Her gaze was drawn immediately to the painting hanging above the mantel of the marble-faced fireplace.

It was a portrait of a woman, a very beautiful woman with copper hair and sparkling hazel eyes. The peach-tinted lips were curved in a breathless smile that embraced life. Yet, despite all the vitality flowing in every slender line, there was a definite air of fragility and innocence.

"My mother," a male voice said.

Jill whirled away from the portrait to face the corner of the room from which Riordan's voice had come. Gray eyes mocked the wary look in her expression as he rose from a wing-backed chair, a glass in one hand.

He had changed from the dusty denims to tailored pants. A long-sleeved silk shirt molded the breadth of his shoulders and tapered to his comparatively slim waist. The top two buttons were undone, revealing dark, curling hairs on his chest. The black thickness of his hair glistened as if still damp from a shower.

Her rapid once-over was being echoed by Riordan, although his slow appraisal of her was more insolent as he inspected the way the clinging material of her loose-fitting dress revealed her full curves without being blatantly suggestive.

His intent gaze was stripping her. Jill felt the heat of arousal warming her face. But she refused to look away even when his mocking eyes stopped at her mouth, as if reminding her of the time he had possessed her lips.

"I've heard of pink elephants, Miss Randall, but pink butterflies?" His mouth quirked with cynical amusement. Unwillingly Jill protectively touched the rose-colored material of her dress. "Would you like a drink?"

"No," she snapped, and regretted her sharpness as a dark brow raised suggestively in her direction. She added more quietly, "Thank you anyway."

It wouldn't do to lose her temper so early in the evening, and on her first night in his house, too.

"I apologize for not being here to greet you and Miss Adams." His low voice was not at all apologetic. "I hope you weren't at your window watching for me too long."

"I wasn't watching for *you*," Jill declared coldly. "I was enjoying the view of the mountains from my window." Satisfaction glittered in his eyes. He had deliberately trapped her into admitting she had seen him and she had foolishly risen to the bait. She turned away, angry with herself for not being better prepared for this encounter.

An older woman was pausing in the doorway, wearing a dress of blue gingham with an apron in a matching blue tied around her large-boned frame. Short blue-black hair was dulled by a suggestion of gray, but nothing dimmed the alertness of her nearly black eyes shining out of a strongly structured face as she glanced from Jill to Riordan. This was obviously the housekeeper, Jill decided.

"Mrs. Benton sent me in with this tray of nuts and olives," the woman explained, walking into the room. "She said you'd be having drinks in here before coming to the table."

"Jill Randall, this is my housekeeper, Mary Rivers," Riordan confirmed Jill's deduction. "She's a full-blooded Crow Indian, the granddaughter of a war chief. Jill is a friend of the young lady Todd brought home."

"I'm pleased to meet you." Jill's smile came naturally, prompted by the friendliness in the woman's expression.

An answering smile crinkled the corners of the intelligent dark eyes. "I hope you enjoy your stay here, Miss Randall." The words of welcome were spoken sincerely—the first Jill had heard. "Despite my ancestry, I seldom go on the warpath! After thirty years in this house, it takes a lot to provoke me."

Jill darted a swift glance at Riordan's impassive face. Mary Rivers had obviously overheard his needling remarks and had offered a discreet word of advice—a suggestion easier said than done.

"May I help you with anything in the kitchen?" Jill offered.

"It's nearly all ready," the woman refused, still maintaining her warm smile. "And besides, too many cooks . . ."

Her voice trailed away, leaving Jill with the impression that the housekeeper believed Sheena Benton already made it one too many cooks. The thought brought a smile she was forced to hide as the chestnut-haired woman entered the room, bestowing a dazzling smile on Riordan.

"I'd best get back to the kitchen," the housekeeper murmured, and withdrew.

The cat-gold eyes of Sheena Benton weren't quite so warm as they blinked at Jill. "Have you been down long, Jill? I'm afraid I was in the kitchen." "Only a few minutes," Jill acknowledged. Silently and partly grudgingly, she admired the gold dress that matched the woman's eyes and sensuously hugged her curves.

Riordan's eyes were watching her above the rim of the glass he held to his mouth. He probably knew his tiger mistress did not like pink butterflies, either, and was waiting for an excuse to claw the fragile wings.

When his gaze slid to the doorway, Jill followed it, seeing Todd get rid of a lipstick-stained Kleenex as he ushered a flushed and radiant Kerry into the room.

Chapter Five

The odd number of people had placed Jill alone on one side of the oval table opposite Todd and Kerry with Riordan and Sheena as host and hostess at the ends of the table. Sheena had dominated the conversation with witty anecdotes of ranch life.

In the main, she had related stories that involved either Riordan or Todd, always subtly pointing out her closeness to the host and silently reminding Jill and Kerry that they were outsiders—Jill more so than Kerry.

Jill's ostracism hadn't ended in the dining room. She should have known Sheena couldn't have cut her out of the group without Riordan's approval. In the living room, Sheena as acting hostess naturally sat on the sofa in front of the silver coffee service and Riordan joined her.

Todd and Kerry took the two chairs opposite the sofa, which left Jill with only two choices. One was

out of the question since it meant sitting on the
sofa beside Riordan. Accepting the china cup and
saucer from Sheena, Jill sat in the chair which
placed her outside their circle.

Seething inwardly, Jill maintained an outward
air of calm and composure. She was not going to
try to force her way into the conversation or draw
attention to herself in any way. It would be what
Riordan expected her to do. Instead she sat in
apparent acceptance of her exile from the group
and listened.

There was satisfaction in discovering that Kerry
was no longer being excluded as Sheena asked
polite questions about her childhood, college life
and studies. Kerry's replies were soft as they always
were with strangers, but she answered without hesitation, a fact that Jill silently applauded, knowing
the courage it required from her shy friend.

"Todd, you'll have to show Kerry the beaver
pool," Sheena declared, glancing at the brunette
after she had given the command. "It isn't far from
the house, a nice walk and it's a perfect swimming
pool. The water is a bit chilly since it's snow melt
from the mountains, but the setting is idyllic. It'll
be something for you to do while Todd is working.
You do swim, don't you?"

"Well, actually, I don't know how," Kerry replied
self-consciously. "I never had the opportunity to
learn while I was growing up."

"What about horseback riding? I'm sure Riordan
could find you a suitably gentle mount. You'll enjoy
an afternoon canter over the open meadow—that
is, if you ride?" A feline brow arched inquiringly.

A hand nervously crept to a dark curl as Kerry

darted a sideways glace at Todd. "I have ridden a couple of times, but I'm not very good."

Sheena smiled faintly. At Jill's angle she couldn't tell if the smile was motivated by satisfaction or polite understanding. The latter seemed very unlikely. Riordan was leaning against the sofa back, apparently content to let Sheena suggest activities to occupy the free daylight hours.

"In any event—" Sheena shrugged away Kerry's lack of enthusiasm for horseback riding, "—I know there'll be times when you'll want to get away from the ranch. I want you to feel free to come to my home anytime. I've installed a tennis court in my backyard—it's an extravagance but tennis is a passion of mine. If I should happen to be gone, you're more than welcome to use it anyway." A reddening pink crept into Kerry's cheeks as she lowered her gaze to the china cup in her lap. "It's very kind of you to offer, but I'm afraid I don't know how to play tennis. You see, I'm really not athletically inclined."

Jill's lips parted slightly in dawning discovery. How could she have been so blind? Riordan hadn't really been interested in separating Jill from the group to make her feel unwelcome. He had wanted her away from Kerry while he subtly pointed out to Todd how little he and Kerry had in common.

"Good Lord, Kerry!" Sheena exclaimed with cutting laughter. "You don't know how to swim or play tennis. You don't like riding. What are you going to do here for a month? You'll go crazy if you spend every day sitting around the house by yourself!"

"You've forgotten Kerry isn't alone." The cup clattered noisily in its saucer as Jill set it on the small table near her chair. Her blue eyes clashed openly with Riordan's metal gray, letting him know she had seen through his ruse and did not intend to sit silently any longer. "I'm sure we'll find plenty to do to occupy the daytime hours."

"And I'm more than willing to entertain Kerry in the evenings," Todd inserted, his previously uncertain expression changing into a smile. "Tomorrow morning I'll show you around the ranch so you won't get disoriented if you go for a walk. I'll persuade Mary to fix a picnic basket for the afternoon. The beaver pool would be a perfect place to have it."

"I'd like that," Kerry murmured, hesitantly returning his warm smile. Riordan scowled. "I'm afraid that won't be possible," he said calmly. "I'm shorthanded right now, so I won't be able to let you have a couple of days to unwind from the end of term, Todd. You'll have to be up and out bright and early in the morning."

"What?" A startled frown crossed the youthfully handsome face. "Why are you shorthanded? Who isn't here?"

"Tom Manson. I fired him last week for drinking."

"Tom's been nipping at the bottle for years and we both know it." Todd's hazel eyes darkened with suspicion. "After turning a blind eye to it all this time, why did you suddenly fire him for it?"

"He was drunk last week and nearly set the barn on fire. I wasn't about to give him a second chance to succeed." The level gray eyes dared Todd to challenge his decision. Except for a slight tightening of his mouth in resignation, Todd made no reply as he turned toward Kerry.

"I'm sorry, honey. I guess that takes care of that."

"It's all right," Kerry assured him, her hand finally stopping its nervous twisting of her hair. "We'll do it another day." "Speaking of other days—" Sheena glanced at the expensive gold watch on her wrist, "—it isn't too long until tomorrow and unfortunately, I still have to drive home. I'll get my clothes and other things from the bedroom."

Whose bedroom? Jill wondered cattily as the woman rose lazily to her feet. Accidentally her gaze met Riordan's. Something of her dislike of Sheena Benton must have been in her expression, because amusement twitched the corners of his hard mouth.

Todd unconsciously broke their exchange of glances by asking what the agenda would be for the following day. The discussion between the two men stayed on ranch business until Sheena reappeared in the doorway.

"Good night, everybody." Her superior gaze swept over all the occupants of the room, stopping on Kerry. "Remember, if you feel lonesome, be sure to call me or come over. It's been a pleasure meeting you. And you, too, Jill." It was added as a deliberate afterthought. Jill's fingers curled. Sheena's cattiness seemed to be contagious!

"It was very nice of you to be here to welcome us, Mrs. Benton," she answered insincerely.

Sheena's gaze narrowed for a fleeting second. "It was my pleasure. Riordan—" a winging brow arched toward him, "—will you walk me to my car?"

He didn't reply but rose to his feet. The suffocating tension that had enveloped Jill seemed to leave the room with him. She hadn't realized how stiffly she had been holding herself until she drew a free breath.

A certain aura of confinement remained, probably brought on by inactivity. Jill knew Todd and Kerry wouldn't object if she left them alone. In fact, they'd probably welcome it.

"I think I'll take the coffee service into the kitchen," she announced without receiving any objections in response.

The kitchen was large and spacious with an old breakfast table and Windsor chairs in the center. Despite the state-of-the-art appliances, the room retained the old-fashioned charm of the rest of the house.

Mary Rivers waved aside Jill's offer to help clean up the few cups and saucers, insisting that it wouldn't require two pairs of hands. Jill stayed for a few minutes anyway. They talked without saying anything.

When she came away from the room, Jill knew her first impression of the matronly housekeeper had been correct. She was a warm, friendly woman and Jill liked her. She hoped the feeling would be mutual.

As she neared the base of the stairs in the entrance hall, the front door opened and Riordan walked in. Nerve ends tensed instinctively. After a fractional pause in her steps, Jill continued forward, her gaze sweeping coolly over his aloof features.

At the base of the stairs, she made a split-second decision and turned to climb them, aware of the long smooth strides carrying Riordan toward her.

"Are you retreating so early?" he mocked softly.

Jill paused on the first step, her hand resting on the polished banister, but she didn't turn around.

"It's been a long day." Silently she added that it promised to be a long month, especially if tonight was any example of what she was to expect.

"Is something wrong, Jill?" Again, ridiculing amusement dominated his voice. Only this time he was at the stairs, stepping to the banister, putting himself in her line of vision.

"Nothing," she shrugged, her gaze striking blue sparks as it clashed with the flint-gray hardness of his. Pointedly she directed her attention to his mouth and the faint smear of lipstick. "You should suggest that Mrs. Benton blot her lipstick. It isn't so likely to rub off."

The grooves around his mouth deepened as Riordan made no move to wipe away the lipstick trace. "Not a very enjoyable evening for you, was it? You're used to more male attention, I'm sure, but spare tires are sometimes flat. Maybe after a month you'll get used to it."

It was one of those horrible moments when words deserted Jill. An hour from now she would be able to think of a suitably cutting retort that she could have made. Seething with impotent anger, she couldn't keep her voice from trembling.

"Please tell Kerry that I'm tired and went up to my room."

"Of course." Riordan inclined his head with patronizing politeness.

Her legs were shaking, but they still managed to carry her swiftly up the stairs to her room. Although she wasn't tired, she changed into nightclothes and climbed into bed anyway.

Later she heard Kerry and Todd saying good

night in the hall and the closing of their respective bedroom doors. It seemed as if she lay awake a long time after that before drifting to sleep, but she never heard Riordan come up the stairs.

After a week, life at the ranch fell into a pattern. The daylight hours were the ones that brought the most pleasure to Jill. She and Kerry often took exploratory walks in the morning, discovering the beaver pool and other places, but wisely keeping the ranch buildings in sight at all times. In the afternoons they lazed in the sun or helped Mary when she would let them. It wasn't a demanding routine but a welcome change from the hectic college schedule of classes and study.

As Jill had expected, Sheena stopped over. Both of her visits coincided with times that Riordan was at the house—deliberately planned, Jill was sure. Neither visit had changed Jill's opinion of the woman.

Part of Jill's pleasure was derived from the fact that Riordan was gone from the house with the rising of the sun. Todd, too, of course. Generally it was nearly dark before they returned. On only three days had they been close enough to the ranch house to return for lunch, an event that Kerry looked forward to and Jill dreaded.

The evenings were blessedly short. By the time Riordan and Todd returned, showered away the day's dirt and had eaten dinner, it was nearly time to go to bed. Still, it was more time in Riordan's company than Jill wanted to spend. He was constantly baiting her with a word or a look guaranteed to set her teeth on edge. Kerry he virtually ignored, intimidating her into shy silence merely with his presence.

Since the object of this visit was ostensibly for Riordan to get to know Kerry better, his indifference annoyed Jill, but she was helpless to do anything about it. She could hardly point out Kerry's good qualities as if her friend were a slave on an auction block.

The Tiffany glass pane in the living room window lacked its usual brilliant color. The thunderheads concealing the mountain peaks had completely blocked out the sun. The fat drops that had been ricocheting off the windows had turned into a sheeting downpour of rain. Serrated bolts of lightning were followed by rolling explosions of thunder that rattled the windowpanes.

Todd had dashed into the house alone more than a quarter of an hour ago, drenched to the skin. Jill hadn't cared where Riordan was. She was curled in a corner of the living room sofa staring at the portrait above the fireplace, wondering how that beautiful woman could be the mother of such very different sons.

"Hi, where's Kerry?" Todd walked into the living room, tucking a clean shirt into his dry trousers.

His brown hair was still damp, gleaming almost as black as Riordan's. For an instant the resemblance between the two brothers was strong. It vanished when Jill met the friendly hazel eyes.

"In the kitchen, making you some hot chocolate," she replied.

"That woman is going to make some man a great wife," he sighed, sinking into the wing chair opposite the sofa. A crack of lightning was ominously close. "Rain, rain, rain!" A smile of contentment turned up his mouth. "I was beginning to think I was never going to have an afternoon off. What have you been doing this lovely rainy day, Jill?"

Her gaze swept to the portrait. "Reading," she answered absently, although the book had been discarded on the cushion beside her for some time. With a curious frown, she glanced to Todd. "May I ask a nosy question?"

"Ask it and I'll decide whether I want to answer it," he grinned, obviously refreshed and in a jesting mood. "Your mother's portrait is still hanging above the fireplace. I guess I was wondering why." She tipped her head to one side, watching Todd's teasing smile fade as he turned toward the portrait, admiring affection in his gaze. "She and your father were separated for nearly eighteen years, weren't they?"

"It's always hung there ever since I can remember. And separated isn't really the right word to use." Todd leaned back in his chair, his expression thoughtful when he glanced at Jill. "They lived separately, which isn't quite the same thing. For nine months of the year Mom and I lived with her father. In the summer, we came here."

"Every year?"

"Every year." He nodded. "I'd wake up one morning in Helena and Mom would say we were going to the ranch. She never called ahead to say we were coming, but I can't remember a time that Dad wasn't there to meet her. It's very hard to explain how very much they loved each other, but they did, genuinely. And every summer it was like a honeymoon. They would laugh, talk in whispers, and Dad would steal a kiss every once in a while. I couldn't begin to count the number of times I saw them simply gazing into each other's eyes. Then on an August morning, Mom would say we were going back to my grandfather's."

"But why?" Confusion clouded Jill's eyes. "I mean if they loved each other so much, why did they live apart?"

He breathed in deeply and gazed at the portrait. "Mother couldn't stand the isolation of the ranch. She needed people around her. She was gregarious, always wanting to see new faces. I can remember her telling me how she used to pray for something to break down when she lived here. It didn't matter what it was as long as it required a repairman to fix it and she would have someone new to talk to if only for an hour. For eight years, she said that she kept thinking she would adjust. Finally she couldn't tolerate it anymore."

"It's a miracle they stayed in love all those years. Being separated nine months of every year would put a strain on any relationship," she declared with an amazed shake of her blond hair.

"Dad did come to Helena every year at Christmas-time for a couple of days. Riordan came, too, until he was about sixteen. On our way up here the other day, you asked me about Riordan as a boy." Todd frowned absently. "I think in a way he believed that mother deserted him and Dad, even though Riordan realized that she had wanted him to live with her. He never said anything to me, but I imagine he thought she had lovers. She never did, Jill. You can't hide something like that for eighteen years, not even from a small boy, and I lived with her all the time. There was only one man for her and that was my father. It was a very special and rare kind of love they had for each other, and one that was very strong."

"It had to be," Jill agreed, staring at the portrait.

"Do you know what Dad used to call her? His butterfly." Everything inside Jill seemed to freeze. A chill seemed to stop her heartbeat. A numb sensation spread through her limbs. A resentment that had been manifested in Riordan's childhood was responsible for his bitter dislike and contempt of her, another butterfly.

"There you are, Todd." Kerry's happy voice came from the open doorway. "I fixed you some hot chocolate. I thought you might like some after your drenching?"

"Remind me to marry you," Todd winked, grabbing her hand as she set the cup on the walnut table between the two wing chairs.

"I will." Kerry laughed but with a breathless catch. Thunder clapped, vibrating the walls.

"Todd!" At the sound of Riordan's commanding voice, Jill nearly jumped off the sofa.

The thunder had evidently drowned out the opening and closing of the front door. He was standing in the doorway, his clothes comparatively dry. A telltale dampness around his shirtsleeves and collar indicated he had been wearing a rain slicker.

"Just because it's raining, it doesn't mean there isn't work to do," he said curtly.

Jill kept her face averted from those discerning gray eyes. All of her senses were reacting to his presence with alarming intensity.

"I've just changed into dry clothes," Todd grumbled in protest.

"If you'd taken your slicker, you wouldn't have

got soaked," was the unsympathetic response. "Come on, we might as well sharpen the mower blades."

"There goes my afternoon off!" Sighing, Todd rose from the chair, smiling apologetically at Kerry. "Thanks for the cocoa, honey, but I'm afraid you'll have to drink it."

When the front door closed behind the two men, a long, resigned sigh broke from Kerry's lips. "Here, Jill, you drink it. I don't want it."

The cup was set on the table in front of the sofa. "Hey!" Jill scolded, catching the look of utter depression on her friend's face. "It's not the end of the world. Todd will be back."

"In time for dinner." Kerry stuffed her hands in the pockets of her slacks and walked dejectedly to the window.

"You knew he had to work when we came," Jill reminded her.

"I knew." The downcast chin was raised to stare unseeingly through the rain-sheeted glass.

"Don't let the weather get you down. Why don't we start a fire in the fireplace? That ought to chase away the gloom."

"It's not that." Kerry turned tiredly away from the window.

"Haven't you noticed?"

"Noticed what?"

"We've been here seven days and in all that time I've seen Todd alone about a total of one hour. He works from dawn to dusk, never has any free time, and at night his brother is always around."

"And me, too," Jill said gently.

She suddenly realized that she had been so anxious to insulate herself from Riordan, she hadn't considered that Todd and Kerry would want to be alone. And it had been one of her prime objectives on their arrival.

"I'm not blaming you," Kerry assured her quickly.

"I know you're not, but maybe there's something I can do to arrange some time for you and Todd."

"If only there was!" Kerry's brows lifted expressively. Surprisingly, an opportunity presented itself that evening. Jill had been deliberately pleasant to Riordan at the dinner table, but not overly so in case he suspected some ulterior motive. Mostly she attempted to avoid exchanging innuendos, asking questions without becoming too personal.

When the four of them left the table to have coffee in the living room, as had become the custom, Riordan glanced out through the night-darkened windows. "The rain's stopped. We'll have to get out and check the stock tomorrow."

"It isn't raining?" Jill repeated, taking hold of the opportunity. "If you three don't mind, I think I'll skip the coffee. After being in the house all day, a walk sounds very welcome." Riordan was behind her, so he didn't see the wink she gave Kerry.

"Of course not," Kerry answered, a secret sparkle of understanding in her brown eyes.

"I'll get my sweater." Jill started for the stairs and paused. "I'd better see if Mary has a flashlight I can borrow." She laughed lightly. "I don't want to stumble over something and break a leg in the dark."

"I'll come with you," Riordan said.

"That's okay," she refused quickly. "I'll be all right by myself, honestly."

"I'm sure you would be, but I'll come with you just the same." The chiseled features were expressionless, almost aloof.

Jill hesitated, deliberately giving the impression that she would like to argue the point. Riordan wasn't as easy to manipulate as some men she had known.

"All right." She gave in after letting him hold her wavering gaze with his long measuring look. "I'll get my sweater."

A pulse was throbbing much too wildly in her throat when she descended the stairs, sweater in hand. She blamed it on the disturbing gray eyes watching every step. Her breathless smile was genuine. She had taken the time to run a brush through her hair and gloss her lips.

With no false modesty, she knew she presented an alluringly innocent picture. This time, unlike the previous time she had tried to trick him, the emphasis was on the alluring rather than the innocent. He might despise butterflies, but Riordan was human—Sheena proved that.

She walked lightly across the hall and through the door he held open, pausing outside long enough for him to close the door and turn to join her. Then, leading the way, she moved down the few steps to the stone walk. As she turned onto the lane, she pretended to ignore the man walking a fraction of a pace behind her.

The course of the rutted lane across the meadow had been a deliberate choice. Here she would be walking directly in the moonlight, its silver gleam catching the sheen of her lips and accenting the blondness of her hair.

Her eyes swept the panoramic landscape. It

wasn't necessary to pretend an enchantment with the night's beauty. A lopsided moon was directly in front of them, dominating the starfire of the black sky. In the distance, Jill could see the bank of thunderclouds and the lightning that played hide and seek within.

"It's beautiful," she murmured as if to herself, but she had not forgotten for one instant that Riordan was with her.

"Yes." A glance at that strong profile told her that he was untouched by the beauty of the night or her. As unyielding as his expression was, the moonlight had softened the rugged lines, giving him a dangerous, ruthless kind of attraction.

Jill had forgotten how tall he was and the way his well-proportioned frame gave a deceptive impression of leanness. Strolling beside him the way she was, she was aware of the solid muscles in his arms, chest and legs.

"Don't you think it's beautiful?" She paused when he did, questioning the reason for his less than enthusiastic response. His silver gaze swung to her face, metallic and reflecting.

"Are you angling for a compliment?" Riordan taunted.

"A compliment?" she repeated blankly.

"Wasn't I supposed to be affected by the vision of your loveliness in the moonlight?" His sly tone was maddening.

Anger sparked in her eyes as she unflinchingly met his steady look. "No." Her voice was calm and completely indifferent.

Smoothly she started forward, feeling his doubting gaze on her profile and knowing that she had intended to prompt some measure of admiration. She'd cut off her arm before she would admit that.

"Aren't we supposed to talk about Todd and Kerry?" The sarcastic inflection of his low voice whipped at the raw edges of her temper.

Jill kept walking, gazing at the mountain meadow without seeing anything. "If you want to," she shrugged carelessly.

"Isn't that why you invited me along?"

"I didn't invite you along, Riordan. You invited yourself," she reminded him, sending him a complacent glance through the sweep of her lashes.

His mouth twitched with amusement. "I know you wanted me to come with you. I just haven't figured why." A gauzy cloud of smoke was blown ahead of them, the wispy trail waiting to ensnare Jill.

"My reason for taking this walk is nothing more than a desire to be outdoors in the fresh air," she defended airily. She tossed her head back to send him a glittering look. "The evening is much too peaceful to start an argument with you."

"You've been a little too nice all evening. Why, Jill?" The husky issuance of her name started a disturbing reaction in her stomach.

"I've already told you."

"You've given a reason, but you haven't told the truth."

The man was too perceptive by far. "Why don't you tell me what the truth is?" she challenged lightly.

"I imagine a girl as beautiful as you is accustomed to lots of admiration from the opposite sex. After a week here, you might be in need of a man's company," Riordan suggested. "A casual flirtation to keep in practice."

"And I'm supposed to have tricked you into coming with me for that purpose?" Jill demanded, her head thrown back, her blond hair glistening in the moonlight.

"You've picked a romantic setting," he pointed out. "A walk in the moonlight on a path that takes us some distance from the house, just the two of us—alone."

She swallowed involuntarily, glancing furtively around, not realizing how far they had walked from the ranch house.

They were very much alone, surrounded by meadow and moonlight.

"If that was my intention, I would have picked a man who at least was attracted to me. You've made your dislike of me very clear," she responded boldly.

"On the contrary, I am attracted to you. I may think you're a scheming little witch—" his mouth curved into a humorless smile while he lazily inspected her upturned face, "—but it doesn't lessen the desire to make love to you. You're a very beautiful woman."

The bluntness of his declaration sent shivers of ice down her spine. "Save your compliments for Sheena. I'm sure she would appreciate them much more than I do," Jill answered sharply, averting her face. His thumb and finger caught her chin and turned her back.

"Jealous?" Riordan said huskily, noting the deepening color in her cheeks that not even the dim light could hide.

Her eyes blazing, she wrenched away from his touch. "You're conceited, arrogant—"

His eyes turned to metallic steel as he clamped a hand over her mouth, shutting off the tirade with the swiftness of a slicing blade. Her hands came up to tear his fingers away and she was crushed against his chest.

"I wondered how long it would take before you lost your temper." Slowly he removed his hand.

"Let me go!" Jill cried wildly.

Riordan didn't. His mouth descended toward her and Jill was helpless to avoid it. A gasp of protest dissolved into murmers as he nuzzled the throbbing pulse in her neck.

"Resist if you must," he jeered, raising havoc with her heartbeat as he nibbled at her ear, "but you know you intended this to happen all along."

"No," she said weakly.

His mouth trailed over her cheek to taste the corner of her lips, the warmth of his breath caressing her skin.

"Why else did you want me to come with you?" Riordan smiled and almost melted her. The tantalizing closeness of his mouth, sensually touching without taking, was unnerving. A purely physical reaction started a trembling through her limbs.

"Don't!" She spoke against his mouth, fire leaping somewhere inside her. "I left the h-house because I wanted privacy—"

"Naturally," he agreed.

"No. Privacy for Todd and Kerry," Jill explained desperately. "I . . . I thought they should have some time alone. That's why I wanted you to come with me."

His head raised from hers, a brow arching in

satisfaction. "Now I know the truth," he murmured, relaxing his hold so she could pull free.

Staring at him, Jill bit into her lip. "You tricked me, didn't you?" she accused in a shallow breath. "You never intended to try to seduce me."

"Could I have?" The grooves around his mouth deepened.

"No!" She spun away.

Her flesh still tingled from the imprint of his strong body and there was a funny empty ache in the pit of her stomach. Could he, a tiny voice inside asked.

"No!" The second vigorous denial was made out loud.

"We'd better head back to the house," Riordan said with silent laughter in his voice, "while you're still trying to make up your mind. If you aren't convinced, then I may become curious enough to find out for myself."

It sounded very much like a threat to Jill. Sometimes it was better to retreat and lose a battle than to stay and lose a war. Right now Riordan was much too disturbing an influence for her to think straight.

As they entered the house, with Jill a hurried step ahead of Riordan, Kerry walked out of the living room. There was no inner glow to her expression as Jill had expected. For a moment she forgot her own haste to reach the safety of the bedroom.

"Where's Todd?" Jill glanced curiously toward the living room. A frown appeared on her forehead as she tried to guess if the two had quarreled.

"He's in the living room," Kerry answered tightly, her lips thinning in irritation. "He was so tired he fell asleep twenty minutes ago."

Jill's lashes fluttered shut in sighing disbelief. A low throaty, chuckle sounded behind her, rolling into outright laughter. She darted an angry look at Riordan, catching the crinkling of his eyes at the corners and the broad, laughing smile. It was a Riordan that she had never seen before.

"Ah, the irony of it, Jill," he concluded with a wry shake of his dark head.

"What's so funny?" Kerry frowned after Riordan had strode away, still smiling, toward the rear of the house.

Jill put a hand to her mussed hair, a faint smile tugging the corners of her mouth. "Don't ask, Kerry," she answered with a short sighing laugh. "From your viewpoint, I don't think it would be very funny."

Chapter Six

"We've changed the bedding in all the rooms except Riordan's, Mary," Jill announced, tucking an escaping wisp of hair under her blue bandanna. "I'm afraid we couldn't figure out which room was his."

Mary Rivers was on her hands and knees in the hallway cleaning and polishing the woodwork. She straightened stiffly upright, a hand pushing against the small of her back.

"I already took care of his room. He sleeps downstairs in the rear . . . I didn't think to mention it. Old age, I expect."

"Want me to put the sheets in the washer?" Kerry asked, holding the armload in front of her.

"You girls have done enough. You're guests in this house, not daily help." The housekeeper shook her head in refusal.

"We enjoy helping," Jill insisted.

"It's much better than sitting around doing nothing. At least this way we can be useful," Kerry added. "Besides, what's involved in washing sheets? All I have to do is stick them in the washer, add detergent and push a button."

"While she's doing that, I can help you with this woodwork." Without allowing time for a protest, Jill bent over to pick up the cloth and polish at Mary Rivers's feet.

"I can't let you girls do this." The housekeeper tried to take the cleaning items from Jill's hand, but she held them out of reach.

"How are you going to stop us?" Kerry asked impishly, turning down the hall toward the kitchen and the utility room beyond it.

"Come on, Mary," Jill coaxed. "Let us help. You said yourself that by the time you do the cooking and regular cleaning, you're lucky to have the spring housecleaning done by fall. We've been here over ten days. We can't keep doing nothing while you work."

"You make the beds and straighten your own rooms. That's enough of a help to me."

"Let us help you with other things. Not all the time but every once in a while, like now. Not much else to do with our time," Jill pointed out.

"I give up!" Mary lifted her hands in the air in surrender. "I'll get another polishing cloth and we'll both clean this entrance hall."

"It's a deal," Jill smiled. "I'll do the woodwork near the floor so you won't have be getting up and down so much. You can do that carving around the wainscoting."

After two hours of scooting along the floor on her hands and knees, Jill's muscles in her back, shoulders and arms started to protest. She hurt, but it was a good kind of hurt, if that was possible. The work was certainly an outlet for the restlessness that had been plaguing both girls.

The evenings had returned to their former pattern with Riordan dominating, by his presence, the other three. Jill didn't make any more attempts to maneuver Riordan away from Todd and Kerry.

Naturally Kerry had, bit by bit, wheedled an account of Jill's disastrous night out. Jill never admitted that she had actually thought Riordan intended to seduce her or that, for a few traitorous moments, her flesh had been tempted to respond to his teasing caresses.

Without these pertinent facts, Kerry had seen the ironic humor of the event. While Jill had been ineffectually trying to fend off Riordan's advances—as Kerry believed they were—she had been listening to Todd snore.

The end result of the episode for Jill had been an increasing awareness of Riordan. She was certain that he could, if he wanted to, arouse her physically as no other man had done. She had always been the one in control of all aspects of a relationship, and she didn't like the sensation of being so vulnerable. He didn't like butterflies. It was a possibility that he might some day decide to capture her, if only for a moment.

A shiver danced over her skin as she remembered the tantalizing warmth of his mouth just barely brushing hers. A dangerous curiosity kept wondering what it would be like to be kissed by him—not the take charge kiss he had subjected her to when they first met, but a kiss of passion.

And there was the silent challenge, too. Every

man she had ever gone after, she had got. But what about Riordan? Was he the exception to the rule?

There was a jingling in the hallway behind her. Brushing a stray strand of hair away from her eyes, Jill started to turn around. What a silly time for Kerry to put on a bracelet, she thought. Then the jingling was accompanied by the sound of long, angry strides closing on her. There was a fleeting glimpse of Riordan's uncompromising and forbidding features.

In the next second, Jill's wrist was seized and she was yanked to her feet, unaware of the startled gasping cry that came from her throat. Her legs were momentarily too numb from the crawling position to support her. She sought to steady herself against his chest with her free hand.

"What the hell is going on here!" Riordan shouted. He pulled the hand from his chest to tear away the polishing cloth still clutched in her fingers and hurl it to the far side of the hall. "Mary!"

Jill stumbled heavily against him, her heart lurching as she came against the solid wall of muscle. His arm automatically released her wrist and circled her waist to catch her, taking her full weight as if it were no more than a child's.

"Mary, what's the meaning of this?" Thunder growled threateningly in his voice. "And you'd better have a damned good explanation!"

His strong male scent was all around Jill, filling her senses to the exclusion of everything but his nearness. It seemed to take all her strength to look away from the compelling features so close to her own and focus on the housekeeper who was the recipient of his stormy gaze. Mary Rivers didn't appear intimidated by his anger. Instinctively Jill leaped to her defense anyway.

"I was helping," she said breathlessly.

Riordan's gaze rested on her for a paralyzing second. "Shut up, Jill. Mary is perfectly capable of answering for herself." His attention was again riveted on the housekeeper. "Well?"

"The girls offered to help," she answered simply.

"You've been working, too?" An accusing glance was thrown over his shoulder. Jill could barely see Kerry hovering uncertainly near the stairs, her brown eyes rounded and stunned at the sight of Jill a captive of this snarling lion.

"I . . . was doing the wash," she murmured.

Riordan muttered an imprecation under his breath. "I'm only going to say this once, Mary." A muscle worked convulsively in his strong jaw. "They are my guests in my house and I will not have guests crawling around on their hands and knees cleaning woodwork or washing clothes!"

Mary Rivers stood calmly before him, straight and tall, her hands clasped in front of her. "They're strong, healthy girls, Riordan. You can't expect them to sit in this house day after day twiddling their thumbs."

"I don't give a damn what they do. I will not have them working like hired help in this house. Is that clear?"

"How can you stop us?" Jill breathed in challenge. "Mary tried and she couldn't. You weren't even here. I took the cloth and polish away from her and demanded to help."

The arm around her waist tightened, crushing her more firmly against his rippling muscles.

"Stay out of this." He looked swiftly back to Mary. "Have I made myself clear?"

"I'm not to blame." The housekeeper held his gaze without flinching. "As you pointed out, they're guests in this house. It's your responsibility and not mine to see that they're entertained. If you choose to neglect that, you have no right to lose your temper because they found their own way to amuse themselves and fill the empty time."

"And you would do well, Mary—" Jill moved away from him as Riordan turned to tower above the housekeeper "—to remember that you are not a part of the family, but a paid employee!"

The spurs on his boots jingled noisily again as long strides carried him to the door. Jill flinched at the explosive slamming of the door, half expecting the rattling windows to shatter from the impact. Her gaze shifted automatically to the housekeeper silently staring at the door.

"I'm sorry, Mary," she offered sincerely, strength finally beginning to flow through her limbs. "We never intended to get you into trouble."

"He'll get over it." Mary Rivers shrugged philosophically. A twinkle sparkled in her dark eyes. "But in the meantime I think you'd better leave the housework to me until he cools down at least!"

The atmosphere in the house remained electrified with invisible tension. Dinner that evening was an awkward affair.

Riordan's disposition hadn't improved. A black mood seemed to hover about the house during dinner. Not even his unexpected departure from the house after the meal put any of them at ease. The tension remained in the house into the following day. Wanting to defy him, Jill was still hesitant to offer again to help Mary. She wasn't quite as convinced as Mary that Riordan was going to get over his anger.

Perhaps that was why his announcement the following night at the dinner table came as such a surprise. Her lips were slightly parted in disbelief as she continued to stare at him.

"A trail ride?" Todd echoed the words Riordan had just spoken.

Riordan appeared indifferent to the stunned reaction to his suggestion. "I thought we could leave first thing Monday morning. That'll give the girls some time to get accustomed to the horses. We can only be gone two days."

"Horses?" Kerry swallowed. "Yes, horses," Riordan affirmed. "Unless you want to walk to the top of the mountain?"

"No, of course not," Kerry said nervously, glancing to Jill to see her reaction.

"You did say you could ride," he reminded Kerry pointedly.

"She can ride well enough," Todd answered for her, reaching out to cover Kerry's hand. "I'll pick out a nice, gentle mount for you."

"And you, Jill?" Riordan drawled, his impassive gray eyes shifting to her. "Can you ride, or will you require a nice, gentle mount, too?"

Despite the casualness of his voice, there was a decided bite underlining the question. She tried to fathom his expression without success. She still couldn't believe that he sincerely meant to go through with it.

"I can ride." Her reply was marred by uncertainty.

"You don't sound very enthusiastic," he commented dryly.

"Maybe—" Jill breathed in deeply, drawing on her reserve of bold courage, "—because I don't think the invitation for this trail ride was offered willingly."

"Jill!" whispered Kerry in a shocked plea for caution.

"Mary's little speech yesterday reminded me of my responsibilities as host," Riordan said, leaning back in his chair and regarding Jill thoughtfully.

"Good," she nodded. "Quite a tantrum. You need to grow up."

"Well, you're quite right in believing that." The hard line of his mouth quirked briefly as he arrogantly inclined his head in acknowledgement. "The question remains, do you want to go?"

Jill definitely wanted to go. Her brother had been the last one to take her on a trip into the high country around her home in Yellowstone. But this wasn't exactly Kerry's cup of tea. Of course, her friend would go to the moon if Todd asked.

Her chin raised thoughtfully, as she met Riordan's narrowed gaze of watchfulness. He was very well aware of Kerry's timidity toward animals, especially something as large as a horse, and her lack of an adventurous streak that made Kerry prefer the security of a house to the unknowns of the wilderness. Jill had been the one who had prompted the exploring walks around the ranch.

Kerry's only dissatisfaction in their stay here had been she hadn't seen as much of Todd as she wanted. She would have been content to putter around the house.

Jill didn't condemn Kerry for being unwilling

to experience other worlds, but Riordan did. He considered it a fatal flaw for his brother's prospective bride to have. It was time he learned that Kerry had a lot of spunk, Jill decided. However much Kerry wanted the security of a house, she would, without a grumble, go wherever Todd led her. Kerry was like a lot of pioneer women had been— she could make a home wherever her man was.

If Riordan expected to hear Kerry complain about the hardships of the long ride and camping out, or give way to fits of terror at crawling insects and the night cries of wild animals, he was going to be in for a surprise. A secret smile teased the corners of her mouth.

"Yes," Jill finally responded to his question with a decisive nod of her head, "I would like to go."

"It's settled, then," Riordan stated, with a faint glitter of curiosity at the almost complacent look on Jill's face. "I'll start making the necessary arrangements."

Dawn was only splintering the sky when they pointed their horses away from the ranch buildings toward the shadowed mountain slopes three days later. Fresh and eager for the trail, Jill's horse snorted, sending vapor clouds into the brisk morning air. She glanced behind her at the wide path they had left in the dew-heavy grass of the meadow.

The silence seemed almost enchanted. Only it wasn't really silent. The grass swished beneath the horses' hooves, scattering diamond droplets of dew. All around was the chirping wake-up call of the birds. Loudest of all was the rhythmic creak of saddle leather.

"Having second thoughts?" Riordan asked in a low voice.

The roofs of the ranch buildings had almost disappeared behind the rise in the meadow as Jill faced the front again. There was a serene glow in her expression when she glanced at Riordan riding beside her, leading the packhorse carrying their supplies.

"None at all," she assured him.

The faint glow of pale yellow lasted only a few short minutes more before the sun popped above the craggy peaks to the east. The mountain seemed to catch the light of the rising sun, reflecting the golden hues. By the time they reached the foothills, it was well up in the sky, flooding the forested slopes with brilliant sunshine, piercing the foliage with golden streamers of light.

The delicate scent of pines dominated the air as the four riders entered the forest. Riordan led the way with Jill behind him, followed by Kerry and Todd bringing up the rear. The narrow, weaving route through the trees was traversed single file which made conversation almost impossible. Jill didn't mind. She savored the solitude of her own thoughts.

The private glimpses of wildlife were many. A jay followed them for some distance through the trees as if inspecting the invaders of his domain. Squirrels hid behind trunks waiting for them to pass before resuming their endless search for food.

At the edge of a small forest glade, Jill's horse stopped. She had been watching a squirrel peering warily around a trunk. Glancing forward, she saw that Riordan had reined in his horse and checked the packhorse's progress. Curious, she looked beyond him.

In the sun-drenched glade, two deer stared

motionless in their direction. Then, with a flick of a white tail, each bounded away, gracefully leaping through the tall rippling grass dotted with brilliant red and yellow wildflowers.

Without a word or glance being exchanged with the others, Riordan nudged his bay horse into the open. Jill followed, keeping single file and not attempting to draw level with him. For a moment, she ignored the scenery and concentrated on the wide shoulders ahead of her.

Riordan sat with casual ease, a part of the horse and environment, the untamed look about him more pronounced than before. The warmth of the sun had made itself felt and his sheepskin jacket was swinging open. A wild tremor shook her senses as she caught a glimpse of his rugged profile. With the golden sun striking the chiseled features of his strong jaw and the faintly ruthless line of his mouth, his virile attraction pulled her like a powerful magnet.

Riordan was in his element in the wilderness, Jill told herself, trying to ignore her purely physical reaction. Her blue eyes swung determinedly away from him to focus again on the landscape they rode through. But more and more often as the morning wore on, her gaze was drawn to the man riding in the lead.

Farther on, the trees began to thin out, giving way to a grassy plateau studded with rocks and colored with mountain wildflowers. It seemed as if their steady climb should have gained them great height, but craggy mountain peaks towered all around them. This was only an insignificant hill dwarfed by its bigger brothers, connected by a dipping ridge to their slopes.

Yet the crest of the hill beckoned Jill. Behind
her, the valley floor was a twisting corridor through
the fortress walls of the mountains. The vista at
the top of the hill promised a look at it and the
untouched wilderness beyond. She urged her
horse even with Riordan, meeting his sideways
glance of inquiry, a black brow lifting slightly.

"Are we riding to the top of the hill?" she asked.
The breathlessness in her question was merely from
the exhilaration of the ride. It had nothing to do
with his considering look, she told herself.

"We can." He reined in his horse and turned
sideways in the saddle toward the slower couple
following them. "We're going to the top, Todd."

Todd waved them on. "We'll meet you at the
ridgeback."

That wasn't what Jill had in mind. She had
intended that the four of them share the view, but
she could hardly protest now. Riordan took a wrap
on the packhorse's lead rope. Clicking to it, he
touched a spur to his bay's flank, and the horse's
striding walk obediently extended into a reaching
trot. Jill followed.

The crest of the hill was farther and steeper than
she had guessed. A lone pine growing out of an
outcropping of jagged rock at the top seemed to
be the point to which Riordan was taking her. The
last few yards she gave her horse his head to pick
his way over the stony ground, always climbing.

"I didn't realize it was so far," she said when
her horse stopped beside Riordan's at the top.
Her gaze was already sweeping the breathtaking
panorama. "But it was worth it."

The ranch buildings far below were almost totally
hidden by the windbreak of pines. The verdant

meadow stretched like a curling green ribbon on the valley floor. The unexplored horizon on the opposite side of the hill was dominated by snow-capped peaks and virgin valleys, wild and unscarred by man, stunning in their casual grandeur.

Riordan dismounted, looping the rope to the packhorse around his saddle horn. "We'll take a breather here and give the horses a rest."

Her dismount was considerably less graceful than his, stiff muscles unaccustomed to extended periods of riding making their protest felt. All of that was forgotten as she spied a dark shape in the crystal-blue sky.

"Riordan, look!" she whispered excitedly. He was loosening the cinch on his saddle and paused to follow her pointing finger. "Is it an eagle or a hawk?"

"An eagle." His sharp gaze remained fixed on the wide span of wings. Unconsciously Jill moved closer, her blood racing with excitement. "I'd say it's a bald eagle. This is one of the few regions you can still find them where they haven't been driven out by civilization."

She was unable to take her eyes from the eagle soaring high on the wind currents above the mountains. "I don't know how anyone can claim to be rich if they haven't seen an eagle flying wild and free."

"That's a profound statement." Something in his voice drew her gaze. In his eyes she saw a glint of admiration. The sight of the eagle had made her spirits buoyantly light. It was like a heady wine, making her feel decidedly reckless.

"You mean coming from me," she returned boldly, "you don't expect such statements." Riordan moved lazily around to her horse. A stirrup was laid over the saddle while he loosened the cinch. A breeze lifted her tousled hair, burnished gold in the sunlight.

"Maneuvering again, Jill?" he taunted softly.

Unbuttoning her medium-weight jacket of lined blue corduroy, she pushed it back so the refreshing breeze could reach her skin.

"I don't know what you mean," she shrugged carelessly.

"You knew when you suggested we come to the top of this hill that Kerry wouldn't willingly make any side trails on her horse." Patting the horse's neck, he ducked beneath its head to stand beside Jill. "Weren't you arranging for her to be alone with Todd?"

"If you say so." With a contented sigh, she tilted her face to the sun, letting its warm rays spill over her, with her hands on her hips holding the jacket open. "I'm in much too good a mood to argue with you, Riordan."

"I wasn't arguing," he replied smoothly.

"Weren't you?" Amusement dimpled her cheeks.

Glancing through the gold tips of her lashes, she met his mocking eyes. They trailed slowly over her face down her neck to her blouse, dwelling on the material straining over the roundness of her breasts. A silvery flame seemed to lick through the material, igniting a rush of warmth in her veins.

"I believe you're trying to flirt with me," he drawled, stepping by her to remove a canteen from his saddle.

Studying the jet-black hair that curled around

his collar, she tipped her head to one side, feeling playfully bold. "And if I am?"

He unscrewed the lid of the canteen and handed it to her, grinning. "I think you're outclassed."

Her eyes sparkled brightly over the rim of the canteen as she took a swallow of the cool water. All her senses were vibrantly alert and ready to take up the challenge. Jill gave him back the canteen.

"I don't think you know me very well," she retorted softly, almost in warning.

Had he not raised the canteen to his mouth at that moment, Riordan would have seen the mischief glittering in her eyes. At precisely the right second, she lifted her hand and tipped the canteen, spilling water over his face. Despite the dangerous flash in the gray eyes, she couldn't keep from laughing.

"Why, you little—" Riordan growled, but without real anger. The lid was replaced on the canteen as he took a threatening step toward her.

The hasty, laughing step Jill took backwards sent her bumping into his horse, who moved only a protesting inch. She tried to elude his reaching hands and failed as they encircled the soft flesh of her upper arms.

"I'm sorry, Riordan, honestly." But the bubbling amusement that remained in her voice belied the assertion. "I couldn't help it."

Her forearms were pressed against his chest as she laughingly tried to struggle free of his hold. Swinging her head back, she turned her mirthful eyes to his face.

The smoldering light in his eyes was not from anger and the smile slowly faded from her lips.

Her gaze slid to his mouth, so hard, so masculine, and so close, and resistance ebbed with a rush.

In the next instant, her hands were curling around his neck and his mouth was closing over hers with a savage insistence. Her lips parted voluntarily in response to his passionate demand. Hands slipped beneath her jacket, sliding smoothly to her back, arching and molding her closer to him.

Any sense of inhibition was forgotten as she yielded to his expert caresses. Passionate desire seared through her veins. Shivers of excitement danced over her skin as he minutely explored the hollow of her throat and the pulsing cord in her neck. Her breast seemed to swell as his hands cupped its roundness, arousing a longing for a more intimate caress. His mouth was hungry and possessive when it returned to hers.

The clatter of hooves against stone shattered the erotic spell. "Riordan, are you coming or not?" Todd called, still some distance away, the pine tree and the horse shielding them from his view.

As he lifted his head reluctantly, Riordan's hands slid to her waist, holding her against him. Jill nestled her head against his chest, a soft smile curving the lips that still throbbed from his ardent kiss.

"We'll be right there," Riordan called in a voice that was husky and disturbed. Excitement shivered over her skin. Beneath her head she could feel his ragged breathing and hear the uneven beat of his heart, very much in tempo with her own. She could have him.

In that exultant moment, she knew she could bring this man to his knees. It mattered little that he disliked her because now she knew he desired her. The knowledge provided an immense power she could use to gain her own ends.

Then Riordan was setting her away from him and walking to the horses to tighten the cinches. Outwardly he seemed completely unmoved by the charged embrace they had just shared. The gray eyes were cool and aloof, like impenetrable granite, when they met the brightness of hers. His control was remarkable. If she hadn't had those few seconds in his arms after he had broken off the kiss, she might not have guessed that she had so successfully aroused him.

"Mount up," he said, swinging into his own saddle.

His eyes narrowed thoughtfully as Jill gave him a bemused smile and complied with his order. This trail ride was going to be much more interesting and exciting than she had thought. She met his gaze with an alluring sweep of her long lashes, then moved her horse into the lead.

Chapter Seven

The green meadow was nestled high in the mountains, a miniature valley where the mountain hesitated before soaring toward the sun. Cutting a path near the encroaching forest, a stream tumbled joyously over itself, crystal clear and cold from melting snow.

"I almost wish we never had to leave." Jill turned regretfully away from the scene.

"Do you feel like going primitive?" The gray eyes slid to her briefly as Riordan pulled the saddle from Kerry's mount.

"Something like that," she agreed, smiling at his choice of words. "What's wrong with returning to nature and the basics?"

"It's easy to do as long as you've brought supplies, but not quite so romantic when you have to forage for food like any other animal." He set the saddle out of the way and tossed a short blanket to Jill. "Rub the horse down and make sure he's dry."

The horse stood docilely as she began to wipe dry the dark stain of perspiration where the saddle and pad had lain. "So you don't think I would like the life in the rugged outdoors?"

As he glanced over the seat of Todd's saddle, his mouth twisted dryly. "You tell me. After a month, your nails would be broken, your hands would be rough and callused. That beautiful complexion of yours would probably be burned by the sun. And who would fix your shiny golden hair?"

Jill laughed. "Why couldn't you have pointed out the hardships and dangers? You could have attacked something other than my vanity." Inside she was secretly pleased that he had noticed so much about her.

"Want some help, Riordan?" Todd paused in front of the horse his brother was now rubbing down. "The camp is all set up and Kerry is gathering more firewood from the deadfall."

"No," Riordan answered after glancing at the site that had been chosen for the night's camp. "You might as well get those telescoping rods from the pack and start catching our supper. Jill and I will finish up here."

"What will we eat if Todd doesn't catch any trout?" she said lightly when they were again alone with the horses.

"The contingency menu consists of the old western standby—beans." His eyes crinkled at the corners.

It was only the second time Jill had seen him smile naturally. Her heart quickened at how devastatingly attractive it made him.

Tapping the rump of Todd's horse to move it out of the way, Riordan walked around it to his own saddled mount. Jill finished her horse and walked to the bay's head, absently stroking its nose. It blew softly in her hand, the dark brown eyes almost curious in its inspection of her.

"What's your horse's name?" she asked, running her fingers through the horse's tangled black forelock.

Riordan shrugged indifferently. "Boy. Fella." Mockery gleamed in the eyes that glanced at her face. "At times, some other names a gentleman shouldn't repeat in front of a woman."

"Doesn't he have a name?" Her head tilted to one side in surprise.

"No. He's only an animal. There are a few horses on the ranch that supposedly have names, the ones that happen to be registered stock." He lifted the saddle off the horse's back, swinging it onto his shoulder and carrying it over to the others. He returned to start rubbing the horse down. "This one is just a mountain-bred horse with no pedigree."

"You honestly don't name your horses?" Jill persisted.

"Why?"

The brim of his hat was pulled low, throwing his face into shadow. She couldn't be certain, but she thought she saw his expression momentarily harden. For long seconds he didn't answer. She thought he was going to ignore her question altogether.

"I was about five when Dad gave me my first horse, a buckskin named Yellowstone Joe. Like any boy I imagined he was the best horse in the world. When I was twelve, one Indian summer day I rode him into the mountains to go hunting. I didn't pay any attention to the time until I realized that it was afternoon. I was miles from the ranch with little chance of making it back before dark, unless I took a shortcut. It meant going down a steep slide area, with a lot of loose rock. I'd taken Joe down it before, but I'd forgotten to consider that there'd been a storm recently. When we started down, the ground slid out from beneath us. I was thrown clear and rolled to the bottom. Joe was there, too, with both front legs broken.''

Her chest constricted sharply, her blue eyes darkening to mirror the unendurable pain she knew he must have felt. But for all the emotion in his voice, he could have been discussing the weather.

''I was miles from home and help, not that there was anything that could be done for Joe. I couldn't leave him like that, suffering and helpless. I knew he had to be put out of his misery and there wasn't anyone around but me. My marksmanship was off, and it took two shots to kill him. I started walking for home. Dad and a search party found me around nine o'clock that night.''

Jill could hardly distinguish his impassive features through the blur of tears, but she could tell his face was turned to her.

''I don't put names on something I might have to destroy, not anymore. Horses are only animals, like cattle you slaughter to eat. It was a lesson that had to be learned,'' Riordan concluded unemotionally.

''Yes. Yes, I see.'' Her voice was choked by the knot in her throat, hoarse and raw with sympathy for that twelve-year-old boy. She knew any minute the tears would spill from her eyes for Riordan to scorn. "I . . . I think I'll go and help . . . Kerry."

"Go ahead," he agreed blandly. "I don't need you. I can finish up here."

Jill wondered if he had stopped needing anybody that day when he was twelve. Two years before that, his mother left him for a reason he couldn't understand. Was it any wonder he had grown up so hard and cynical? She wanted desperately to reach out and gather that little boy in her arms and ease his hurt and grief. Only Riordan wasn't a little boy anymore and he didn't allow himself to be hurt.

Try as she would, Jill couldn't forget the scene his indifferent voice had described. It haunted her, dulling the beauty of the meadow and marring the serenity of the mountain stream. That long-ago event didn't hurt him anymore. She was a fool to let it hurt her.

It didn't change the fact that she had the power to bring him to his knees. She could still use the physical attraction he felt for her to manipulate him into approving of Todd and Kerry's marriage.

A cold, ruthless streak had become embedded in him and he would not hesitate to use any means within his grasp.

It wasn't as if she could hurt him again. He was beyond being hurt. He pitied no one, so why should she pity him?

Todd's catch of trout had been spitted and cooked slowly over the glowing embers of the campfire, then served with canned tomatoes and piping-hot bannock biscuits Riordan had fried. It had been a delicious meal, only Jill's appetite had been dulled.

She stared at the speckled gray coffeepot suspended at the side of the fire. Kerry had enlisted Todd's aid in carrying the dishes to the stream to be washed. They had not camped close to the stream because Riordan had explained that animals came down at night to water and he didn't want their camp obstructing the animals' right of way to the stream. The explanation had not put Kerry at ease.

"More coffee?" Riordan stooped beside the fire and refilled his cup from the gray pot.

"No." Jill shook her head absently, her hair catching and reflecting the amber flames of the fire.

From the stream, she heard a startled shriek from Kerry, and Todd's laughing admonition that it was only a harmless raccoon. The corners of Riordan's mouth turned up crookedly.

"Your friend is a little jumpy."

His faintly derogatory tone made her heart harden against him. The time of indecision was thrust away. How dare he criticize Kerry's feelings of fear toward the unknown when he possessed no feelings himself?

"What can you expect, Riordan? Camping in the wilds is completely outside Kerry's experience." Her voice was low and tautly controlled. "She's frightened—that's normal."

"You aren't frightened."

"No." She turned her head, sharply challenging his hooded look. "But my family camped a lot, backpacking into Yellowstone on weekends, so this isn't a totally new experience for me."

"I see you're still intent on defending your

friend." Riordan was in the shadowy circle beyond the fire, the sardonic amusement in his voice mocking her.

"I see you're still intent on breaking them up," Jill retorted smoothly, keeping the anger from her voice.

"I didn't realize butterflies could be so irritable. What's the matter, Jill?" he taunted.

Closing her eyes against the impulse to snap, she took a deep breath, releasing it in a shrugging sigh. "Most butterflies probably never spend a day in the saddle riding up a mountain."

"Stiff?"

"Brilliant deduction," she responded dryly, unconsciously arching the protesting muscles in her back. She stared into the crackling flames of the campfire.

Pine needles rustled beside her, warning her a second too late of Riordan's approach. As she started to turn, a pair of hands closed firmly over her shoulders and began to spread the taut muscles in her back. A soft moan escaped her startled lips, a mixture of pain and enjoyment.

"If you weren't so biased because Kerry is your friend, you would see that they aren't right for each other and you would join forces with me in separating them before they make a big mistake."

His fingers were working magic on her aching flesh. Jill almost wished there wasn't any need for conversation, but she shook her head determinedly.

"You don't know your brother well, Riordan," she murmured. "I think you somehow believe that he survived the separation of your parents relatively untouched. But you're quite wrong. He's chosen a wife whom he knows will be at his side through anything. If you thought this trail ride was going to reveal their differences to Todd, you've failed. If it revealed anything to him, then it's the fact that Kerry joined in without one word of complaint, adjusting as best she could to the surroundings.''

"But will she continue to do that?" Riordan spoke as if he already knew the answer.

His strong fingers had sent a lethargy creeping through her bones, but at his question Jill stiffened, holding herself motionless as a light flashed in her eyes.

"It isn't Kerry you object to, is it, Riordan?" She answered the question herself. "It's marriage. No matter who Todd chose, you wouldn't approve."

"No," was his simple and uncaring reply, laced with a touch of amusement.

A short breathy laugh slipped from her throat. She hadn't expected him to admit it so nonchalantly. Tilting her head to one side, she glanced over her shoulder at him.

"Do you really dislike women that much?" Her eyes searched the carved, imposing features, the enigmatic gray of his eyes.

The hard, masculine mouth curved into a cold smile. "What do you think of men, Jill? Do you admire them? Look up to them? View them as equals? Or do you enjoy twisting them around your pretty little finger and letting them fall when they no longer amuse you?"

His mocking accusation struck too close to the mark. She did tend to play with men, but not the way Riordan suggested. Deep down there was always the hope that the man she went after would be the one she loved. Only with Riordan did she want to be the unfeeling enchantress.

Her tongue nervously moistened her lower lip, unconsciously sensual until she saw the smoldering light darken his eyes. A wicked sparkle flashed in her eyes, enticing and challenging.

"And you, Riordan," she murmured with husky suggestiveness, "do you find that women have occasional uses?" He smiled, recognizing the invitation on her gleaming lips.

A dark brow arched, the massaging hands on her back sliding near her ribcage.

"Occasionally," he responded coolly.

Jill fixed her blue gaze on his mouth, feeling her heartbeat quicken. "Like this morning on the hilltop?" Forgotten for the moment was her own sensual response to his embrace. Only the memory of the way she had aroused him was considered.

His eyes narrowed thoughtfully as if measuring the strength of the trap she laid for him. The rakish thickness of his hair gleamed blacker in the firelight, a faint arrogance hardening his impassive features. "Did you enjoy it?"

"Did you?" Jill breathed.

The hands tightened on her ribs, lifting and turning her into his arms. The initial shock of having physical contact again with his hard-muscled chest made her mind spin. Her head rested against his arm, the tawny gold of her hair spilling over his shoulder while he inspected the perfection of her face with slow deliberation. Jill let herself relax pliantly. A hand slid across her stomach to curve over her hip.

Then his mouth was closing over hers. That seductive, searing fire that she had somehow for-

gotten consumed her again. There was no fierceness in his touch this time, only a series of long,
drugging kisses calculated to undermine her sensi-
bility to everything but his virility. Without a doubt
she was losing control. Riordan was seducing her,
not the other way around. The insanity of it was
that she didn't care. She wanted to go on drowning
in the sensual oblivion of his caress.

From this admission came the strength to resist.
With a tremulous gasp, she twisted away from his
mouth using her arms to wedge a space between
them. Her skin felt hot to the touch, the raging
fire within refusing to be banked.

Strong fingers cupped her jaw, tilting her chin
upward. Not daring to meet his eyes for fear she
would be captured by their silvery sheen, Jill stared
at his mouth, so cool, so self-composed compared
to the trembling softness of hers. The tanned fingers trailed down her neck until his hand rested
lightly and deliberately on her breast.

"I want you," Riordan said with soft arrogance.

Yes, he wanted her, Jill silently acknowledged,
but not enough, not yet. Straightening toward him,
she let her lips flutter submissively against his
mouth as if in surrender to his dominant strength.
Then, with a single fluid movement, she was out
of his arms and on her feet standing in front of
the fire. She could feel him watching the uneven
rise and fall of her breasts and tried to stabilize
her breathing. Her limbs were treacherously weak
beneath her.

Riordan made no move to follow her, his long
male length stretched in a half-sitting position,
seemingly relaxed and undisturbed. She forced

herself to play by the rules of her game, the rules that would allow her to win.

"You'll have to forgive me, Riordan," she sighed, giving him a half-smile over her shoulder. "I'm afraid I got a bit carried away."

"Why should I forgive you for that?" he returned evenly. "I enjoyed it."

"So did I—a little too much." That was the absolute truth, but it served her purpose to say it. "Todd and Kerry should be back soon. Would you care for another cup of coffee?"

"Since there's nothing stronger," he agreed.

Forgetting that the pot had been sitting above the flames for a long time, she tried to pour the coffee without the aid of a pot holder. She had barely closed her fingers around the handle before she released it.

"That's the way to get burned," Riordan drawled, tossing her a towel.

Jill could have told him there was more than one way to accomplish that as she successfully filled his cup and one for herself as well. She had just sat down, a discreet distance from Riordan, when Kerry and Todd returned.

"Ah, coffee!" Todd kneeled beside the pot, wisely picking up the towel before he attempted to pour a cup. "Was that a cougar I heard a while ago?" He directed his question at Riordan as he settled on to the ground near the fire, pulling Kerry down beside him and nestling her in the crook of his arm.

"Yes," Riordan agreed. He caught Jill's startled glance, the glitter in his eyes mocking the fact that she had obviously been deaf to everything when she was in his arms.

"Aren't you going to organize a hunt to go after him?" Todd frowned. "He could raise havoc with the spring calf crop."

"So far he's restricted his prey to the deer. I certainly don't object if he keeps them to a manageable number. That way there aren't so many deer to compete with my cattle for graze. If he shows a taste for beef, I'll have to get rid of him," Riordan shrugged.

Kerry shuddered. "I hope he doesn't."

"So do I," Riordan responded dryly. "As far as I'm concerned, the range is big enough for both of us. I respect the cougar's right to survive. If it's possible I'll drive him out of the area rather than destroy him. That isn't always possible."

Unwillingly a tightness closed over Jill's throat. So Riordan felt compassion for wild animals and none for humans. Was it his affinity for the land that made him that way?

Later, snuggled in her bedroll, the fire dying beside her, she stared at the stars, the question still unanswered. There was so much about Riordan she understood. His cynicism, his hardness, his aversion to any lasting relationship with a woman. Yet was there more? Was that little boy still hiding somewhere inside, sensitive and alone?

The morning sun made Jill forget all her unanswered questions of the night before. The answers were really of little consequence anyway. She was still determined to go ahead with her plans. But she did recognize after last night that it was a dangerous game she was playing, luring Riordan with implied promises she had no intention of fulfilling. It served to make the game more exciting and the vivid color of her eyes revealed it.

While Kerry poured water on the remains of the campfire, Jill stirred the coals to be certain no live ember remained. Todd was saddling the horses a few yards away and Riordan was loading the pack-horse.

"It's all out," Jill announced with a bright smile.

"Last night . . ." Kerry moved restively, drawing a curious glance from Jill. "Last night, I saw you with Riordan. Jill, what are you doing?" Anxious brown eyes searched Jill's face, as if she was certain her friend had taken leave of her senses.

"Exactly what it looked like. I was letting Riordan chase me," she replied. Her gaze moved thoughtfully to the broad shoulders of the man in question. "You know the old saying, Kerry, a boy chases a girl until she catches him. Well, I'm going to catch Riordan."

"Do you mean you've fallen in love with him?" Kerry breathed incredulously.

"No, silly," Jill laughed softly. "I'm not that big a fool. But I think I can get him to agree to your marriage before the month is up. It's impossible to reason with that man. That only leaves female trickery."

"Oh, Jill, do you think you should?"

"Should has nothing to do with it. I'm doing it."

"Come on, honey. We're ready to start back." Todd stood holding the reins to Kerry's horse, effectively ending the conversation between the two.

The mountains in the east were reflecting the glow of a setting western sun when the four rode into the ranchyard. During the ride down Jill had not attempted to force a conversation with Riordan or even lightly flirt with him. This was the time to be slightly inaccessible, to be friendly if he made the move but never to imply an intimacy.

One of the ranch hands was there to take the horses. Jill smiled easily when Riordan helped her from the saddle, deliberately ignoring the fraction of a second his hands remained on her waist after she was on the ground.

"I hope Mary has fixed an enormous roast with potatoes and gravy and the works," Todd declared. His arm was nonchalantly draped over Kerry's shoulders as they all started toward the house.

"I hope she's a mind reader and has a hot bubbling tubful of water waiting for us," Jill said. "The food can wait."

"You girls can laze in the tub if you want," Todd grinned. "I'll take a quick shower and eat."

"Not all of it. I'm starved, too," Kerry laughed.

"There's a car in the driveway. Oh, oh!" Todd arched a brow expressively at his brother. "Looks like you have a visitor."

Jill recognized the gold Mercedes. It belonged to none other than Sheena Benton. This was not exactly the way Jill had wanted to end the day. She slanted a glance at Riordan and caught the watchful glimmer of his gray eyes on her. He expected her to be disappointed.

"Maybe she can stay for dinner," she suggested in a deliberately casual vein.

"I'll ask." Riordan's mouth quirked.

Todd's eyes shifted from one to the other. He had seen what Kerry had seen the night before, and unless Kerry had enlightened him, which Jill doubted, he had put his own construction on it.

"It ought to be an interesting evening," offered

Todd dryly. His comment was followed by a sharp
dig in his ribs by Kerry's elbow.

Entering the house through the rear door, they
found the kitchen empty but with all sorts of delicious smells coming from the oven. In the entrance
hall, they could hear Sheena's voice. Jill couldn't
make out what she was saying, but it was obvious
she was talking to Mary.

"Oh, Riordan, there you are," Sheena declared
with purring delight when the foursome walked
into the entrance hall.

"Hello, Sheena," Riordan greeted her blandly.
"I didn't expect to see you here."

"I was just leaving, actually. Mary told me you'd
gone on a trail ride and, of course, I had no idea
when you would be back. Did just the four of you
go?" Her tiger eyes swerved to Jill, hostility sparkling in their almond shape.

"Just the four of us," Jill answered with a challenging smile.

"It must have been a long ride back. You certainly look grimy and saddlesore," Sheena replied.
Miaow! Jill thought, catching the snapping humor
of Mary Rivers's black eyes and trying not to let an
answering sparkle enter her own. It would simply
not do for Sheena to discover that she and Mary
were laughing at her, however silently.

"You're right on both counts," Jill agreed.
"Although—" an impish demon made her glance
at Riordan, "—it was certainly worth it."

Emotional fire flamed over her face and Jill knew
she had thoroughly evoked Sheena's jealousy. So
did Riordan. His gray eyes were unmistakably
amused.

"What brings you here, Sheena?" he asked. "Business or pleasure?"

"Business, mainly." The fires were banked as she swung her gaze to him, the light in her eyes adding that just how much "business" depended on him. "I was hoping I could persuade you to come over one evening and go over my accounts with me."

"Will Friday night be soon enough?" He didn't seem surprised by the request, which led Jill to believe that it was a common one or a smokescreen for a more intimate rendezvous. Or both.

"Friday will be fine," Sheena purred, sending a cool, sweeping smile that bordered on triumph to the others in the room. "I'll be going now to leave you all free to wash the trail dust off."

"Aren't you staying for dinner?" Clear blue eyes widened innocently. There was immense satisfaction in turning the tables on Sheena and pretending to be the hostess this time. "I'm sure Mary can stretch the food."

"You're welcome to stay if you like," Riordan said, a faint twitch of amusement near one corner of his mouth as if he knew the intent of Jill's invitation.

"Thank you, darling," Sheena purred. "But I know you're all on the verge of collapse. I'll see you Friday."

Chapter Eight

A bee made a downward swoop towards her head and Jill ducked quickly away from his buzzing path. Raising a hand to shield her eyes from the sun, she looked again to the truck parked beside the fence, its tailgate down. Beyond it and partially hidden by it was Riordan's dark head. Her fingers tightened their grip on the unopened bottle of cold beer.

Since the trail ride, she had seen next to nothing of Riordan. Myriad small obstacles had littered her path, ranging from sick animals to mechanical breakdowns of ranch equipment. Her plans were threatening to derail. Today was Friday and it was imperative that she make an impression on Riordan before he visited Sheena tonight.

Given enough time, Jill knew she could easily overcome the competition presented by the older woman. The problem was she didn't have much

time. In a little more than a week, she and Kerry
were due to leave. Lucky for her that Riordan was
fixing a fence close to the house today.

As Jill drew nearer the truck, she ran a hand
along the edge of the blouse she had tied just
under her breasts. On the surface, the tied blouse
was a concession to the blazing hot sun overhead,
but actually it was intended to draw attention to
the slenderness of her waist and other suggestive
curves.

"Hello!" Jill called, hooking a thumb in the belt
loops of her jeans as she rounded the rear of the
truck. "Are you working hard?"

Straightening from the fence, Riordan glanced
over his shoulder, an odd light flickering briefly
in his gray eyes. Jill halted beside the truck, the
world spinning crazily for an instant. A naked
expanse of bronzed torso glowing with the sheen
of sweat met her eyes. Riordan's shirt was slung on
the fence post.

"Out for a walk?" There was a substantial degree
of male interest in his question.

Leather gloves were pulled off with slow deliberation to join a pair of pliers in one hand as he moved
lazily toward the truck and Jill. His gaze slid to the
brown-tinted bottle in her hand.

There was a roaring in her ears that she couldn't
explain. She gladly shifted her attention to the
bottle and away from the hypnotic sight of the
tightly curling black hairs on his chest. Good heavens, she'd seen her brothers wearing less than that.
Why on earth was she letting it disturb her?

"Yes, I was feeling restless and thought I'd walk
it off," she admitted, tossing her head back with
an air of careless indifference. "Since I had

nowhere in particular to go, I thought I'd bring you something cold. The sun is hot today."

"That was thoughtful of you." He leaned against the side of the truck near Jill, laying his gloves and pliers near a roll of barbed wire in the back of the truck before taking the bottle of beer she offered. "I try to be useful," she smiled, attempting to sense the emotions behind his dry-voiced response. Riordan could be positively impenetrable at times. This was one of those times.

She watched him unscrew the lid and toss it in back, then lift the bottle to his mouth. As he tilted his head back to drink, she studied the tanned column of his throat, the cords rippling sinewy strong. Wiping the mouth of the bottle, Riordan offered it to her.

"Have some. You must be thirsty after your walk." Her throat did feel dry and tight. Accepting the bottle and raising it to her lips, she could almost feel the warmth of his mouth imprinted on the glass as she took a drink of the cold beer.

"Where's Kerry?" Riordan asked, his fingers accidentally—or on purpose—touching Jill's as he took the bottle from her hand.

"At the house." *Still insisting that I'm out of my mind for attempting such a thing,* Jill added to herself.

An uneasiness settled over her. She glanced away from Riordan, pretending an interest in the distant mountains sculptured against a wide blue sky. The gray eyes watched silently, leaving her with the unshakable feeling that it had been a mistake to come out here.

"I suppose I ought to let you get back to your work," she offered, for want of anything better to say.

"Not yet," Riordan drawled.

Jill glanced in surprise at the wrist that was suddenly a firm captive of his hand. "I . . . only came to bring you something to drink. Mary thought you might like a cold beer."

"Mary thought?" A brow arched quizzically, a dark glitter laughing at her in his eyes. "She must be getting forgetful, otherwise she would have remembered the cooler of beer she sent with me at noon."

Damn! Why had she allowed herself to be tripped up in her own lie? That was a teenager's mistake.

"Maybe that's what she said and I misunderstood her," she bluffed. "In either case, I'm keeping you from your work."

"I'm not objecting."

The bottle was set half-full inside the truck. Applying pressure to her wrist, Riordan drew her toward him. Short of struggling Jill couldn't resist.

The initiative of any embrace was supposed to have been at her invitation and not this soon. She let her legs carry her reluctantly toward him, almost sighing in relief when he let her stop a scant foot from him. At the moment her senses were clamoring too loudly at his nearness. She needed a few seconds to regain her sense of objectivity before coming in physical contact with him. His superior height forced her to tilt her head back to meet his hooded gaze. "Riordan, I—"

A hand touched her cheek, halting her words as effectively as if it had covered her mouth. "How many men have told you that your eyes are the color of the sky?" he mused. "A Montana sky, vivid blue and pulling a man into the promise of heaven beyond."

No sooner was Jill aware of her wrist being released than she felt his hand on the bare flesh of her waist. The strong male scent of him was an erotic stimulus she didn't want to feel.

"Please!" Her effort to appear indifferent was thwarted by the involuntary catch in her voice.

"Didn't you wander into this meadow with the intention of bestowing some of the honey from your lips on me, butterfly?" Riordan taunted.

A tiny gasp parted her lips. His hand curved around the back of her neck, drawing her upward to his mouth. The brawny chest was satiny smooth and sensual beneath her fingers, hard muscles flexing as he molded her against him. Her lips moved in response to his to deepen the kiss until a wild, glorious song burst in her heart.

The melody raced through her veins. Jill was only half aware of Riordan pressing her backward. Spiky blades of grass scratched her bare back as his weight pinned her to the ground. The caress of his hands was arousing, exhorting her to give—and to plead with her body to receive—more in return.

The tails of her blouse were untied and the buttons undone with careless ease. Her nipple hardened under his touch and she moaned in surrender. The reason she had come was completely lost under the spell of ecstasy flaming through her.

When his head raised from hers, she locked her arms around his neck to draw him back. His fingers closed over her wrists and firmly pulled her hands away, his mouth twisting harshly.

"Sorry, butterfly. I'm not satisfied either, but we're about to have company."

Rolling to his feet, Riordan stood above her.

Dominated as she was by raging emotions, it took a full second for Jill to realize the significance of what he had said. The sound of a car engine could be heard crossing the meadow and drawing nearer. She scrambled to her feet, cheeks flaming at her complete lack of control, and turned away from his taunting gaze to hastily button her blouse.

The task was barely completed by her shaking hands when the car stopped beside the truck. Self-consciously brushing golden hair away from her face, Jill turned. She wanted to scream in frustration at the sight of Sheena Benton.

"Am I interrupting something, Riordan?" Sheena said archly, leaning against the steering wheel of her car, fingers curling like unsheathed claws over the wheel.

"It'll keep." Riordan shrugged, slanting a mocking glance at Jill's still flushed cheeks. "What can I do for you?"

"I wanted to remind you about tonight." Her statement was directed at Riordan, but the hatred in her eyes was solely for Jill.

"I hadn't forgotten," Riordan assured her smoothly, an intimate dark light entering his eyes.

"If you can get away, why not come early?" Sheena suggested. A purring entered her voice at his look. "You can check the accounts over dinner."

"I should be able to arrange that," he agreed coolly, and was rewarded with a dazzling smile. Nausea churned Jill's stomach.

"I won't keep you," Sheena murmured, shifting the car into gear and glancing with feline spite at Jill. "Can I give you a lift to the house, Jill?"

"No, thank you," she retorted coldly. "I prefer to

walk." The red mouth tightened with displeasure. "Suit yourself." Sheena tossed her chestnut mane. Blowing a kiss to Riordan, she reversed to turn back the way she had come.

"Are you going back now?" Riordan asked with insinuating softness.

"Yes," Jill answered decisively, wishing the heat in her cheeks would ease. "Right away."

"Better fix your blouse before you get back to the house," he pointed out. "You've buttoned it crooked."

A mortified glance at the front of her blouse confirmed his statement. There was not the slightest chance that the sharp-eyed Sheena had not noticed it. "Thanks, I'll do that," Jill retorted defiantly, refusing to show any guilt about her action.

But guilt hounded her steps all the way back to the house. She had intended to entrap Riordan with his physical attraction for her. Despite the way his lovemaking had aroused her in previous encounters, she had never expected he would awaken her inner desires and the extent of her womanhood. In all honesty, her confidence was badly shaken.

Riordan wasn't at the dinner table when she entered the dining room with Kerry and Todd. She left it to Mary Rivers to explain where he was. There was a noticeable lack of desire to mention her meeting with Riordan that afternoon and she avoided the questing look from Mary.

The perfectly prepared meal was utterly tasteless, but Jill forced down nearly everything on her plate. She didn't want to parry any questions about a lack of appetite. After the meal, she retreated to a corner of the living room with a book, ostensibly affording Kerry and Todd some privacy.

Her thoughts were as jumbled and confused as they had been earlier. The printed lines on the book page blurred. She simply couldn't concentrate . . . on anything. The only thing that seemed to register was the portrait of the copper-haired woman with sparkling hazel eyes that hung above the mantelpiece. A butterfly like herself.

Suddenly restless, Jill snapped the book in her lap shut, drawing startled glances from Todd and Kerry. "I think I'll go and see if Mary needs some help in the kitchen," she said in explanation.

But the kitchen was sparkling clean and the housekeeper was nowhere to be seen. With the half-formed idea to take a walk outside, Jill wandered down the back hall towards the rear entrance. A closed door drew her hypnotically. She knew it was Riordan's room. Mary had mentioned it one day in passing, but Jill had never been inside. Curiosity surged to the forefront, a sudden need filling her to see his room.

Cautiously she opened the door and walked into the room, touching the light switch. The small light overhead left the corners of the room in shadows. Jill stared silently around her, taking in the single bed against one side of a wall with a small table beside it and the chest of drawers against another wall. A rigid, straight-backed chair occupied one corner.

Compared to the quiet elegance of the rest of the house, the stark simplicity of this room was unexpected. It was almost monastic. Very quietly Jill closed the door behind her, aware that she was trespassing but unable to leave.

Riordan was a man of basics. She had always guessed that. Yet, walking to the single bed, she couldn't stop wondering why he had chosen to shun the more luxurious creature comforts offered by the rest of the house for this. Did he need to sleep here to remain hard and cynical? Was he avoiding the gentle, feminine touches she had noticed in the rest of the house?

Fingering the agricultural book on the bedside table, Jill smiled at herself. She was crazy to come in here. The room revealed no more about Riordan than he did himself. She was being overly imaginative to believe otherwise.

A striped Hudson Bay blanket covered the bed. Without being consciously aware of what she was doing, Jill sat down on the edge of the bed. The mattress was firm without being rock-hard, a fact she noticed absently as she gazed about the room.

A movement caught her eye, and freezing with cold dread, she saw the doorknob turning. She couldn't breathe and as the door opened, she offered a hurried prayer that it would be Mary Rivers she saw. It was much too early for Riordan to come back.

But it was his broad-shouldered, lean-hipped frame that filled the opening. Gray eyes met the startled roundness of her blue ones. Jill's heart was in her throat. She couldn't think of one legitimate reason she could offer as an excuse for her presence in his room. With a speculative glitter, his gaze swept over her.

"This is an unexpected invitation," Riordan murmured dryly, stepping into the room and closing the door.

Heat flamed through her cheeks as Jill suddenly

realized she was sitting on his bed. She rose hurriedly to her feet.

The hard line of his mouth quirked mockingly. "There's no need to get up. I would have joined you."

"I . . . I was just going," Jill stammered.

"You don't need to slip into something more comfortable."

His steel-gray eyes studied her with lazy intensity, lingering on the trembling parting of her mouth, the pulsing vein in her neck and finally the vee of her blouse.

Her hand protectively covered the vee. "You don't understand," she protested nervously. "I didn't expect you back so soon. I thought you . . . I mean, Sheena . . ." There simply wasn't any way she could put into words exactly what she thought he and Sheena would be doing.

"After this afternoon, did you honestly think I would prefer the scratching of a jealous cat when I could have the fluttering softness of a butterfly?" He took a step toward her.

"No!" Her breath was fast and uneven. "I know what you must be thinking, finding me in your room and all," she said wildly. "I only came in because I was curious." The grooves around his mouth deepened. "It's not at all what you're thinking, I swear."

"Don't bother to bat those innocent blue eyes at me," he retorted. "You were maneuvering again, Jill. We both know it."

She opened her mouth to try to protest the truth of his statement. It would be futile. There were too many disturbing emotions stirring inside her for her to lie convincingly.

"Excuse me, but I really must go," she murmured unsteadily, keeping her eyes downcast as she started toward the door.

"Now what's the game?" Riordan was in her way, blocking the path to the door. "Are you playing hard to get?"

"I'm not playing anything. Please let me by." There was room to pass him, but Jill didn't trust him.

"I see." He was laughing at her, silently—she could see it in his eyes. "You simply flitted into my room by accident, drawn only by curiosity. Now you want to fly away, so I can remember how sexy you looked waiting on my bed."

"Riordan, please!" Jill swallowed tightly.

Trading words with him was useless. She had to escape before she became enmeshed in the backlash of her plans. At this moment she was too unprepared to cope with Riordan or her wayward reactions to him.

Jill started for the door. As she drew level with him, she held her breath, flinching when his hand moved. But it didn't reach out for her. Instead it snapped off the overhead light, throwing the room into darkness.

Stopped by the unexpectedness of his action and her own momentary blindness, Jill wasn't able to move. The suggestive intimacy of the bedroom, isolated from the living area of the house, washed over her like shockwaves.

"Once you trap a butterfly—" his low voice was closer, a soft and seductive weapon, and she gasped at his hands gripping her shoulders, "—you must take it by the wings."

"Let me go!" she cried breathlessly, frightened

by her sudden desire to lean submissively against his chest. She tried to wrench free of his grip, but Riordan used her twisting motion to pivot her around, easily drawing her unbalanced body against his.

His dark head bent and he brushed his mouth against the sensitive skin below her right ear. Jill couldn't control the shudder of delight. The heady male scent of him enveloped her, earthy and clean. Tilting her head to one side, she tried to elude his provocative caress, but only succeeded in exposing more of her neck to his exploring mouth.

"No," she pleaded, shaking back the feathery length of her gold hair and increasing the pressure of her hands that strained against his chest.

Riordan laughed softly, a deep delicious sound that shivered down her spine. His mouth lifted to the averted line of her jaw.

"Isn't this the way you planned it, Jill?" he taunted. His warm breath fanned across the already hot skin of her cheek.

"I didn't plan this," she protested in a desperate whisper. Her eyes were beginning to adjust to the softness of the starlight streaming through the windows.

"You didn't *plan* to make me want you?" Riordan said. Jill breathed in sharply. "I know you did. The idea has been in the back of your mind since the first time we met. Everything you've done has been calculated to blind me with desire for you so you could twist me around your finger, take what you wanted and fly away."

"No," Jill gulped.

She bent her head backward, trying again to escape the disturbing nearness of his mouth.

Strong fingers spread across the small of her back, molding her arching body more fully against the male vigor of his. A dizzying weakness spread through her limbs. Her tightly closed lashes fluttered open, focusing her gaze on his rugged features. Half-closed eyes studied her upturned face with a silvery fire that stole her breath.

"Please!" she begged to be released.

His hand held on to the long silken hair at the back of her neck. Jill could not avoid his kiss. Her hammering fists glanced harmlessly off his chest and shoulders.

At last his conquering mouth had her fingers curling into the thin material of his shirt, clinging to him weakly in surrender. Riordan wasn't content with submission as he parted her lips with persuasive mastery, exploring her mouth until Jill responded with demanding hunger.

Reason was banished completely under the molding caress of his hands. There was only the whirling, mindless ecstasy of his embrace urging her to new heights of sensual awareness. She was achingly conscious of her need for physical gratification, and the hard maleness of Riordan made her aware of his.

The trailing fire of his lips burned over her eyes, cheek and throat, branding her as his possession, and she didn't deny it. Her hands were around his neck, fingers winding into the thick blackness of his hair. His hard mouth closed again over hers, uniting their flames into a roaring fire of passion that sang in her ears.

Like a drowning person, Jill made one last attempt to be saved when his mouth blazed a path to the hollow of her throat.

"I can't—"

Her thoughts were too chaotic. What couldn't she do? She couldn't stop. She couldn't think. She couldn't breathe. She couldn't exist without the wildfire of his touch.

"I'm insane," she ended with a sighing groan.

His head lifted briefly, fingers sliding to her throat. "That's the way I want you to be," Riordan muttered harshly. "Driven to madness until you can think of nothing else but me." He spoke against her lips, his mouth moving mobilely over them in a caress that was designed to make her ache for his kiss. "I want you to want me so much you won't fly away until sunrise."

Jill breathed in sharply, knowing she didn't ever want to fly away, yet realizing how dangerous it would be to give in to her emotions so completely.

"Kerry . . . Todd . . ." she offered in protest.

Riordan's mouth shut off her words until she stopped caring about Kerry and Todd. Only then did he answer.

"They'll enjoy being alone at last. They won't miss you. I doubt if Todd even expected me back tonight."

Weakly Jill shook her head, unable to deny the truth of what he said. Lowering her head, she felt his lips against her hair, their moistness tangling in the silken gold.

"Riordan, I—"

The support of his hard, masculine body was taken away from her and she swayed toward him. Her movement was checked as an arm slid under her knees and she was lifted into the air, cradled against his chest. Automatically her hands circled his neck.

As he turned toward the small bed, a shaft of starlight illuminated his face. The strength of purpose stamped in the forceful, handsome lines caught at Jill's throat. Nothing could stop him. The same erotically charged mood had her in its spell and she knew she didn't want to try to prevent what seemed so inevitable and paradoxically so right.

Sitting on the side of the bed, Riordan held her on his lap. His face was in shadows, but she knew the gray eyes were studying her. This was her last chance to protest. Instead her fingers began exploring the blunt angles of his features, feather-soft and caressing.

He seemed to be prolonging the moment when he claimed her as if to make the possession sweeter. Feeling wantonly bold, Jill leaned forward and pressed her lips against his mouth. He smiled.

"The bed isn't made for two," Riordan murmured huskily, the grooves around his mouth deepening in satisfaction, "but tonight I don't think either one of us will care."

An almost inaudible moan of complete surrender slipped from her throat as Riordan bent her backward onto the mattress. His hand slid intimately from her thigh to her hip and along to the curve of her breast. The pressing weight of his male body followed her down, his mouth unerringly and possessively finding hers. Jill was lost in an erotic dreamworld of sensations that she never wanted to end. She succumbed with delight to each new touch.

"Jill?" A familiar voice was trying to enter her dream. Jill's head moved in protest to its call. "Jill? Where are you?"

"No!" she gave a muffled cry to forbid the entry. "Sssh." Riordan's strong fingers lightly covered her mouth.

His indirect acknowledgment of the voice that called her made the dreamworld begin to fade into reality.

"Jill?" Now she could recognize the voice as Kerry's, still distant but moving closer. "Where could she be?"

"She did say she was going to the kitchen, didn't she?" Todd was with Kerry.

"Yes, but she isn't here," came the muffled reply of concern.

Reason and sanity came back with shocking swiftness as Jill tried to twist from beneath Riordan's weight. He checked the movement easily.

"No," his low voice commanded near her ear. "You know you don't really want to leave."

"Yes . . . no." The conflicting answers were crazily the truth as Jill was torn in two by her emotions.

"Maybe she went outside for a walk," Todd suggested.

"It isn't like her not to tell me. Oh, Todd, let's check."

Kerry rushed down the hall that led past Riordan's room to the rear door of the house.

Jill's hands pushed frantically against the stone wall of his chest. "They'll find us," she whispered desperately.

His warm breath moved over her cheek in silent laughter. "They won't look for you in here," he mocked, his mouth following the curve of her throat to the tantalizing hollow between her breasts.

"N-n-no!" Her protest was shaken by the violent surge of desire brought on by his intimate touch.

"She could have gone up to her room, too," Todd said as they walked by the bedroom door.

"Let's check outside first," Kerry replied anxiously.

"She's a grown woman. She can take care of—" The "herself" was lost as the closing back door cut off the rest of Todd's statement.

"I told you they wouldn't find us," Riordan murmured against her skin.

"B-but they'll keep on looking," Jill moaned softly, her hands still straining against him. "Please let me go."

"No." His fingers closed over her chin, holding it motionless as his mouth closed over hers in a drugging kiss that sent her floating nearly all the way back into her dreamworld. The click of the bedroom doorknob splintered through her. The alert tensing of Riordan's muscles told her he had heard it too, but he didn't lift his mouth from hers nor allow her protesting lips to twist away.

"Riordan, they're looking for her." Mary Rivers spoke from the doorway.

His hold relaxed slightly as he raised his head, his gaze glittering, holding Jill's pleading blue eyes. Hot waves of shame licked through her veins.

"Get out of here, Mary," Riordan ordered smoothly.

"Don't talk to me that way. Unless you want a smack."

Tearing her eyes from his face, Jill twisted her head toward the housekeeper, her tall, stocky build outlined by the light streaming into the room from the hallway. Her throat worked convulsively, but nothing came out. Part of her didn't want to be rescued.

"You can't do it, Riordan," Mary sighed, but with firm conviction.

"Can't I?" he said arrogantly. "The lady is more than willing," he added with sarcastic emphasis.

"Let her go."

He smiled coolly down at Jill. "She's free to leave," he rolled away from her, only a hand remaining spread on her stomach as his wicked gray eyes held her gaze captive, "if she really wants to leave."

Perhaps if he hadn't been so confident she would stay or if he had asked her not to leave him, Jill would have remained where she was. Instead, with a frightened sob at what a fool she had nearly made of herself, she scrambled to her feet.

Two wavering steps toward the door were all she had taken before the soft flesh of her upper arms was taken in a strong grip. Weakly she allowed herself to be pulled back against his chest, her head lolling against his shoulder, unable to deny the disturbance his touch caused.

"Riordan," Mary warned swiftly.

"No, she can go," he interrupted in an ominously low voice laced with contempt. "She and I both know that I wasn't seducing her. She was letting me seduce her. Almost since the day she came, she's been inviting me to make love to her, deliberately holding back so she could lead me on. She knew I found her as physically attractive as any man would and she intended to use that attraction to get what she wanted. Isn't that right, Jill?" he demanded savagely.

She didn't have the strength to disagree even if

he was wrong, but he wasn't wrong and she didn't argue. "Yes, yes, that's right," she admitted in a breathy whisper. "But it didn't work." The calm voice slashed at her pride. Didn't he want her? His arousal had been very real—as real as her response to him. He released her with a slight push toward the door and Mary. "You can go. But I'm not quite through with you yet."

With that half-threat and half-promise ringing in the air, Jill stumbled forward. Mary wrapped a supporting arm around her shoulders and led her from the room. Drained of all emotion except the cold feeling of dread, Jill was barely aware of the housekeeper's presence.

"I'll take you upstairs to your room," said Mary.

Jill was suddenly conscious of how disheveled she must look. Her clothes were in a revealing state of disarray and her lips had to be swollen from his passionate kisses. She knew she had the look of a woman who had been made love to. A sob strangled her throat. She very nearly had! She cast a surreptitious glance at the housekeeper, wondering what this proud woman thought of her. The only part of Riordan's accusation that had been a lie was when he had suggested that she had intended that he seduce her. Jill had never contemplated going that far, but she *had* planned to make Riordan want her so badly he would do anything.

When they reached her bedroom, Jill caught the look of gentle compassion in Mary's dark eyes. In shame and humiliation, she knew guiltily that she didn't deserve the woman's understanding.

"I'm all right," Jill asserted forcefully, averting her face from the housekeeper's concerned gaze. Her legs now strong enough to deny the need for a supporting arm, Jill stepped forward. "Would you tell Kerry that you saw me and that . . . that I have a headache and have gone to my room?"

"I'll see that you're not disturbed," Mary nodded perceptively, "by anyone."

By anyone, Jill knew she meant Riordan, too. And she didn't doubt that the woman would figuratively stand guard at her door. When Mary left, Jill buried her face in her hands, but she didn't cry.

Hysterical laughter sobbed in her throat. She barely smothered it with her hand. The irony of the situation struck her forcibly. All along she had believed Riordan was chasing her. Instead, she had been chasing him and he had caught her. She was the one who had been brought to her knees.

Never once in all her planning had she ever seriously considered the possibility that she might fall in love with Riordan. Yet that was exactly what she had done. She knew it as clearly and as certainly as she knew her own name.

Tonight had not been the result of a sudden desire for physical experience or the arousing attention of an experienced lover. They were a potent combination but not an explanation for her complete abandonment of reason. Love was the answer, no matter how foolish and painful the emotion might be.

Chapter Nine

Jill stared at the rising sun on the eastern horizon. Blue eyes were glazed with pain, faint etchings of red at the corners. Not from tears. She hadn't cried. Not a single tear had come forward to ease the ache in her heart.

The redness was from exhaustion. She had not slept, not even attempted to sleep nor made the pretense that she would. Still dressed in the same clothes, she had alternately paced the room and stared out the window. Sometimes she thought of nothing except what it had been like in Riordan's arms. At other times, her mind raced wildly to come up with a scheme to make Riordan love her. All were rejected eventually. He would see through them just as he had seen through all of her other maneuvers.

There was a subdued knock at her door, and she spun from the window. It couldn't be Kerry. She would use the connecting door. Todd was out of the question. Mary?

"W-who is it?" she called shakily.

"Riordan," was the low response.

A shaft of irrational joy pierced her heart. She wanted to race to the door, fling it open and throw herself into his arms. She told herself not to be a fool.

"Go away," she said tightly.

The doorknob turned, but for some unknown reason Jill had locked it last night. Now she bowed her head in thankfulness.

"A locked door isn't going to stop me, Jill. Open it!"

It wasn't an idle threat. Still, she hesitated before walking over and turning the key in the lock. Control was the key, she told herself as she walked quickly away. She had to remain calm and controlled. She mustn't let her emotions surface, nor the love she felt for him.

Again at the window, she halted. He was in the room, the door closed behind him.

"What do you want?" she demanded.

"If you had trouble sleeping last night, why didn't you come downstairs?"

Jill glanced sharply over her shoulder just as Riordan turned away from the bed that bore not the slightest imprint of having been slept in. Aloof gray eyes caught her look and held it, but not for long.

"Leave me alone, Riordan," she snapped harshly at his arrogant expression, then breathed in deeply to regain the control she needed so desperately. Yet it seemed that the only way she had of concealing her love for him was to lash out in anger.

"Not yet," he answered quietly. "I've come to

tell you that you can move your things down to my room this morning. I'll have a larger bed and another chest of drawers moved in."

Slowly Jill turned from the window, her head tipped to one side in disbelief. "What?" she breathed incredulously.

A brow arched higher. "I thought I'd made it clear. I'm not the type to go sneaking around after midnight."

"So you're simply arranging for me to sleep with you?" Her hands moved to a challenging position on her hips.

"Spare me the pretense of indignation." He gave her a wry look. "I'm sure your friend Kerry is aware of the facts of life. No doubt she'll find it romantic. If you prefer, I'll explain to her and Todd."

"And what will you explain? That I'm your new sleeping partner, your lover, your mistress?" Jill demanded coldly. "I'm dying to know exactly what position you're offering me."

The dark head was tipped arrogantly back, the gray eyes clear and piercing like an eagle's. "Whatever label suits you," replied Riordan.

"What is the duration of this position?" A cold clarity filled her heart and, momentarily at least, eased the pain. "Until you're through with me?"

"I'm not setting any time limit, butterfly." There was faint contempt in his tone. "Whichever one of us tires of the other first can call it quits."

"I see," she said tautly. "And you expect me to fall all over myself accepting this arrangement?"

Riordan moved slowly to stand in front of her and it was all Jill could do to hold her ground and not retreat. He towered over her for a long moment.

His hand reached out to touch the petal softness of her cheek. Something melted inside her at his caress and she had to steel herself not to visibly react.

"You were eager enough for me to make love to you last night," Riordan reminded her softly.

The peculiar light in his eyes made her heart skip a beat. Yet the indecision of what to do that had plagued her all night was gone. Under these circumstances, there was only one thing she could do.

"Yes," she admitted calmly, "I did want you to make love to me last night."

There was a satisfied look on his face. "Do you want me to send Mary up to help you pack your things?" Jill moved away from the hand that was still resting on her cheek and walked to the center of the room. She clasped her hands in front of her, staring at her twining fingers for an instant before she met his alert gaze.

"Please do send Mary." A strange calm spread over her. "I would like to pack and get out of this house as soon as possible."

The room crackled with a stunned silence. His gaze narrowed fractionally, followed by a short, sardonically amused sigh.

"Are you flying away already, butterfly?" He smiled indifferently. "Even that was too much of a commitment for you to make?"

His aloof comment stung. If he had indicated in any way that he cared for her, Jill would have willingly committed her life to him. She felt the moistness of tears on her lashes.

"There is one more thing," she squeezed the words out through the lump in her throat, "before

I ask you to leave my room. I want you to give your approval of Todd's marriage to Kerry.''

Again he walked to stand in front of her, not touching her this time, as his gaze focused on a crystal drop threatening to fall from a dark-gold lash.

"Tears?" Riordan jeered. "That must be the oldest female maneuver in the book. Didn't have to dig too deep in your bag of tricks to come up with that one!"

Jill stared at her hands, unable to meet his satirical look. "I don't doubt that you find them amusing. I don't think you're capable of understanding anything but your own needs."

She took a deep breath, not raising her eyes. "You don't know your brother very well either, because if you did, you would know he's capable of very deep feelings. He cares about you, but he won't let you stand in the way of his happiness forever. You can threaten him with money or any other thing you want, but in the end he will marry Kerry and hate you. Maybe you don't care. Family probably means nothing to you. If it doesn't, then it can't matter what Todd does with his life."

"Are you finished interfering?" Riordan snapped.

"Yes." Jill turned away, her shoulders slightly hunched forward, a terrible coldness in her heart. "Will you go now? And . . . and I would prefer not to see you again before I leave."

"That makes two of us," he agreed mockingly.

The bedroom door slammed and another tear slipped from her lashes. Jill wiped it determinedly away. She wasn't going to cry, not when she knew she was doing the only thing possible. She walked to the closet and started yanking out her clothes.

A few minutes later Mary was there, silently helping her, not needing the reason for Jill's sudden departure explained.

The last suitcase had been snapped shut when there was a knock on her door. Jill couldn't move, terrified that it might be Riordan and her resolve to leave would crumble if she had to be near him again. But when Mary opened the door, it was Todd who stood in the hallway.

"Riordan said that as soon as you were ready, I'm supposed to take you home," he said quietly. "He said you had an argument." But his hazel eyes said he knew it was more complicated than that.

"Yes . . . well," she ran a shaking hand over her forehead, "I'm ready." She glanced hesitantly toward the connecting door to Kerry's room.

"I'll explain to Kerry if you'd like to leave now," Todd offered.

She darted him a grateful look. "Thank you, Todd. And you, too, Mary." She gave the housekeeper a quick hug before picking up one of the smaller bags and hurrying toward the door.

With the rest of her luggage under his arm, Todd started to follow, then glanced back at Mary. "When Kerry wakes up . . ."

The housekeeper smiled gently. "I'll tell her you'll explain everything when you get back."

Butterflies could fly away and never look back. Jill didn't feel very much like a butterfly. She doubted if she ever would again.

Taking her foot off the accelerator, she gently applied the brakes to ease the car around the curve in the snow-packed road. The Christmas-wrapped packages on the seat started to slip and she put out a hand to stop them. She didn't feel in the holiday spirit either. She just hoped that once she was home with her parents and brothers and sisters, she would catch the festive mood.

After the way she had moped around the house this past summer when she had left the ranch, her parents were entitled to expect some improvement in her disposition. They had been wonderfully understanding, although they couldn't really believe there was a man who wouldn't love their daughter. Of course, Jill hadn't told them the whole story. Kerry was the only one who came close to knowing all of it.

The car she was driving had been a consoling gesture from her parents. They had shrugged it off by saying that they were tired of making double trips back and forth to Helena to pick her up on the holiday vacations. They would not be too pleased, though, when they discovered she had made this trip without Kerry's company.

Her engagement to Todd was still on, even though Todd had transferred to Harvard and Kerry had remained in Helena. They had made the decision not to marry until Kerry had finished college, even though it meant a separation. Jill had never had the courage to inquire whether the waiting period had been Riordan's idea, although she had guessed that it was. His name was never mentioned unless by Jill.

Todd had flown back from Harvard to spend Christmas with Kerry. Jill had invited both of them to come home with her, but Todd had declined. He wanted to be certain to catch his flight back. With the unpredictability of winter storms, he didn't object to being snowbound at the airport as long as he wasn't stranded two hundred miles away from it. Naturally Kerry preferred to stay in Helena with him, especially after he had given her his mother's engagement ring.

Jill touched the antique cameo suspended by a delicate gold chain around her neck, Todd's Christmas present to her. It, too, had belonged to his mother—she remembered how startled she had been when he told her that. She had held it for long minutes, unwilling to put it around her neck.

"Does Riordan know you gave me this?" she had asked finally. A cold hand had closed over her heart to keep it from beating.

Shortly after Todd had arrived in Helena, he had driven to the ranch to see his brother and to select Kerry's engagement ring from his mother's jewelry.

"Yes, he knows," Todd had answered quietly. His eyes had examined Jill's frozen expression. "After I'd taken Kerry's ring from the box, I mentioned that I wanted to buy a gift, so Riordan told me to pick out something I thought you might like from Mother's jewelry."

Jill had forced a bright smile. "It's very lovely, and I do like it," she said, fastening the cameo necklace around her neck. "Are you and Kerry driving out to the ranch for Christmas day?"

"No, Jill, Kerry and I want a peaceful Christmas," he had said with decided emphasis.

"I'm sure Sheena will keep him company," Jill had shrugged, but a shaft of jealousy had drilled deep.

"She's gone to Palm Springs for the holidays.

She came to see Riordan while I was there," Todd bad explained.

Later Jill had summoned the courage to ask if Riordan had given his approval of their engagement. It had seemed likely since Riordan had evidently permitted Todd to give Kerry their mother's ring.

Todd had breathed in deeply, a slightly closed look stealing into his expression. "Let's just say that he's reconciled to the fact that be can't change my mind."

Sighing heavily, Jill couldn't help wondering if Riordan hadn't relaxed his opposition to their engagement just a little bit. He might not have given his wholehearted approval, but at least he was not taking such a hard line against it.

And the necklace she wore, did it have any special significance? Was it an indirect and private way of apologizing? Whoever said that hope sprang eternal certainly was right, Jill thought wryly. Here she was hoping for a miracle. Of course, Christmas is a miracle time, she reminded herself, so maybe it was only natural.

Christmas. It was a time for family gatherings and enormous dinners. Jill could visualize her own home with holly strung on evergreen branches all through the living room, dining room and hall. Her father would have mistletoe hung in every archway and from every light fixture. And her mother would have the stockings they had used as children hung over the fireplace, waiting for Santa.

The tree would be gigantic, covered with tinsel, angel hair, and the ornaments that had become old friends over the years. Plates of Christmas candy and bowls of colored popcorn balls would be all over the house, promising an extra five pounds of weight to anyone who dared to touch them. Logs would be in readiness in the fireplace, but a fire wouldn't be started until Christmas morning, after Santa Claus had safely made his visit.

That was Christmas to Jill.

Unbidden the question came—what was Christmas to Riordan? Todd had told her Riordan was in his teens when he had stopped accompanying his father to Helena to spend Christmas with his mother. How many lonely Christmases had he spent in that big house without family and with only Mary Rivers as company? No family and probably no decorations. Men didn't take the time to do such things on their own, and what would there have been to celebrate?

And what about that twelve-year-old boy who had been forced to shoot his horse when it had broken its legs? That little boy who had grown into a man, a man who wouldn't give horses names in case he had to destroy one again. That same man was spending Christmas alone again this year. His own brother had chosen the company of the woman he loved over Riordan, just as their father had done.

Suddenly it didn't matter whether Todd's decision was warranted or not. It just seemed so totally unfair that Riordan was going to be alone again.

Jill turned into the first plowed side road she found and drove back the way she had come. A couple of miles back she had passed the crossroads intersection and the highway that would take her to the Riordan ranch. One of the packages on the seat contained a sweater for her father. With luck, it would fit Riordan. Another contained a hand-crafted shawl she could give Mary.

His present would be a conciliatory gesture on her part. He might just meet her halfway. There was that eternal hope again! She smiled sadly. More than likely, Riordan would think it was another trick she was playing, a maneuver of some sort. But she didn't care. She simply had to see him.

The lane leading from the cleared county road to the ranch house had not been plowed. Several sets of tracks ran over each other in the general direction of the buildings located on the other side of the meadow, presently out of sight behind the rise. Jill offered a silent prayer that she wouldn't get stuck as the car crunched over the tire-packed snow.

The winter sun set early in the north country. It was barely past mid-afternoon and already there was a purpling pink cast to the snow-covered mountains. Jill refused to think about the rest of her drive home in the dark.

The house, nestled in the protective stand of snow-draped evergreens, looked somehow bigger and emptier than she remembered. A tense excitement gripped her as she selected the packages from the rest and stepped out of the car.

At the front door, she hesitated, gathering her courage before she opened the door. Maybe it was a subconscious wish to catch Riordan unawares that had prompted her to enter without knocking, or maybe she had become accustomed to simply walking in after spending those fateful weeks in the house that summer.

The house was silent and empty. A fire crackling in the entryway hearth would have made the house seem warm, but there was none. Slipping off her snowboots, Jill listened attentively for some sound of human occupation.

It suddenly occurred to her that Riordan might not even be here. He could be at one of the barns or at another section of the ranch altogether. That would only leave Mary Rivers. She would undoubtedly be in the kitchen. Jill slowly exhaled the breath she had been unconsciously holding. It was probably just as well that she hadn't seen Riordan, she decided, but she would speak to Mary.

The awesome silence of the house had her tiptoeing on the hardwood floor of the hall leading to the kitchen in the rear. As she drew closer, she caught the aroma of cooking and smiled. Mary was there.

Her hand was on the kitchen doorknob ready to turn it to open the door when she heard Riordan's voice come from inside the kitchen.

"I don't care what you're fixing. I told you I'm not hungry," he snapped.

"Then have some coffee and stop grouching about like a grizzly," Mary replied evenly.

"I am not grouching," Riordan answered tightly.

"Snapping my head off every five minutes is not grouching?" the housekeeper inquired dryly. "You either have a severe case of cabin fever or you're thinking about that girl. Which is it?"

Jill held her breath, unable to move until Riordan had answered. There was a heavy silence before he spoke in a cuttingly indifferent voice.

"What girl?"

"Jill, of course, as if you didn't know."

"I wasn't thinking of her," Riordan replied.

"Weren't you?" Mary countered. "When are you going to give up and ask the girl to marry you?"

Jill's heart exploded against her rib cage, pounding so fiercely it seemed impossible they couldn't hear it.

There was a sudden scrape of a chair leg. "I'm not that crazy!" he jeered. The pounding of her heart stopped almost abruptly.

"I don't know about that. Why don't you call her?"

"You know why, Mary." Riordan sighed angrily. His cryptic statement was followed by a long pause as though he was waiting for the housekeeper to comment. Bitterness and contempt laced his next words. "I remember one August when Mom left unexpectedly. I was thirteen or fourteen at the time. Dad came in the house after saying goodbye to her, looking all hollow and beaten. I demanded that he go and get her and make her stay with us, but he said he couldn't use force to keep her or beg or bribe her to stay. The only thing he could do, he said, was to simply love her."

"He was right, Riordan," Mary agreed quietly.

"Right!" he returned with a scoffing laugh. "In all the times she left him, I never saw Dad cry once—only when she died. Then he became half a man. When she was alive, you know how many winter evenings he sat in front of her portrait and how impossible it was to get him to leave that room when she died. No woman has a right to bring a man down like that. He was strong and intelligent, a giant, and she had no right to make a fool of him."

"She loved him," Mary said.

"She used him," Riordan corrected grimly. "If

she'd loved him, she would have stayed here where she belonged."

"But she never belonged here . . . I think that's something you were never able to understand. No matter how much she loved your father, your mother would never have been happy on this ranch. It wasn't her environment. As much as your father loved her, didn't you ever wonder why he didn't move to the city to be with her?" Mary answered her own question. "He would have been miserable because he didn't belong there. Their love for each other was the bridge between the two worlds, and it was a very strong one."

"Well, my mother flew over that bridge every spring and left every fall." His voice was savagely harsh. "Should I live in misery for nine months of the year the way Dad did? Maybe I inherited his curse for falling in love with butterflies, but I will never marry one!"

The fragile hope that had been building inside Jill began to crumble. It was just as she had told herself last summer. Although Riordan was passionately attracted to her, he also was afraid of her.

"Butterflies," Mary murmured with amused disbelief. "You believe Jill is a butterfly?"

"Picture her in your mind, Mary," he sighed. "Her hair is as golden as the sun and her eyes are as big and as blue as the sky. She's so fragile, I could snap her in two with one hand. Men are drawn to her just like they were drawn to my mother."

"Riordan, you're blind!"

"Oh, no," he declared. "Well, maybe. But I'm not stupid. I could see all the traps she laid for me." "Since when do butterflies have to lay traps?"

Jill had to strain to hear the housekeeper's soft voice. "Jill is very beautiful, but she isn't a butterfly. Look at the way she fought for her friend and stood up to you. She's as tough as you are, in her womanly way."

In the silence that followed, Jill's mind raced to assimilate Mary's words. Finally she came up with the same verdict. She was not a butterfly. She not only loved Riordan but she loved his home and life as well. She had never needed to feed on the admiration of others to survive as his mother had. Elation swept over her.

The silence was shattered by Riordan's retort. "You don't know what you're talking about!"

Long striding steps were carrying him to the hallway door where Jill stood. Suddenly she didn't want him to discover she had been there listening. She stepped hurriedly away from the door, intending to retreat to the front of the house, but it was too late. The door was yanked open.

Riordan stopped short.

The harsh lines of anger on his face changed to stunned surprise, but his features were nonetheless forbidding. Jill blinked at him uncertainly. This couldn't be the same man whom she had heard say that he loved her. There was not even a flicker of gladness in the wintry eyes at the sight of her.

"What are you doing here?" he demanded coldly.

Her fingers tightened on the packages in her arms. "It's Christmas," she offered in hesitant explanation.

His gaze slid to the brightly wrapped presents. "Get out, Jill," he said with the same freezing calm. "I don't want anything from you."

Chilled by his cold command, Jill swayed to carry out his order. Then a voice warned that this was her last chance. If she left him now, there would never be another.

"Did you . . ." She paused to chase the quiver from her voice. "Did you mean it when you said you loved me?"

"You were listening?" A dark brow arched quizzically. Jill nodded numbly. "Yes, I meant it," Riordan acknowledged, "but it doesn't change anything."

"It has to," she breathed fervently, taking a step toward him, then another, all the while anxiously searching his face for some indication of his love. "I did try to trick you and maneuver you and do all those things you accused me of, but I never intended to let my own emotions become involved. Riordan, you must believe me. I mean, whoever heard of a butterfly coming back in the dead of winter?"

Her feeble attempt at a joke failed miserably as he remained withdrawn. "I never meant to fall in love with you. It just happened. I love you."

He reached out and took the packages from her arms, flipped them onto a table in the hall, then gathered her to him, saying not a word and letting the blazing light in his eyes do all the talking. Covering her mouth with a hungry kiss, he lifted her off the floor and carried her into the living room.

It was much later before anything other than incoherent love words could be spoken. Jill was nestled against his shoulder, the long length of him stretched in a half-sitting position on the sofa.

The thudding beat of his heart was beneath her head, the most blissful sound she had ever heard.

"Do you think she really loved him?" Riordan murmured.

Peering through her lashes, Jill could see he was gazing at the portrait. "I think she did. She gave him all the love she had."

His arms tightened around her. "And you, angel? Will you promise to give me all the love you have?"

"Yes," she whispered achingly. Her fingers crept to his face, caressing the rugged features she loved so much. "Oh, Riordan, that will be the easiest promise in the world to keep."

"I'll probably be jealous and possessive and you'll start to hate me," he smiled wryly.

"I don't think so." She outlined his hard, passionate mouth with her fingertip and sighed. "I wish I didn't have to leave. Riordan, please come home with me. We'll drive together and you can meet my family."

He moved her hand away, tucking a hand under her chin and lifting her head so he could plant a tender kiss on her lips.

"I don't intend to let you out of my sight." His low voice vibrated with emotion, and delicious shivers ran over Jill's skin at its intensity. "We'll get married at your parents' house and be husband and wife before the New Year comes."

Jill glowed. "Are you sure you want to marry me?"

"Sure?" His gray eyes, warm and vibrantly alive, caressed her face. "I knew I had to have you that morning I came to your room. What I didn't realize was how completely I wanted you . . . forever. That was something I learned in the last six months—painfully, I might add. Besides, you don't know what it's like to have you haunting my bedroom every night."

"I think I might have an idea," she murmured, snuggling deeper in his arms, unbelievably content. "I can hardly wait to tell Kerry that we're getting married."

"I never expected to beat Todd to the altar," Riordan chuckled. Her eyes had been half-closed, savoring the dreamlike sensation of being in his arms and loved by him. Her lashes sprang open suddenly, tension darkening the blue shade of her eyes.

"Riordan, what about college?" she breathed uncertainly. "I only have a half a year to go to get my diploma."

He stiffened for an instant, then untangled her from his arms and rolled to his feet, walking to the fireplace. His hand rubbed the back of his neck, ruffling the jet-black hair curling near his collar.

"You don't want me to go back, do you?" she said, sitting up and gazing at his broad shoulders sadly. "No, I don't want you to go back!" Riordan said ruefully. "I've just found you. How could I possibly want to let you go!"

Jill swallowed tightly. She knew better than to give up her own hopes and dreams but she could guess how much the separation would hurt him. "It's all right." She lowered her head, pretending to give in. "I don't want to quit, but—"

"Like hell you will!" He pivoted sharply toward her. "You'll finish college. I'm not going to let you quit."

"You don't know what you're saying." She studied him thoughtfully, noting his unrelenting gaze.

"It's only for a few months. I'll . . . I'll move into town."

"You'd hate it." Jill shook her head.

"I could stand it." He walked back to the sofa, his hands digging into her shoulders as he pulled her to her feet. "But I couldn't stand being without you, not for a day." She cupped his face in her hands. "But I won't let you leave this ranch. I love you too much to ask that of you, Riordan." She breathed in, ready to offer the compromise she had in mind. "I know what I'll do. I'll transfer my credits to the university in Dillon and drive back and forth every day from the ranch."

His mouth tightened with concern. "And drive me crazy with worry about you out alone on the roads?" Jill slipped her arm around his neck, lifting her face invitingly towards his. "But I'll be home every night, Riordan. And I've got a thousand ways to drive you crazy indoors . . ."

SHOW ME

Chapter One

The asphalt road snaked along the ridge, winding its way towards Dewey Bald. Here and there the trees fell away to allow a panoramic glimpse of the Ozark mountains of Missouri. The sylvan hillsides were colored in a myriad spring greens, from the deep hues of the cedars all the way to the pale greens of newly budding trees, an array as spectacular as autumn's bold splashes. The burgeoning world was highlighted by the mauve shades of the redbud tree and the symbolic white blossoms of the flowering dogwood, while the rock-strewn ground burst forth with an explosion of wild spring flowers.

"Can we stop at Sammy's Lookout?"

The small, questioning voice drew Tanya Lassiter's wandering gaze away from the road and scenery ahead of them. Her mouth curved into a smile as she gazed into the rearview mirror at the silently pleading blue eyes staring so earnestly back at her. Baby-fine brown hair covered his forehead, softening the effect of his pointed chin.

No one else could have a little boy as beautiful and intelligent as her John, Tanya thought to herself with a warm glow of satisfaction. At seven, he was as impish and happy and curious as anyone would want their child to be. Who could remain immune to the entreaty of those trusting eyes that invariably reminded her of the clear blue color of warm summer skies—so unlike Jake's, his father, whose eyes held the metallic sheen of blue steel.

"Can we?" John repeated.

"Okay. For a little while," Tanya agreed. Her lips had tightened fractionally and she forced them to relax. "But Grandma is making supper for us, so we can't stay too long."

There was no enthusiastic response from John, causing Tanya to glance wonderingly at his averted head. His thoughtful pose, as he gazed out the side window of the station wagon, meant something was troubling John. She knew it would soon be confided to her once he had methodically thought it through on his own.

Tanya unbuckled John, who got out and waited impatiently a few feet away from where the station wagon was parked along the road. Sliding out from behind the wheel and closing the door, she smoothed her hair into its band and hurried to join the slender boy.

Together they traversed the few hundred yards back to the big gray stone overlooking Mutton Hollow and the section of the Trail That Is Nobody Knows How Old that led here. While John made straight for the large, slate-gray rock, Tanya sought the seclusion of a small boulder farther up the hillside. It denied her the view of the valley, but it hid her from the sight of passing motorists on the road just below. The traffic was mostly local now. The tourist crowds would come with the summer sun.

The boy stood on the rock, gazing out over the scenery, his legs spread apart in a proud stance with his hands on his hips. In some ways, John was a lot like her. On the surface he possessed an outgoing personality—gregarious, fun-loving and always curious—but he, like Tanya, had those moments when he enjoyed being alone with his own thoughts. There were times when she felt that at seven years old John was too serious, too contemplative and too much in the company of adults; but when he was with children his own age in school, he made many friends. So she had marked her worry off to an overactive maternal conscience.

Leaning back against the slanting hillside, Tanya watched the sun slowly settling on the western slopes. The bright plumage of a male robin darted in front of her as he flew in attendance on his chosen mate. A surging ache rose from deep inside, shooting through her limbs until she wanted to hug her arms about her to ward off the pain. Spring was the mating season, after all, and Tanya recognized the inexplicable longing inside was the same desire for a mate of her own. She was a twenty-six-year-old female of her species, in need of a male to love, the simplest and oldest truth of life.

And she was beautiful, without having to work at it.

Tanya's long hair hesitated between light brown and blond with occasional natural streaks of shimmering honey, and was brushed straight back from her smooth forehead, showing her perfect features. There was a classic lift to her cheekbones and nose, and her sensuous mouth could transform the cool, marble beauty of her face with a smile. But it was her tawny, gold-flecked eyes that kept the shutters closed on the smoldering passions that lay below the surface.

Nothing remained of the haunted, slightly vengeful young girl who had come to these hills over seven years ago with a boy child in her arms. The influence and example of her mother-in-law, Julia Lassiter, had erased the schoolgirl image and replaced it with a poised, sophisticated young woman. Just one thing remained, Tanya thought with a flash of bitterness, and that was her loathing of Jake Lassiter, the man whose name she bore. The only saving grace of her marriage had been that she had John. He belonged to her and could never be taken away—as long as she remained married to Jake.

"Mom?"

Her burnished eyes opened. Tanya straightened to sit erectly as John settled on the ground beside her, one hand plucking at the sprouting grass.

"Yes, John?" Tanya curled her arms around her knees and waited.

"Do I really have a dad?"

Only for a second did the shock of his question register on her face. "Of course you do." Her heart thudded a little louder in her chest, but there was no other outward sign that his question had disconcerted her.

"I mean, is he really alive?" This time the troubled blue eyes stared into her face, earnest and searching.

"Yes, he's alive. You have his letters. What made you think that he wasn't?" Tanya tried to laugh lightly, but it came out shrill and without amusement.

"Danny Gilbert said he must be dead or in prison or he'd come home. He isn't in prison, is he?"

"No, honey, he isn't in prison. He's somewhere in Africa right now." Her arm went around the slim shoulders, drawing the tense boy against her body, afraid he would see that she had no wish to talk about Jake Lassiter. "He works for your grandfather, remember? And there's a big dam or bridge or something being built over there and your grandfather's company is supervising the work. Your father is over there making sure it's done right."

"But why doesn't he ever come home? And why don't we ever go to visit him? Doesn't he want to see us?" He pulled away from the hand that was stroking his head to gaze in confusion at the frown creasing Tanya's forehead.

"He'll come home someday," she attempted to reassure him, but the very ambiguousness of her answer defeated her. "He's very busy."

"Everybody gets vacations. Why can't he take a vacation and come visit us?"

"He did do that once." She didn't dare add that Jake had ostensibly come home for a month's stay and had left after a week.

"I was a baby," the boy pointed out in a disgruntled tone. "Three years old, Grandma said. I don't remember him at all."

"Did you talk about this with your grandmother?'' Tanya asked hesitantly. One more black mark would go against Tanya in her mother-in-law's book if he had.

"No." John lifted his shoulders in an expressive little shrug. "I only asked her how old I was when I got that ivory statue of an elephant. You told me my father brought it home to me as a present."

Yes, Tanya remembered his question several days before, but had given it no special significance. A tiny sigh of relief escaped her lips. "Can we visit him this summer after school is finished?" She thought desperately to find a way of refusing the request without confirming John's growing opinion that his father wanted nothing to do with him. It was there in the defeated dullness of his eyes. "Well, no . . . the political situation over there—maybe your teacher has talked about it, John—"

"I knew you'd say something like that." The pseudo-adult bitterness in his voice lashed out at her with the smarting flick of a whip.

"Okay," Tanya swallowed nervously, hating the suggestion that was forming on her lips, "how about we write a letter to your father tonight and see if he could arrange to come home for a couple of weeks this summer." She ruffled his silken brown hair away from his forehead as John turned to stare into her face, a half-hopeful expression in his eyes. Unwillingly, her gaze strayed to the crooked little finger, the mark that from birth had affirmed his right to the Lassiter name.

"Do you really think he'd come?" he asked.

Secretly she hoped he wouldn't, but her silent prayer that Jake would refuse died as she gazed into the boy's face. "If it's at all possible, I'm sure he will, especially if you write to ask him." Tanya had never tried to encourage any correspondence between father and son, unwilling to share John's love with the man she loathed. Only at Christmastime and birthdays did she prompt John to send a thank-you note for the packages that dutifully arrived in the mail.

"We'd better get home." John hopped to his feet, a wide smile on his face.

"John, just because we write your father," Tanya spoke quietly several minutes later as she turned the station wagon onto the lake road leading home, "there's no guarantee that he'll be able to come back to the States."

"I know. But he'll come, I know he will!" The determination in the small boy's voice reminded her how strong the bond was between a father and son. Much as she wanted to ignore her husband's existence, for John's sake she couldn't.

"Besides," John went on, "I've been thinking that maybe he thinks I don't care about him. If he knows how much I want to see him, he'll come home. I'm sure of it."

"Well, perhaps if not this summer, he might be able to come in the fall or even at Christmastime. Don't build your hopes up too high, John. He may not be able to get away."

"I wish he could come home now so Danny Gilbert could see that I really do have a father and that he really has been in Africa." He glanced earnestly at her. "Can we write that letter right after supper?"

"Yes, right after supper," Tanya promised though her heart sank at the thought.

"And we'll send it express mail so he'll get it right away?"

"All right." She nodded reluctantly.

"Uncle Patrick's car is in the drive," John announced happily at the sight of the silver Blazer parked in front of the ultra-modern ranch-style home. "It's been ages since he's been here."

"Only a little over a week," she corrected, her eyes sparkling too, at the sight of the familiar SUV.

Patrick Raines wasn't really John's uncle, although he had called him that ever since he could talk. Now that Tanya's father-in-law, J. D. Lassiter, was semi-retired, going to his firm's office in Springfield only two or three times a week, Patrick Raines was head of the engineering firm in all but name. Tanya had a feeling that J.D. was keeping his hand in the operation until Jake returned to the States, at which time he would turn it over to his only living son. It had been her father-in-law's persuasion that had brought Jake home for an brief stay four years ago. But no one had been able to ignore the chilling and hostile atmosphere that had surrounded Jake and Tanya. They hadn't been able to carry on a civil conversation, let alone be comfortable in the same room.

As she and young John walked onto the highly polished tiled floor of the foyer, Tanya felt her heart skipping a beat at the sound of Patrick's rich voice in the next room. John went dashing ahead of her, calling out a greeting to his grandparents and to the dark, handsome man just coming into Tanya's sight. Her mouth curved into a welcoming smile under the warm regard of Patrick Raines.

"Good to see you again, Patrick." Her hand reached out naturally for his, enjoying the firm, lingering touch that reinforced the glow in his brown eyes. "John was thrilled to see your car. Said you hadn't been here for ages."

"Then you did miss me while I was out of town," his resonant voice declared with satisfaction.

Tanya was about to say that she didn't even know he'd been away, when her mother-in-law broke into the conversation. "We were beginning to give you two up for lost. Where did you and Johnny wander off to?" Only Julia Lassiter ever called John Johnny, and Tanya was sure her mother-in-law did it because Julia knew how it irritated her.

"We went on a little side trip that took longer than we expected," she replied calmly, turning towards the woman firmly holding John's hand. Her eyes flickered over the aristocratic face with its professionally dyed blue-gray hair, knowing Julia expected a detailed account of their every movement. "Is dinner ready?"

"We were just finishing our beers before going in," J.D. announced, unfolding his tall form from the velvet sofa and rising to his feet, an imposing figure of a man, like his son.

"Give us a few minutes and we'll be down." Tanya held out her hand for John and flashed a smile aimed generally at the trio, but resting a shade longer on Patrick. In record time, she changed out of her jeans and T-shirt into a dress that did her figure justice in an eye-catching shade of carnelian red. She pulled off the confining hairband and brushed her tawny hair straight back from her forehead to fall around her slender neck and shoulders, curling just at the ends. The simplicity of the hairstyle and dress bespoke sophistication and poise.

Tanya went immediately to the kitchen, knowing

full well that Julia expected her to be there. The Lassiters could afford a maid or a cook or a gardener, but Julia Lassiter's home was her private castle. The work was either done by herself or under her watchful eye. The woman was perfect, Tanya decided grimly. There was nothing she couldn't do as well as the best and better than the average. Her meals were a gourmet's dream, but she grudgingly permitted french fries now and then to satisfy her husband's palate. The house was always immaculately clean with never a smidgen of dust hiding in any forgotten corner. The garden, a unique and imaginative creation, was tended only by Julia, although she graciously allowed Tanya or her husband to do the more mundane chores of mowing the expansive lawn. And she kept herself elegantly groomed, never a hair out of place, no loose buttons and above all, no sweatsuits.

There was ample evidence Julia was not only a perfect wife and housekeeper, but also a mother. Never once did she question Jake about the naive young girl he had brought home as his wife, nor commented on the baby boy he had identified as his son. Without raising an eyebrow, she had carried out Jake's wishes that he and Tanya have separate rooms. Not one word of recrimination had been directed at Tanya when her son had left within a few days of bringing his bride home, nor in the years that followed when he stayed away.

Yet Tanya had the distinct feeling that she was only tolerated in Julia's home because of John, who had become the center of Julia's universe. Tanya always heard an underlying disapproval in her mother-in-law's voice whenever it was directed at her, and after all these years in the same house together, never once had a hint of affection or friendship penetrated the cool reserve of Julia's gray-blue eyes.

Jake's father, J. D. Lassiter, was altogether different. Tanya had once said with biting cynicism that Jake could charm the fangs off a cobra, and after meeting J.D., she knew he got his power to persuade from his father, though J.D. was more honest and open with his feelings. When she had first come to his home with little John, he had been openly skeptical of the arrangement and decidedly disapproving of his son's marriage to her.

J. D. Lassiter was an autocrat and a powerful one—there was never any doubt about that. A shrewd businessman, a recognized expert in his field, and a keen judge of character, he had observed her transformation from an unworldly girl barely out of school to a sophisticated young woman.

Gradually his thinly veiled disapproval of her had changed to respect and admiration. A quiet hand of friendship had been extended to Tanya almost five years ago. Although there never had been any questions from J.D. about her relationship with Jake, she sensed that he knew the circumstances that had surrounded their marriage.

Of course, he couldn't know the whole truth. That secret was hers alone and she guarded it tenaciously, just as she guarded John. Yet it was her father-in-law's droll wit and affection that had made it bearable to remain. But she would have gone through any hell that would have given John a name, a family and a future.

Julia already had the first course of their evening meal on the table when Tanya arrived in the kitchen. Her apology for arriving too late to help was drowned out by her mother-in-law's announcement that dinner was to be served. John was already taking his seat next to his grandmother as J.D. held out the chair on his right for Tanya. She smiled across the table at the square-jawed man sitting opposite her, a warmth pervading her at his answering smile.

"You look gorgeous in that dress, but then you would no matter what you wore," Patrick remarked.

"Thanks for the compliment. A little flattery always makes my day." Her voice was warmly teasing as her gaze rested briefly on his strong features and his dark, curling hair with a premature touch of gray around the temples.

That undercurrent of electricity was flowing between them, its tingling existence a nearly tangible thing that couldn't be ignored. The Lassiters entertained company executives often, and it had become an accepted thing that Patrick and Tanya should be paired together automatically. Her husband was in Africa for an indefinite period and Patrick Raines had been divorced for three years with his ex-wife remarried. Tanya tried not to notice whenever his dark gaze strayed to her, reminding that Patrick was the only really attractive single male she knew, and it was consistent with her romantic, secretly passionate nature to weave fantasies about such a handsome, charming man.

The few times they had been alone together, not an indiscreet word had been uttered, yet Tanya knew their relationship was not exactly a platonic friendship. They were both too aware of the sexual chemistry between them, but Tanya's old-fashioned morals wouldn't allow her to disregard the diamond wedding ring on her finger and her vows of fidelity, regardless of the manner of man she had given them to.

"Tell me," picking up her soup spoon and playing the perfect lady, "where your travels took you to this time, Patrick. I had no idea you were going on a trip."

"Oh, a spur-of-the moment journey to Scotland for the company,"—he paused—"with a major side trip to South Africa."

There was a hairline fracture in Tanya's poise, so minute that only J.D. noticed it, his iron-dark head inclining towards his wife at the other end of the table. "Julia doesn't allow business talk at the table—a rule of the house, Patrick. As if anything could detract a man from your onion soup, honey. It's delicious as usual." His fulsome compliment was intended to tactfully shift the conversation.

"Did you say you went to Africa, Uncle Patrick?" John piped up, a suppressed excitement in his voice.

"John!" Tanya softened the sharp reprimand in her voice. "You heard your grandfather. Wait until after we've eaten."

"Right." He hung his head obediently, but Tanya knew his sudden interest in his father would erupt the minute the dessert dishes were cleared. She wasn't quite ready to tell the rest of the family that they intended to write Jake asking him to come home.

A quick glance at Julia Lassiter's averted gaze indicated the source of the slight chill in the air. Tanya sighed inwardly, guessing that she must have thought the reprimand a little too much. John was only going to ask about his father. She had to admit to herself that it probably was, but she didn't want Jake's name spoiling her dinner as it undoubtedly would.

"Before you and John arrived tonight," J.D. had picked up the conversation again with the adroitness of an expert at table talk, "we were discussing the possibilities of having a small dinner party to celebrate our thirty-fifth wedding anniversary on the eighth of May."

"I think that's an excellent idea," Tanya agreed.

"I'm glad you think so," J.D. nodded with a twinkle. "Julia thought it would be in bad taste to throw a party for our own anniversary, but I didn't agree."

"Weather permitting, Julia, we could have it out on the patio. All your spring flowers would be blooming by then and it would be ideal," Tanya suggested, noticing the grudging agreement in her mother-in-law's eyes.

"And you could do some of that baked trout that I like so much," J.D. interposed, "and serve the meal buffet style."

The topics of guests, food, and decorations for the proposed party dominated the conversation through the salad course, the exquisitely prepared standing rib roast and the crème-de-menthe parfait. The telephone rang just as Julia was about to serve their after-dinner coffee in the living room, and Tanya was delegated to pour while her mother-in-law went to answer it. The caller wanted to speak to J.D., which left Tanya and Patrick alone together when John dashed off to his room on some secret errand.

"Patrick—" Tanya nervously cupped her hands

around the delicate china cup, tossing her tawny
brown hair over her shoulder with a flick of her
head, "when you were in Africa—did you see
Jake?"

He darted a lightning-quick glance at her as he
leaned against the back of the sofa. "Yes, yes, I did."
His dark gaze showed the same intense interest in
the black liquid in his cup as she did.

"The project he's working on, how is it coming
along?" It was cheating, she knew, to try to deter-
mine what the chances were that Jake might take
her up on her invitation to return home, but she
had to know.

"Which one?" Patrick asked dryly. "The one
he's finishing or the one that's just starting?"

Relief raced through her and unknowingly she
sighed. "I didn't know he was working on two
different projects. It must keep him very busy."

"Lonnie Danvers is a very capable assistant, but
Jake still has to do a lot of commuting between
sites, at least for the time being."

Tanya was glad of Julia's return. It saved her from
explaining the reason for her questions, and the
curious glint in Patrick's eyes had indicated that
he was about to ask it. J.D. entered the room within
seconds of his wife, sent her a quick smile of apology, and launched into a brief business discussion
with Patrick that excluded the two women.

As Julia seemed preoccupied with thoughts of
her own, Tanya took the opportunity to study the
man sitting opposite her. During the years she had
lived with her in-laws, she had noticed the way so
many people kowtowed to the Lassiters' wealth and
power. One of the first things she had admired
about Patrick Raines was his refusal to be a yes-

man for J.D. Lassiter. He never hesitated to voice
an objection and stick with it if his views didn't
match those of the firm's CEO. Yet Patrick wasn't
so independent that he wouldn't seek the older
man's advice and experience if he felt he needed
it. There was more than just charm and intelligence
behind the handsome facade that drew Tanya.

A small hand touched her shoulder. She glanced
up into a pair of clear blue eyes.

"Can we go and do it now, Mom?" His oblique
request only made sense to Tanya.

"Go and do what, honey?" Julia inserted, her
slightly raised voice drawing the attention of the
two men.

"I'm going to write my dad a letter asking him
to come home on his vacation." His young voice
was filled with importance.

Tanya studied the proud tilt of his head, a rosy
hue coloring her cheeks as she felt the eyes in the
room looking at her. Patrick had only guessed at
her animosity towards her husband, but his parents
knew of it only too well. Their curiosity about her
reaction to John's announcement weighted the
silence.

"I think that's an excellent idea, Johnny," Julia
Lassiter said firmly, the tone of her voice daring
Tanya to disagree.

Tanya turned her cool amber gaze towards her
mother-in-law, her marble-smooth features composed. "So do I, Julia," she agreed with freezing
calm, "which is why I suggested it to John."

She wanted no further discussion on the matter,
no questions asked by Julia about her motives or
even by J.D., so she rose from her chair, resting a

hand on John's slim shoulders as she guided him out of the living room.

"You want to write the letter, don't you?" the boy asked hesitantly when they had arrived in the alcove off Tanya's bedroom.

"Yes, John," she smiled down at him, swallowing the distaste the words caused. From what Patrick had said, there was little chance that Jake would come or could come. A twinge of guilt raced through her as she forced herself to be cheerful. "We'll both write to him."

John fumbled in his shirt pocket for a photograph which he handed to her. "I thought we could send this picture Grandpa took when I got my new bike . . . so Dad'll know what I look like."

John wasn't the only one in the picture. Tanya was there too, laughing into the camera, her dark-blonde hair ruffled by the wind and looking well-dressed and confident, though almost too young, somehow to be the mother of a boy old enough to ride a bicycle.

"He has your school pictures, John," she reminded him gently, strangely unwilling to send the photograph in her hand.

"But they don't look like me and I had a tooth missing," he protested. "Please, can't we send it?"

With those pleading blue eyes looking at her, Tanya knew she would always give in. A part of her admitted guiltily that John was getting to the age where he needed the guidance of a man, something only a father could give.

An hour later the feelings of guilt had subsided as she sealed the envelope containing the letters from John and herself. His was a heart-tugging, scrawled message politely inquiring if his father could come home this summer. Hers was as simple, stating John's sudden doubts that he really had a father and impersonally adding that perhaps Jake should come home for a few weeks if he could find the time. Tanya felt her conscience had been assuaged. She loathed Jake Lassiter for the things he had done in the past, but for John's sake she would tolerate his presence—if Jake came. And Tanya was almost positive he wouldn't.

Chapter Two

"You look beautiful, Mom," John declared as Tanya set the portable television on top of the small desk in his bedroom.

"Do you like the dress?" A graceful pirouette sent the brilliant silk chiffon of the skirt swirling about her knees. Her long, tawny-blond hair was brushed back from her forehead and behind her ears where two simple hoops of gold dangled from her lobes. "I bought it especially for your grandparents' anniversary party tonight."

"It's terrific. I wish I could go to the party," he sighed.

"And think of the television programs you'll miss. *Star Trek* is on tonight," Tanya teased.

"Is it?" His eyes lit up. John was typically boy when it came to TV. Most other programs bored him as he preferred to generate his own adventures, but not *Star Trek*. "Some of the guests have already arrived. You'll be all right, won't you?'' she smiled.

"Sure," he shrugged.

"Lights out at ten o'clock," Tanya reminded him. "I'll be back to make sure they are."

"Okay, Mom," he grinned as she lifted her hand in goodbye before stepping out of his room into the hallway.

They both knew it was an excuse to return at ten because John considered himself too old to be tucked in, although neither one wanted to discontinue the nightly ritual.

Tanya and John's rooms were in a separate wing of the house, originally designed as guestrooms with the Lassiters' master suite on the other side of the house. Now they were more or less separate apartments, though without kitchens, which gave John and Tanya some privacy.

The house itself, built of native stone and wood, was situated on a point of land jutting into Table Rock Lake. The sheltered cove of water contained a private dock and enclosed boathouse. There were no neighbors as J.D. Lassiter had bought up the adjoining land to ensure his privacy and isolation. Any invitation to the home was treated as a royal summons and was never declined, hence the houseful of guests that evening.

The doorbell rang as Tanya's heels clicked onto the tiled foyer. "I'll answer it, Julia," she called, hearing her mother-in-law's footsteps approaching from the kitchen. She swung the embossed-wood entrance door wide, admitting Patrick Raines and the petite, dark-haired girl who accompanied him.

"Sheila, I'm so glad you could come!" Tanya exclaimed, reaching out to take the hand of Patrick's sister. "Your dress is so pretty," she added, taking in the white eyelet summer dress that set off the young girl's dark beauty. "Kind of colorless next to yours," Sheila commented, a glint of envy and something else in her brown eyes as she made a quick and thorough appraisal of Tanya's appearance.

There was only four years' difference in their ages, Sheila being twenty-two, but Tanya had never felt accepted by Patrick's sister. Tonight there was a look in her dark eyes that made Tanya believe her welcome should have been a bit more sophisticated.

"We aren't late, are we?" Patrick asked, his blandness overridden by the admiring expression in his eyes as they wandered over the sheer sleeves and low neckline of Tanya's dress.

"Not at all. The others are out on the patio."

The foyer—Julia preferred to call it a breezeway—ran the full width of the house, culminating in sliding glass doors that opened on to the patio and the surrounding rock garden. With the lake less than a hundred yards away, the Lassiters had never installed a swimming pool. Julia hadn't wanted it anyway for fear it would spoil the aesthetic effect of her garden.

As the trio joined the rest of the guests, J. D. Lassiter immediately excused himself from the couple he was with to come forward to greet the new arrivals. Julia appeared a few minutes later, carrying a replenished tray of her hors d'oeuvres.

For the next hour and a half, Tanya was occupied answering the doorbell, helping her mother-in-law arrange the food on the buffet table, later clearing the half-consumed dishes away, and chatting with the twenty-odd couples who were attending the party. It was something of a relief when Patrick appeared with a pair of drinks in his hands and ordered her to sit down on the cushioned redwood bench and relax.

"I don't know why the Old Man doesn't have these affairs catered," Patrick declared, leaning against the rear cushion and trailing his arm along the back near enough to Tanya's shoulders to cause a disturbance not revealed by her outward poise. "It would be much less work for you and Julia."

"But then the credit wouldn't be Julia's," Tanya sighed before grimacing ruefully. "That sounds catty! It's true, though. If this party was catered, she would still supervise everything. It's her nature."

"What's your nature?" he asked softly, the look in his eyes shutting out the rest of the people chattering about them.

"Hmm." She paused, gazing out past the lanterns that lit the patio to the silvery moonlight on the lake. "I would have probably invited one-fourth as many people and grilled steaks and shrimp."

"Invite me to your next party," Patrick smiled. "That sounds great."

"I will." Tanya had to look away from the hypnotic mouth so far away and yet so incredibly close. "Beautiful night, isn't it?"

"Very," he replied, without taking his eyes off her. "The moonlight matches the music."

Tanya paused to listen, hearing a haunting, romantic melody filtering softly through the steady din of voices. The sound filled her with an aching desire to be held in the warmth of a man's arms, if only for a little while.

"How many eyebrows do you think we'd raise

if we danced over in that empty corner by the speakers?'' Patrick asked, the dark brilliance of his sideways glance chasing over her face.

"Probably everyone's,'' she breathed, wondering if she had betrayed herself by look or word.

"Let's chance it,'' he suggested quietly, his hand reaching out to claim hers and draw her to her feet.

A magic spell seemed to be wrapped around them. Only Sheila looked their way, a knowing expression in her brown eyes. Tanya couldn't remember the last time she had been held in a man's arms or simply didn't remember as she willingly surrendered herself to Patrick's guidance. He kept to simple steps that didn't require much concentration, so Tanya was able to enjoy the feel of his firm grip on her waist, holding her as close to him as he dared.

The gentle caress of his breath against her hair made her want to lay her head against his chest, but she steeled herself against it, although she did allow her hand to creep a little further along his shoulders.

"Tanya.'' The softness of his voice brought her chin up so that she was gazing into his tanned face, now dangerously close to hers. That delicious sensation of being held by a man made her glow, especially since she was gazing into such a handsome face.

"You're so incredibly beautiful,'' he murmured. The ardent light in his eyes made her heart beat faster. For one treacherously weak moment, she wanted to forget convention, but only for a moment.

"Patrick, don't say anything." Her slender finger reached out to touch the firm line of his mouth.

He captured it with his hand, pressing a kiss against the tip, then staring deep into her hazel-gold eyes. "I haven't said a thing for over a year," he said quietly.

"But then I don't have to say anything, do I? We're adults. We don't have to play games, do we?"

"Please don't say anything," she replied, moving an inch or two away. She noticed the argumentative set of his jaw. No doubt he was about to remind her that her marriage was only words on a piece of paper. "It won't do any good."

"Have dinner with me next week." His request was almost a plea as his gaze roved possessively over her face. "I'll meet you anywhere you say."

"It's . . . it's not possible," she said weakly with a confused, negative shake of her head. Desperately she wanted him to sweep away her arguments with sure, masculine strokes, to be a knight slaying all the dragons.

A fragile stillness danced briefly between them. 'Am I wrong?" Patrick asked grimly. "Aren't you attracted to me?"

The song ended, the last chord of the piano ringing mournfully in Tanya's ears as she slipped out of his unresisting arms. She knew she should have sought the company of the other guests, but she really didn't want the hopeless conversation to end.

"What woman wouldn't be attracted to you?" Her light tone was forced and brittle. "You're strong and handsome and unmarried—that's a potent combination, difficult for any woman to resist. Yes, I find you very attractive, Patrick," she said quietly, "which is why I won't meet you outside the walls of this house."

"What kind of a hold does Lassiter have on you?" he demanded harshly. "Why are you so afraid of a man you've seen only seven days out of seven years?"

They were standing in the shadowed corner of the patio, among and yet apart from the other guests.

"Jake has no hold over me." Her reply was cool. Not even to Patrick, a man she was half in love with already, could Tanya confide the true reason for her loveless marriage. "My life is my own business."

"And none of mine," he queried her. "Not even if I want to make it mine?"

For so long, Tanya had stood figuratively alone without anyone but herself to lean on. And Patrick was so strong, so very strong. She pressed her lips tightly together to keep words of surrender from tumbling out.

His quiet, persuasive voice came from near her shoulder, the distance between them lessened. "John needs a father, Tanya," he struck at the vulnerable chink in her armor, "not someone who's never around like Jake."

"You're not playing fair," she accused in a voice that was shaking with anguish and self-doubt.

"All is fair, Tanya?"

"Excuse me, I have to go check on John." She hurried away from him, suddenly afraid she would give in to the temptation dangling so tantalizing in front of her. As she approached the sliding glass doors, Julia Lassiter intercepted her. "We need some more ice at the bar. Would you bring it out, Tanya?''

"I'll get it," Patrick spoke up, a step or two behind the women. Tanya glanced at him quickly, surprised to find he had followed her. "Tanya wants to check on John."

"Thank you, Patrick," the older woman smiled. "And Tanya, give Johnny a goodnight kiss for me."

"I will, Julia," Tanya promised, hoping her inner agitation wasn't showing.

Only one light cast a dim glow in the foyer and it was at the opposite end near the entrance door. Tanya turned to face Patrick as he closed the sliding glass door behind them.

"There are bags of ice in the freezer," she told him quickly. When she would have turned away, his hand reached out and stopped her, drawing her instead into a corner of the room to take her in his arms. Her lips moved to protest, but Patrick silenced them with a gentle, probing kiss that left her breathless and unable to speak. There was sweet ecstasy in the contented sigh that sprang from his lips when he broke the kiss, cradling her face in his hands so he could gaze into her dazed eyes.

"Jake must be insane to leave you behind," he murmured.

"Yes, I must be."

With a horrified gasp, Tanya tore herself out of Patrick's arms to stare in the direction from which the voice had come, its insolent arrogance immediately recognizable. Still she stared in disbelief at the man leaning so negligently in the living room archway, yet in total command of the situation.

"You've been gone too long. She isn't yours any

longer, Lassiter," said Patrick in a voice that was deceptively soft.

There was no answering comment. Tanya watched with an unnamed fear paralyzing her throat as Jake slowly straightened into an upright position, noticing for the first time the cigarette held in his hand. He moved out of the shadows of the arch to snuff it out in an ashtray, looking taller and broader than Tanya remembered.

He stopped where the light fully illuminated his aristocratic features. The dark tan of his skin made his blue eyes take on the color of cold steel. "Come here, Tanya," he ordered.

His compelling gaze held hers as she unconsciously closed the distance between them, too stunned by his sudden appearance to do anything else. Only two feet separated them when she stopped, her eyes examining his face, noting the changes. It had been four years since she had last seen him.

His face was leaner and more uncompromising than before. The softness of youth had been stamped out by the hard experiences of life, the lines in his face now exhibiting a harshness and unrelenting strength. Jake was still handsome, but now with more rugged overtones. A virile masculinity was the dominant factor in his attraction—that along with a world-weary cynicism.

His study of Tanya was just as thorough. "You can go now, Raines," he directed, his gaze never leaving Tanya's face.

The sound of the glass door sliding shut released Tanya from the shock that had held her silent. Disdain glittered coldly in her eyes. "Nothing has changed," she stated, knowing it would anger him.

"You damn little bitch," he muttered savagely, reaching out to grasp her shoulders, his fingers digging through the fragile material of her dress. "I expect more of a welcome from my wife than that!"

He pulled her against his body until every muscular inch was pressed against her, evading, then capturing the hands that would have clawed at his eyes. Roughly he covered the mouth that had moments before trembled under the sweetness of Patrick's kiss. The iron band of his arms crushed her so that Tanya had no breath to struggle, however uselessly, as Jake continued taking his pleasure with her lips.

Then he let her go, seemingly amused that he had conquered her so easily. "Tell me something," he said, openly laughing at the burning hate in her face as Tanya fought for the breath that had been denied her.

"You pig!" she spat, striking out with her hand at the sarcastic expression on his face and thoroughly enjoying the biting sting as her palm made contact with the hollow of his cheek.

With the swiftness of a striking cobra, he captured the guilty hand, while his other hand grabbed the silky strands of her hair and twisted her stiff body against his.

"I knew that sophistication was a pose," he sneered. "You're the same little hellcat I brought into this house seven years ago."

"Let me go!" she hissed, struggling to escape his hold on her.

"Let her go, son." J. D. Lassiter's quiet voice came from the patio doors. One corner of Jake's mouth curled contemptuously at the sigh of relief from Tanya, rescued at last, or so she thought, from her husband.

"In a minute, Dad," he answered arrogantly. "I want to make sure my wife knows how good it is to be home." Mockery underlined every word. His hold on her slackened. Her eyelids fluttered down as Tanya relaxed for a fraction of a second. Then, through the thickness of her lashes, she caught a glimpse of his face, the only warning she received before her lips were taken again. His mouth was sensually masterful. Tanya didn't respond nor resist, jolted by the fire born inside her from the spark of his touch. The contact was brief, ending before she had recovered sufficiently to struggle free.

Anger flared immediately in her amber eyes, drawing a throaty, mocking chuckle from Jake. His finger lightly touched the tip of her nose.

"That's the way to welcome a man home, honey," he grinned, turning away from her before she could retaliate, to walk to his father. "It's good to be back, Dad."

Tanya watched the warm reunion between father and son, her body trembling with the violence of her emotions while her hands were clenched in useless fists at her side.

"Can't begin to say how glad I am to see you, Jake," J.D. declared fervently, their hands still clasped together in greeting. "You've come back none too soon."

"That thought occurred to me. Several times, in fact," Jake agreed cryptically, sliding a glance at the volatile expression on Tanya's face. "And never more than tonight."

Her usually soft mouth was set in a grim line,

refusing to rise to his baiting reference to the scene
he had witnessed between her and Patrick. That
last kiss had made it evident that he hadn't been
living a celibate existence these last years, and his
subtle criticism only put her temper on a shorter
fuse.

"Your mother will be so happy to see you." The
older man shook his head, chasing the last rem-
nants of disbelief away as he continued to gaze
into Jake's face, drinking his fill like a thirsty man.
"Damn this party!" J.D.'s voice was choked with
emotion. "I have half a notion to send everyone
home."

"And I thought you'd killed the fatted calf to
welcome me back," Jake smiled.

"I would have if I'd known," his father returned
gruffly. "Did you know, Tanya?" he asked, finally
releasing Jake's hand and turning towards her.
"Was this a secret present for our anniversary?"

For all the outward air of rejoicing in her father-
in-law's expression, Tanya saw the searching look
he gave her, assuring himself that she was
unharmed. Some of her anger faded as she remembered that J.D. had ordered his son to let her go.

The smile she gave him was tremulous but sincere in its warmth. "It was as much of a surprise
to me as it was to you."

"That's true, Dad." Jake's eyes seemed to rest
on her face with lazy indulgence, but Tanya saw
the metallic hardness gleaming through and
returned it with a glittering challenge. "Tanya was
undoubtedly even more surprised than you."

Tanya wished in fuming silence that there was a
way to end his double-edged comments without
having to reply in kind. Sensing the electricity

crackling invisibly in the air between them, J.D. walked over and put an affectionate arm around her shoulders.

"Your wife is an absolute gem," he declared. "And that boy of yours—he keeps your mother and me both young." The glass doors to the patio slid open, distracting the three to the woman entering the house, and interrupting any caustic comment Jake might have made.

"Hello, Mother," Jake said quietly.

Julia Lassiter brushed a hand in front of her eyes before letting it fall to the blue brocade bodice of her dress. "Jake?" Her voice broke, as she took a hesitant step towards him.

"I'm home. Happy anniversary." Then he was folding his arms around the happy, sobbing woman. Tanya's blood ran cold as she glimpsed the tender, charming smile given to her mother-in-law, recalling too vividly the effect it had once had on her. "No more tears," Jake teased, lifting her quivering chin with his hand. "I don't want them spoiling the face of the most beautiful mother in the world."

"I'm so happy," Julia declared, smiling despite her now-streaky makeup. "When did you get back? Did you know he was coming, J.D.?"

"I had no idea."

"I didn't let anyone know," Jake explained, planting a lingering kiss on his mother's damp cheek, "in case something happened and I couldn't come."

"How long will you stay?" Her eyes moved to Tanya, who guessed Julia was really wondering if she was going to drive Jake away again.

"I don't know for sure." A hint of harshness laced his voice.

"Oh, Jake, please, you must—"

"Now, now," J.D. placed a restraining hand on his wife's shoulder, "we'll save those discussions for another time. Let's just be grateful he was able to come home."

The trio of Lassiters seemed to huddle together, drawing a circle that put Tanya outside its circumference. She had always known she didn't belong, that her presence was suffered only because of John. That was the way she wanted it, she told herself, asserting her independence with a proud lift of her chin.

With Julia monopolizing the conversation, Tanya slipped quietly from the foyer, walking quietly down the hallway to her bedroom, assuring her pride that she was only leaving to look in on John. But the instant the door closed behind her, she leaned against its firm support. The mirror on the opposite wall reflected the pallor in her face, and she had to admit that Jake's unexpected arrival had taken a considerable toll on her nerves.

A surge of loneliness rose up, threatening to tear out her insides. She closed her eyes against the aching emptiness that assailed her, opening them to see that her reflection had a self-deprecating smile on its face.

Only two weeks ago she had been sitting on a rock near the top of Dewey Bald Mountain. There, with the spring mating calls all around her, she had acknowledged her own growing longing for a mate, accepted that the never-satisfied restlessness consuming her was the desire for a man's attention.

After seven years of abstaining from any form of

caress, she had been kissed three times in one night by two different men. It would have been amusing if it wasn't for the sickening knot in the pit of her stomach. Why was it that her lips remembered so vividly the provocative caress from Jake and so vaguely the sweetness of Patrick's? Shame and self-disgust ate away at her. The desires of her flesh had made her weak enough to become aroused by the powerfully erotic kiss from a man she loathed. Tanya had always believed she exercised complete control over her senses. She had for seven years.

Of course, there had been mitigating circumstances. She had, only moments before, suffered the humiliating punishment of Jake's first embrace, if it could be called that. The shock of his return, the intimate scene he had witnessed, and his cold-blooded assault had all combined to wear down her defenses. Rationally she could see how her guard had slipped when freedom from his touch seemed imminent.

Now that Tanya realized how susceptible she evidently was to any man's caress, she convinced herself that she was better able to cope with it. Jake Lassiter was a dangerous man, more so now than he had ever been because there seemed to be a ruthless determination about him. His actions quite plainly said that he would take what he wanted, his years in Africa stripping away the veneer of civilization.

As she mulled over the sudden turn of events, a degree of composure came back to Tanya. The quaking anger had receded, allowing her hand to pick up the hairbrush from the dressing table without trembling. A few quick strokes through her tawny mane put it back to its usual state of order, although the back of her head still tingled where Jake had tugged at her hair.

The bathroom off her bedroom had a connecting door into John's room. Tanya used it, quietly entering the room to see the boy sound asleep, the light still on beside the bed, but the television was off. Love brought a warm smile to her lips as she tiptoed over to draw the bedcovers around the pajama-clad figure. She lingered for several minutes before brushing a light kiss on the smooth forehead and whispering "good night." She flicked the lamp off as she left the room.

One step inside her own room, Tanya froze, staring at the long, lean form stretched out on her bed. An overhead light fully illuminated the room and the lazy, mocking expression on the face Jake turned towards her, his head resting comfortably on his hands. The rich blue of her satin quilted bedspread emphasized the white of his shirt opened at the throat, tapering from the wide shoulders to muscular abs. Potent, masculine virility struck out at her with the force of a body blow.

"Aren't you going to order me off your bed?" he taunted softly.

Tanya bit back the angry words that would have done just that. Instead, she chose to take a calmer attitude. "Why should I?" She shrugged indifferently, walking over to the mirror to flip the ends of her hair needlessly with a comb.

"You didn't expect me to come back, did you?" Jake swung his legs over the edge of the bed to sit on the side, at the same time joining his reflection in the mirror with Tanya's.

"No, I didn't," she said, coolly meeting the mockery in his eyes.

"I don't know why you didn't. I practically heard a trumpet fanfare when I received your letter." His humor didn't negate the sarcasm in his voice.

"You make it sound as though you never heard from me," Tanya snapped. "I wrote you a letter every week, which is more than could be said for you."

"A letter? Is that what you called those impersonal pieces of paper I received?" Jake laughed in his throat, the chill of his blue gaze contemptuously holding hers. " 'I took John to the dentist today. John enjoyed his first day of school. John is learning to swim.' "Never once was there a 'How are you' or 'What have you been doing', just short messages to fulfil your duty. What was I supposed to write back? 'The bulldozer broke down today? I stopped off and had a beer with the boys last night?' "

"If you had, John wouldn't have this ridiculous notion that he doesn't have a father!" Her temper flared in spite of her determination to keep it under control.

"You would have liked that, wouldn't you? It would have suited you just fine if I never returned," he jeered. "Must've been hard to write that last letter to me reminding me of my duties as a father!"

Tanya didn't trust herself to speak. Her sense of outrage would only make an intolerable situation worse. She watched Jake uncoil and walk over to tower behind her.

"If I wanted to duck my responsibility as a father, I would never have married you!" His heartless statement made her face go pale. "Or did you forget that in your attempt to make me look bad?"

Their eyes clashed in the smooth glass of the mirror. "I never suggested that you take that job in Africa," Tanya answered calmly. "Nor did I ever tell you to stay."

"Why did you marry me, Tanya?" His eyes narrowed with icy contempt. "From the first, there was nothing but hatred in your eyes when you looked at me. You never gave our marriage an opportunity to work. Why should I have stayed? John was a baby. He needed his mother, but not me. And you made it clear every time you looked at me how much you despised me."

"I never asked you to marry me," she reminded him acidly, "only to acknowledge John as your son."

"The instant you had my money you would have run away to the remotest place on earth taking my son with you so I could never see him again." His perception brought a quick rush of color to her cheeks. "The reason I married you is the same reason that I'll never divorce you. I want my son, even if it means putting up with you."

It was Tanya's turn to lash out. "Your son is seven years old. He doesn't even know what his father looks like, outside of a photograph, and he isn't even sure he has one. Explain that to me, Super Dad."

The sudden tightening of his jaw told her that her arrow had found the target. "We've been married seven years," Jake said dryly. "A lot of things have changed, me included. I admit I didn't intend to stay away so long, but John really does need both parents, as you pointed out in your letter. You've come of age too, Tanya." His hands spread around her waist, their scorching touch turning her to face him.

She stared down at his arms, slowly raising her

eyes to his face so he could see her distaste of his touch even while her heart thumped wildly against her ribs. "There's no point to this discussion," she declared in a frosty voice. "It's time I was returning to the party."

His hold tightened fractionally when she started to move away. "Is Patrick Raines your lover?" The metallic hardness of his gaze belied his casual tone.

"No!" The explosive denial came too quickly, accompanied by an uncomfortable rush of warmth to her face. "Tonight was the first time—" she bit back the rest of the words, suddenly angry that Jake had drawn any kind of an explanation from her.

A wide, triumphant smile split his face, his eyes gleaming with amusement as he released her waist. "Then I did come home in time!"

"You came back because of John," she asserted sharply.

"I'm not about to forget the reason I'm here," he agreed smoothly. He picked up the jacket he had tossed on a chair, slipped it on, and turned with a mocking bow towards Tanya. "Shall we join the party?"

Chapter Three

Julia caught sight of them before anyone else as Jake and Tanya walked through the sliding glass doors. She hurried over to them, her hand reaching out for her son's arm while her gaze rushed lovingly to his face.

"Did you look in on Johnny?"

"Actually John was asleep," Tanya began, only to have Jake lightly touch her arm to stop her.

"I looked in when I first arrived," he said, sliding a mocking glance at Tanya's surprised expression. "He'd fallen asleep before the captain and crew fixed the hyperdrive on the *Enterprise.* How come the hyperdrive never works?"

"Isn't he a beautiful child?" Julia declared, ignoring Tanya's sudden silence. "He looks just like Jamie when he was a boy. There's no mistaking that little Johnny is a Lassiter."

"None at all," Jake agreed. There was no amusement in the expression he turned to Tanya. "He looks like a great kid." Was he praising her? she wondered, finding the ensuing rush of pleasure at the thought unsettling. But at that moment, Jake's unexpected presence was noticed by some of the other guests and Tanya's attention was distracted from that disturbing discovery.

All the other men wore suits and ties, which made Jake stand out all the more. Yet Tanya was forced to acknowledge that even in evening attire he would be conspicuous. There was an aura of power and self-possession about him that rejected the restrictions of convention.

His hand rested on the curve of her hip, keeping her at his side as he renewed old acquaintances and made new ones. It was a gentle and unnecessary reminder that she was his wife and one that she resented while parrying the comments of the guests.

Mrs. Osgood had just declared, "You must be so happy to have your husband home after all this time," when Tanya spied Patrick walking towards them with his sister.

"Not half as happy as John will be," she qualified, forcing her gaze away from Patrick's rigid face to the woman standing in front of her.

"That's your little boy, isn't it? Does he know his daddy is home?"

"He was sleeping when Jake arrived." Tanya started to edge away from the light hold, not wanting Patrick to see the possessive touch, but her movement was stopped by Sheila's airy voice. She managed a passing nod in the direction of the departing Mrs. Osgood while turning to stare at the brunette bestowing a more than affectionate kiss on Jake's cheek.

"You're full of surprises, Jake," Sheila scolded provocatively. "You could have mentioned that you were going to be flying home. I would have kept your little secret."

"I hadn't made my decision then," Jake replied, amused and even pleased at the intimate look the dark-haired girl was giving him. "And I hadn't realized how many reasons I had to come back."

To Tanya's knowledge, Jake and Sheila had never met. Sheila would have only been fifteen when Jake had married Tanya and it was inconceivable that he had met her on his only other trip home four years ago.

Sheila cast a sideways glance at Tanya, her dark eyes amused by the confusion written in her expression. "Didn't Patrick tell you?" Sheila asked with pretend innocence. "I went along with him to South Africa a month ago. That's when I met Jake."

Tanya darted a quick glance at Jake's unrevealing profile before looking to Patrick for confirmation, noting the hint of exasperation in his brown eyes. "I thought it was a company trip," addressing her half statement, half question to Patrick.

"It was," he asserted.

"I persuaded him to take his little sister along for a little vacation." Sheila spared an overly affectionate glance at her brother. "Of course, he was so busy flying back and forth between Europe and Africa that I finally stopped trying to keep up with him and stayed in Africa. I would have been bored to tears if Jake hadn't been able to take a few days off."

A slow boil was seething through Tanya at the

implication behind Sheila's words. "Well, Patrick didn't mention that." The undertone in her voice added that her husband hadn't either, which placed a smug smile on Sheila's artfully bowed lips.

"Lucky for you that Jake was able to get free."

"I think Sheila would have been able to keep herself amused if I hadn't been there," Jake smiled lazily, his eyes roaming familiarly over the girl's face. "But since I did have some free time, I thought it was only right to keep an eye on the sister of the firm's acting manager."

"Is that what you were doing?" Sheila murmured seductively. "Keeping an eye on me?"

Jake must have felt Tanya breathe in deeply to control her temper at the sly innuendoes Sheila was making because there was a fractional tightening of his fingers on her waist. She arched him a speaking look. He couldn't possibly think she cared one way or another whether he had had an affair with Patrick's sister. She merely found the Sheila's suggestive comments irritating.

"I'm glad you enjoyed my husband's company," Tanya declared with cloying sweetness. "It would have been awful to be in a strange country with no one to show you the sights."

"We didn't do much sight-seeing." Sheila flashed a coy look at Jake before looking back at Tanya. "Although I did want to tour the construction project Jake was working on. But he explained to me that some of the crew hadn't seen a woman in weeks and there was no reason for them to be needlessly aroused when the job was so near completion and they would all be returning home to their wives and families soon. I'm glad Jake didn't think it was necessary to impose those restrictions on himself. Of course, he didn't decide to return home until after I left. I wonder why."

Tanya wanted to gag.

"Let's say you reminded me of some of the compensations there would be to returning home." White-hot anger seared through her at Jake's drawling reply. The haughty expression in her tawny eyes taunted him with the knowledge that his supposed concern for his son wasn't the only thing that had brought Jake back. It was obvious silly little Sheila had been a contributing factor. But his indifferent smile mocked her indignation.

"How long will you be staying, Jake?" Patrick inquired with the same deceptive softness he had used earlier.

"Are you asking me just out of interest or as an executive of the firm?" There was a knife-edged challenge in the look Jake threw at him.

"A little of both."

There was a noticeable tightening of Patrick's square jaw as the two men silently took each other's measure. Then Jake let his gaze slide over to Tanya, curving the sensuous line of his mouth into a smile that didn't change the hardness in his eyes.

"Danvers has more than enough experience to handle the road project, so don't think it isn't in capable hands." He studied his competition through narrowed eyes. "There's every probability that I'll be staying here a very long time."

Each word of his statement was slowly and carefully enunciated so there could be no mistake about what he was saying.

Tanya stared at him helplessly, trying to fathom the unreadable expression in his face as Jake allowed the impact of his announcement to make its mark. Not an hour ago he had told his mother he didn't know how long he would be staying. Had Sheila's presence influenced his decision? It seemed obvious, and yet was it? Tanya had no doubt that Sheila was a factor, but not the deciding one. It was clear that Jake didn't intend to enlighten them as to the cause.

"I believe that calls for a drink," Tanya announced, finding herself in need of a little alcohol to restore her shaken composure. "Excuse me."

"I'll help you," offered Patrick, moving quickly to her side.

"Make mine something festive and bubbly," Sheila ordered flirtatiously. Her words only confirmed what Tanya already knew—that she found Jake's announcement something to be celebrated.

Patrick stepped behind the portable bar to mix the drinks as if sensing that her hands weren't steady enough for the task. She gripped the padded edge of the bar fiercely, turning her knuckles white in the process.

"Why didn't you mention that Sheila went with you on your trip?" she asked, lowering her voice so that her question was for Patrick's ears alone.

"She is my sister, in spite of the gap in our ages. It was a case of Sheila wanting to take a trip as I was leaving on one." His dark gaze raised to dwell thoughtfully on Tanya's face. "Or are you really asking why I didn't mention that she had become acquainted, shall we say, with Jake?" Tanya found it difficult to meet his look squarely. Patrick continued when it became obvious that she wasn't going to reply. "I had the impression that you didn't care what your husband did as long as he stayed away.

I'm beginning to think I need to revise that opinion."

"He means nothing to me!" she said quickly, 'I just felt so idiotic standing there with everybody knowing what was going on but me."

"Tonight—when I all but told him to get lost— why did you go to him when he called? Why did you leave me standing there like a fool while you rushed to his side?" Patrick demanded.

"It was shock." Tanya ran a nervous hand over her tawny hair. "A nightmare. I couldn't believe he was really there. I never thought he would come back. Not even when I wrote—"

The muttered expletive from Patrick stopped the tumbling torrent of words. "You asked him to come back?" he ground out harshly.

"I had to." Her eyes begged for his understanding. "Not for myself—for John. He had this crazy notion that Jake was dead or in prison, and insisted on writing a letter asking his father to come home. What else could I do?" she ended with a resigned shake of her head. "You'd mentioned how busy Jake was. I hoped ... I thought he wouldn't be able to get away."

"Yes, I remember," Patrick sighed, running a hand wearily through his dark hair. "It's just when I think about you being alone with him later on tonight, I—"

Her face heated at Patrick's implication and Tanya hurried to banish the image of her in Jake's arms.

"His bedroom is across the hall. We don't—"

"Got those drinks mixed yet, Raines?" Jake's voice slashed out at them from his position just

behind Tanya. She spun around to stare into the
cold anger on his face.

"Ooh, you two look guilty," Sheila declared with
kittenish delight. "What were you whispering
about?"

"Scotch and water all right with you, Jake?" Patrick asked, deliberately ignoring his sister's jibe as
he handed her a drink.

"Scotch and water is fine." Tanya met his chilling
gaze defiantly, refusing to feel the tiniest pinprick
of guilt over her completely innocent conversation
with Patrick.

"What shall we drink to?" Sheila demanded,
darting a coquettish look at Jake over her upraised
glass. "To your homecoming?"

"Let's make it something we can all drink to,"
he suggested dryly. "Shall we say—to better days
and brighter tomorrows."

Their glasses made a semblance of touching
before they were raised to their lips. The bracing
swallow of liquor had little effect on Tanya, not
with the way Jake kept watching her—that and the
sullen silence from Patrick.

They were still standing near the bar, so there
was always someone stopping to have a word with
Jake and eliminating the opportunity for any more
double-edged exchanges. Tanya moved to the side,
appearing to be a part of the quartet but holding
herself aloof while deliberately avoiding any eye
contact with her husband and wishing she had
never written the letter that had precipitated his
return.

"Well, Jake," a man exclaimed with a good-
natured slap on his shoulder. "What are you going
to do with yourself now that you're back?"

"The first thing I'm going to do is spend some time with my family," he announced. Sliding a glance at Tanya, he added, "and get acquainted with my son.'

"It's too bad he's in school right now," Sheila murmured. "You're going to have a lot of empty hours during the day."

"I'll think of ways to fill them." A twisted smile lifted the corners of his mouth as Jake stared into the veiled promise in her dark eyes.

The man missed the interchange between Jake and Sheila as he laughed, "I imagine your wife will have a lot of plans that will only include the two of you. Isn't that right, Mrs. Lassiter?"

The color washed out of Tanya's cheeks as she met the amused smile on Jake's face.

"Jake makes the plans," she smiled, not caring that she sounded like a dutiful wife bowing to the wishes of her husband. He would know that what she really meant was his plans didn't include her.

"Wish my wife thought that way!" The man widened his eyes expressively.

"Oh, Tanya's one of a kind," Jake declared with a mocking glint in his eyes.

"Jake, the Harrises are leaving," his mother touched a hand to his arm. "Come and say goodbye to them."

"Of course." He nodded politely to the gathering as he wound his way through the thinning guests towards the sliding doors.

"Come on, Sheila. It's time we left, too," said Patrick, reaching out to take his sister's arm. His dark head inclined towards Tanya. "I'll see you?" he murmured.

A coldness closed in on her heart, making her

feel very strange. Her troubled eyes met his. "Yes, Patrick," she nodded absently, acquiescing because her thoughts were too tangled to make any coherent protest. Sheila flicked her an amused glance as she bade her an airy goodbye.

Their departure seemed to signal an end to the party and a general exodus of the remaining guests began. As she repeated the polite words of parting, Tanya kept glancing towards the doors, expecting Jake to return before the last of the guests left. But there was no sign of him when the final couple departed and she breathed a sigh of relief.

There was still a sound of voices in the foyer and in the front of the house, indicating her mother and father-in-law were occupied, probably along with Jake. Tanya didn't want to chance a meeting with him inside, so she busied herself with collecting the glasses and scattered dishes on the patio, placing them on a trolley to be later wheeled into the house.

Not a breeze stirred the air. The silence of the night was broken only by the distant, eerie cry of a screech owl. Tanya paused near the far edge of the patio, turning her face up to the midnight sky with its smattering of stars and shimmering pale moon, savoring the stillness of the moment before a dim red glow caught her eyes among the trees. As she turned towards it, she saw a dark form separate itself from the shadows to make its way to the steps, artfully constructed to appear like natural stone formations. Tanya stiffened when the moonlight revealed Jake's face.

"I thought you were saying goodbye to the guests," she said, with a note of accusation.

"I slipped away when nobody was looking." He

didn't glance her way as he reached the empty patio and sank into one of the cushioned chairs, taking a last drag on his cigarette before crushing it out in an ashtray. He was still carrying his drink and held it in both hands to stare with a frown into its pale amber depths.

"Why?" Tanya demanded, feeling an uncontrollable urge to bait him the way he had done all night. "Were you trying to figure out ways to meet Sheila on the sly? It shouldn't be too difficult. She usually spends the summers on Patrick's houseboat tied up at one of the marinas. Very convenient for you!"

He swallowed the remaining liquid in his glass. "Actually I was tired," Jake said with thinly disguised impatience. "I've crossed quite a few time zones since I left Africa."

There were unmistakable signs of fatigue in his face, but Tanya could summon no sympathy for him. Instead she directed her attention to the empty glass in his hands.

"Are you through with that, or do you want another drink?"

A bitter smile touched his mouth. "One is my limit now."

"Really?" she deliberately made her voice sarcastic as he rose to his feet to place the glass on the trolley in front of her. "That doesn't sound like the Jake Lassiter I remember."

"No, it probably doesn't. I recall a night when I got so drunk that I couldn't remember a thing, and less than a year later a girl shoves a baby under my nose and tells me it's my son. An experience like that has a sobering effect on a man."

Her gaze fell under the austerity of his. Her stomach twisted itself into knots as she tried to appear as calm as Jake, but her hands were trembling visibly. Tanya clasped them together, vividly aware of the way he towered over her and the muscles that rippled under his jacket.

"I've often wondered," Jake continued when his statement was only met with silence, "what you recall about that night." Tanya stared at her hands for a minute more before defiantly tossing back her head to meet his bland gaze. "I try to block out the unpleasant memories."

He didn't appear the least disconcerted by her biting voice, lazily meeting the contempt in her blue eyes. "Was everything about the evening unpleasant?" he asked without giving her time to reply. "The whole night wasn't completely blacked out for me by drink. The first part is relatively clear. I remember meeting a very lovely and shy young girl at the Sedalia fair and asking her to dance with me. I even remember how prettily she blushed when I told her that her hair reminded me of antique gold. We didn't talk very much, though. I just held her in my arms and pretended to move my feet so it would seem as if we were dancing while I stared into those topaz eyes."

His voice was like velvet, weaving a magic spell that turned back the clock to that long-ago night. Tanya had only to shut her eyes to have that deliciously heady sensation take possession of her at the thrill of being in his arms. She remembered that first tender kiss and the second, that had been filled with such fierce passion. That was when she had fled from him, frightened by her own response and the desire that flamed inside her.

"What are you trying to make me believe?" she

demanded bitterly. "That you actually cared about me? That I meant something to you? Was I really any more to you than a one-night stand?"

His hands captured her shoulders, giving her a hard shake. "Tanya, damn it! I—"

"You were going to come and see me the following weekend—or so you said!" she accused him shrilly. "You never meant to, and we both know it."

"My brother was killed in a car crash. I couldn't come," he ground out savagely.

"Not then. Not later. Not ever."

Exasperated by the sarcasm in her voice, he dropped his hands from her shoulders, running a hand through his hair. "I don't even remember telling you I'd come back. But I intended to until Jamie was killed." The weariness in his voice was not caused only by lack of sleep. "To be perfectly honest, nothing seemed to matter very much after he died. I'd almost forgot you existed until I accidentally ran into you."

"That I can believe," Tanya agreed bitterly.

"That's why you hate me, isn't it?" He held her gaze, refusing to let her look away. "Your ego was hurt because I took you and forgot you. You couldn't even forgive me for that when I married you. You felt I owed it to you to marry you, to partially pay for one reckless night."

"That's not true," she protested, stung by the heartless picture he had painted of her. "I never intended you to know about John, not until we met accidentally . . . I never wanted to marry you, but when you found out about John, you threatened to take him away from me. The only reason I told you about him was—" the muscles in her

slender throat constricted and she had to wait a
moment before continuing. "I told you because I
wanted you to squirm, to feel some of the guilt
and fear that I had. I only wanted money to take
care of the bills. But you wanted the baby! You
and your Lassiter money and Lassiter power and
Lassiter name! First you treated me like I was
nobody and forgot all about me, and then I'm
supposed to be forgiving when you make me marry
you in order to keep John! You ask the impossible."

His mouth was drawn into a grim, forbidding
line. "You've never tried. We've never regarded
our marriage as anything more than a masquerade.
For our son's sake, it's about time we did. You
admitted that much when you wrote that letter
suggesting I come back, even if you didn't think I
would come."

"It won't work, Jake." He seemed too close to
her and Tanya took a quick step backwards, an
unreadable light in his eyes sending her senses
reeling.

"I never said it would work!" he exclaimed with
a flash of angry impatience. "I said we should try.
No marriage will work if the two people involved
won't try. You're a beautiful and desirable woman,
and I can't believe you find me totally repulsive."

If only she did. Tanya wished silently, looking
anywhere but at his compelling face. "What are
you asking, Jake?" She spoke quietly, the hidden
fear showing in her eyes when she glanced at him.
"That I go to bed with you?"

A cynical noise that resembled laughter sounded
in his throat. "The answer is no, I'm not asking
you to go to bed with me, although it might be
the ultimate answer. What I do want you to do—

or suggest that we do—is to treat each other like friends instead of enemies. To try to get to know one another at last, for our son's sake. each other is like. Call it a trial period or a truce or whatever, but we need to bury the past.''

"Great theory,' Tanya agreed, hoping he couldn't see the slight wistfulness in her eyes. "I might even have considered it if it weren't for the contemptible way you treated me tonight."

"You mean when I caught you kissing Raines?" Jake looked at her with studied nonchalance.

"He has a first name. It's Patrick!"

Her quick defense only drew an amused smile. "I probably do owe you an apology for the way I manhandled you. We may be married in name only, but I still consider you to be mine. Seeing you in his arms was a blow to my male pride."

Tanya was quick to note that Jake never actually apologized, only admitting that he should, but it did mollify her a bit.

"Well? Will you consider a trial period?" Jake repeated, watching her carefully.

"What about Sheila?" she asked stubbornly.

"She doesn't enter the picture at all."

"Doesn't she?" She arched an eyebrow in his direction. "You seemed glad to see her tonight. Looks like you got to know each other rather well when you were in Africa together."

He seemed to hesitate before replying. "Well, there are times when a man needs a woman, and that's the only explanation you're going to get." His admission of some kind of intimacy with Sheila didn't carry the least note of remorse. "But our agreement would be strictly between the two of us."

"Are you saying that you won't see Sheila?"

"Are you saying that you won't see Patrick?" Jake countered swiftly, his eyes narrowing on the rosy hue of her cheeks.

"I told you I haven't been seeing him!" Her temper flared at his implication that she was as unprincipled as he.

"After tonight, I don't think he's going to be satisfied merely to gaze at you from afar. The taste of honey is addictive," a sardonic smile touched his mouth. "But that's beside the point. You still haven't answered whether you'll agree to my proposal for a truce."

"What happens at the end of this trial period if I still despise you?" Tanya demanded.

"If, at the end of two or three months, we don't feel our marriage could be in any way successful, then we'll have to explore the alternatives," Jake told her.

"Divorce?" Tanya wondered why the word seemed to stick in her throat.

"That would be the obvious one." Nothing could could hide the piercing sadness in his eyes.

"And if I don't agree to your so-called truce, what then?"

"Then things will continue on exactly as they are." There was no mistaking the inflexibility in his words.

"That isn't much of a choice, is it?" Her amber eyes smoldered with her outrage.

"It depends on the way you look at it," he said smoothly. "Think it over and give me your answer in a couple of days."

The next instant Tanya was staring at his retreating back.

Chapter Four

Tanya rolled over, pressing a hand against the dull ache in her head as golden sunlight streamed from her bedroom window. She sighed wearily without knowing exactly why. An odd depression seemed to be casting shadows over the morning and only when she blinked her eyes open did she remember the cause.

Jake was home.

With a little moan she buried her head in the pillow, her memory racing back over the events of the previous evening. He was back with the intention of staying. No longer would she be able to ignore the existence of her husband. The worst of it was, she couldn't summon any hatred for him, only a nameless fear of the repercussions his return could bring and the terrifying thought that living with her day in and day out might enable him to guess the secret she had guarded so carefully.

The door to her room burst open and John came tearing in. He catapulted himself to the side of the bed, stopping there to catch his breath as Tanya pushed herself into a sitting position.

"Is it really true? Is my dad really here? Grandma said he'd come home. Where is he?" The rapid-fire questions were hurled at her with unrestrained eagerness.

John was too excited to notice that Tanya's smile was forced. "Yes, he is here. He's in the other bedroom sleeping."

"I'm going to go and see him!"

Before Tanya could reach out to stop him, he had whirled around and headed for the door. "John, wait!" she called sharply, swinging her feet onto the floor and reaching for the layered white chiffon robe to cover the silk of her nightgown.

By the time she could cover the same distance to her bedroom door, John was flinging open the door on the opposite side of the hall. He stood poised inside the door, one hand still holding the knob when Tanya reached him.

"Don't wake him, John," she whispered firmly, her fingers settling on his shoulders to draw him silently out of the room.

Then she saw the reason for John's transfixed stance. Jake was standing in the doorway to the private bath. Dark blue jeans molded his thighs and hips, but his chest was bare and very tanned. His thick, tobacco-brown hair still glistened from a shower while the clean scent of soap permeated the air. Amused blue eyes took in Tanya's disheveled appearance as an uncomfortable feeling of warmth stole over her face. Then his gaze swung down to the boy standing in front of her.

"Good morning, John. You are John, aren't you?" Jake asked with a decided twinkle in his eyes.

The silken brown head nodded affirmatively as John continued to stare at the man whose presence dominated the room. "Are you my dad?" his small voice asked, a hint of doubt in his words that indicated that he was bracing himself for a denial.

Jake's answer was a simple and unequivocal, "Yes." But he made no move towards the boy.

Tanya discovered she was holding her breath. Very quietly she expelled it as she gently removed her hands from John's shoulders. The room was so still a feather could have been heard landing on the carpet. Finally John released the doorknob and walked slowly towards Jake, stopping when he was directly in front of him to tilt his head back and look up at Jake.

"Will I be as tall as you are when I grow up?" he asked seriously.

Jake smiled, a slow smile that transformed his carved features into an expression of unbelievable tenderness. He kneeled down to be at eye level with the boy.

"You might even be taller," he answered just as seriously. There was another period of silence, but without the tension of the first. Tanya watched the pair, knowing they had completely forgotten she was there in the room. They were so close together, yet not speaking or touching. One was standing, his gaze questing and exploring the face of the stranger who was his father, and the other kneeling with a confident and understanding expression.

"Have you had breakfast yet?" Jake finally asked.

"No."

"Neither have I. Why don't you run and ask your

grandmother to put another plate on the table and we'll eat together?''

John nodded a quick agreement and turned to leave, then stopped and turned back to the still-kneeling man. A frown creased his forehead.

"I'm glad you came home, Dad," he announced firmly, then spun around and dashed from the room.

Jake slowly straightened to his feet. Eyes as calm as a summer sky met her tawny gaze.

"I'm sorry," Tanya murmured helplessly, clutching her robe tighter about her throat.

"Why?"

"John's welcome wasn't exactly enthusiastic, I—" she stared down at the carpet, —"I'm afraid he doesn't know you very well."

"Did you expect him to throw himself in my arms? I would have been disappointed if he had." He met her startled glance. "I'm a stranger to him. I wouldn't want him to give me his trust and affection simply because he's been told that I'm his father. It's a much more precious gift if it's earned."

Tanya sighed. "I suppose you're right." Her fingers raked through her tousled hair. She couldn't shake the feeling that she was ultimately to blame for the rift between father and son. She didn't even hear the soft steps that brought Jake nearer to her.

"Give him time to get to know me, Tanya."

Her pulse raced in agitation as she realized how close he was to her.

"Have you thought any more about our discussion last night? A friendly truce would be the best thing for John."

From the corner of her eye, Tanya could see the

even movement of his bare chest calmly breathing in and out. Part of her mind couldn't concentrate on what he was saying because of the potency of his animal attraction.

Her voice was a hoarse whisper when she did reply. "We can never be friends, Jake." She found the strength to look warily into his face and saw the tightening of his jaw at her adamant stand.

"I never said we could be friends," he corrected sharply. "In fact, I would be the first to admit that it's practically an impossibility. All I want to do is get rid of this damned hostile atmosphere that we're both guilty of fostering."

"I don't know. I just don't know," Tanya asserted with a shake of her head, her eyes looking everywhere except at the man standing beside her. His semi-nakedness was arousing her senses, making her too vulnerable to his talent for persuasion.

She expected storm clouds to descend at her indecisive answer. She wasn't prepared for the sudden softening of his tone, like the caress of velvet over her skin.

"Is peaceful co-existence so much to ask?" His hands reached out to grasp the upper portion of her arms.

The thinness of her silken robe couldn't ward off the scorching fire of his touch, nor could she fight the desire to be drawn against the muscular strength of his chest. Tanya closed her eyes tightly and cringed to elude his hold, her hands raising upwards to protect herself from any further advances.

"Don't touch me!" she gasped, her voice trembling violently at the traitorous response of her body. "I can't stand it!" Her eyelids fluttered

open to see the fists clenched rigidly at his side
while his cold gaze froze the expression of pain in
her eyes.

"How and why did I ever marry you?" Jake
sneered. His eyes mercilessly raked her from head
to bare toe. "You have the wrappings of a beautifully passionate woman, but there's nothing inside
except ice!"

"No!" Her pride protested, unable to let his
scathing words stand without a denial, knowing full
well her problem was she was too susceptible to a
man's attention. "That's not true!"

His face took on a cold, seductive quality that
chilled even as it attracted. "I'm from Missouri.
You're going to have to show me." His softly spoken
words carried an unmistakable invitation to come
into his arms to prove her claim.

Her breath caught in her throat as Tanya swayed
closer to him, drawn by an irresistible magnetic
force. His gaze held her captive, pulling her nearer
when every instinct cried for her to flee.

As his warm breath fanned her cheeks, her
glance moved to the sensual line of his lips. She
ached for his kiss, longed to satisfy the desires she
had kept banked for so long. At the last second,
Tanya knew she couldn't let Jake discover her dangerous vulnerability to a man's caress.

He must have sensed the beginnings of her withdrawal and reached out to fold her in his arms,
the blue fire in his eyes dwelling on the parting
softness of her mouth. "Don't say no now, honey,"
he chided softly.

There was a rush of footsteps in the hall before
John came to a halt in the open doorway, his eyes
opened wide at the seemingly embracing couple.

He blinked twice before stammering out his message.

"Grandma says . . . your breakfast i-i-is ready." Jake smiled down at Tanya's lowered head. "Don't worry," he whispered scornfully in her ear, "you've been saved." As he relaxed the steel band of his arms that had held her, he told his son, "I'll be right there."

John shifted uncomfortably from one foot to the other, unsure whether he was supposed to stay or go. Tanya's feet were rooted to the floor as an embarrassing wave of shame and humiliation washed over her. But Jake was very calmly putting on a shirt, buttoning it and tucking it into the waistband of his trousers, not the least bit shaken as Tanya was over what had almost occurred. Before he left the room with his son, he walked over to her and raised her chin to gaze into her tear-blurred eyes with maddening satisfaction.

"You did try, Tanya. Maybe next time," he murmured.

"There won't be a next time," she retorted.

He merely raised an eyebrow, indicating more plainly than words his disbelief, then he released her and turned away.

"Are you ready, John?" he asked.

"Are you coming, Mom?"

"No," Tanya quickly swallowed the rising sob of panic, adding more calmly, "I have to get dressed yet. You go ahead with your father." She brushed a hand over her cheek, wiping away a tear that had fallen from her damp lashes. A small hand touched her arm.

"Mom, are you all right?"

"Yes, I'm fine." But the weak smile she gave him wasn't reassuring.

"Why are you crying?" John darted an accusing look at Jake standing in watchful silence at the door, his expression deliberately unrevealing.

One word. That was all it would take, and Tanya knew John would turn against his father. One spiteful word and she could destroy the tenuous thread of their relationship. For a moment there was a glitter of vengeance in her eyes. How simple it would be to pay Jake back for every wrong she believed he had done. She glanced towards Jake, seeing the hardness in his eyes that knew the power she had over his son's love.

"I'm crying—" Tanya took a deep breath and looked down into the thin, apprehensive face, "I'm crying because I'm happy, John. Because your father has finally come home."

There was a hint of uncertainty in his face before it was wiped away with a large smile. His perception was still that of a child's and he couldn't see the defeat dulling her eyes.

"So am I, Mom," he agreed.

"Your breakfast is getting cold," she reminded him. The hand that touched his cheek affectionately was trembling. "Run along before your grandmother sends out a search party."

"Come on, Dad," John called, waving to Jake to follow him as he hurried past.

But Jake was looking at Tanya. Her sense of fair play had brought her figuratively to her knees, but it hadn't bowed her head. He studied her for a minute more before he turned to catch up with the small boy. Tanya wondered if Jake realized she had just declared him the victor before the battle had begun. But not all the spoils of war would be his. At all costs she must ensure against that.

The days following Jake's return fell into a pattern. When John was in school, Jake spent hours with his father, at the company office in Springfield or staying at their lakefront home. Late afternoons and early evenings were devoted to John. Sometimes they went fishing or played ball or, if spring rains forced them inside, they watched television together or played video games.

The late evening hours, the ones Tanya dreaded most, had been entirely in the company of his parents. Only for odd moments were they alone and Jake had allowed her to keep the conversation on a safe topic. But she had the feeling that he was only biding his time, waiting for his own moment to force an agreement out of her.

She shuddered to think what the consequences might be if she should consent to a trial period for them to get to know one another. Tanya wanted to spend no more time alone with him than she had to in order to maintain an outward appearance of peace to his parents. And her pride wouldn't let her bolt every time he stepped into a room where she was.

Today—Saturday—Jake had taken John boating. Fortunately, Tanya had a previous commitment to help with a sale held by the women's organization of their church. Each woman had volunteered for a three-hour shift and hers was about over. She scanned the small crowd for a glimpse of her mother-in-law who should be arriving to take her home.

Instead Tanya saw a tall, dark-haired man weaving his way towards her. With a start of guilt she realized she hadn't given Patrick Raines a single thought since that first night when Jake returned. Looking at the dark hair with its silver wings at the temple and the strong, handsome face, she felt the familiar feeling of warmth encompass her as it did every time she saw him.

"Patrick, what are you doing here?" Her cheerful smile was completely natural and not the least bit forced.

"I was out at the house with your father-in-law. Julia was getting ready to leave just as I was, so I volunteered to come in her place," he explained. "Are you ready to leave?"

Tanya said her goodbyes to her replacement at the cake-laden counter and walked with Patrick to his car. He flashed her a warm smile as he opened the door for her, then walked around to the driver's side.

"I've missed you," Patrick said simply as he slipped the car into gear and reversed out of the parking lot.

"It seems much longer than last week since I saw you," Tanya answered truthfully, tilting her head back to feel the refreshing breeze blowing in from the car window.

"I wasn't sure I would be welcomed if I came. I know Jake wouldn't be glad to see me," he laughed without amusement. "And I couldn't help wondering if his return had changed your thinking as well." He tossed her a quizzical look that Tanya was oddly reluctant to meet. It was funny how before last week when the silence had been broken and the first tentative words had been spoken, she had imagined them meeting like this, stealing a few minutes alone. Now she found herself uncomfortable and unwilling to bite into the forbidden fruit.

"You know you're always welcome as far as I'm concerned," she managed to answer with an air of unconcern that ignored the deeper meaning of his question.

"Why did he have to come back?" Patrick muttered, his strong fingers closing over the wheel in a death grip. "You're already withdrawing from me. I know that coolness in your voice. I've heard it before at parties when someone got overly friendly and you wanted to put them in their place. I thought you felt something for me."

With a stab of guilt she knew she had let him believe she did. In truth, she was drawn to him, but too afraid of the consequences.

"I do . . . that is, I could," she corrected quickly. Her words threatened to tumble over themselves in a rush to get out. She breathed in deeply to gain control. "I have more than just myself to think about, Patrick."

"You mean John. Well, you can't honestly say that Jake has been much of a father to the boy," he grumbled.

"That's as much my fault as it is Jake's."

"I find that hard to believe," he sighed. "Do you believe in love at first sight?"

"No!" The violence of her answer surprised her until she remembered how completely she had been taken in by Jake's charm so many years ago, before he had so unutterably destroyed her illusions about life and love. "No, I don't," she repeated more calmly.

"In a way, I believe in it." His dark eyes roamed over her perfect features. "I was still married the first few times I remember seeing you. Even then I found you attractive. I kept growing more curious about you, about why you and the Lassiters maintained this idea of a perfect marriage between you and Jake, and yet you still never visited him and he never came to see you. I found myself growing jealous that you might have a lover on the side and couldn't figure out why until I realized that I wanted to be that man. That's when I began to see that shimmer of loneliness in your eyes. You are lonely, aren't you, Tanya? That self-possession is just a front, isn't it?"

"Everyone is a little bit lonely," was as much as she could admit before holding her head up proudly to show it didn't matter.

"You don't have any family, do you? I want to know everything about you," Patrick said with grim determination. "Were you an orphan?"

"Not really. My parents were killed when I was nineteen. I was already out on my own by then supporting myself," she answered calmly. College, career—she'd given up the dream of both to raise the little boy she loved.

"No brothers or sisters?"

"I had a younger sister," Tanya stared out the window. "She died of pneumonia a few months after we lost our parents."

"You were about nineteen when you married Jake, weren't you?" But Patrick didn't look to her for confirmation. "That must have been a rough time for you. I can see how you could have wept on the first shoulder offered. That's a blow anyone would have trouble handling. What happened, angel? Did you fall in love with love and only realize when it was too late that it was a mistake?'' The sympathy in his voice cried out to her. She very nearly told him the whole story with every sordid detail, but somehow she held back.

''Yes, it was something like that,'' she agreed.

''Sometimes it's a mistake to hold a marriage together for the sake of a child, which is what you're trying to do. Have you ever asked Jake for a divorce?''

''We've discussed the possibility.''

''I'm—'' Patrick began.

''Please, let's change the subject,'' Tanya interrupted, the beginnings of a headache pounding in her temples. ''I'll be glad to drop the subject,'' sighed Patrick, giving her a look that was both passionate and stubborn, ''if you'll tell me where I stand.''

They had already turned off the main highway on to the road leading to the Lassiter home. Patrick slowed the car down and parked by the road overlooking Table Rock Lake.

''Well, Tanya?'' he repeated.

''I don't know.'' She pushed her long tawny hair behind her ears and stared at the mirrorlike body of water reflecting the surrounding hills in the afternoon sun. White clouds danced gracefully in the blue sky. ''I haven't had time to think.''

''I'm a man, Tanya. Now that I've touched you, I can't be content to gaze at you from afar.''

He was close beside her when he made the last statement, his hand on her shoulder slowly turning her towards him. His words were so nearly the same as Jake's that Tanya wanted to laugh hysterically. Only when she looked into Patrick's eyes, it wasn't so funny.

Without a protest she allowed him to draw her against his chest, hoping to find solace there. But her uncertainty only seemed to be intensified. The lips that touched her hair and moved down to brush her eyelashes produced a warm sensation, yet not nearly as soul-destroying as Jake's caress.

"I'm not the kind of man to beg," he murmured against her cheek. "But I want you, Tanya."

She moaned a protesting "no" as his mouth moved to cover hers and his arms tightened when she tried to pull away. All emotion drained away as she lay passively in his embrace, knowing that subtly she had invited this advance and finding she didn't really want it. Yet her lack of response didn't discourage Patrick. There was still an ardent fire in his dark eyes when he released her and shifted back to his own side of the car.

"Now do you understand the way I feel about you?" he asked, his breathing ragged and uneven. 'I don't want to sneak around any more than you do. I understand how you feel about your son and I respect you for it. You want him to have a good home, a decent education, and a future. The Lassiters can give him all of that and the security of a family. You just say the word and I'll give him the same things. Young John likes me. I think he would accept me as his father. He's certainly seen more of me than he ever has of Jake."

Tanya stared at him in bewildered amazement, not believing that he was actually proposing to her.

"Are you asking me to leave Jake and marry you?" she breathed.

"That's exactly what I'm asking." He smiled at her tenderly, his strong features made all the more handsome by the love shining in his eyes. "I would even get down on one knee and repeat it."

"But I'm not exactly sure that I love you," she protested weakly, looking away before she succumbed to his persuasive charm.

"I'd be the last one to ask you to change one husband for another that you don't love either," Patrick nodded, wisely not pushing her on a decision. A wistful smile played over his mouth. "You have no idea, Tanya, how badly I want to win your love. I want to see you again, alone, like this, where we can talk and not be afraid what we say will be overheard, even if it's only for a half an hour or an hour—whatever you can arrange. Say you will. Say yes."

"I don't know when I—"

The sound of another car's tires on the gravel halted her hesitant agreement. She saw the quick frown that appeared on Patrick's forehead even as she turned her head to see the approaching car. Her stomach fell with sickening suddenness as she recognized Sheila sitting beside Jake at the same moment that they saw her with Patrick. Jake said something to Sheila that elicited an expression of displeasure as the car halted beside them. The grim look on his face when he stepped out of the car did little to ease the frightened hammering of Tanya's heart.

"You don't have to explain anything," Patrick said quietly, a reassuring hand closing over hers.

She cast him a grateful glance as her door was

opened and Jake leaned down to mockingly look at the occupants. Tanya braced herself for the tirade that was to come.

"Admiring the view?" Jake inquired calmly, his steel-blue eyes glancing towards the expanse of lake water below them. "Lovely this time of year."

"Very beautiful," Patrick agreed, the challenging gleam back in his eyes.

"Sheila got tired of waiting for you to come back, so I volunteered to take her home. It's a good thing I ran into you. It saves both of us making the trip." His hard blue gaze turned on Tanya. "You can ride back to the house with me."

Patrick's expression was plainly saying she didn't have to go with Jake if she didn't want to, but Tanya smiled to let him know she didn't mind.

"Thanks for picking me up," she told him. Before Tanya had a chance to change her mind, Jake's hand closed over her arm, propelling her out of Patrick's care to his own. Sheila looked a little sulky as she got reluctantly out of the car to make room for Tanya.

"I was looking forward to you taking me home, Jake," she sighed meaningfully, "but I know you want to get back to your little boy. I had a great time. Maybe we can do it again?"

The last was accompanied by a bewitching smile directed solely at Jake, who returned it with a half-promising, "Maybe." Tanya found her anger rising as Sheila blew him a kiss and got into her brother's car. Patrick's car was nearly out of sight by the time Jake walked leisurely around his own and slipped behind the wheel.

"Did she go with you and John today?" Tanya

demanded, her eyes flashing a glance at the man calmly starting the car.

"As a matter of fact, she did, although it wasn't planned that way,' Jake replied with a slight smile.

"John must have put a terrible crimp in your style," she retorted sarcastically. "What a pity you promised to take him along."

"It was Sheila who wasn't part of the plan. John and I bumped into her when we stopped at the marina for lunch." His gaze explored her face. "The time we spent together was as innocent as your few minutes with Raines." Tanya turned away from his searching eyes, knowing the warmth in her cheeks had betrayed her sense of guilt.

"Of course," Jake continued, a chilling coolness invading his tone, "you didn't have the benefit of John as a chaperon, so perhaps yours wasn't quite as innocent."

The accusation in his voice infuriated her.

"Our meeting was motivated by more respectable reasons than yours," she retorted.

"Respectable?" he jeered. "Would you like to explain that?" She shifted uncomfortably in the leather-covered seat. "Patrick asked me to marry him." Her voice was coolly composed. Jake merely shrugged.

"I have to give the man credit. I didn't think he would move that fast," he said, surprising Tanya with the indifference in his voice.

"What was your answer?"

"That's my business." She stared down at her hands, trying to figure out why she felt so disappointed by Jake's calm acceptance of her announcement.

"It's mine, too, Mrs. Lassiter." He underlined

the last with mocking emphasis. "If not as your husband, then as the father of our child."

"If you must know, I didn't give him an answer!" Her anger returned as quickly as it had fled.

"Why?"

"Because I didn't have a chance. You and Sheila drove up as—"

"If you'd had the chance, what would it have been?" Jake persisted.

With a belligerent toss of her head, Tanya turned to stare at him, the false words of her acceptance of the proposal forming on her lips. But she found she couldn't be less than truthful under his penetrating regard.

"I don't know. I need time to think it over," she said, keeping the defiant lift to her chin.

"It doesn't sound to me as if you're really in love with the man or you wouldn't need time to think." His comment was accompanied by a wry smile. "You certainly can't plead that you don't know him. You've known Raines as long as you've known me."

"But I don't know you," she protested artlessly.

"Do you want to?" Jake asked softly.

Tanya sat motionless, afraid she would say something else that she would regret as much as her previous admission. Very slowly she gained control over her clamoring nerves and shook her head.

"No, I don't," she said firmly. "What I do know about you, I don't like. No point in expending energy on a lost cause."

"Are you saying our marriage is a lost cause?" There was speculation in his narrowed gaze.

"What would you call it when we can't even be

in the same room together without starting something?'' she countered nervously.

"Is that the way you feel?" But he didn't seem at all upset by her description and merely shrugged when she nodded her assertion. He turned the key in the ignition. "Maybe you're right."

Chapter Five

Tanya slipped out the patio door into the warmth of the moonlit night. She had just tucked John into bed and the idea of returning to the living room where Jake and his parents were was too oppressive. A solitary walk along the lake's edge was much more inviting. She was determined not to let her problems spoil the beauty of the evening.

Streamers of stars adorned the heavens while the moonshine cast silvery shadows on the rocks and boulders along the path that she walked. Crickets and cicadas sang out their shrill songs, drowned out now and again by the distant scream of a screech owl, or the baying of a hound. A breeze tickled the tops of the trees, an assorted collection of oaks, cedars and hickorys, but it didn't get through the foliage to cool her face.

It was a languid night, warm and humid and still. A lopsided three-quarter moon gave the lake's mirror surface a pearly sheen. Tanya paused near the private pier leading out to the boat dock, then turned to wander out over the water, her footsteps on the planks sounding unnaturally loud. She stopped at the end and leaned over the railing to stare into the hidden depths.

Her skin felt hot and sticky where her clothes persisted in clinging and the water looked so deliciously cool. There were no other homes or resorts on their little cove and no running lights from boats were visible. Tanya was completely alone. She removed the leather clasp that held her tawny hair back, swept it on top of her head and secured it again. The small locker on the dock always had a towel inside which she quickly removed and laid near the railing. Before she could have second thoughts, she stripped off her clothes, placed them near the towel, then used the ladder to slip into the water.

After the first shiver had passed from the cold water touching her bare skin, a sensuous kind of enjoyment took over. Treading water for only a few seconds, she struck out for open water with the rhythmic strokes of an experienced swimmer. For over a quarter of an hour she alternately swam and floated in the moon-kissed water. When the initial spurt of energy passed, the cold water began to make itself felt. She turned with a leisurely sidestroke to head towards the dock.

Perhaps it was a sixth sense or the betraying glow of a burning cigarette or the creaking of a wooden plank caused by human weight that made her aware that she wasn't alone. She stopped several yards short of the ladder, her eyes searching the shadowy areas near the boathouse for her intruder.

"Who's there?" she called out sharply.

There was a movement as a tall figure walked out of a dark corner and walked to the railing directly in front of her.

"I didn't know mermaids could talk." Even before the softly spoken words were carried across the water to her, Tanya had known the voice would belong to Jake. She very nearly reversed her course and struck out for the opposite shore, but she knew she was too cold and tired to make it.

"Please go away, Jake." The chattering of her teeth made the demand sound more like a plea.

The moonlight played over his wide forehead and prominent cheekbones, throwing the hollows of his cheeks in sharp relief as his mouth opened in an amused smile.

"It's not a mermaid," he teased with a regretful sigh, "only Mrs. Lassiter skinnydipping in the moonlight. That water must be cold."

"It is!" she snapped, trembling with cold and anger. "Will you go away so I can get out?" But Jake continued to lean against the rail staring at her. Tanya was infinitely grateful for the dark water that hid her nakedness, fighting the embarrassing sensation that his gaze was piercing the darkness. "If you won't go away, then toss me the towel from the ladder." She hated the desperate ring in her voice, but her limbs were beginning to feel numb and she didn't know how much longer she could continue to tread water.

Jake glanced where she had indicated, took a step, then leaned down and picked up the towel. He held it in his hands and looked back at her, laughter etched in every carved line of his face.

"If I throw you this, you won't have anything to dry off with," he couldn't resist pointing out.

"I'll worry about that later," she retorted, hating him for catching her in such a humiliating predicament.

With a shrug, he tossed it in the water ahead of her, forcing her to swim closer before the towel became soaked and sank beneath the surface. It was impossible to remain afloat and wrap the towel around her in the open water. She had to move to the ladder where she could slip a leg through the lower rung, thus keeping herself upright while leaving her hands free to maneuver the towel. She looked daggers at Jake, who continued to stare arrogantly down his straight nose at her. She longed to order him to turn his back to her, but knew such an edict would be met with open mockery. Instead she twisted around so her back was to him, fighting the sopping towel until she managed to pull it tightly around her chest and tuck in the end flap. Even secured, the heavy weight of the sodden cloth threatened to pull it off as she struggled up the ladder.

"Such modesty!" Jake chuckled. "I've seen naked women before."

Tanya tossed him a venomous look as she stalked soggily past him. "But not me!" she snapped.

"That's a strange thing for the mother of my son to say." The softness of his voice didn't hide the curious speculation her statement had aroused.

For a split second Tanya froze, a white-hot rush of heat enveloping her shivering body. She managed to put the right degree of contemptuous disdain in her voice. "Women get seduced with their clothes on all the time, Jake."

"Damn you!" The phrase was muttered beneath his breath. In one fluid stride, Jake was at her side, grabbing her shoulders. Tanya was made vividly aware again of his superior height and physical strength, tempered into sinewy muscle by the years spent in Africa. "Why do you keep making it sound as if I raped you?"

Her smooth white throat was exposed as she tilted her head up to stare calmly into his angry eyes. "You don't remember, do you?" she taunted, surprised at her own audacity to provoke him further yet knowing her acid tongue was the only weapon she had.

The burning rage faded from his eyes, replaced by a haunted pride. His hands fell away as he remained standing rigidly in front of her. "No. No, I don't remember," Jake admitted through gritted teeth. His gaze roamed with deliberate slowness over her body, half-covered by the wet towel that revealed the mature fullness of her breasts, her slender waist, and the gentle curve of her hips. "God help me, I can't remember." He turned away from her at last.

Without the intense scrutiny of Jake's eyes, Tanya bent down and picked up her clothes. Her eyes kept straying towards the broad, straight back and the rigid shoulders. Something in his proud, lonely stance closed over her heart with a painful squeeze. She tried to ignore the poignant tug as she walked quietly towards the enclosed boathouse. When she reached the door, she knew she couldn't leave him like that, shouldering all the blame.

"Jake." Her low voice asked for his attention. The glint of the moonlight shone over his face as he turned partially towards her. "It wasn't rape," she whispered, slipping inside the boathouse as he turned.

A footstep sounded on the wooden floor of the dock as she quickly closed the door behind her. With apprehensive stillness she waited to see if Jake would pursue her for an explanation. But he didn't seem to be following her and she sighed in relief and flicked on the light switch. The wet towel slipped unheeded to the floor as she shook out her pants. Then a rap on the door had her draw them protectively in front of her.

"There should be a towel you can use on the front seat cushion of the boat, Tanya." Jake's voice came quietly from the opposite side of the door.

She saw it almost instantly. "Got it," she answered, rubbing the rough terry cloth vigorously over her skin.

Once dressed, Tanya stood hesitantly at the door, overcome by a feeling that when she opened the door, something would happen—something beyond her control. But there was no alternative. She couldn't stay in the boathouse all night.

Jake was standing at the far end of the dock where a small bench was attached to the railing. One foot was raised onto the seat, his knee acting as a support for him to lean on. As the door clicked shut behind Tanya, he turned and straightened, and they stared at each other for a long moment before she broke free of his gaze and moved towards the pier leading to the shore.

"Tanya, don't leave yet." The peremptory ring in his voice halted her.

"Please, Jake, I don't want to talk about that night." She turned quickly as he came to a stop before her, her tawny eyes pleading with him not to ask any more questions. Her heart did a somersault at the gentle fire in the depths of his blue eyes.

"I just want you to know that I appreciate your honesty." There was no mistaking the sincerity behind his words. "I realize that you didn't have to admit what you did."

That virile charm was working its old magic on her and Tanya had to look down to break its spell. She couldn't explain to herself why she hadn't been able to let Jake go on thinking as he had. Some inner impulse had compelled her to speak out.

"And I haven't thanked you yet," Jake continued, "for not turning John against me. So many women in your place would have done just that."

"I couldn't," Tanya replied. "A boy should respect his father."

"You're a unique woman. I never realized until now how unique you are. You must have had wonderful parents. I only wish I could have met them."

But Tanya knew that if her parents had been alive she never would have married Jake. She never would have been driven to the point of mental and physical exhaustion from trying to support and care for a newborn baby alone. Her parents would have been there to share some of the burden. It was quite likely that Jake would never have known he had a son. And those thoughts strangely made her shudder.

"You must be cold," he declared with a velvet huskiness.

Before she could protest, he had removed his jacket and placed it around her shoulders. Her senses were assaulted by an intoxicating mixture of cigarette smoke, his musky scent of masculinity, and the warmth of his body heat clinging to the jacket. As he moved closer, drawing the jacket together under her chin, the heat emanated from him as if she was standing in front of a blazing fire. Staring at the white polo shirt, she felt the last of her resistance crumbling. When he removed the clasp from her hair, sending it cascading about her shoulders, she knew she wanted nothing more than to be taken in his arms.

He ran his fingers through her hair, smoothing it down around her neck where his hands halted almost encircling her slender throat. Then his thumbs began moving in a slow circular motion that was hypnotically sensuous. The slightest pressure was exerted on her chin, lifting her face towards his. Through half-closed lashes, Tanya glanced up at him, her pulse leaping as she saw his gaze dwelling on her mouth.

"You're beautiful," he murmured, bringing her closer to him. His breath was like a warm caress, "I have to do this. Don't fight me, honey."

There was only submission as he tilted her head back and covered her mouth with his. Submission, until his deepening kiss touched off the passionate core of her soft body spreading a yielding fire through every fiber of her being and Tanya responded, body and soul. She swayed against the solid wall of his chest, her hands creeping up to his neck to twine about it in her own fierce possession.

Yet his hunger for her was insatiable as his hands moved down her back, waist and hips, shaping her feminine form to the hard contours of his body.

Tanya strained closer, her heart pounding like thunder in her chest while her mind whirled at the exquisite pain of his crushing embrace. With a driving mastery, Jake parted her lips and began a sensual exploration of her mouth, drawing a moan of sheer ecstasy from deep in her soul.

The jacket fell into a heap on the dock near her feet, no longer needed to provide its impermanent warmth. They were surrounded by a heat wave of their own making, as they kissed and kissed again. His mouth left a scorching trail over her eyes and ears and neck, then returned to consume her mouth again. Tanya recognized the throbbing weakness in the lower part of her body as the time-less desire for a woman to know a man. The com-pleteness of the intimate longing frightened her and her hands made a fluttering protest against his chest.

His arms tightened fiercely about her, conquer-ing her weak opposition with arrogant sureness. There was a tiny sob of surrender as her lips melted under his and her hands began a tremulous and exploring caress of his rugged features. Then his mouth was dragged slowly away from hers and a hand pressed her tawny head against his chest, holding her possessively against him. The rush of his heart was in tune with the frenzied pace of her own. A wild, sublime peace encircled them for endless minutes, neither wishing to break the mindlessly magic spell.

Then his harsh, uneven breathing became more natural and controlled beneath Tanya's head. His chest rose and fell in one long, shuddering sigh as his hands clasped her arms and reluctantly moved her away from him. Their firm grip prevented her from swaying back to him while she stared at her hands still resting on his waist.

"Look at me, Tanya," Jake ordered.

Unwillingly she lifted her chin a fraction of an inch, knowing her desire for him was still glazing her eyes. But she obeyed, looking into the smoldering blue flames that burned with the certainty of the power he had over her. His gaze made an intimate exploration of her face, satisfying himself of the response he had aroused.

"Is this the reason for the electricity between us?" he said tenderly. A smile tugged at the corners of his mouth as even in the moonlight he saw the heightened color rush into her cheeks. "Do you still believe our marriage is a lost cause?"

This moment, more than ever before in her life, Tanya wanted their marriage to be real. Tears sprang to her eyes as the terrible pain of hopelessness struck her. With a sobbing sigh, she shook her head.

"It's impossible, Jake." Her voice quivered with defeat.

She could feel the freezing rigidity flow through him. It was like a knife wound to her heart.

"Impossible?" he echoed angrily. His fingers dug into her arms, giving her a shake. "What do you mean?"

"It can't work." The constriction in her throat made her voice sound very small and weak. "There's too much you don't know about me." She hesitated, afraid of the questions that statement might bring, then rushed on to cover it. "And I don't know about you."

"I won't accept that." His haughty arrogance had returned, to her dismay.

"Please, please," Tanya begged, "can't you leave things the way they were?"

"No," Jake said grimly. "It's too late to turn back now." The unrelenting hardness of his eyes seemed to pierce through her skin into the hidden secrets of her mind. "I should have taken you just now and made you mine."

"No!" She took a frightened step backwards, terrified that he might decide that it still wasn't too late to do it.

"I'm trying to understand you, Tanya, but you're making it awfully hard." He shook his head in a sort of angry bewilderment and made no attempt to move nearer. "You said yourself that John needed a father. Well, he needs a mother, too. You can't expect us to spend the rest of our lives sharing a child and still remain strangers to one another."

"I don't really expect that," she said with a hopeless shrug.

"What do you expect then? No, no, don't answer that," he added with a wry shake of his head. "You'd probably send me back to Africa."

In spite of herself, Tanya smiled. "Maybe Antarctica this time," she suggested softly.

A slight twinkle accented his quiet contemplation of her. "Today John asked me if you couldn't come along with us some time like Sheila did. Not all the time, but every once in a while." Jake paused, not really waiting for an answer as he studied her subdued expression. "We do need time to get to know one another—I said it the first night I came home. That's also why I didn't make love to you the way I wanted to a few minutes ago. If you don't want to spend time alone with me right away, what better chaperon could you ask for than a seven-year-old boy?"

"Oh, Jake, I don't know. I just don't know." The admission was wrenched from her heart. She wanted to agree, if for no other reason than to find out if the attraction between them was more than physical. But if it was, what would she gain? She turned away, letting her hands close over the railing.

"Right now we have a son and a marriage certificate. I don't know if we can have a future together or not." His solemn voice was directly behind her. She made no protest when his hands turned her back around to face him. "But I do know if we never try, we'll always wonder if our marriage could have worked. Our chances of making it a success are slim." His finger gently raised her chin, compelling her to look at the resolution on his face. "I don't know about you, Tanya, but I'm a true Missourian. I'm going to have to be shown that it's impossible. And I haven't been convinced so far."

For so many years she had told herself that she hated him. Her mother had often said that it was a very fine line that divided the emotions of love and hate. Had one been disguised as the other all these years? At the moment that answer eluded her as she tried to find the courage to answer Jake.

A frown of impatience swept fleetingly across his forehead at her continued silence. "If you're afraid that I'll take advantage of you, then I promise you right now that I won't touch you."

"It's not that," she assured him hastily, finding the thought of being near him and not having him touch her was intolerable. His regard of her deepened, almost as though he could divine her thoughts. Tanya swallowed hard, trying to appear composed and not at all shaken by the sensuous line of his mouth. "I don't mind being kissed, although I . . . I . . ."

"We won't go further than we did tonight." Jake rescued her from her stammering attempt to qualify her words. "Unless you specifically ask me to make love to you."

The amused and knowing glitter in his eyes stole away her poise, leaving her standing defenseless before him.

He smiled down at her. "Are you agreeing to my proposal to get to know one another?"

"Yes," Tanya sighed, a strange peace settling over her as she made her commitment. Her doubts about the sanity of her decision were momentarily banished.

"This calls for a kiss to seal our bargain, doesn't it?"

Jake gave her time to reply as his head slowly lowered towards hers, but every inch of her wanted to feel that passion his lips could evoke. The kiss was short, but without haste, lasting long enough to set her pulse racing before he gently released her mouth. His hands were on her shoulders and she trembled with longing. Jake misinterpreted the movement, deliberately, Tanya thought, as he bent down to retrieve his jacket, placing it back around her shoulders.

"Ready to go back to the house?" he asked.

Tanya nodded, knowing that to stay here alone with him would be flirting with temptation. A thrill of gladness swept through her when she turned to retrace her steps and discovered his arm was possessively encircling her shoulders, keeping her beside him as they walked the tightrope of the narrow pier. Nor did it fall away on the rocky path to the house. She stole one quick glance at his face, noting his pleased, nearly triumphant smile, and wondered if she'd made a fool of herself again.

"You won't be sorry," Jake said quietly, perceptively reading her thoughts. There was a teasing twinkle in his eyes. "You might even find I'm a likeable guy."

Tanya laughed shortly, sending him a rueful glance. "Hm. You could charm the stripes off a zebra if you set your mind to it," she declared.

"In that case," he grinned, "my own wife shouldn't be too much trouble."

The way she felt just then, she could agree with him, but she wasn't about to admit it. "The trouble is I don't have any stripes," she reminded him.

"Not what I want anyway," Jake replied as they reached the patio. Tanya was prevented from replying that defense-destroying remark by J. D. Lassiter, as he moved to let his presence be known. "Hello, Dad," Jake greeted him calmly, as though it were the most natural thing in the world for him to have his arm around his wife.

"Beautiful night, isn't it?" his father replied after one brief, surprised glance at Tanya. He, too, had a rather pleased smile on his face as he gazed absently at the starry sweep of the Milky Way.

"We took a walk down by the lake," said Jake, glancing down at Tanya as she shifted uncomfortably away from him. He obligingly let his arm fall to his side, an understanding look in his eyes.

Tanya didn't feel capable of discussing the trivialities of the weather. She slipped Jake's jacket from

her shoulders. "Excuse me. I feel . . . a little tired.
I think I'll turn in."

There was something very warm and intimate in
the look that Jake gave her as he wished her a good
night. It went a long way in restoring her shaken
composure.

Chapter Six

The first week under their new agreement passed very smoothly, almost as though it didn't exist. Tanya initially thought that Jake might be giving her a chance to back out—which was ridiculous, because Jake wasn't the kind of man to allow anyone to go back on their word.

There had been one short outing, an after-school fishing expedition with John. His delight in having both of his parents along was so clear that Tanya felt guilty for not accompanying them before. Not a single I-told-you-so look had come from Jake, only an occasional glance of shared satisfaction at the boy's happiness had been exchanged.

Tanya strolled along the winding private lane, enjoying her leisurely walk to the mailbox. Two o'clock. In another three hours Jake would be coming home from his almost daily journey to the firm's office in Springfield, sometimes in the company

of his father, but more often alone. It was frighten-
ing the way she had begun to look forward to the
hour of his arrival.

The shadow of a circling hawk flitted across the
ground in front of her as she neared the mailbox.
She glanced up at it, admiring his gliding flight
while shivering at the sinister silence of his
approach.

She opened the mail box and riffled through the
assortment of envelopes and catalogs. Her name
leaped out at her from the face of one of the
envelopes. There was no mistake that it was meant
for her and not Julia. It was addressed to Mrs. Tanya
Lassiter. Even as she ripped it open, she knew who
it would be from. These last few days she had tried
several times to compose a letter to Patrick, only
to have the words flow stiff and impersonally formal
from her pen. With a sinking heart, she read the
short message: "Meet me Wednesday at twelve
noon at the Persimmon Tree Restaurant. If you're
not there, I will know you couldn't get away.
Signed—Patrick."

Furtively, Tanya stuffed the letter in the pocket
of her jeans. She resisted the impulse to dash back
to the house and phone him. His assistant was a
stickler for details, and it would be impossible to
get through her without divulging her name. Since
Tanya had never had cause to call Patrick before,
her sudden interest in him would cause gossip.

Tomorrow was Wednesday. She had little time
to decide whether she was going to meet him or
not. To not go would only postpone things. Patrick
would no doubt send another, similar note. She
might not be so lucky the next time and someone
else might see it first. She had occasionally gone

shopping in Springfield, and she would arouse no one's suspicions if she went tomorrow. In that instant, Tanya knew she was going to meet Patrick without confiding in anyone the true purpose of her journey, least of all Jake. Somehow she just didn't believe that he would understand.

Her casual announcement that evening of her plans was taken very matter-of-factly, even by Jake. But she didn't escape quite as easily as she had thought she might after Jake spoke up.

"Why don't you meet me for lunch tomorrow?" he suggested.

A quick, apprehensive frown marred her poised expression. What excuse could she possibly give him for refusing his invitation? Her hesitation spoke for itself as did the slight narrowing of his gaze.

"On second thoughts, you'd better not plan on it," he said, offering her a way out as he leaned back in his chair. "I might not be free. Lunches have a way of turning into business meetings these days. Maybe another time?"

"Another time," Tanya nodded, smiling weakly in relief.

Did he suspect another reason, namely Patrick, for her obvious unwillingness to meet him? She seriously doubted it. Jake was more apt to blame it on a reluctance to be alone with him. Part of her wanted to assure him that that wasn't it at all and explain exactly why she was meeting Patrick, but there was a stronger, cold voice that kept saying it wasn't any of his business.

Dark clouds blotted out the sun. There was an ominous rumble of thunder in the distance increasing the drizzling rain to a steady pour, then allowing it to slack off again. A more melodramatic setting couldn't have been staged for her clandestine rendezvous with Patrick. Tanya had chosen to wear a simple navy blue dress, attractive but not eye-catching. She had sleeked her long hair back into a neat French braid that added severity to her features without taking away their perfection. If the sun had been shining, she thought wryly, she would probably have hidden behind dark glasses.

Still, when she looked at her reflection in the small car mirror, it was hard to believe that the poised, sophisticated woman looking back was herself. No one would guess that beneath that cool exterior she was a trembling mass of confusion and apprehensions. She had never done anything like this before and it made her feel oddly unclean, regardless of how innocent her reasons were. She resolutely thrust aside those feelings of embarrassment and shame that kept bringing unnatural color to her cheeks. But as she got out of her car, she glanced unconsciously around to see if anyone was watching. Then she used the umbrella to hide her face as she stepped over the puddles, not feeling safe until she reached the restaurant doors.

It was twelve o'clock on the dot when she deposited her raincoat and umbrella in the cloakroom. With a deep breath to calm her churning stomach, she walked towards the hostess, her gaze flitting about the room for a glimpse of Patrick.

"How many in your party?" the woman inquired politely.

"Two," Tanya replied. "I'm supposed to meet Patrick Raines here at noon. Would you know if he's arrived?"

"Mr. Raines, yes, of course," the hostess nodded. "Come this way, please."

As she followed the woman leading her down the long, narrow room, Tanya understood why Patrick had picked this particular restaurant. Despite its airy decor, there was also an air of intimate seclusion owing to the high backs of the leather booths and the concave chairs that closed around and hid their occupants from view. Patrick's table was in the rear, allowing little chance of their being seen. He rose briefly as she took the seat opposite him.

"I didn't think you would come," he murmured, an ardent fire darkening his eyes which Tanya couldn't meet.

"I—" she began, only to be halted by a person stopping at their table. She glanced up in alarm.

"Would you like a drink, miss?" an attractive waitress inquired.

"No, a cup of coffee, please." To quiet her jumping nerves, she added to herself.

"We'll order later," Patrick dismissed the waitress quickly, noticing the sudden pallor in Tanya's face followed by an immediate rush of bright pink. He moved to put a reassuring hand over hers, but she hastily drew it into her lap. Neither spoke until after the waitress had returned with their coffee.

"I'm sorry you're so uncomfortable, Tanya. I wish there was some other way we could meet," Patrick apologized.

"It doesn't matter," she shrugged nervously. "I only came to tell you this would be the first and last time I would meet you."

"What did you say?" A stunned disbelief underlined his words.

"I'm sorry, Patrick. But I just can't see you any more, like this."

"Why?" he demanded with that incredulous sound still in his voice.

"I tried to write you a letter and explain, but it sounded so cold and trite on paper. That's why I decided to meet you today, so I could explain—" Tanya glanced over at the rigidly set lines of his face, "that Jake and I have agreed to see if we can't make our marriage work."

"What?" Patrick's anger exploded around her. He leaned forward, controlling his temper with obvious difficulty. "You pretty much told me that you stayed married to Lassiter only because of your son. What's all this about?"

"It's about giving it a fair try," Tanya corrected stiffly, reacting to his sharp sarcasm. "It may not work out at all."

"If you feel that pessimistic, why did you bother to agree?"

Her motives were too uncertain to bear close scrutiny. If she was falling in love with Jake, as she suspected, there would come a time when she couldn't fool him any longer. Then the little affection and trust she might gain in these next few months would be destroyed. How would she be able to hold him except through John? And could she do that knowing the disgust Jake would feel for her?

Tanya drew a deep, shuddering breath. "I agreed because Jake indicated that if, after a few months' trial period, we didn't think our marriage could be successful, a divorce would be the obvious alternative."

Her explanation visibly abated his anger.

"Has divorce ever been mentioned before?"

"No, because of John. Since Jake's come home, he's seen that I don't say anything negative about him in front of John. I think Jake feels now that a divorce won't mean losing his son's affection and trust." And that knowledge depressed Tanya. "The Lassiters have a very strong sense of family ties. Unless I was willing to give up John, Jake would never have divorced me before."

"Then I'm sorry I got so angry." Patrick smiled apologetically. "I guess I can understand now why you agreed to go along with Lassiter's proposal. But where does that leave me?"

She had known that question would eventually arise. Some instinct told her it would be futile to ask him to wait—futile for Patrick.

"I can't see you anymore," she explained, meeting his gaze evenly so he could see the determination written in her eyes. His strong features took on a bleak look.

"Do you honestly believe Jake is going to stop seeing Sheila?"

Inwardly Tanya reeled from the almost physical impact of his question.

"I don't know if he is or not," she said, surprised by the calmness of her response. "It doesn't affect my decision to not see you again."

"Is there a reason why I should wait?" He methodically searched her face, a grimness stealing into his expression even before she replied.

"No, I'm not asking you to wait."

"That says it all, doesn't it?" he asked bitterly.

"I'm sorry, Patrick. I really am. I know you're fond of me—"

"Fond of you! That's the understatement of the

year!'' he muttered, turning abruptly away from the guilty look that appeared in Tanya's eyes. Then in an ominously quiet aside, he asked, ''Did you tell Jake you were coming here?''

''No, of course not,'' she replied in a startled voice.

''He's just walked in. No! Don't look around!'' he hissed as she started to turn in her seat.

Her stomach lurched with sickening nausea. ''Has he seen us?'' she whispered.

''No, I don't think he has. He's with that McCloud man from Denver. They just sat down at a table and Lassiter has his back to us.'' He darted her a cynical glance. ''I take it you don't want him to know that you met me today?''

''No,'' she murmured weakly, not able to draw a secure breath, knowing that any moment Jake could walk up to the table and confront them. ''What are we going to do?''

''We can't leave without being seen, so I suggest we have some lunch.'' Patrick shrugged, signaling to the waitress that they were ready to order.

Tanya picked at the salad she had ordered and ended up leaving most of it uneaten. Conversation was pointless, considering there was nothing left to be said and it was not a time to be discussing the weather. It seemed as though Jake was lingering an excessively long time over lunch and the minutes went by with nerve-racking slowness.

''I think they're going to leave,'' Patrick announced, darting a quick glance at their table. ''They are. They're walking to the front now. We'll give them a few minutes.'' Tanya felt as if she had been given a reprieve from the death sentence. In all they gave them ten minutes before Patrick went to get her raincoat and umbrella.

"We should probably leave here separately," he said.

"Yes," she nodded in numb agreement. Hesitantly she extended a hand to him. "I'm sorry the way things worked out, Patrick."

"Not half as sorry as I am," he replied, holding her hand for a brief second. "Good luck, Tanya. I'm afraid you're going to need it."

Tanya counted to a hundred before she left the restaurant alone. The drizzling rain had diminished to a light mist, so she didn't bother opening her umbrella for the short walk to her car. She paused at the narrow drive to allow an approaching car to pass before crossing. As it drew closer, she recognized with a growing terror that was her own car, and the man behind the wheel was Jake. Escape was impossible.

The car halted in front of her and Jake stepped out to walk around and open the passenger door. The fury in his expression sent shivers of fear down her spine while the coldness in his eyes froze any hope that she could explain.

"At which hotel are you supposed to be meeting him?" His mouth curled into a sneer.

Pride guided the hand that slapped his face and seconds later kept the tears at bay when he grabbed her by the shoulders. The cold glint in his eyes warned her of the rage she had aroused, but the humiliation his accusation had brought wasn't lessened by his anger. Jake shoved her roughly in the car and slammed the door.

Minutes later they were speeding down the highway, Tanya guessing that he was taking her home.

She was too miserable to care as he took the scenic back roads at an unlawful pace. His freezing silence was more condemning than his words, and she could have wept with pain. It was an agonizing journey, made more so by the stolen glances in his direction. Every time she gathered the courage to explain why she had met Patrick, it died before the words could ever reach her lips, cut down by the unrelenting set of his jaw.

The instant he stopped the car in front of the garage, Tanya bolted for the house, praying to reach her room before her control collapsed and the tears washed down her cheeks. But Jake was faster, his hand closing over her arm and jerking her back under the overhang.

"Where do you think you're going?" he ground out savagely.

Her words came out with bitter swiftness, uncaring that she was only adding salt to her own wounds. "To call Patrick, of course, so he won't worry when I don't show up! What else did you think?"

He clenched his fists. "The bargain we made didn't cover a lover on the side. What did you intend to do? Play both of us along?"

"For your information, I wasn't playing anybody along." Indignation gripped her throat. "I met Patrick to tell him I wouldn't see him any more, and I don't care whether you believe me or not!" He stared warily into her tawny brown eyes, which shimmered with unshed tears.

"I can't tolerate being lied to," Jake growled. "If this isn't the truth, I'll find out eventually." Tanya closed her eyes, feeling a tear escape her lashes and made a watery trail down her cheek.

"It's the truth, Jake," she murmured. He was

studying her face, openly seeking a sign of false-ness. "I thought it was only fair to let him know about our decision to—" Her voice broke in a sob. She bowed her head to fight for composure while brushing the tear from her cheek.

"You crazy, idiotic female," Jake declared with a humorless laugh. "When I saw you in that restaurant with Raines and realized that was why you had panicked when I asked you to meet me, I could have cheerfully beaten up both of you. Rad McCloud had to keep repeating himself because I couldn't concentrate on a thing he was saying. All I could think about was the two of you brazenly meeting in a public restaurant and you thumbing your nose at the agreement we'd just made."

"It wasn't like that," she declared. Her voice was choked, but she drew her head back to stare up at him with pride. His hands reached out, almost touching her shoulders before they fell back to his side. There was an enigmatic quality to his eyes that only told Tanya that the anger was gone.

"I know that now." He took one of her hands and held it gently in his own. The unconscious circular motion of his thumb had an oddly seductive effect. "I owe you an apology and this time I do apologize. I should have given you the benefit of the doubt, or at least heard your explanation before I laid into you."

"You believe me?" Tanya breathed. She hadn't expected that and it caught her unaware. She wanted to fling herself in his arms and be held there until all the coldness and pain melted away.

"Yes, I believe you." A ghost of a smile curved his mouth.

"Thank you," she said, withdrawing her hand

and lowering her gaze before she succumbed to her impulse. She moistened her lips, feeling his eyes catch the movement. "I should have told you what I intended to do."

"We don't trust each other yet," Jake said. "But look at it this way. Maybe we're learning to."

"How do you mean?" Tanya glanced at him warily.

"You've always known I have a bad temper, but I can admit I was wrong when I've made a mistake." His expression was friendly but nothing more. "And I've learned that you aren't the type of woman to deceive me deliberately. I'm glad you're honest, Tanya, because I don't like to be used."

"I think I guessed that," she swallowed and turned away.

"You didn't have a chance to do any shopping," Jake's low voice followed her. "Since I have to drive back to Springfield, you're welcome to come along."

"No. Thank you, but I don't really need anything." She managed a small, forced smile in his direction.

She thought he might follow her, but as she reached the front door, she heard the car door shut and the motor start. Jake was reversing out of the drive as she entered the house.

Tanya was setting the table for the evening meal when Jake returned in the company of his father. The tapping of her mother-in-law's shoes sounded in the hallway as she made her way to the foyer to greet her husband and son. There was a rush of smaller footsteps and Tanya knew John had heard them come in. Setting the last tumbler on the table, she wished that she could casually go meet them too, but she remained in the dining room listening to their voices.

"What have we here, Jake?" she heard Julia ask in a bright voice, followed immediately by John's, "What's that?"

"It's a present," Jake replied easily. "Where's your mother?"

"I don't know," John answered.

"Setting the table," Julia replied, a little coolly, Tanya thought, her curiosity aroused.

There was a rustle of paper and John saying, "They're pretty." Then firm footsteps approached the dining room and Tanya held her breath. Jake was coming to see her. She turned away from the open doorway until the quick glow of pleasure subsided from her eyes. Her fingers moved nervously, needlessly adjusting the silverware beside the china plates as he walked in to stop behind her.

"The table looks fine to me," he commented lazily, almost as though he knew her readjustment was a pretense to keep from looking at him.

"Hello, Jake. I heard you and J.D. come in," she said, beginning to turn to face him. "Dinner will be ready shortly."

Her calm expression turned to stunned surprise as she stared at the bouquet of tangerine-colored roses in his hands—a pure tangerine that was startling in its perfection.

"They're for you. Aren't you going to take them?" There was a gentle amusement in his voice. Numbly Tanya took the bouquet, a faint rose fragrance tickling her nose. One finger touched the velvet-soft petal of a full bloom to assure herself the tangerine roses were real.

"Do you like them?"

"They're beautiful," she replied in an awed tone, "But you didn't have to b—"

"I wanted to do it," his low-pitched voice replied quietly.

"Because of this afternoon," Tanya supplied, feeling a little sad.

"Oh, Tanya," Jake smiled, the caressing touch of his gaze making her heart beat faster. "We can't make up for the hurt we've done to each other in the past. We can only try not to hurt each other in the future."

"Then why the roses?" She stared into the depths of his eyes, trying to find a motive for his unexpected generosity.

"Simply because I wanted to buy some unusual flowers for an unusual woman. Is that all right?" The tenderly teasing words reached out to enfold her in their warmth.

"Yes," Tanya breathed, lowering her gold-flecked gaze to examine a rose. "No one's ever given me flowers before," she mused, not really realizing she had said it aloud.

"Not even a prom corsage?" he mocked.

"That's not the same thing," she said wistfully. Jake redirected his gaze to the rose she had been studying, touching its softness lightly with his hand, while Tanya watched.

"No, I guess it isn't the same thing," he agreed quietly. The amused line of his mouth held her mesmerized even as she recognized it coming closer to her. Then his mouth was brushing hers in an infinitely sweet caress that ended much too soon. The swiftly rising color in her cheeks made it difficult for her to look at him with any degree of composure.

"I'd better put these in water," she murmured, taking a hasty step backwards and nearly bolting from the room.

Julia was in the kitchen. A curious, almost doubting gleam came into her eyes when Tanya walked in with the roses. She followed her over to the sink, as though waiting for some explanation from her daughter-in-law—which didn't come.

"They are lovely, aren't they?" Julia finally spoke. "Why don't you arrange them in the Oriental vase? They would make a beautiful centerpiece for the table."

"If you don't mind, Julia, I'd rather take them to my room." Tanya darted a glance at the older woman, reluctant to share her first gift from Jake with the rest of the family while knowing she was being absurdly sentimental.

Julia Lassiter drew back coldly; her expression was one of just being slapped down after making a friendly gesture. "Well, of course you may take them to your room. I was only making a suggestion. Jake did give them to you." Her hurt tone plainly added that she thought she was a more worthy recipient of such a gift.

Tanya sighed, stubbornly refusing to let the hint of rebuke sway her decision to take the flowers to her room. She knew they weren't red roses, the flower of love. They were only meant as a friendly gesture on Jake's part, but that didn't count as much as the fact that he had given her something that he hadn't felt obligated to do.

"May I still use the Oriental vase?" she asked politely, knowing the exotic orange blooms would look exactly right with the brilliant patterns of greens, golds, blues, and oranges in the vase.

"Certainly," Julia smiled calmly, letting Tanya know that she could be generous and share her things even if Tanya would not.

Later that evening, in the solitude of her room, she singled out the special rose that Jake had touched and pressed it between the pages of her parents' Bible, the only possession she had kept of theirs. She chided herself for giving in to the romantic impulse that had prompted her actions. It was an open admission of love for her husband, a love that she had been fighting because she knew it would eventually bring her unbearable pain.

There was consolation in knowing that love wasn't really love until she had given it to Jake and had it returned. And she was determined that he would never know she found him more than physically attractive.

Still, it was in the hope of finding Jake that Tanya slipped out on to the patio, trying to fool herself into believing that she only wanted to see him to thank him once again for the roses. But it was his father she found relaxing in one of the cushioned redwood chairs on the moonlight-bathed patio. "Looking for Jake?" he inquired with a twinkle in his eyes, and didn't wait for her reply. "He's in the study looking over some blueprints and specifications on a new project. I don't think he'd mind the interruption."

"No, I wasn't looking for him," Tanya lied quickly, oddly embarrassed by J.D.'s acute perception. "John is in bed and I thought I'd step out for a breath of fresh air before doing the same."

He gestured towards a nearby chair. "Sit down.

It's a peaceful night.'' Tanya took the chair he had indicated and leaned against the cushioned back, finding he was right; it was a very peaceful night. For long moments they sat in silence. The fragrant scent of pipe smoke was the only thing that reminded her she wasn't alone.

"You and Jake seem to be getting along better," J.D. commented quietly. Instantly alert, she slid a quick glance in his direction.

"You don't hate my son any more, do you, Tanya?"

"No," she replied without elaborating further. She tried looking the other way, hoping to end the conversation before it had begun.

"When you first came here, I believe every breath you drew was a reminder to hate him for as long as you lived. Of course, time has a way of making that impossible.

"Perhaps that's true," Tanya sighed. "Or maybe time puts things in their proper perspective."

"I'm glad you said that." There was a smile in the older man's voice. "Maybe there's a chance the two of you can make your marriage work the way it should."

"I wouldn't count on that, J.D." Her face was clouded with a wistful sadness. "That's asking too much of vows taken without love."

"Love can grow in the most unlikely places, places where it doesn't seem to stand a chance of surviving. And a love like that, able to overcome all obstacles, is the most precious kind."

"Don't—please!" The words seemed torn from her throat. "I know you're trying to assure me that something good can happen after seven years, but don't get your hopes up." Tears were scorching the back of her eyes. "A love like that would be a miracle, and I don't think God is giving them away this year."

"I didn't mean to upset you, honey," J.D. frowned, but Tanya was already rising from her chair to race inside the house. She couldn't let his impossible dream take hold of her heart. Realistically she knew it didn't stand a chance of coming true.

Chapter Seven

The voices of both small boys were clamoring to be heard at the same time. Jake finally put two fingers in his mouth, emitting a shrill whistle that brought instant silence. Tanya bit back a smile, knowing firsthand how lively two seven-year-olds could be.

"The first place we're going to go is to Tom Sawyer's Landing," Jake decreed, holding up his hand as John groaned, "But I wanted to go to Fire-in-the-Hole first!"

"Me too," Danny Gilbert chimed in.

Jake repeated firmly. "We'll work our way around the park to Fire-in-the-Hole." His tone of voice brooked no opposition and the boys meekly gave in, setting off ahead in the direction of the general store. An eyebrow raised in amusement as Jake put a guiding hand on Tanya's elbow. 'What a pair!'

"I wondered if you knew what you were letting yourself in for when you suggested that John bring a friend along to Silver Dollar City," she laughed.

"You didn't think *I* was going to take him through Fire-in-the-Hole, did you?" Jake grinned.

"I should have known there was a method to your madness." Her smile accented the already radiant glow in her face that had nothing to do with the warm June sun, nor with the fact that she looked very attractive in her slim-fit jeans and a tightly crocheted lace blouse that hinted at the golden color of her skin without revealing it. It was based on the warm friendliness of the man at her side and the easygoing relationship that had developed between them. their

"Danny's a very curious kid." Jake was watching with amusement as the two youngsters entered the topsy-turvy fun house with gleeful abandon. "I had the impression I was being interrogated on the ride here."

"You were." Her gold-flecked eyes danced as she met his curious glance. "Danny Gilbert is the boy who had serious doubts that John had a father in Africa or that he had a father at all. So, all the questions about lions and tigers and zebras."

"Don't forget the elephants," Jake reminded her with an amused shake of his head.

"And the giraffes. I think you let John down when you told Danny that most of the animals were in game preserves and parks," Tanya scolded him with mock dismay.

"You should have warned me beforehand that Danny was the instigator of the letter that brought me home. I could have made up a tall tale of a safari into the jungle."

"I think John is quite satisfied just to have you home."

Jake's eyes traveled lightly over her face. "How about you? Are you glad I'm home?" There was a watchful stillness in his expression.

"There are moments when you're handy to have around," Tanya replied, refusing to answer his question seriously.

"It's nice to be useful," he commented with a teasing smile, not pressing for any other kind of admission. "Hey, here they come."

Danny and John burst from the side exit door with the same exuberance as when they had entered, dashing like a pair of whirlwinds towards Jake and Tanya.

"Where to next?" John asked in breathless excitement.

"The candy shop," Tanya answered.

"We have a sweet tooth in the crowd," Jake teased.

"Not really," she demurred. "I like to watch them make it, though."

Over a quarter of an hour later, the foursome walked out of the shop, all munching on sample pieces of freshly made peanut brittle.

"Can we go see the wooden Indians next?" Danny asked. At Jake's nod of agreement, he grabbed hold of John's arm. "Come on. Let's go over the swinging bridge."

Jake and Tanya set out after them at a more leisurely pace. Two teenage girls came walking towards them, giggling behind their hands and glancing over their shoulders, not paying the slightest bit of attention to where they were going.

One girl would have walked right into Jake if he

hadn't put his hands out to stop her. She glanced up at him in surprise, her face turning a brilliant shade of red as she mumbled a stammering "Excuse me."

"No problem." Jake winked, a wide smile on his face as he released his hold on her shoulders. Tanya knew by the dazed look on the girl's face that the Lassiter charm had made another conquest. She heard the awed exchanges after they had continued on their way and she smiled in secret agreement at the compliments they gave Jake.

"What's that smug smile for?" he asked, his gaze running possessively over her face.

"Oh, those girls thought you were cute," she mocked, reaching out to put a trailing hand on the bridge railing. The boys were just ahead, their heads hanging over the railing as they gazed into the ravine below.

"Do you agree?" he asked with lazy interest. She pretended to study his face as though she'd never seen it before. "I think," she tipped her head to one side to get a better view of his artfully carved features, "you're a little too arrogant to be truly handsome."

A low, rumbling sound of laughter followed her words as Jake reached out to enclose her waist with his hands. "Tanya Lassiter, you're flirting with me," he accused. Rolling waves of warmth spread out from where his hands touched her.

"I wasn't," her breathy protest was enforced by her fingers moving out to touch the tanned flesh of his bare arms in an attempt to ward him off.

"Yes, you were, and you're going to have to pay the consequences," he averred, his gaze centered on her parted lips.

"Jake, there are people watching." She glanced around quickly and couldn't see a soul anywhere near them. "And . . . and I don't see the boys."

"If those are the only reasons you have for not wanting me to kiss you, I'll wait," he agreed, flicking a finger over the pink color in her cheek.

They caught up with the boys at the woodcarver's shop, lingered with the youngsters as they watched a woodcarver at work, strolled through the area where the carvings were for sale, and paused in front of the wooden Indian at the entrance door. It was every bit as tall as Tanya, dressed in buckskins and a feathered warbonnet, implacable and proud, his hands folded in front of him.

"How would you like to have him guarding the foyer at home?" Jake asked John, who was studiously examining every hand-carved detail. "I think it would be great, but I bet Grandma wouldn't," the silken brown head nodded sagely.

"You're probably right, John," Jake agreed, ruffling the soft hair affectionately. He glanced at Tanya, an enigmatic expression on his face. "I envy that Indian."

"Why?" Her smile was curious.

"I don't have a wooden heart like he does."

Her pulse responded to the softly worded statement, pounding at a furious pace at the base of her throat. He was only flirting with her as she had done with him, but it disturbed her more than she cared to have him know. Luckily the boys were there and she could transfer her attention to them and ignore the gleam in Jake's eyes.

"Do you want to go on the Water Toboggan ride next?" she asked, knowing she would be met by instant agreement. Tanya turned a composed smile towards Jake. "I'd suggest the glass-blowing factory, but I'm afraid they'd be like bulls in a china shop."

"Oh, boy, the Water Toboggan!" Danny yelped.

"Are you two going to come along this time?" John asked, looking hopefully at his father.

Tanya was about to agree when Jake put a hand on her shoulder, his sudden touch stealing away her voice. "No, you and Danny go by yourselves," he commanded.

Minutes later Tanya stood near the fence protecting the Water Toboggan, watching as John and Danny disappeared around a corner. Jake was standing directly behind her, the heat from his body almost as warm as the sun's rays.

"Do you?" he asked cryptically.

"Do I what?" She half-turned to look at him over her shoulder. The light breeze blew a lock of hair across her cheek which Jake gently pushed back behind her ear.

"Do you have a wooden heart?"

"Of course not." Tanya laughed, trying to make his question a joke while her nerves vibrated from his nearness.

"Supposing I fell in love with you, what would you do?" Jake asked calmly. Her eyes widened with surprise and a little fear. "Don't look so frightened," he mocked. "I didn't say I was, only supposing I was in love with you."

She turned abruptly away from him, her gaze searching wildly about her for some avenue of escape, even as her heart plummeted at the overpowering thought. "I don't know what I would do," she murmured.

Jake continued to talk. "You're a beautiful and desirable woman. We've got along very well these last couple of months. I already know you're an excellent mother. You have a decidedly old-fashioned outlook on things which I admire and respect. In fact, you have most of the qualities I would want in a wife. A real wife, I'm talking about.'

"Now you're the one who's flirting with me," she teased, but her legs were beginning to refuse to support her.

"Maybe," he agreed smoothly. "What I said is also the truth. Now that I'm home, I want to stay here—with you. When I look at John, I think it would be good for him to have a brother . . . maybe even a sister with tawny eyes and long blond hair." His breath was stirring her hair with a devastating effect on her senses.

"Don't . . . don't talk that way," Tanya breathed, starting to move away before his fantasy could wreak more havoc, but his hands closed over her shoulders, bringing them back against his chest.

"Why not?" he murmured near her ear. "After these last few weeks, would it be so hard to love me?"

"No . . . I mean, yes . . ." The nibbling on her ear was destroying her ability for coherent thought.

His low chuckle rippled over her. "Make up your mind. Is it yes or no?"

"Please, Jake," she gulped, moving determinedly away in a desperate need to put space between them. "I can't think straight when you do that."

"That's a step in the right direction," he murmured with a lazy smile.

"It doesn't mean anything. Every human being responds to a caress," she corrected quickly. Deprived of his touch, she was fighting the withdrawal pains attacking her heart. "I like you. I think you're a good father. You're an attractive man as well. But I don't think I want to complicate my life by falling in love with you."

The frown on his face was a mixture of curiosity and amusement.

"How would falling in love with me complicate your life? Wouldn't it simplify it, since you're already married to me?"

"You don't understand," Tanya protested, finding herself caught in a trap of her own making.

"I'm trying to," Jake answered patiently. "Go ahead. Explain it to me."

"No," she shook her head in desperation, "I don't think so."

"Why not?" His gaze had become sharp and the hooded look was back in his eyes.

"I just don't want to," Tanya shrugged helplessly. "Not now anyway."

"I'm not playing games with you, Tanya," Jake said quietly. "I'm deadly serious when I say I want to make our marriage work. It hasn't been easy, but lately we've been able to put the past behind us. Don't try to hang on to that old bitterness. Think about the future for a change."

"I know," she sighed, a look of wistful sadness in her eyes when she met his gaze. "But there are some things a person just can't forget, no matter how hard they try."

"You've got to, Tanya," he said grimly. "You've got to, or else all this is worthless."

"You said yourself, Jake, that it would take time. Wishing won't make it happen faster," she murmured.

"Do you believe that we have a chance?" he

asked softly. Tanya glanced up to see he had moved a step closer to her.

"Sometimes," she breathed, gazing into his half-closed eyes. "Sometimes I do."

"I'm just going to have to change that "sometimes" into "most of the time'," he smiled, the confidence in his voice indicating that he could do it with a snap of his fingers.

"I wish you could." Tanya lowered her chin only to have him capture it in his hand and raise it back up.

"All you have to do is meet me halfway. I've never asked you to do all the giving," said Jake. "But marriage isn't a fifty-fifty proposition, as some people say. It has to be one hundred per cent on both sides to be a success."

"Have you ever considered that you might be asking too much from both of us?" she whispered the question.

"Have you ever considered the possibility that you're making mountains out of molehills?" His teasing question was accompanied by an exasperated shake of his head. "You can question something to death, you know. Let's take it day by day."

"Guess you have faith in the future." Tanya smiled.

"Don't you believe?" But he seemed to sense her unwillingness to reply to that question, knowing it would require an admission that she wasn't ready to make. Instead he reached out for her hand. "Here come the boys. Prepare yourself for the onslaught. Fire-in-the-Hole is the next stop."

Fire-in-the-Hole, Treetop House, the Buzzsaw Falls roller coaster—they made all the rides except for the Steam Train. They stopped to watch the construction of a log cabin, candles being made, and a potter at his wheel.

At the spinning shop, a woman demonstrated the use of a spinning wheel to make wool into yarn and showed them the weasel used to measure yarn into skeins. Forty turns of the weasel's wheel equaled a skein. The woman pointed out the notched metal disc in the wheel, explaining that there were forty notches to save the pioneers from counting each revolution. On the fortieth turn, a block fell into place, preventing the wheel from turning. The woman smiled warmly, "Or to quote the nursery rhyme—pop goes the weasel," to the delight of the crowd.

John was the one who signaled the end of their excursion through Silver Dollar City where unique rides were combined with exhibits of old-time crafts.

"I'm hungry, Mom," he declared, an announcement that quickly brought agreement from Danny.

"So am I, Mom," Jake added his laughing voice to the pleas of the two boys, his eyes twinkling at Tanya's blush.

"One picnic lunch coming up," she declared cheerfully, trying to cover the attack of embarrassed shyness his teasing words had evoked.

When they were all in the car ready to leave, Jake turned to her. "Where are we supposed to have this picnic?"

"Inspiration Point," she suggested.

"Inspiration Point it is," he agreed.

The picnic basket contained ample helpings of fried chicken, baked beans, and potato chips with the plastic plates and silverware. And there was potato salad, cole slaw and cider in the ice chest.

It didn't take long for the hunger pangs to be satisfied.

"Let's go up to the top of the hill and see the statues," John piped up the instant the food was cleared away.

Jake looked over at Tanya, tilting his brown head to one side. "Are you game?" he asked. "Or have you tackled enough hills for one day?"

"I'm never too tired to look at the view from this hill," she assured him, lightly accepting his outstretched hand. Once on top, she drew a deep breath. "It's beautiful, isn't it?" Tanya commented, her voice softly pitched. Even John and Danny stood in silence, the scene impressing them, too.

"Okay, listen up. This is your tour guide speaking." Jake's hand stole around her waist, drawing her into the shelter of his chest and arm. "Geologists claim that these Ozark hills are the oldest mountains or highlands on this Continent. It's amazing how after all these years they still manage to look untouched by civilization."

"Dad." John looked up, his face drawn into a quizzical frown. "How old is the Trail That Is Nobody Knows How Old?"

"You've answered your own question," Jake smiled. "Nobody knows how old it is."

"Why don't they?" he persisted.

"Well, when the first settlers came here in the late eighteen-hundreds, the trail was here, curving along to Dewey Bald and on to the outside world miles away. Those settlers said the fur traders and trappers used it before them. The trappers said the French and Spanish explorers traveled over it, guided by the Indians who had used it before the explorers. And the Indians said the trail was there before them when the Old Ones walked the hills. So you see, it was named correctly—The Trail That Is Nobody Knows How Old."

John nodded, and stood there gazing intently at the scene.

"He's an intelligent kid," said Jake, lowering his voice so that his comment was for Tanya's ears alone. "But too serious sometimes," she added absently, enjoying the gentle rise and fall of his chest beneath her head as she stared dreamily at the panoramic view.

"Right now he looks like a normal, healthy boy to me," Jake chuckled, bringing her gaze around to John. The moment of inactivity had passed and he and Danny had erupted into a noisy game of tag. "You worry about him too much, honey." His lips brushed the top of her hair in an affectionate caress.

"I suppose I do," she agreed ruefully, resisting the impulse to snuggle closer. "But that comes from having to stretch yourself from one parent into two."

"You don't have to do that any more." His arm tightened, drawing her nearer.

She tilted her head back to look up at him, delighted by the brightness in his eyes. "I know I don't," she said, letting the slow smile of happiness widen her mouth.

"One of these days," Jake murmured, "I'm going to accept that invitation written on your lips no matter who's watching."

A wave of radiant confusion colored her face and she wondered if he could feel the sudden leaping of her heart.

"Look, there's a persimmon tree over there."
She spoke to distract his attention away from her.

"We'll have to go persimmon and paw-paw picking this autumn after the first good frost," Jake nodded.

"I'd like that."

"You don't think we're planning too far ahead?" he whispered, nuzzling her ear playfully. Tanya drew back in surprise. "It's too late!" Jake laughed. "You've already committed yourself to going with me and I'm not going to let you back out. We have a date for this fall, so, my little honey, you'd better plan to stick around."

"That's not fair," she protested.

"All is fair," he mocked.

Tanya would have pursued her argument if John hadn't come running towards them with Danny only a step behind him.

"Can I trade my pocketknife to Danny for Harry? He said I could have him if I gave him my knife. Can I, please?" he urged.

"First of all, who is Harry?" Tanya asked with an indulgent smile. "He's my pet—" Danny replied, sliding a sideways glance at John. "You don't want to give away your pet, do you?" Jake asked, amusement and suspicion in the gaze that encompassed the pair.

"My mother says I have to get rid of it anyway," Danny shrugged.

"Can I trade him my pocketknife?"

"I don't know—" Tanya began, only to have Jake interrupt.

"Exactly what is Harry?"

"Exactly?" Danny repeated, shifting uncomfort-

ably from one foot to the other. "Harry is my pet
. . . tarantula."

"A spider?" A violent shudder quaked over Tanya's shoulders and down her spine.

"Tarantulas don't hurt you, Mom," John rushed
in. "They aren't poisonous. Dad told me so. He
said the ones in the jungle are, but these around
here don't hurt you when they bite you any more
than a wasp sting hurts. They just crawl up your
arm and make friends."

"No, absolutely not!" she stated unequivocally.

"Ah, Mom, please," John wheedled. "I'd keep
him outside."

"Your mother said no, John," Jake stepped in.
"There won't be any more discussion about it, all
right?"

His head bobbed glumly in agreement as he
scuffed his shoes in the gravel. "Come on, Danny,"
he grumbled.

As the pair trotted away, Tanya shivered again
and began vigorously rubbing her arms. "I can
almost feel that horrible thing crawling on me right
now," she shuddered.

"Little Miss Muffet," Jake teased. "Are you afraid
of spiders?"

"Phobic," she declared fervently. "It doesn't
matter how harmless they are. Even a daddy-long-
legs can get me standing on a chair. I know it's
silly, but I can't seem to help it."

"Well, be glad John asked before he made the
trade. The poor kid would have been minus a
pocket knife and a spider the second you found
out about it," Jake grinned.

"I can be thankful for that," she agreed, shuddering again.

"Or you could keep me around as your official spider-slayer," he suggested with a decidedly tongue-in-cheek expression.

"That's the best proposition you've made," Tanya laughed.

"With a little encouragement," his eyes made a slow, deliberate appraisal of her curved figure, "I'd make a few more."

"I think . . ." His lustful look made it difficult to speak. "I think it's time we took Danny home."

"You're good at dodging the issue, aren't you?" Jake said, but got no reply from Tanya. "Okay, we'll call it a day. A very enjoyable day."

"Yes, it was," she agreed softly.

That day spent almost entirely in each other's company seemed to put their relationship one plateau higher than before. Jake paid more little attentions to her, greeting her specifically when he came home and not including her any more in a general greeting, holding her hand when she was standing or sitting next to him. A lot of little things that were not significant on their own, but very special when looked at as a whole. Tanya could almost believe that he wanted to love her as a person, not as the mother of his child.

It was becoming more and more easy to turn her face to his for the goodnight kiss that was slowly becoming a habit. He was always gentle and controlled, never demanding more than she was willing to give. Yet her reticence, born of fear, increased in the same proportion as her love for Jake. The rapport between them was bittersweet agony, made all the more painful by the shattering secret that kept pushing itself forward every time she thought she and Jake had a chance for happiness together.

Perhaps if she had told him at the beginning, Tanya thought to herself as she idly plucked at the cord around the cushion of the redwood lounge chair. But where was the beginning? She only knew she had kept it from him too long for Jake to understand and forgive her.

The patio door to the house slid open, drawing a casual glance from Tanya. Her eyes widened as Sheila Raines walked confidently towards her, dressed in the latest thing from the mall.

"Hi," she greeted Tanya cheerfully. "Is Jake around?"

"No, he hasn't come home yet." A stillness crept into Tanya's expression, instantly on guard at Sheila's familiar tone.

Red lips pursed in a pout. "Too bad. He said he was coming home early today, and I hoped to catch him here. Do you know how long he'll be?"

"No, I don't." Tanya wasn't about to let Sheila know that Jake hadn't confided his plans to her. "Would you like to wait for him?"

"No." Sheila glanced at her diamond-studded watch. "I really have to run." A dramatic sigh shuddered through her. "I really, really wanted to see him this afternoon."

"Was it important?" Tanya asked archly, disliking the possessive ring in the girl's voice. "I could give him a message for you."

"Would you?" The voice gushed as though Tanya were doing her an enormous favor. "I could phone him later on, of course, but I don't like to intrude on the time he spends with his son."

"That's very thoughtful of you," Tanya murmured, her temper seething closer to the surface.

"He can call my cell phone—he has the number—but tell him it's one o'clock Saturday instead of two at the Country Club."

"Saturday at one. I'll give him the message." Tanya nodded curtly.

"Thanks," Sheila purred, turning as if to leave only to stop and add, "I almost forgot. I looked at that piece of property he was interested in buying. Tell him that it just won't do at all. It's practically inaccessible. The lakefront part is all submerged trees and the view is totally boring. I'll give him the rest of the details on Saturday. Maybe then we'll have time to go look at the property together."

Tanya was too angry to trust herself to speak. Jake had never mentioned that he was looking at land for sale in the area. Had these last months together been a trick intended to lull her into believing Jake cared while he continued to carry on his affair with Sheila? Sheila's unexpected visit had made the affirmative answer to that question very apparent.

Something in her expression must have betrayed the doubts and jealousy in her heart, because the brunette's dark eyes glittered with spiteful satisfaction as she waved goodbye and started for the patio door.

"I'll tell Patrick you said hello," she chirped.

Chapter Eight

Sheila had been gone only a half hour when Tanya heard a car in the drive. Since Sheila had told her that Jake was coming home early today, she guessed that it had to be him. The anger that had seethed to the boiling point demanded she rush out to confront him with her knowledge of what was going on with Sheila, but she remained in the lounge chair, the fury in her eyes hidden by sunglasses.

It was several moments before the patio door opened and closed and Tanya glanced up to see Jake carrying two iced drinks in his hands. His gaze slid over her bare legs to the white shorts and the blue polka-dot top. In other circumstances his raking gaze would have disturbed her. Now she knew its falseness.

"Cold nectar for the sun goddess," Jake mocked, handing her one of the glasses as he continued to stand above her. That lazy smile pierced her guard and sent her pulse leaping. Tanya suppressed a shudder over how completely she had succumbed to his virile charm.

"I hadn't expected you home so soon," she murmured, allowing only a saccharine smile to tug the corners of her mouth.

"Mom stopped into the office this noon to have lunch with Dad. She mentioned she'd dropped John off at one of his friend's house for a birthday party. I knew I wouldn't have a better opportunity to be alone with my wife, so I persuaded her to do some shopping and drive Dad home later when she'd picked up John."

Tanya rose to her feet on the opposite side of the chair where Jake was standing. Bitterness rose in her throat, with the knowledge that once such a statement would have elated her.

"I had a visitor this afternoon," she announced casually, minutely examining his face through the protective darkness of her glasses.

"Oh? Who was it?"

"Sheila Raines." Her mention of the name brought a brief moment of guarded stillness to his face as his eyes narrowed.

"What did she want?" His tone of voice sounded curious but indifferent.

"Actually she didn't come to see me. It was you she was looking for." Tanya was glad he didn't try to look surprised. In fact she found malicious pleasure in the grimness of his expression.

"Did she say why?"

"She did leave a message," Tanya nodded, glancing down at her drink, then she tilted her head back at a challenging angle. "Meet her at one o'clock instead of two at the Country Club on Saturday. She didn't say which one, but I'm sure you know." His blue eyes glittered with ominous coldness at the edge in her voice. "And she also said she looked at that piece of property you were interested in and—in her words—it won't do at all—something about submerged trees in the lake and bad roads. She said the two of you could look over some other property on Saturday."

"I intended to tell you about that this afternoon." The muscle twitching in his jaw indicated the tight check on his temper.

"Well, now you don't have to tell me, do you?" she mocked sweetly. "I already know."

"You only know the part that Sheila told you, and you seem to have put the wrong spin on that," he snapped.

"Oh, spare me the explanations!" Tanya cried angrily, letting go of her temper. "I know you can twist things around to make it sound as if you've done nothing wrong."

"I haven't. Not the way you mean," Jake bit out.

"You told me you couldn't tolerate being deceived," she laughed bitterly. "That same day Patrick told me you were still seeing Sheila, but I refused to take him seriously. I accepted your word that you were going to try hard to make our marriage work. I should never have trusted you!"

A string of muttered imprecations came from Jake as he covered the distance between them with the swiftness of a striking cobra. "Listen to me!" he growled, grabbing her shoulders and shaking her. But Tanya was just as quick to twist free, her anger pumping strength into her body.

"I've listened to your lies for the last time!"

"You're doing the very same thing I did—accusing me and convicting me without even waiting for my explanation." His tall form loomed over her, formidable in his leashed fury.

"How stupid do you think I am?" Tanya asked, bitter shame bringing tears of anguish to her glittering gold eyes. "Do you expect me to believe you again when you make up some story to explain away the intimate relationship Sheila made so clear." Jake opened his mouth to speak, but her hand forestalled his words. "No, don't say anything. You never once said you were giving Sheila up—in fact, you avoided the answer the only time I asked, so it really was only a white lie. Maybe I deceived myself. It doesn't matter any more now that I know the truth."

"But you don't know the truth! You won't listen to the truth!" His husky voice was harsh with angry exasperation. The shrill ring of the telephone sounded from inside the house. Jake determinedly ignored it. "You'd better answer that," Tanya murmured coldly. "Sheila said she might call later."

His gaze was ruthlessly thorough as it swept over the implacably firm expression on her face; the line of his mouth was grim as he turned away to stride into the house.

After his departure, the anger that had sustained her began to ebb away and Tanya could have wept at the unbearable pain in her heart. Without the support of her avenging rage, she sagged weakly against the patio railing, knowing she had a few minutes' respite to regain her strength before Jake returned. Or so she thought, until the patio door slid open.

"Tanya, come in here," he ordered in an uncompromising voice. She didn't even glance in his direction as she shook her head no. "Come in here or I'll come and drag you in!"

Something in his voice told her he would do that very thing if she refused him again, so she walked slowly towards him, keeping her shoulders squared and her gaze averted from the harshness of his. She didn't attempt to shake free of the hand that closed over her arm and led her forcibly towards the telephone in the foyer, the receiver off the hook lying on top of the small stand.

Jake picked it up and spoke into the mouthpiece. "Repeat what you just told me, Dad." Then he thrust it against Tanya's ear.

"Repeat it?" J. D. Lassiter's voice echoed with surprise. "All I said was that the meeting for the executives and area engineers of the firm was changed from Saturday at two o'clock to one o'clock. It's an informal meeting with the wives invited, so be sure to let Tanya know. She'll want to make arrangements for a babysitter for John. What's so difficult to remember about that?"

The rigidity went out of her body, carried away by the shuddering sigh that acknowledged the grievous error of her accusation. "Thanks, Dad," said Jake, taking the receiver back.

"Wait a minute," said J.D., his faraway voice carrying to Tanya's ears. "Your mother just reminded me that Sheila left a list of unimproved land for sale on my desk. I won't be coming to the office tomorrow, so be sure to pick it up from my secretary. I never believed she'd actually get her real estate license," he laughed. "But she's a hard enough woman to be a success at selling. Beauty and ruthless perseverance are a potent combination."

This time Tanya's eyes flashed open, rounded in shock and pain as she stared into Jake's implacable. Anger still glittered in his blue eyes. He was speaking into the telephone, but she was too stunned to hear what he was saying.

"I'm sorry, Jake, I'm very sorry," she whispered, taking a frightened step backwards before pivoting to stumble clumsily outside.

She couldn't face him, not now, not after she had so wrongly misjudged him. Her mumbled apology couldn't adequately make up for all the horrible things she had said. As she sped down the path leading from the patio to the lake, she knew she should have waited until she had heard Jake's explanation. But her jealousy ran so deep that she probably wouldn't have believed him even then. And Jake guessed that.

Tears spilled over her cheeks, blurring her vision until she couldn't see where she was going. At the layered shelf of rocks a few yards away from the lake's edge, she stopped, her feet crumpling beneath her as she sagged to the ground to weep freely. Unconsciously she pushed away the sharp, loose rocks that jabbed into her body. The grief and misery and frustration that had been building up over the last seven years were released in a torrent of racking sobs that shook her body until there weren't any tears left.

As the last shuddering sobs faded away, she pressed a hand to her temple and leaned back against the rocks to stare at the brilliant blue summer sky. She felt like a lost child who had run away and only wanted to find her way back again. The

numbness began to leave as a fly landed lightly on
her arm, then buzzed away. Irritatingly it came
back to flit around her face until she moved her
hand to flick it away.

Something brushed her leg once, then again.
Tanya leaned forward to rid herself of the fly—
and horror rose in her throat as she stared at the
large hairy body of a tarantula. Basically a night
creature, the scattering of loose rocks had disturbed his burrow and now he was preparing to
cross the obstacle in his path—her legs. Tanya was
too terrified to move, frozen by the sight of the
mammoth spider. But when it began to crawl on
to her petrified legs, she screamed.

In her terror, she didn't recognize that she was
calling Jake's name over and over again. Nor did
she hear the sound of footsteps racing towards her.
The only thing that registered was the tanned hand
brushing the spider off her leg and the pair of
arms that reached down and pulled her to her feet.
Then she was crushed against a muscular chest,
the arms wrapped around her, a hand stroking her
hair as she gasped in shuddering breaths against
the warm body.

"It's okay. You're all right now," a soothing voice
whispered in her ear.

"Jake, Jake," she moaned.

"I'm here. Take it easy now, nothing's going to
happen. The spider's gone," he assured her quietly. "There's nothing to be afraid of any more."

"I can still feel him crawling on me," she cried
softly, her voice still trembling from the depths of
her unreasoning fear. Although it was impossible,
Jake seemed to draw her close against him, and
her arms circled his waist to cling tightly to him.

"Are you all right now?" he asked, gently tucking her hair behind her ear.

Tanya nodded numbly, keeping her face pressed against the reassuring solidness of his chest. "I know it's silly to be so frightened, but I can't help it," she murmured. "Hold me a little while longer, please, Jake."

"As long as you want," he agreed with real warmth in his voice.

It was several more minutes before Tanya reluctantly untangled her arms from around his waist. Her legs still felt weak and unsteady, but enough of the shock had worn away to make her feel self-conscious over the way she was clinging to him.

"I think I'm all right now," she murmured, keeping her eyes downcast as he let her move to arm's length.

"Have you forgiven me?" Jake asked softly as he caressed her warm cheeks with his hand.

"F—for what?"

"For not being here in my official role as spider-slayer," he teased.

An embarrassed laugh slipped from her mouth. "Of course. I thought you were talking about Sheila."

"We won't talk about her now," he said, tilting her chin as he ran his thumb along her lower lip and gazed deeply into her gold-flecked eyes. "You aren't up to the discussion I want to have."

"I want you to know that I realize how wrong it was not to you explain earlier," Tanya persisted.

"I told you we'd discuss it later." Mock exasperation beamed from his face.

"I know." Like a child, she needed the reassurance of his forgiveness. "But I had to tell you how badly I feel."

"You're stubborn," he smiled slowly, pulling her gently into his arms again.

His warm, moist mouth covered hers, moving sensually against it until her lips parted in response. But when her hands moved up to his neck to draw him into a deeper kiss, Jake halted them with his own hands, slowly raising his mouth from hers.

"Your apology is accepted." Thick lashes acted as a smoky veil to conceal the smoldering fire in his gaze. "Now, do you want to walk up to the house or shall I carry you?"

"I'd better walk," Tanya declared breathlessly, knowing that if she were cradled in his arms the way she was feeling at this moment, she would be shamelessly caressing him.

"You don't feel safe in my arms anymore, hm?" he mocked, and chuckled when she didn't answer.

He kept a steadying hand on her arm as they traveled over the rocky path back to the house. Inside, he escorted her to her room.

"Go in there and freshen up," he ordered. "We'll have a talk when you're done."

"What talk?" she asked, but he had already gently shoved her into the room and was closing the door.

Was it about Sheila? Tanya wondered, then shrugged. She was too drained of emotion at the moment to think straight. The thought of a brisk shower to chase away the last creeping sensation of the tarantula was very inviting.

She had just toweled herself dry and slipped on her ivory satin robe when there came a knock on her door. "Come in," she called, untying the ribbon that bound her hair on top of her head, shaking the damp tendrils loose with her fingers.

"You look much better," Jake declared, pausing for a moment in the doorway, his tall figure imposing itself in the suddenly small room. He walked on in, handing her a tall, frosted glass of lemonade. "There isn't any fear in your eyes now."

Tanya couldn't keep the sudden light from springing into them when she looked into his ruggedly handsome face. "Guess I made a complete fool of myself," she murmured, turning away to take a sip of the drink, then set it on the dressing table to begin brushing her hair. 'I wish I could get over that childish fear of spiders. But those tarantulas are so grotesque."

Her composure had returned and she was grateful for it. There was a rustle of paper near the bed. As she glanced behind her, she noticed for the first time the roll of blue paper Jake had carried under his arm.

"What's that?" she asked, watching curiously as he unrolled it on the bed.

"Come and look."

He stood quietly beside her as she stared down at the rectangular drawing. "It's a blueprint of a house," she said.

"Not of a house," he corrected. "It's our home." His gaze steadfastly met her startled glance. "Since Sheila insisted on telling you that I was interested in buying some property, I decided I might as well tell you the rest."

"What do you mean—our home?" Tanya breathed.

"Aren't you getting tired of living with my parents?'' he asked. ''Not that I don't love them dearly, but wouldn't you like a home of your own?''

''Of course, but—'' she hesitated, recognizing the implication of his words.

''Then you'd better give me your opinion of this layout. There may be something you want to change.'' Jake didn't give her an opportunity to comment as he pointed out the location of the living room and family room, the kitchen and the proposed location of its appliances, the bathrooms, and the bedrooms, showed her where the fireplace would be and the washroom area. ''Do you like it?'' he concluded.

''It's beautiful,'' she murmured, ''but—'' Her voice trailed away as she shook her head to keep from falling under the enchantment of the dream house.

''What's the matter, honey?'' His hand raised her chin so he could look more closely into the troubled expression in her eyes. ''Don't you think it's about time we jumpstart our marriage?''

She was suddenly tense, too afraid to speak and equally afraid not to. She stared at him as if memorizing his face, knowing how very much she loved him. ''Oh, Jake,'' she murmured helplessly.

Instantly he drew her into his arms, his mouth passionately raining kisses over her face as though every perfect feature was precious to him. Her heart pounded wildly against her ribs at his touch. He nibbled at her earlobe, then sent an erotic trail of fire along her neck as he nuzzled the sensitive skin.

''I've wanted to do this for so long,'' he murmured huskily into her ear, his breath fanning the flames already racing through her.

The satin robe was like a second skin covering her nakedness as his hands caressingly molded her to his lean body, sliding over her hips and up to her shoulders. All the while his mouth sensually explored the hollow of her throat, pushed aside the satin to kiss her shoulders until Tanya was lost in desire. With a passionate cry, she captured his face in her hands and brought it to her mouth, letting him take it captive with his own.

For long moments, Jake tasted her succulent lips, bruising them with the fierceness of his passion, parting them roughly so he could know the full response of his lovemaking. Her fingers twined themselves in his hair as she moaned his name against his lips. There was wild joy in their intense hunger of each other's caress, a hunger that went beyond the bounds of the physical to a joining of their souls.

Reluctantly Jake pulled his lips from hers, roughly dragging his kiss along her face to the top of her hair. "You don't know the self-control I've exercised to keep myself from making love to you like this before now." His ragged breathing and his voice, raw with desire, only confirmed how completely Tanya's response had aroused him.

Her fingers ran ecstatically over his shoulders and arms, glorying in the muscles that swelled to bind her tighter in his embrace. Then she directed them to the open collar of his shirt, pushing it aside to kiss the hollow of his throat above the dark hair on his chest.

"Kiss me, Jake," she commanded in a husky whisper as her mouth moved upwards to the strong chin.

"Tanya," he groaned, resisting the pull of her

hands that would have brought his mouth down on her again. "I want more than kisses from you."

His gaze moved from the tempting invitation of her mouth to search her eyes for the answer to his unasked question. The advantage was all Jake's. If he had chosen to possess her, Tanya wouldn't have resisted. Now he was giving her a choice and fear sliced through her heart. She wanted to fight her way out the arms that held her in a tender but not confining embrace. Bitter tears burned her eyes. She felt his strong arms circle her waist and pull her against his chest. She was glad her back was to him and he couldn't see the misery and pain in her eyes.

"Don't be frightened, Tanya." His mouth moved over her hair so that his velvet-rough voice whispered near her ear. "This is about more than just sexual desire, although I want you desperately."

"Oh, Jake!" His name was a pleading cry of protest drawn achingly from her heart. It was not his touch that she feared, but his anger.

"Hush, love," he murmured, tightening his arms so she was molded more firmly to his muscular body. "You're entitled to the words. We both need them to take away the last of the bitterness."

"Jake, I—"

"Don't talk. Just listen," he scolded her tenderly. "I love you. Maybe I always have. I don't know. I only know that I'm in love with you now, more deeply every minute."

A moan of intense longing escaped her lips as she sagged weakly against him, knowing her own love was as strong as his. "Don't say any more, Jake, please," she begged, wishing only to have this moment last for an eternity.

There was a moment of hesitation and Tanya sensed that Jake wanted action to take over where his words had left off.

"Let me finish," he demanded huskily. "Because after this moment I never want to bring up the past again." He drew a deep, shuddering breath. "I didn't come home because of that letter you sent me. I used it as an excuse. Not that John wasn't a factor, too, because he was. I wanted to see my son. But even more, I wanted to see my wife, that beautiful woman in the photograph. You, Tanya. The woman who had haunted me for seven years with the golden rays of sunlight in her hair and eyes."

There was a bittersweet song in her heart. Perhaps their love was strong enough to overcome the anger and hostility of the past and enable him to understand why she had deceived him all these years. "This is what happened—and understand that my brother and I were very close. We were more than brothers. I don't remember telling you I would come back that night at the fair, but I intended to—until Jamie was killed." Tanya could feel the pain in his voice and her heart cried for his loss. "He was so young, Tanya, with so much of his life ahead of him. I became terribly cynical and bitter. What memory I retained of that shy, sunshine girl I met became tainted by those emotions. Then when I saw you that day, more beautiful than I remembered, I cursed myself for not looking for you before, especially when I saw the baby in your arms. And that cold contempt in your eyes unnerved me. I knew you wanted me to go away and leave you alone, but I couldn't. That's why I pretended to take such an interest in the baby."

His arms tightened about her as he rocked her gently against him, as if it would ease the pain in both their hearts.

"I'll never forget that first wave of shock that went through me when you said don't you recognize him? He's your son! At first I thought you were lying, that you'd found out about the relative wealth of the Lassiter family and wanted it for your illegitimate baby. DNA testing would be the final test, but I wasn't convinced even when you showed me the crooked little finger, the Lassiter birthmark. Not until later when I went to that squalid apartment where you were living did I accept the fact that he was my son, even if I couldn't remember the act of conception. Tanya, can you ever forgive me for that?" he whispered.

"There's nothing to forgive," she answered fervently, trying to turn to face him, but his arms held her where she was.

"When I asked you at your apartment if he was really my son, I can still remember that light shining in your eyes when you confirmed it again. In that moment I knew you weren't lying, that you weren't capable of lying." His mouth moved along her neck. "That's the one thing that's stood out in our marriage—your honesty. It was one of the first things I loved about you. It became the foundation of my love for you."

"Oh, no, Jake, no," Tanya groaned. Her heart that had been singing so joyously sank with sickening swiftness. The room reeled in front of her eyes as she wished the ground would open up and swallow her.

"I don't blame you for hating me at first," Jake murmured. "I did force you to marry me. I can't even be sure now if I did it to have my son or to have you as my wife. I only know that I despised myself for all you must have suffered because of me. Every time you looked at me I was reminded of why you loathed me. You didn't drive me away, Tanya, I drove myself away. None of that was your fault. The blame is strictly mine." There was a moment of hesitation as he gently squeezed her waist. "You do see why I had to tell you all this, don't you? You've been so honest with me that I had to do the same."

Honest! Honest! The word was haunting her. There wasn't any way she could tell him the truth now. Her supposed honesty was the one thing he admired about her. She couldn't destroy it or it would destroy his love for her.

"Why? Why did you have to tell me all this?" she sobbed, wrenching herself free from his arms. "Don't you see it doesn't matter?"

"Honey, what's the matter with you?" The surprised and gentle concern in his voice only increased the pain.

"Oh, Jake, Jake!" Her head moved from side to side in anguish. There was only one way out of this situation. He would hate her for it, but not nearly as much as he would if he found out the truth. "Please, I want a divorce."

"A divorce?" he repeated in disbelief, taking a step to erase the distance between them. His gaze was staring holes into her. "Is this some kind of a joke?"

"No, it's not a joke. I want a divorce."

His hands closed over her shoulders, spinning her around to stare into her face. "I just told you I love you! Are you trying to tell me that you don't love me?'' he demanded angrily. ''Is that what you're saying?''

''I'm saying I want a divorce,'' she answered more firmly, not able to meet the piercing regard of his eyes. ''Isn't that answer enough?''

''No, dammit! It isn't!'' He looked at her warily. ''I'm not so inexperienced that I don't know when a woman wants me, and I know that a moment ago you wanted me as badly as I wanted you.'' The angry and confused expression on his face made Tanya's heart weep with pain. ''I know you love me. Admit it!''

''Stop it, Jake.'' Her hands moved to his chest, trying to push herself away as he pulled her to him.

''I want an explanation!'' One hand moved to the small of her back, arching her against his hips, while the other hand wound its fingers in her hair, twisting her head up towards his.

''You're hurting me,'' she whispered, frightened by the cruel line of his mouth.

''I love you,'' he growled, angry fires leaping in his eyes. ''I'll make you love me!''

He swung her into his arms, warding off the futile efforts of her hands to prevent him as he carried her to the bed. The blueprints were brushed aside before he dropped her onto the blue satin coverlet. The rough handling loosened the sash around her waist and the robe opened to show the tanned length of her legs. As her hand reached down in a frightened effort to cover herself, his fingers closed over her wrists, thrusting her backwards onto the bed while the full weight of his body pressed down on her.

His gaze was hard and alien as he stared into her face, without the seductive light that usually thrilled her. His head came down to capture her mouth, but Tanya twisted her head away.

"You wanted my kisses before," he jeered, maneuvering her hands until both wrists were held by one hand and he used the other to move her face to his.

"Please, Jake, don't do this," she whispered in a trembling voice. "It won't change anything. I'll still want a divorce. Please, Jake, please!"

"I don't believe you," he said coldly.

Tears gathered in the corners of her eyes. "I don't have the strength to stop you, Jake."

He stared down at her for a long moment. "Damn you!" he muttered savagely as he broke free from the pleading look in her eyes and rolled off of her onto the floor. A shuddering sob moved through her as his footsteps carried him away from the bed. The door of her bedroom opened, then closed with a resounding slam.

"Oh, Jake, I love you," Tanya sobbed into her pillow.

Chapter Nine

There was a lot of door-slamming in the course of the next days as Jake refused to be in the same room with Tanya. A brooding anger followed him like a dark cloud wherever he went until even John hesitated to approach him. Tanya wondered if he even slept, because she could hear the restless pacing at night coming from the room across the hall.

The blue circles under her own eyes were evidence of her insomnia. Countless hours she lay awake, staring at the ceiling, wishing she could cross the hall and admit her love. But she didn't. Jake would never understand. So she suffered through the sleepless nights, and the reproachful glances from Julia that plainly placed the blame for her son's departure before breakfast and his return after the evening meal on Tanya's shoulders. J.D. was the only one who looked at her with anything resembling sympathy. Yet he too seemed a bit grim and withdrawn.

Poor John was the one who was suffering the most. The hostile atmosphere in the house was something he hadn't experienced before. Danny Gilbert had asked him to spend the night at his house and Tanya had agreed—somewhat reluctantly, it was true, because she selfishly wanted him around her to deflect as much of her attention as possible from Jake.

She was on her way to John's room to make sure all the necessities for an overnight stay had been packed when she passed Jake's doorway and glanced in. Her steps faltered, then stopped. Jake was standing in front of a mirror patiently tying a silver and blue striped tie to complement the perfectly tailored gray summer suit he was wearing. The elegant suit seemed to accent the cynical, world-weary hardness of his chiseled features. Tanya hadn't even known he was home yet and it looked as though he were getting ready to leave. His flint-hard eyes caught her reflection in the mirror.

"Are you going out?" she asked, feeling the need to say something since he had noticed her standing there.

"Yes."

"Danny Gilbert asked John to spend the night with him."

"So?" His eyes flicked over her reflection as he secured the tie clasp to his shirt.

"I thought perhaps you could take him," Tanya suggested, not really sure why she was saying it at all except to have an excuse to talk to Jake a little while longer.

"Can't anyone else take him?" he asked coldly.

"Well, yes, of course," she fumbled. "But John would like it if you did. He doesn't quite understand why you're so seldom home now, and when you are, you're always going off by yourself."

"Maybe you should enlighten him," he jeered, turning so the mirror couldn't soften the effect of his contemptuous glare.

"Jake, please!" Tanya averted her eyes from the freezing disdain of his look.

"Please what?" he snapped bitterly. "What do you expect of me? Am I supposed to say Sorry, babe, that it didn't work and go my merry way? A man has only two things he can give a woman, Tanya—his love and his name. You're rejecting both! And you don't even have the decency to give me an explanation." His mouth curled with disgust.

Not one word crossed her lips, although a thousand flooded from her mind. Her chin trembled as she murmured a very weak, "I'm sorry," and crossed the hallway to her room. Moments later his striding footsteps could be heard in the hall signaling his departure.

Somehow Tanya dried the tears his embittered words had aroused and recovered a sufficient amount of composure to enable her to drive John to the Gilbert house. On her return, she avoided entering the house, choosing to circle it to arrive at the patio in the rear. It didn't matter that Julia would probably want her help in the kitchen to prepare the evening meal. She needed to be alone.

She walked to the railing and stared absently at the glasslike surface of the lake shimmering beyond the trees. Tears of self-pity stung her eyes as she suddenly felt overwhelmed by the mess she had made of her life. She made no attempt to wipe the dampness from her cheeks, feeling entitled to shed a few tears on her behalf.

"I didn't know anyone was out here," J.D.'s smooth voice sounded behind her, causing her to turn with a start. "You're crying, child," he murmured sympathetically.

Tanya quickly wiped her face with the back of her hand. "It's nothing," she shrugged.

"Here," he said, handing her the drink he held in his hand. "You look more in need of this than I am. Take a big swallow." She did as she was ordered, choking on the potent liquor in the process. "Burns all the way down, doesn't it?" he smiled. "But it momentarily revives you."

"Thanks," she said huskily, her throat still feeling the scorching effect as she started to hand the glass back.

"No." He waved it off. "You might need another dose. You and Jake had another quarrel, am I right?"

"More than a quarrel, I'm afraid," she nodded, taking a deep breath to fight the shooting pain Jake's name caused.

"There couldn't be much doubt about that. He's been like an elephant with a toothache, angry at everybody." Tanya could feel his speculating gaze move over her face. "You're in love with my son, aren't you?"

She darted him a quick glance, but neither confirmed or denied it. She couldn't. She didn't think J.D. would accept her lie that she wasn't in love with Jake and there was too much chance of the truth getting back to Jake.

"You'd rather not say, is that it?" J.D. chuckled. "Surely you know that he's in love with you?"

"Yes," she admitted in a tight voice.

"Would you consider me a nosey in-law if I asked what the quarrel was about?" His expression was friendly and warm when Tanya glanced at him.

She met his eyes squarely. "I asked Jake for a divorce."

One dark brow shot up in surprise. "Why?"

"Personal reasons," Tanya hedged.

"May I ask you another personal question?"

"What's that?" She couldn't keep from tilting her chin at a slightly defiant angle.

"Does Jake know that you aren't John's mother?"

The glass slipped from her hand and shattered into a hundred fragments on the patio floor. Icy fear held her in its paralyzing grip.

"Obviously he doesn't," J.D. said dryly.

"H—how . . . did you know?" she gasped, her hand slipping up to her throat in an oddly protective gesture.

"Let's say I wasn't as willing as my son to believe that this strange girl we'd never seen or heard of before was who she professed to be, and more important, whether the baby was really my grandchild. As far as I was concerned there was a very real possibility that you were only passing the boy off as Jake's son. Jake wouldn't discuss it with me except to admit that the baby had been born before you two were married. So I did some checking on my own." His eyes looked kindly at her. "Why was it that Jake never asked for a DNA test—to see John's birth certificate?"

"He did once," Tanya breathed, unable to

believe any of this was really happening. "But I didn't show it to him."

"You can imagine my shock and anger when I saw that the birth certificate listed your sister as John's mother," J.D. said with a rueful smile.

"Why didn't you confront me or Jake with your discovery?"

"You were legally married to Jake. No, I hinted a few times in my letters to him that there might be something he didn't know, but he wrote back that John was his son. I guessed from that that he knew the truth. By then," he sighed, "I could already see how very much you loved the boy, as if he were really your own."

"When did you find out that Jake didn't know?" she whispered.

"That time I persuaded him to come home. I asked him one night about your sister, and he said he'd never met her."

"He was drunk," Tanya murmured. All the bitterness was gone and only sadness was in its place. "He couldn't remember anything about that night except meeting me."

"Why didn't you tell him the truth then, Tanya?" he asked quietly.

"Because he said he wanted his son." She swallowed back the lump in her throat. "And I knew that because he was John's father, with the Lassiter wealth and name to back him up, I didn't have a chance of keeping John. I loved John. Deanna, my sister, never got to hold him once. She came down with drug-resistant pneumonia in the hospital and died. It doesn't happen often, but it happened to her. I took care of him. He was my baby and Jake would have taken him away from me!"

She broke into sobs and found herself being drawn into her father-in-law's arms where he patted her shoulders and comforted her.

"I understand, child," he soothed. As the last of the sobs faded away, he handed her his linen handkerchief. "And now you're afraid to tell Jake what you did."

Tanya nodded, blowing her nose gently in his handkerchief. "Yes. He'd hate me for it." A blankness swept over her face as if she were beyond feeling. "He said I was honest, that I always told the truth. How can I tell him that I've been living a lie for seven years?"

"I'm afraid you have to."

"I couldn't," she shuddered.

"My dearest daughter-in-law," J.D. said gently, lifting her chin with his finger, "my son couldn't be more hurt or angered than he is right now because you rejected him. Do you really believe he's going to hate you more for telling him the truth?"

"I suppose not," she murmured. "I just don't know if I can face him, or if he'll even talk to me."

"I'll arrange to have him come to my study tomorrow night at seven o'clock. I'll act as a referee for the first few minutes," J.D. suggested.

"Maybe . . . maybe it would be better if you didn't tell him I was going to meet him there. He might not come otherwise."

"You may be right," he smiled. "Jake can be as stubborn as the proverbial Missouri mule. Now, I have your word that you're going to tell him?"

"Yes," Tanya sighed, more frightened by the prospect than she cared to admit.

* * *

It was the longest night and day she had ever lived through. It was six-thirty the following evening and Jake hadn't arrived home yet. Tanya kept hoping he wouldn't come even though she knew it would only prolong the agony. Now that his father knew the truth Jake would find out whether she told him or not. She almost wished she had asked J.D. to tell him, if it weren't such a cowardly thing to do.

Three times she had changed her clothes, unable to decide what to wear. When she looked in the mirror, a hysterical bubble of laughter rose in her throat. She was wearing black with her amber-streaked hair coiled on top of her head. She looked as if she was going to a funeral; it felt as if it was her own.

She fussed with concealer, trying to hide the dark smudges under her eyes without success. She felt sick to her stomach and her hands were trembling like aspen leaves. The muscles were knotted at the back of her neck from the overwrought state of her nerves.

At ten minutes before seven o'clock, she stepped into the hall, her knees barely supporting her as she walked down the hallway across the foyer to the secluded study on the opposite side of the house. J.D. was sitting behind the desk, his head resting against the back of the chair as he stared into space.

"He isn't home yet," she spoke softly from the door, bringing his startled gaze around to her.

"No," he sighed heavily. "He isn't home. You might as well sit down. We can wait together."

The leather-covered cushions seemed to close

around her when she sat down, swallowing her up in its oversize proportions. It was a pleasant sensation marred by the ticking of the antique clock on the mantelpiece.

It was half past seven when they heard the sound of a car in the driveway. Tanya's fingers curled into the arm of the chair as she glanced fearfully at her father-in-law.

There was a grim smile on his face as he returned her look. "It'll all be over soon," he said.

"Yes," she whispered, not wanting to agree. Her eyelashes fluttered tightly down over her eyes at the sound of the front door shutting. There was a sickening cramp in her stomach and she was afraid she was going to be sick. She kept waiting for the sound of footsteps in the hall—Jake's footsteps. But the clock kept ticking in the silence.

After nearly ten minutes had gone by, J.D. began tapping a pencil impatiently on the desk top while glowering at the closed door. Tanya's nerves were stretched to breaking point. The knock on the door brought her to the edge of her chair.

"Come in," J.D. called, motioning to Tanya to remain seated.

As the door swung open, the atmosphere threatened to stifle her. Jake looked so powerful in the slim-fitting trousers and the white shirt that was half unbuttoned to accentuate the bronzed color of his skin, it took her breath away. His hair gleamed with rich brown tones, damp and slightly curling from a shower. But it was his face that Tanya stared at, so arrogantly carved and so disturbingly attractive.

"Sorry I'm late, Dad," he said, without a hint of sincere apology in his voice as he moved through the doorway. His gaze had moved from his father to Tanya, changing from indifferent blandness to glittering cold. His mouth snapped shut into a grim line as he glared at J.D. "I thought you were alone. Excuse me."

He pivoted sharply to leave, his rigid carriage announcing his refusal to be in the same room with her.

"Come back in here!" J.D. barked.

"I'll come back when you're alone," Jake retorted, the muscles in his arm rippling as he gripped the side of the door.

"You are not leaving," his father declared in a tone that brooked no opposition. "And Tanya isn't leaving either." She saw the muscle twitching in Jake's tightly clenched jaw and knew the tight rein he held on his temper. The knowledge that he couldn't stand to be in her company was a physical pain in her heart.

"I don't mean to be disrespectful, Dad," Jake declared. His back was still turned to his father as he spoke through gritted teeth. "But this is none of your damned business."

"I beg to differ with you, son," J.D. answered with the same note of ominous softness in his voice. "I have a stake in the future of my grandson, so that makes me involved."

"If you're trying to act as a marriage counselor, I suggest you have a talk with Tanya first," Jake sneered, tossing a venomous look at Tanya, who cringed inwardly at the malevolence in his eyes.

"I already have—that's why I asked you here tonight. Now close that door and come in here and sit down." She knew that only Jake's father could get away with ordering him around like that. No one else would dare that smoldering anger.

The door closed with a resounding slam as Jake turned on his heel and walked to the chair near Tanya's. He reclined his long length in it, looking amazingly relaxed, but she knew it was the watchful stillness of a jungle cat.

"Let's get this over with," he muttered, glancing at the gold watch on his arm. "I have a dinner date tonight."

"With Sheila?" Tanya didn't realize she had spoken the question out loud until Jake's blue eyes bored into her.

"Do you care?" he said nastily.

"That will be enough of that," J.D. reprimanded. "We aren't here to trade insults."

Tanya had lowered her chin nearly into her chest, breaking free from Jake's look of scorn and contempt that slashed at her heart.

"Exactly why am I here?" Jake demanded. "Are we supposed to be discussing the divorce settlement or what?" She felt utterly miserable. "Because if so, I want you to know that I won't give you one penny of alimony and I intend to fight you every inch of the way for custody of my son."

The bitter vengeance in his voice brought Tanya to her feet, her hands twisting together like the knots in her stomach. How he despised her!

"Tanya," J.D.'s gentle voice reached out to her, reassuring and warm, promising her all his support. Her beseeching gaze sought out the craggy features of the still handsome older man.

"I don't think I can do it," she whispered as hot tears scalded her eyes.

"Tears," Jake scoffed with cynical amusement. "How touching!"

"Of course you can, Tanya." J.D. sent a sharp, reproachful look at his son. "That is if my arrogant son will keep his mouth shut long enough to listen."

"Why do you insist on butting into this?" Jake nearly exploded. "You don't even know what's going on."

"I know more than you do!" his father retorted just as angrily. "And if you'll shut up and listen you might find out something, too!"

"Stop it!" Tanya cried, unable to stand the angry bickering between father and son. "I won't have you yelling at each other because of me!"

"You've made my relationship with my family difficult since the first day I married you. Why should it suddenly be different now?" Jake lashed out at her. But he didn't wait for her answer. "Now tell whatever story it is you have to tell. I'm getting tired of all this melodramatic suspense." Tanya looked helplessly at the man behind the desk, praying that he would speak up and make the onerous explanation. But her father-in-law only nodded for her to go ahead.

"I don't know how to start," she hedged weakly.

"For God's sake, just say whatever it is you're going to say so I can get the hell out of here!" Jake snarled, shifting restlessly in the chair.

"You're not making it easy, Jake," Tanya replied, sending him a slightly angry glance of her own.

"When have you ever made my life easy?" he asked coldly. There was a moment of silence as her retaliatory anger faded at his harsh reminder of her own past treatment of him. She took a deep breath and wiped the tears from her cheek. Her feet put more distance between them as she stared down at her tightly knotted fingers.

"The other day wh-when we were talking," she began quietly, "you said you admired my honesty. I haven't been honest with you, Jake—in fact, I've led you to believe something that isn't true at all." She glanced at him apprehensively, seeing his reaction to her statement. He was watching her, his gaze cold as he impatiently waited for her to continue.

"It's about John." Her teeth bit into her lip.

"What about John?" he prompted her.

From the corner of her eye she could see the uncompromising line of his mouth. She forced herself to meet his gaze, unconsciously squaring her shoulders as she made the half turn towards him.

"He is not my son."

The words had barely been spoken when Jake loomed to his feet, gliding across the distance separating them like an avenging angel. His hands closed over her soft upper arms, his fingers digging in as he drew her up on tiptoe until she was inches away from his enraged face.

"What is this? What are you saying?" he demanded, shaking her roughly. "Are you trying to make me believe that John isn't my son?"

"No," she murmured, the tears running down her cheeks again. "He is your son. I've never lied about that."

"Then what are you talking about?"

"John isn't *my* son. I'm not his mother," Tanya repeated more forcefully.

"You're not making any sense." His forehead

drew together in a disbelieving frown. "If you're not his mother, then who is?"

She swallowed the painful lump in her throat and lowered her gaze to his chest. He was so near to her, yet so very far away.

"My sister," she mumbled, gasping with pain as he suddenly increased the grip on her arms.

"That's a lie!" Jake snarled. "I don't believe a word you're saying!"

"It's the truth. I swear it," she whispered fervently.

"No!" he shouted, causing her to shrink away from him. He released her abruptly. "I don't believe you."

"She's telling you the truth, son," J.D. said quietly, and Jake turned towards him.

"What do you know about this? Don't tell me you believe this crazy story?" he nearly shouted.

The older man didn't answer immediately, picking up a document from the desk and holding it out to Jake. "I don't think you've seen this," he said calmly.

Tanya waited with paralyzed stillness as Jake frowned over the paper. She guessed it was John's birth certificate—her father-in-law had no doubt obtained a copy of it several years before. A suppressed anger remained in Jake's eyes as he turned to look at her.

"Deanna Carr is your sister?" he snapped.

All she could do was nod.

"Why?" he snarled. "Why did you let me believe all these years that you were John's mother?"

"Because you were his father. You would have taken him away from me. I didn't have any family, no decent place to live, no means to support myself or John. I didn't stand a chance of him being awarded to me legally through the courts, not when Jake Lassiter was his father."

"First," Jake said with deadly calm, "I had to live with the fact that you gave birth to my illegitimate son." Anger and shock made his voice vibrate. "Now you tell me his mother was some girl I don't even remember!"

The birth certificate was crunched into a tight ball in his hand. The room became filled with an oppressive silence that pounded as loudly as Tanya's heart. In the next instant the paper was hurled across the room.

"You ask too much!" his tight voice declared, every muscle in his body rippling with the violence and tension of the moment. A tiny sob escaped as a moan from Tanya's lips. She couldn't face him any more, not after all the hurt she had caused him.

"I'm sorry, Jake," she murmured numbly, whirling away from him to rush out of the study door.

Chapter Ten

"Tanya!" Jake's angry voice called after her, but she didn't stop. Her steps quickened when she heard the sound of his in the hallway, following her. She couldn't stop, not even when his commanding voice called her name again.

"Tanya, come back here!" Jake already despised her for rejecting his love. His loathing would only double after learning of the way she had used him for the last seven years. And she couldn't find it in her heart to blame him.

Intent on reaching the safety of her room, Tanya nearly ran into her mother-in-law, who had hurried into the hallway at the sound of her son's strident voice. Quickly she brushed past her, seeing the startled, questioning look on Julia's face with uncaring pain. Her mother-in-law's voice followed Tanya on the flight to her room.

"Jake, what's going on here? What's happened?" she demanded.

"Not now," he brushed her aside impatiently.

"I want to know what's going on. I have a right to know what goes on in my own house!" Julia declared angrily.

"Let him be," J.D.'s calming voice joined in.

"But I want to know—"

A hand was raised to shush her. "I'll tell you all about it. Now where is John?"

"Out in the garden."

Tanya heard the last as she opened her bedroom door and closed it quickly behind her, turning the lock. An instant later she heard Jake's footsteps at the door and saw the jiggling of the doorknob.

"Open the door, Tanya!"

She cringed at the still angry tone. "Please go away, Jake. Just go away."

"Open this door or I swear I'll break it down!"

She hesitated for only a minute before reaching out with a trembling hand to unlock the door. The click sounded loudly in the sudden silence. As the knob turned in response to the sound, she moved swiftly away from the door, her eyes bright with unshed tears while she fought for the strength to make it through his inquisition. Silently she resolved not to cry nor attempt to gain his sympathy. She wasn't entitled to it, not after the way she had abused his trust.

He was in the room. Even with her back to him, she could feel his presence in the room before she heard the closing of the door. Breathing in deeply, she looked up at the ceiling and blinked away the tears in her eyes, while she waited for him to speak.

"Look at me, Tanya," Jake ordered in a tone of tightly controlled anger.

Very slowly she turned around, not knowing how

completely composed her rigidly held features made her appear.

"Can't this wait until tomorrow, Jake?" she asked, clasping her trembling hands tightly so they wouldn't betray her. "You'll be late for your dinner appointment."

"The instant I left, you'd pack your suitcases and leave," he stated what had only been a half-formed thought in her mind, and her cheeks colored. "We'll finish this discussion right here and now."

"I don't know what more I can tell you." Her chin lifted instinctively. "I can only say how terribly sorry and ashamed I am that I didn't tell you the truth sooner."

"I'll bet you are," Jake mocked. "You've somehow managed to convince my father of the sincerity behind your actions, but you have yet to convince me."

"Convince you of what?"

"Why you married me."

"I married you because of John. I told you that," she replied in a hurt voice. "Once I made the mistake of telling you that he was your son and realized you weren't going to treat it lightly, I felt I had no choice. I loved him as if he were my own son."

"The idea of being Mrs. Jake Lassiter didn't enter it at all?" he jeered. "Not when you knew it would mean living in a beautiful home, being free of any financial worries, enjoying the status or a member of the Lassiter family, wearing clothes that you wouldn't even have dreamt of trying on before? That had no bearing on your decision?"

Pride gleamed brightly in her gold-flecked eyes. "I won't pretend that I didn't know the Lassiters were a wealthy and respected family, because I did," she answered calmly. "But I can't make you believe me when I say that those things mattered only because of John. They were his birthright. He was entitled to them. I knew I never was."

"It's funny the way it didn't stop you from using them for yourself," he murmured sarcastically.

"If you want to brand me as a scheming gold-digger, I can't stop you, Jake." She forced herself to meet the diamond sharpness of his gaze. "I can only tell you that my concern was for John's future."

Jake stared at her for a long moment, finally breaking away to shake his head in disgusted exasperation. "I don't know why I believe you, but I do," he muttered angrily.

The constriction of her throat made it impossible for Tanya to speak for a moment. "Thank you," she whispered tightly. Running his fingers through his tobacco-brown hair, Jake turned and walked to the window, staring absently out at the gathering crimson dusk.

"I could accept you as John's mother. I could believe that. But to find out that she's really someone I don't remember—" He sighed as if his heart would break. "I want to know about that night, Tanya."

The grimness of his voice reached out and placed a cold hand on her heart.

"Oh, Jake," she murmured in a weak protest at what he was asking.

"Did she—did your sister tell you I was the father?" he persisted.

Tanya realized he was determined to know every bit of the story.

"Yes, she did."

"Tell me what happened that night. Tell me everything you know," he commanded harshly, not turning away from the window.

Her eyes lovingly caressed the back of his squared shoulders and even the arrogant tilt of his head. She longed to rush over and put her arms about him and take away some of his pain. But Jake had asked her to inflict more. At this point she couldn't refuse him.

"Deanna and I went to the fair and the dance together. She was with some friends when you met me." She began the explanation hesitantly, not knowing anywhere else to begin except at the beginning. "I'm sure she wasn't around those first few times you asked me to dance. You were very handsome and charming. Every time you looked at me you seemed to steal my breath away. I'd never met anyone like you before."

"Why did you run away from me?"

"It sounds foolish now," Tanya sighed. "You'd kissed me several times on the dance floor, but the last time—well it was different. It frightened me. It frightened me because of the way it made me feel. I wanted you to go on kissing me. All of those feelings of desire made me afraid so I ran."

"I looked for you," Jake said with a strange, faraway indifference in his voice. "Where did you go?"

"I went to our car. Our parents had let us use their car and I went to it with the intention of leaving. But I couldn't go because Deanna wasn't with me. And I was beginning to feel silly for mak-

ing such a production out of a kiss, so I came
back—not right back, because I argued with myself
for quite a while in the parking lot. It was probably
a half an hour or more.'' She breathed in deeply
remembering the misery and confusion of those
moments. ''When I came back, there was this boy
I knew standing near the entrance. I asked him if
he had seen Deanna and he told me she was over
by the bar. I walked over there and saw her standing
beside you.''

''Are you sure she was with me?'' Jake asked
sharply. ''Couldn't she have simply been standing
next to me?''

''No,'' she replied quietly, and swallowed the
lump in her throat. ''Dennis—the boy at the
door—had followed me. He said, Isn't that the guy
who was hitting on you a few minutes ago? I don't
remember if I answered him or not. Then he said,
'You'd better warn your sister. Those Lassiters like
to play. If a girl isn't willing, they'll find one who
is.''

Jake turned sharply around at that statement, his
face angry and grim. ''Do you believe that?''

''Not so much any more,'' Tanya shook her head
quietly. ''At the time I think I did and more so
later.''

''Which is why you despised me so much before,''
he said coldly. ''When I wasn't successful in getting
what I wanted from you, I used your sister. That's
what you thought, wasn't it?'' There was a puzzled
expression on his face. ''How did you know for
sure that your sister was with me?''

''About the time I decided to walk over to where
the two of you were standing, some boy came up

to ask Deanna to dance. You put your arm around her and told him hands off—she was yours for the night." There was a heavy, almost groaning sigh from Jake as he turned swiftly towards the window. Tanya wanted to stop, but she knew she had to go on. "Later I managed to see Deanna alone. I tried to warn her about you, but she wouldn't listen to me. She told me she was old enough to know what she was doing and for me to go home. I did. It was nearly five o'clock in the morning when she came home. All she could talk about was that you were coming to see her the following weekend. Then you didn't come or call or write. Our parents were killed in a car crash a few weeks later, and after that she told me she was pregnant."

"Why can't I remember?" His irritated thought was spoken aloud. He glanced over his shoulder with a narrowed gaze at Tanya. "Did she look like you? Could I have confused her memory with yours?"

"She was dark, a brunette, and shorter than I am," she answered quietly. "You'd been drinking quite a bit when you were with me and you had a drink in your hand when I saw you with Deanna."

A silence hushed the room, stretching out over long moments during which Tanya listened to the sound of her own breathing. Jake drew back the sheer curtains, leaning his hand against the windowsill as he watched John playing with a toy bulldozer among the rocks.

"Why," he began at last, still staring out the window, "did you agree to try to make our marriage work? Was that only for John's sake, too?"

"No." Somehow she endured his cold glance. "I agreed at first because you said if it didn't work then we would explore the alternatives of ending our marriage. To me that meant a divorce. I wanted that very much."

"Why didn't you say so before?" Jake snapped savagely. "Or was the taste of vengeance so strong that you wanted to bring me all the way to my knees?"

Tanya flinched. "Seven years ago I would have answered yes to that. Today, a week ago, even a month ago, it wasn't true," she murmured. "Lately I thought we had a chance to have a good marriage, that you might regard me with some affection, or enough to understand why I lied to you in the beginning."

"You underestimate your ability." Jake laughed bitterly, walking away from the window in her general direction.

Tanya closed her eyes for a brief moment. "When you told me you loved me and why, all I wanted was to crawl into a hole and die rather than have you find out the way I'd deceived you."

"Why did you bother to tell me at all? Or did Father force you into it?"

"He told me I had to tell you," she admitted, lowering her gaze to her hands.

"You could have gone on letting me believe John was your son. Why didn't you?"

Unconsciously her gaze strayed to the bed. "If I hadn't told you and became a real wife to you— a wife who took more than just kisses," she glanced back at him, pallor robbing her face of color as she watched him, "you would have learned anyway that I . . . I hadn't given birth to your son." Jake stared at her, his head tilted to one side almost as if he didn't understand what she said. Then he took the step that brought him nearer, his hands closing over her shoulders. His gaze held hers with burning intensity.

"Do you mean . . . Are you telling me that . . ." Then he groaned as he read the answer in her face. With a convulsive movement he drew her against his chest, burying his face in the coiled knot of her tawny hair.

And she clung to him, hopelessly praying that he would never let her go, that he would hold her like this forever. She felt his mouth moving in a rough caress over her hair as he whispered her name.

"I wish you could forgive me," she murmured, her heart singing a bitter sweet melody. "I love you so very much."

"Why? Because of John?" he demanded. "You still want him?"

"I love John," she admitted, understanding his reason for doubting the sincerity of her love. "But my love for you is separate from him. I know you can't forgive me for deceiving you about him. But I love you, Jake."

"No, no," he protested savagely, dragging his head away from her. "I'm the one who needs forgiveness, for what I did to you and your sister."

"I'm not bitter about it any more." Her hands tenaciously gripped his waist, refusing to let him push her aside.

"But it's there, between us. We can't pretend it didn't happen." He stared down at her coldly, the muscle in his jaw twitching in his fight for control.

"I love you, Tanya, maybe more now that I realize what you sacrificed for my son."

"Jake," her fingers lightly touched his cheek, "isn't that important? That we love each other?"

"Dammit, don't you understand?" Angrily he brushed her hand away. "The blankness of that night haunts me. I don't know why I expect you to believe me, but I've never had sex with a woman who didn't already know the score. It was bad enough thinking I'd somehow had sex with you you in a night of drunkenness. The only thing I thought about that night was you. I don't remember looking at anyone else."

He reached out instinctively to touch her trembling body. Tanya felt his anguish as if it were her own. All the love that burned within her was shining in the eyes that looked into his. The hands left her shoulders as he turned away, making a small gesturing shrug of helplessness.

"Do you have a picture of her?" he asked in a more subdued tone. "Maybe if I saw it I could remember."

"In my wallet." Her handbag was on the dresser. Taking out the leather wallet, Tanya hurriedly flipped through the photographs to Deanna's. She handed it to Jake. He stared at it for a long moment, then shook his head.

"It's vaguely familiar," he muttered, handing it back to her, "but she has your smile."

She started to put it back in her bag as his hand reached out to close over her wrist.

"Wait a minute!" he ordered sharply. He looked at it again, then at Tanya.

"Do you recognize her?" she breathed slowly.

"Think carefully," he said, his eyes watching her

closely. "Did she say that it was me she was with that night? I mean me specifically, my name."

"I guess so," she shook her head in confusion. "What are you getting at?"

"I'm asking you if she said she was with Jake Lassiter, or did you assume she was?"

"I don't remember. I was hurt and bitter. I didn't want to talk about you."

"Is it possible she called me Jamie?"

"Jamie is your brother," Tanya frowned. "Why would she call you that?"

"Because my brother was with me that night. I vaguely remember that we didn't go back to the hotel together, but I imagined it was because I was with you."

"But I saw you with Deanna!"

"Was there anyone else with us?"

"I can't remember," she admitted.

"I know he met a girl there, but I was so wrapped up in finding you that I can't say whether she was fat or thin or short or what," he grumbled. "Jamie introduced her to me."

"Jake," she spoke hesitantly, her own mind racing now with doubts, "where was Jamie going the night he was killed?"

"I don't know. I think he had a date somewhere north of Springfield."

He shook his head, then stopped to stare at Tanya.

"When was he killed? Not the time, but the day."

"Saturday." His face began to clear. "The weekend after the dance when I was supposed to have seen Deanna. It was Jamie!" Jake declared vehemently.

"When she told me she was pregnant, all I asked

was whether the father was that Lassiter man she met at the dance. Of course she said yes, and we never mentioned a name again.'' The pieces were beginning to fall into place. ''When John was born, Deanna was so ill that I was the one who gave them the information on the birth certificate. Your name. And all these years I blamed you,'' she said in a horrified whisper. ''Oh, Jake, I'm sorry.''

''I'm not,'' he sighed heavily. ''We can't be sure it was Jamie.''

''But we can't be sure it wasn't,'' Tanya smiled. ''We do know that John is a Lassiter and your mother has shown me baby pictures of you and your brother. His resemblance to Jamie is remarkable.''

''His car was wrecked between here and Sedalia. I'd like to believe he was going to see Deanna. Maybe they did fall in love that night. DNA testing can confirm that John is my brother's son but I don't doubt it for a minute,'' Jake murmured, a rueful smile curving his mouth. ''If for no other reason than to assuage my conscience.''

''It's not so hard to believe. And I fell in love with you that night, for a little while at least,'' she admitted.

He drew her gently in his arms, holding her tenderly against his chest. ''I wonder what would have happened if you'd told me the truth seven years ago,'' he murmured.

''I don't think we'll ever know,'' she sighed, but it was a happy sigh.

''I love you, Tanya, my sweet, honest wife. I think I would have loved you anyway.'' A tantalizing kiss touched her mouth. ''We might have discovered the truth about Jamie and Deanna then and not wasted so many years. But that's over now."

"I like to think," she whispered, inching closer in his arms, "that this has made our love stronger because it was born and survived where it had no right to, don't you?"

His answer was by deed, not words.

Dear Reader,

When my fifth-grade teacher gave the class an assignment to write a story, my dream to one day become a writer was born. From that moment on, I was always either writing a story or coming up with ideas for one. I admit, few of them were ever finished, but I never stopped putting words together.

During high school, I was constantly turning in essays and short stories to my English teacher for extra credit. I remember all of her blue pencil marks and the side notes in the margin, always instructive and always encouraging.

Unfortunately she also gave me—what I thought at the time—was the worst advice in the world. She told me that I should write what I know. I lived in Iowa, for goodness sake! A small town with a population of only five hundred people. Nothing interesting ever happened there! I couldn't think of anything more boring than a story set in Iowa. It literally froze my writing career in its tracks. Instead of going on to college, I went to secretarial school.

Years went by before I realized that the best advice I ever received came from that very same English teacher who told me to "write what you know." Why the change in attitude? Because there is no limit to her advice, thanks to that magic word: Research.

Most people look at the word "research" and think only of printed material, whether that would be books, newspaper articles, or Internet sites. It's true that you can learn a great deal from those sources, but I soon discovered that the written word can't always give you the true feel of a given location, its sights, sounds, and smells. The same is true with a particular occupation. It's not always possible to walk in someone's shoes, but sometimes you can tag along and in that way acquire a sense of the job's day-to-day challenges, stress, and even the unique terminology associated with that job.

Research has become my favorite part of the writing process. Probably because it is the most fun and because it's prompted me to do and try things that would likely never have occurred to me.

While working on a book set in Alaska, I toured a museum that had once housed "ladies of the evening," walked on a glacier, and saw the salmon run. In Barrow, I saw the midnight sun and rode with Joe the Water Man while on his route through town—and nearly got caught in a shootout between the police and a man barricaded in his home. Most exciting of all, I went along with a bush pilot while he made his milk run (into various Eskimo villages accessible only by air or dog sled). On that trip, we landed on the frozen Bering Sea between the islands of Little Diomede and Big Diomede. Siberia could be seen in the distance. It was the trip of a lifetime.

I've been on cattle drives (never overlook working dude ranches for that western experience), toured winery after winery in the Napa Valley and elsewhere, hung around movie sets and television studios, attended Arabian horse shows, visited Thoroughbred horse farms in Kentucky, and retraced the routes of the Chisolm Trail and the Cherokee Trail of Tears.

Perhaps the most exciting, exhilarating—and scariest—thing I ever did was when I went rafting through Class 0 rapids on the Rio Grande. I doubt that I will ever be able to explain what it is like being tossed around like a cork, dancing past boulders that were bigger than most houses. On that same trip, I made a wrong turn (women never get lost while driving; they simply have "unexpected adventures") and ended up on a dead-end road. After consulting my road map, I noticed there was an intersection with a state road about a mile from where I was that would be a shortcut back to the highway so I wouldn't have to backtrack. I took it. The first part of the road was asphalt, the second part was gravel; then I topped a hill and the road became a rutted track into the nothingness of West Texas.

I couldn't find a place to turn around so I kept going, thinking all the while of the headlines—NOVELIST MISSING. It seemed that I drove forever following those two ruts before I finally reached the highway. I later learned that heavy rains had washed out the road, and the one I had traveled was considered "impassible." I'm sure glad I didn't know that at the time.

Doubtless, I will never forget my first trip to Montana. Having grown up in Iowa's rich farmlands, I thought I already knew how big the sky could seem when the land beneath it was more or less flat. I forgot that in Iowa there is invariably a silo or grain elevator visible somewhere, not to mention all the barns and farmyards.

That wasn't true in Montana. The land was big, open, and empty of just about everything but the occasional power lines. Then came the upthrust of the mountains. Montana truly deserves to be known as Big Sky Country. Naturally that became the title for my book in this anthology, BIG SKY COUNTRY, but it only marked the beginning of my fascination with the state as those of you know who have read my Calder series.

Now, in the case of the second novel in this book, SHOW ME, and its location of Branson, Missouri, my first visit to the area came after my mom and step-dad retired here so he could go bass fishing in Table Rock Lake. Prior to that, I had never been to the Ozarks. My late husband and I had once vacationed at Lake of the Ozarks, slightly north and east of Branson, so I thought I had been in the Ozarks. There are some rocky hills there, but it isn't really the Ozarks.

The Ozark Mountains are among the oldest mountain ranges in the United States, although it would be more accurate to refer to them as highlands, and they are home to one of the last hardwood forests in the country. Honestly, I think it was the thousands of trees that first fascinated me. Then I learned that sometime in the 1920s, novelist Harold Bell Wright came to Branson and wrote a best-seller, SHEPHERD OF THE HILLS, which Hollywood later made into a movie starring John Wayne.

During the late twenties and forties, people traveled to Branson to visit the place where the book and movie were set—and returned to enjoy the area's natural beauty. In 1950, a dam was constructed along the White River, creating Table Rock Lake and drawing more tourists. And the town of Branson evolved into a vacation destination with the SHEPHERD OF THE HILLS book being made into an outdoor pageant, a local cave growing into a major amusement park called Silver Dollar City (the site for an episode for the TV show *The Beverly Hillbillies*) and music shows providing nighttime entertainment for tourists.

I had no choice. I had to write a book set in Branson; the backdrop was simply too unique. And that novel is the second book in this anthology—SHOW ME. My sisters have used SHOW ME for years as a kind of measuring stick. Whenever they read my latest book, they rate it by how they think it compares against SHOW ME—not as good as; as good as; or better than.

Needless to say, we came to Branson at least twice a year to visit my parents. Each time I had this sense that I was coming home. There was something about these hills that made me want to put my feet up and stay. And that's exactly what Bill and I finally did after more than five years of traveling the country.

So enjoy these two novels that have been set in locations that are definitely favorites of mine.

Happy reading,
Janet Dailey

A single name stopped him short.

Erin.

Wow. His Erin?

Bannon shook his head to clear it. Then he looked up at the painting of wild horses on the mantel. The artist wasn't his by any stretch of the imagination, and this might not even be the same Erin. But . . . he hadn't called anyone at the Art Walk committee, after all. What if it was her?

He accepted her request. Then got busy. He wasn't going to glue his eyes to the laptop waiting for an instant message like he had nothing better to do.

An hour later he got one.

Hello. Erin here. I saw you on the news.

Bannon winced, wondering what she'd thought of the segment. Only a conceited jerk would ask. She was adding a little more. The typeset sentence appeared in bits.

Sad story. I know it was a long time ago. I hope you
find out something.

Interesting response. She didn't automatically get
misty, thinking a missing victim would be found just
like that. Erin was smart. And if she was as beautiful
as he remembered, well—If one good thing came
out of reopening this case, he hoped like hell it was
her.

I'm working on it, believe me.

Not a bad answer. He didn't want to sound like
he was playing hero or putting himself in the lime-
light just for the hell of it. Mulling over what else he
could say, he took the time to check out the hand-
ful of photos she'd posted. It seemed like a profes-
sional page, not personal. For one thing, it wasn't
loaded with the usual girl's-night-out shots of happy
inebriated pals squeezed together.

There was one photo of her at an easel, dressed
in a loose, tattered shirt that looked like it belonged
to a man, with jeans under it. It was a little frustrat-
ing to not see more of her, but that was beside the
point. She was working on a half-finished water-
color, using a magazine image of horses that was
propped to her right. Not his painting, but one that
was about as good. Bannon jealously wondered
who'd taken the picture—or given her his old shirt
to paint in. He didn't see a single mention anywhere of a significant other.

His hands poised over the keyboard, he thought
some more. His goal was to see her in person, not

chat online indefinitely. But at least they were communicating.

It's great to hear from you, Erin.

He waited. She wasn't the kind to rush through an answer, and he was grateful she didn't use those dumb-ass acronyms to reply, because he couldn't remember any of them.

Thanks.

One word. He tried not to read more into it. She asked about the painting he'd bought. He assured her that it had pride of place on his mantel. And so it went. An hour went by without his realizing it. Then she typed something that made him sit up straight.

Bannon—I almost forgot to say why I contacted you.

He sucked in a breath, watching the rest of her typed words appear one by one.

I painted the Montgomery mansion for the Wainsville historical society. They're doing an illustrated book on grand old houses in the area.

That was information he didn't have. It called for an immediate reply.

I hadn't heard that.

Brilliant, he told himself wryly.

Do you know the director? She went to high school
with your mom in Arlington. They're e-buddies
now (she's Mrs. Judith Meriweather—I don't know
her maiden name).

His mother was all over the Web lately, he knew
that. But he didn't know Mrs. Meriweather. He was
grateful to her, though. Obviously he had been thoroughly vetted in advance. That fit the wariness he remembered about Erin.

Want to go to the house? I can get the
combination for the keypad from her. It's not tour
season yet.

Bannon's eyes widened. *Down, boy. Don't sound too
eager*, he told himself.

Sure.

Erin suggested that they meet at a country restaurant north of Wainsville and he grinned, glad she
couldn't see him. He knew the place, though he'd
never been inside. It was a converted barn by the
side of the road, famous for its traditional American
fare with a gourmet twist. Sign him up. Then she
asked a question that stunned him.

Today?

Did she mean it? He typed an answer fast.

Hell yes. Looking forward to it.

She replied after a minute, as if she'd gone off to do something else in the meantime.

Me too.

Bannon signed off with an oh-so-casual *see you there*. Then he realized that he still didn't know her last name or anything much about her at all.

Bannon Brothers: Honor

Rugged. Tall. Built to last. Linc Bannon has it all—and he's there every time Kenzie needs him. They share a mission: to serve their country stateside, Linc in high-level intelligence and Kenzie as an expert trainer of combat dogs. Independent and sexy, Kenzie is definitely one of a kind—and the only one he wants. But if you ask her, she doesn't need a hero in her life.

Until two of her friends, thousands of miles apart, are suddenly struck down. One, a soldier, is dead; the other, a civilian, is barely alive. Linc goes into action and uncovers a lethal web connecting the tragic events. A killer is at large, unhinged, and with unfinished business. Kenzie has no choice but to join forces with the one man who can get past her defenses . . .

As a hidden conspiracy threatens to explode with devastating consequences, Linc is honor-bound to protect Kenzie. With all his heart, he vows to risk his life for hers . . .

He reached her floor and opened the fire door onto a long hall. Another shadow appeared at the other end, then vanished so swiftly he thought he'd imagined it.

He was dead beat by now. Tired wasn't the word. The mad dash down too many roads and the stop at the hospital had disoriented him. Linc didn't like feeling so off-balance.

There were no more shadows. The fixtures in the hall provided even light. He heard nothing except the faint sound of water running somewhere in the building. Linc walked halfway down the hall before he realized that her door was ever so slightly ajar. A thin slice of golden light edged it.

He tensed. Had someone else noticed it was unlocked and tried it from the outside, then run away just as he'd opened the stairwell door? No telling.

His hand moved automatically inside his jacket for a weapon that wasn't there. His fingers brushed the smooth lining of his tux. No gun, no nothing.

And no sound from inside. Linc shoved the door open.

He choked as an unseen arm shot around his neck and pressed against his windpipe. Linc felt like someone was climbing his back, fast. He reached up to yank the arm away but in a split second his wrist got grabbed and forced behind his back. Gasping, he arched his back until he broke free of the steel-strong hold and—damn. Cracked his head against the door. The pain was blinding.

He whirled around, dizzy, and swung a fist. Didn't connect. Something wet slapped his arm . . . long, wet, whipping hair. His attacker was on the small side and had ducked the roundhouse punch. He stared at her, collecting his wits.

"Kenzie?"

She immediately straightened, standing with her arms akimbo and her clenched hands braced against her hips, Kenzie's breath heaving in her chest.

"What the hell do you think you're doing?" she snapped. "Did you pick my lock or something?"

He sucked in air, his throat swelling from the pressure she'd applied, raw on the inside.

"No. Door—was open. Thought I—saw—" He gasped for the words, recovering slowly. "Somebody out here." He waved at the hall. "Maybe running away."

Her green eyes widened. "What?" She moved to look down the hall for herself, both ways. "There's no one there."

"Hope not."

She came back in and shut the door hard, then slid the inside bolt into place. "Sometimes it doesn't latch unless I kick it. Are you all right?"

"Maybe."

Kenzie kept her distance, but came a little closer. He noticed, vaguely, that she was wearing something white and short. "You scared me half to death."

He patted her shoulder, which seemed to be bare, for some reason. She smelled awfully good, but it didn't seem like the right time to nuzzle her or anything like that. At least she didn't pull away or whack him.

Reassured by the thought, he stumbled to her couch and dropped down heavily. "Had to come. Too bad I didn't know your first name." He looked up at her, still not able to think straight. His head hurt like hell where he'd cracked it. "B is is for—?"

"Babe," she replied. "My dad thought it was cute. I can't stand it, never could. So don't switch."

"Okay, okay. Sorry, Kenzie."

"Why are you even here?"

She seemed more mystified than angry.

"For a very good reason. I saw the accident on TV."

Someone who kinda had it coming, a car thief or a stupid punk, had been taken away on that stretcher. Not Kenzie. She was right here, real as could be. He felt relief wash through him.

"What accident? You're not making sense." She came over and sat beside him, her bare arms folded across her chest.

Linc took a deep, rasping breath, then another. "Don't you ever answer your phone?"

"Not in the shower."

He finally figured out that she was wearing only a terry wrap thing tied in a knot above her breasts.

Shower. Right. So that was why she hadn't heard him.

But that didn't explain why the door had been

cracked open. Her explanation—that it had to be
kicked to latch right—didn't do it for him. Kenzie
wasn't an airhead.

But everybody made mistakes. He'd spent most
of the last hour doing just that.

Ow. He was hurting way too much to form a coher
ent thought. And he was distracted. The wrap was ex
tremely short, at least from where he was sitting. Out
of respect and the growing awareness that he'd
made a world-class fool of himself by coming here
unannounced, he did his best not to look too long at
her bare legs, as slender and shapely as her arms.

No fluffy slippers for her—her feet were bare too.
And recently pedicured. Golden-bronze toenails,
polish flawlessly applied, not a chip to be seen.

That could be why she hadn't kicked the door.
He told himself not to ask if that was the reason, for
fear of sparking her self-protective instincts a
second time. He forced himself to look up, all the
way up. Her dark, wet hair trickled little rivers over
her shoulders. Linc felt weak.

"Kenzie—ah—you do have a helluva chokehold."
His voice was coming back but he stopped to
breathe. She was alive, even if she'd half-killed him.
That was good. "I seem to remember you telling me
you aced hand-to-hand back in basic."

"Yes, I did. And I still practice."

"Good for you." Linc coughed. "But you need to
work on recognizing friendlies. Make yourself a
chart or something."

She got up again and tugged at the wrap. Was it
slipping?

"How was I supposed to know it was you, Linc?"

"God, I'd hate to be your enemy." He blinked

"Now I'm seeing sparks." He forced his eyes closed, but the sparks didn't go away. "Blue sparks. Wow."

She seemed unimpressed. "How much champagne did you have at the reception?"

He didn't answer the question. "It was fun. But I kept thinking about you." He rubbed his eyes, then his neck. "Ouch. Those nerves are waking up. You know how to hang on."

Bare, bronze-polished toes tapped impatiently on the carpet. "I'm waiting for an explanation. Right now would be a good time."

"You bet. Here goes." He launched into a fast recap of his search for her, starting with the news report.

"That can't be—" The rosy glow left her face and she stopped him before he could finish. "Linc, I loaned my car to my friend Christine."

"What?"

He could see her struggling to stay in control. What was going through her mind right now, he couldn't imagine.

"You heard me. That was her you saw on the stretcher. Unless—"

She didn't crack. But she avoided his eyes. "Damn it, where's my cell phone?" Suddenly she was frantic, searching over and under every surface. He didn't see a landline.

"I left mine in my car." He got up, feeling rocky.

Ugly twist. Not a joyrider, not a thief—a friend of hers had been at the wheel. Another possibility that hadn't occurred to him, and he had been trained to think outside every box there was. But Christine had survived. As far as he knew. "I'll go get it."

"No! Stay here!"

She grabbed a pair of jeans that had been slung

over the flat-screen TV and shook them upside down. A small cell phone bounced on the carpet and she scooped it up, flipping it open and staring at the messages listed on the tiny screen. "Two texts. Nine voicemails. Oh no."

She pressed the key for call return and got one of Christine's parents almost immediately. Linc saw her shudder and dash away tears. She turned away from him after that. "Critical condition—I understand— Mrs. Corelli, I am so sorry. I just found out—no, from a friend—and picked up your message. Where is she? Where are you?" She grabbed a pencil and notepad and jotted down the replies. "I'm on my way." Then she looked at Linc. "Yes, I have someone who can come with me."